BEHIND A CLOSED DOOR

Also by J.D. Barker

Forsaken
She Has A Broken Thing Where Her Heart Should Be
A Caller's Game
Behind A Closed Door

4MK Thriller Series
The Fourth Monkey
The Fifth To Die
The Sixth Wicked Child

with Dacre Stoker
Dracul

with James Patterson
The Coast to Coast Murders
The Noise
Death of the Black Widow

J. D. BARKER

BEHIND A CLOSED DOOR

I planned to dedicate this book to my family,
but then I drank a cup of Carpe Diem coffee.

Sorry, family.
This book is dedicated to Carpe Diem coffee.

Continuing beyond this point confirms your
understanding and acceptance of our terms of service.

Sugar & Spice™

1

"When was the last time you had sex?"

"Together?"

The word slipped from Brendan's mouth before he could stop it. His arm dropped to his gut to block the inevitable blow from Abby's elbow, but none came. Instead, Abby glared at him from her designated spot on the therapist's couch at his side, her cheeks burning red.

Dr. Laura Donetti, who had a face built for high-stakes poker, remained expressionless in a fancy leather bound chair across from them.

"I'm sorry," Brendan swallowed. "I sometimes say stupid shit when I'm nervous."

"Brendan!" Abby groaned.

"Stupid *stuff*," he corrected. "Stuff. I'm sorry, I'm not used to this sort of thing."

Donetti ignored the back-and-forth and tucked a loose strand of dark hair behind her ear. "Therapy?"

"Talking," Abby replied, crossing her legs. "He's not used to *talking*."

"That's not true. We talk all the time."

"No. You tell me things. Things like *grab some milk at the store.* Or *I'm gonna be late.* Or *I'm heading to Stuckey's to catch the game.* You *tell* me things, you don't *talk*."

Brendan shook his head. "See what I'm dealing with?"

Donetti's head tilted slightly to the side. "What's…*Stuckey's?*"

"His best friend's house," Abby answered before he got a word out. "Stewart Morland. Everyone calls him Stuckey. They work together, they play together. Sometimes I think they're the ones who are married."

"Not like I'm the only one at his house. You go into withdrawal if you don't spend at least an hour a day chatting it up with Hannah. You're over there *way* more than me."

"I take it Hannah and Stuckey are married?"

Abby nodded. "They live across the street from us."

"And you're in…" Donetti glanced at her notes. "Chestnut Hill? Where is that, exactly?"

"About ten miles outside Boston. Between Newton and Brookline."

"Fairly affluent area?"

"We do okay," Brendan muttered.

"That's not what I asked."

It was Brendan's turn to flush. He and Abby had been fighting about a lot of things lately, not the least of which was money. His job paid well, but not enough to cover everything. They'd been okay when they were both working, but—

"He's been mad at me since I quit my day job."

"That's not true; I told you to quit."

Abby rolled her eyes. "Yeah, well maybe we should have *talked* about it rather than you *telling* me."

Donetti raised her hand, cutting Brendan off. "This is our first session together, so it's important we air as much of this out as possible. At the same time, let's try not to be confrontational about it. That's difficult when discussing things that upset you, but I need you both to try. Choose your words carefully. No need to push each other's buttons—I only need to know what those buttons are. Does that make sense?"

Abby nodded, then Brendan.

"Good." Donetti turned back to Abby. "Why did you quit your job?"

"I wrote a book a few years ago, and it did moderately well. I self published it, but I guess the sales were strong enough for some of the big publishers to take notice. I signed with an agent, and she managed to secure a two-book deal. There was a modest advance, so Brendan suggested I quit work so I could write the next one faster." Abby chewed the inside of her cheek. "I was working as an event coordinator at the Harland Hotel in the city. I wrote the first book before work, after work, on my breaks…whenever I managed to scrape a few minutes together, but it took me the better part of two years. We both figured if I was able to focus, it would be easier."

Donetti understood before Brendan had to say anything. She leaned back in her chair. "And now you're having trouble writing that book, the advance is running out, and money looks like it might get tight."

Again, Abby nodded.

Something clicked in the doctor's eyes. Her brows shot up behind her thick-framed glasses. "*Understanding Ella*. You're *that* Abby Hollander?"

"That's me."

"I love that book."

Brendan cut in before the doctor asked about the book's ending. *They always asked about the ending.* "I want her to succeed. Don't get me wrong. That's why I suggested her quitting. But at this point, she doesn't have an idea for a second book, let alone pages, and we're burning through our savings trying to get by on my salary alone, and that creates a lot of tension."

Abby looked down at her hands. "I can't write with a ticking clock. Can't think. Can't focus…"

"Have you considered going back to work? Writing in your spare moments like you used to?"

"Someone else has my job. I gave the Harland two weeks' notice, and they replaced me in less than three days. It's a competitive market. They'll never hire me back. I'd have to put a resume together, interview…"

Brendan sighed. "The money is tight, but it still makes sense for her to try and knock out the novel before going back to full-time somewhere. There's a second advance when she turns it in. It's enough to carry us over. Gives her enough time for her to work on a third book. She can go pro if she can make this all work."

"Brendan's right," Abby explained. "This is my only shot. I'm sure once I start, I can do it. I just need the right idea. The perfect opening."

"Ella always assumed dying had a smell to it, but nothing like this." The doctor quoted the first line of *Understanding Ella.* "Not exactly a normal opening for a romance novel."

Abby shrugged. "That's probably why it worked, but who knows…"

Donetti tapped her pen on the side of her notepad. "Okay, this is good. You both agree Abby should continue to work on the book. Now you just need to agree on the money. At your current burn rate, how long before the advance is gone?"

Brendan and Abby had done the math an insane number of times. Even factored in things like cutting cable, no more dining out, grocery shopping on the cheap—coupons and sales. No more Trader Joe's or Whole Foods. No more artisan this or milk from nuts for twice the price of good, old-fashioned cow juice.

"Two months," Abby said flatly.

"Three if we really make things stretch."

For the first time in more than thirty minutes, the doctor smiled. "Abby, this is your husband being supportive. I know men aren't always good at expressing that sort of thing, so take note—this is what spousal support looks like."

Brendan felt a smile creep across his face.

Donetti turned to him. "Before you get all smug, I want you to promise your wife something. From this moment forward, for the next thirty days, you are not allowed to bring up money. You are not allowed to ask her about her book. No progress reports unless she volunteers the information. No pressure. Give her space to work. Do you understand?"

Brendan nodded.

"Tell her, not me."

Brendan turned and faced Abby. A soft sigh fell from his lips. "I want you to write the book. I know you can do it. I want to help you succeed."

The smile that filled Abby's face made him forget all those other things, and for one brief second, he remembered just how much he loved her.

The doctor put an end to that when she said—

"Now, we need to talk about the sex thing."

2

"When was the last time you had sex," Doctor Donetti asked again, adding, "together."

Brendan hoped Abby would answer that. He felt strange talking about their sex life with someone they'd only met thirty minutes earlier, and he had no idea what she'd already told this woman prior to today, but when Abby said nothing, he finally gave up the goods. "Going on three weeks now."

"Is that a long time for you?"

"Lately, no. But a few years ago, it was more like three or four times a week."

"And how long have you been a couple?"

"Married for ten years," he told her. "But we've been together for almost thirteen. We met in college. Northeastern."

Donetti scribbled something on her notepad, and Brendan fought the urge to get up and read whatever it was. The idea of someone taking notes on their personal life felt like an intrusion. Like he was eight again, confessing to something in the principal's

6

office, and the comment made the short list in his permanent file.

When the doctor looked back up, she said, "Did your sex life change when Abby quit her job?"

Brendan nodded. "Yeah."

Abby shuffled forward on the couch. "That's not true, Brendan. If she's going to help, she needs to know the whole story."

The whole story.

He knew where she was going with this, because it was where she always went with this.

Every fight.

Every night when she scurried across the bed and slept as far from him as she could without falling over the side.

Every silent stare.

This.

Abby cleared her throat and told the doctor, "Brendan slipped."

The blood rushed to Brendan's face, and he tried to bite back the anger that always came when she said that. Those two words. Like a double-edged knife she enjoyed twisting in his gut. "I didn't slip. I *almost* slipped. There's a difference."

Donetti scribbled again.

Her and the goddamn scribbling.

How was this supposed to make things better?

She'd side with Abby, then both would sling handfuls of guilt his way. You didn't need to be a rocket scientist to see that coming. Didn't need to be a shrink with a notepad.

The doctor leaned back in her chair and tapped her pen against her bottom lip a few times before speaking again. "Tell me what happened, Brendan. And remember, our first step is getting *all* the facts out on the table. No judgment. I just need to understand the details."

Brendan drew in a deep breath and let it out slowly. He looked down at his hands. "I work for an investigative unit of the SEC, that's the Securities and Exchange Commission. I'm in their financial crimes division. They call that one FCID. Government agencies love their acronyms. My job involves a lot of travel. When we're investigating a company, we typically spend a few weeks on-site gathering information, then we bring it back here to our office in Boston to dig in deeper. Two months ago, I was in Chicago with a co-worker—"

"A very attractive *female* co-worker," Abby chimed in.

Brendan wasn't about to take the bait. He ignored the comment and went on. "We'd received a number of complaints about a peer-to-peer lending company and felt it warranted a site visit."

Donetti looked puzzled. "A peer-to-peer lending company?"

"It's an online thing. They pair borrowers and lenders directly, without the involvement of a traditional financial institution in the middle. If you have money sitting in your bank, they can help you loan it out to a stranger and earn some interest. They vet the borrowers for you. The worse their credit score, the more interest you can earn. Some borrowers prefer it because they dislike banks. Others go there when nobody else will lend to them. It's a little Wild West, but it's catching on. Anyway, we received enough complaints to justify a visit. Guilty or not, things can get tense. We usually arrive unannounced and have full access to the company's employees and financial data. They obviously don't want us there. The more we find, the more stressful the situation can become. It creates an *us against them* vibe. This company was no different. They greeted us the first day with fake smiles, and things went south from there. It was like the two of us were trapped behind enemy lines. So Friday night comes around, we'd dealt with this for the better part of a week, and we're both wound tight. I broke protocol and ordered some drinks with dinner."

Donetti raised her hand. "You broke protocol? Or you *both* broke protocol?"

"She's my subordinate in her second year. I've got a decade on the job, six pay grades above her. I was in charge, and she followed my lead. It's on me." Brendan wasn't about to skirt that, he owned it. "There were drinks, food, conversation…"

"You kissed her," Abby said flatly.

Brendan rolled his eyes. "I didn't kiss her. She kissed me."

"There's a difference?" the doctor asked.

"Yes. There's a difference. She kissed me. I told her I was happily married; we had a little laugh over it, and that was that."

Abby let out a soft groan. "That was that…"

More scribbling, then Donetti looked at Abby. "You feel betrayed."

"Damn right, I feel betrayed."

"I didn't do anything!"

Abby wasn't about to back down. "You put yourself in a position where something could have happened."

"But it didn't! Christ. Why won't you let it go? Guys hit on you all the time."

"I've never kissed any of them."

"She kissed me!"

"Then why didn't you report it?!" Abby fired back, her voice shrill now.

Again, the doctor's hand came up. Her face softened, but only slightly. "I know this is hard, for both of you, but it's best if we all keep our emotions in check. Do you need to take a minute?"

Abby glared at Donetti, and Brendan thought she might go off on the doctor, and wouldn't that be perfect? Maybe if the doctor caught a whiff of Abby's temper, she could keep her feet firmly planted in neutral territory. Abby didn't go off on the doctor, though; instead, she slumped back in her seat and managed to rein it back in. "He should have reported it."

More scribbling, and this time Brendan swore he caught some underlining before the doctor looked back up at him. "Why didn't you report it?"

Brendan fought the urge to sink deeper into the couch and instead sat up straight. He did the right thing. He did nothing wrong. "Kim is two years into her career. Something like that would ruin her. It was a non-event. She was embarrassed enough, so I didn't see the point. Nothing happened. Not really."

"Kim…" Abby muttered.

"I told Abby because I didn't want to keep it from her. I thought we were the kind of couple who preferred honesty over secrets, even the harmless ones. Maybe that's where I was wrong."

"Oh, don't put this on me. I—"

Again, the doctor's hand came up. "Okay, time out. Let's just take stock of all this and find a solution. I think we came up with a plan on the money you're both comfortable with, right?"

At first, neither Abby nor Brendan acknowledged that. Both were running defense and didn't want to concede an inch. That was silly. They were here to fix this, not make it worse. Brendan finally nodded and realized Abby was nodding, too.

"Good." Donetti grinned. "That's good. Here are my thoughts on the rest; feel free to disagree, but also try to be each other's champion. Put yourself in your partner's shoes before you respond. You need to back each other up, not back away." She glanced at the clock, then turned to Brendan. "Whether this woman kissed you or you kissed her or you let her believe it was okay to kiss you…none of that matters. You knew something was wrong enough about the situation to feel guilty, and you wanted to unburden yourself by telling Abby. So you did that. It's bad you allowed it to happen, it's good you didn't keep it to yourself. You were right to share." She let that sink in for a long moment, then swiveled toward Abby. "You feel betrayed. Your husband travels a lot for work, that conjures up all kinds of fears, not the least of which is cheating. Something like this happens and validates those thoughts. But here's the thing. Regardless of how it happened, he didn't follow through. He put an end to it. He confided in you. This comes down to one simple question—Would you have preferred not to know?"

Abby shook her head. "Of course not."

"Absolutely. It was painful to hear, but secrets in a marriage are worse. Secrets end marriages."

"He should have reported it, though," Abby said softly. "Not just told me."

Donetti tightened her lips, nodded, and faced Brendan again. "Tense situation. Benefit of the doubt...I understand why you didn't say anything at work, but you need to make a promise to your wife right now. If something else happens with this woman, even the smallest thing, you will take the entire matter to your superiors and let the chips fall where they may. Protecting your marriage is far more important than protecting this woman's career. Husband first, job second. She does it again, you put it out there. Understand?"

Brendan nodded.

"Good. Now here's a simple question for both of you. Do you believe you'll still be married ten years from now?"

That hit Brendan like a gut punch. Abby, too. Her face went white.

Doctor Donetti answered before either of them could. "I think you'll still be married, and here's why—you came here. Both of you recognized a problem and were willing to take action to resolve it before it got out of hand. The couples who fail don't do that. They let things fester. Maintaining a good marriage is hard work, work you've both demonstrated you're willing to do. Be each other's champion in all things. Remember that." She smiled curtly. "We have a plan, and I'm confident you will execute that plan. Which brings us to our final hurdle. The sex thing."

Brendan stole a glance at Abby and found she was doing the same. Both quickly turned back to the doctor.

"A marriage without sex means you're roommates legally bound to each other. Nobody likes a roommate. Sex isn't just about some physical gratification; it brings people closer together. An unmatched intimacy. Good sex teaches you to work together, great sex teaches you to act as one."

She scribbled yet again on her notepad, but this time she wrote in the bottom corner of the page. When she was done, she tore it off and handed the note to Abby.

"That's an app I've found to be extremely helpful in situations like yours. Think of it as a marital aid. A continuation of the work we started here today. It's popular in the app stores, so you shouldn't have any trouble finding it. Read the description, give it a try if you think it's a good fit. Or don't, if it's not your thing, that's fine too. Either way, the two of you need to reconnect on a personal level, and I think it could help. Can you do that?"

Abby looked down at the paper and nodded.

"Brendan?"

He nodded too.

Doctor Donetti smiled. "Good. Now, one last thing. Homework. The two of you are going to have sex tonight. Remember what it is you like about each other. Don't be afraid to try new things. Experiment." She nodded at the paper in Abby's hand. "Give the app a go."

A timer on the desk behind her chimed, and Brendan realized it was ten minutes until noon. Somehow, she'd managed to wrap their session at exactly the fifty-minute mark. She reached over and retrieved a Day-Timer from the corner of her desk. "I'd like to see you both back here next Tuesday. Does eleven in the morning work for you?"

3

"An app, huh? How exactly does that keep his dick out of other women?" Hannah licked some salt from the side of her margarita glass, took a drink, and leaned against the kitchen counter. "If Stuckey pulled that shit with me I'd buy a big pair of scissors and keep them on top of my nightstand, tell him to sleep tight. Men are animals. Back when we were dating, Stuckey told me when he was thirteen he actually fucked a bowl of Jell-O. There are so many things wrong with that it makes me wonder why God bothered to give men opposable thumbs. Maybe you and me should go dyke and move to Costa Rica, open a B&B." She ran her fingers through Abby's dark hair. "You'll need to do something about this, though."

"What's wrong with my hair?"

"Oh, nothing's wrong with it. It's beautiful. *You're beautiful.* It's just a little Plain Jane. If we're going to be seen together in a biblical sense, you need to step up your game."

Two years ago, Hannah Morland was a teller at the local branch of United on the fast track to *remaining* a teller at the local branch of United for the rest of her life. She hated her job, hated her boss, and began posting about it daily on TikTok; these funny videos she'd shoot in the bank about her co-workers and the people who came in. By the time someone reported her, and her boss handed her a pink slip, she had amassed nearly a million followers and was making more on social media in a month than she made in a year at the bank. Now she had nearly four million followers and a slew of sponsors. Companies sent her everything from smoothie blenders to clothing in hopes she'd mention it or wear it or stage it in the background of some shot. Last week a plastic surgeon had offered her free Botox for a year, and by the looks of Hannah's forehead, she'd returned that call.

Hannah had it dialed in.

"Hey, Schmoopy," Stuckey bellowed out from the living room. "Bring me another beer when you finish talking about me behind my back, will ya?"

A forced smile rolled across Hannah's lips. "You got it, Papi Chulo!"

Abby frowned. "Schmoopy? Papi Chulo?"

"We're doing this thing where we're not allowed to call each other by name, only pet names, and to keep things interesting, we're not allowed to repeat the same pet name."

Abby took a sip of her margarita. "What happens if you lose?"

"The loser has to give the winner head at the time and place of his or her choosing."

Abby's cheeks flushed. "That doesn't sound so bad."

"Well, Stuckey's a bit of a freak. The last time he won, he made me do it in the McDonald's drive-thru. Said I had to make him cum before we reached the window, or I'd have to buy."

"And did you…"

Hannah cocked her hip. "I'm not paying for no damn McDonald's.

I pulled some tricks from my high school playbook and got things done in under a minute. Made him buy me a sundae, too."

"That's my girl." Abby clinked her glass against Hannah's, then frowned. "Should I be worried you went to McDonald's?"

"Don't judge me. It was our cheat night."

In the living room, Brendan let out a loud laugh.

Abby hadn't heard that sound in weeks. It was kinda nice.

Hannah's voice dropped low. "Was it weird talking to a shrink?"

"You've never talked to a shrink?"

"Are you saying I should?"

"I just figured…"

"You're saying I'm messed up? I need help? Professional help? Wow. Is that how you see me? *What you think of me?*"

Abby tried to backpedal. "No, of course not. I didn't mean—"

"My God, Abby. I thought you were a friend."

"I didn't mean to imply—"

Hannah squeezed Abby's arm and grinned. "I'm just messing with you. Of course I've seen a shrink. A few, in fact. Got my personal therapist. Couples therapist. Had one back at the bank as part of my benefits; I was on his couch twice a week. He was older than dirt and smelled like rubbing alcohol, but he was a good listener. It's good to talk to a professional. I'm glad you're doing it. God knows you shouldn't be taking advice from me." She glanced down at the crumpled paper Abby had shown her. "An app to fix the sex life and a thirty-day reprieve from money talk to get your book going; sounds like it went pretty good."

Abby took another sip. A long sip. "I still haven't written a word. I have no clue what to write about."

Hannah let out a sigh. "You will. It will come to you when you least expect it. Isn't that how you said it works?"

"That's what happened with the first one, but it's been months and I've got nothing. I'm beginning to think I only had the one book in me."

"You can always write about me."

"I don't do trashy erotica."

"Oh, snap!" Hannah smirked. "Alcohol gives you game. I like it. Maybe you should consider developing a drinking problem when you fix your hair, like a whole *You* makeover."

"Still looking for that beer, Jellybean!" Stuckey called out.

A moment later, Brendan chimed in. "Abby, can you grab me one, too? While you're in there?"

Abby took another drink and licked her lips. "You got it, Tater Tot!"

4

"Juliet, baby, what's wrong with this picture?"

Juliet stood in the doorway, leaning against the wood frame, backlit by some light they'd left on down the hall. Romeo could only make out her silhouette, just the general shape of her, but she had a habit of wearing tight-fitting clothing and her silhouette was something to behold. She gave good shadow; always had. She'd left her shoes in the van, and he caught the faint movement of her toes kneading the plush carpet. She had a thing for all things soft. When she spoke, her voice gave him honest-to-God goose bumps up and down his arms.

"She got the knot wrong."

Romeo nodded slowly, let the next words roll off his tongue in a lazy drawl. "She got the knot *all* wrong."

"You told her a square knot, and that there is a slip. I'd know it from a mile."

The bedroom was a little on the ordinary side. Neutral colors, lots of taupe, too much taupe. A few paintings up on the walls, nothing special. Romeo was pretty certain if he flipped them over he'd find price tags from HomeGoods or IKEA or some shit. While Juliet had decided to watch from the doorway, he had pulled a chair right up to the foot of the bed, twisted it around backward, and straddled the high back. He didn't want to miss anything.

"Square knot can be a bitch to get out of, slip knot is easy," Juliet pointed out. "I hate pointing fingers, but I think she did that on purpose."

"I don't know how to tie a square knot! It's a knot! What do you want from me?"

There was a hitch to the woman's voice, a bit of fear mixed with urgency.

Romeo liked that.

It meant she was on her toes.

She was in the moment.

Sometimes they checked out, and if their head wasn't in the game this sort of thing wasn't much fun, and he'd promised Juliet some fun. He cleared his throat. "If you don't know how to tie a square knot, tie something you do know. As long as it's not that bullshit that comes undone easily, we're all good. I'd hate to think you were trying to pull one over on us, making it easy for your man to get out."

"I'm not!"

"When we got here, you seemed like a straight-up kinda woman to me. Trustworthy. But you get all loosey-goosey with the rope, and Juliet and I may need to reevaluate your role in the current situation. Maybe you're not as important to us as we first thought."

The woman shook her head, or maybe that was the trembling, it was hard to tell. Either way, she leaned back over her husband, untied the rope fastening his wrists to the headboard, and went at it again. This time she tied a respectable knot, some cross between a bowline and a fisherman, and when she pulled it tight her husband winced. He might have cried out a bit too, it was tough to tell with the gag crammed in his mouth.

"That's better, don't you think, Juliet?"

"Much."

Romeo had taken it upon himself to secure the man's legs and torso to the bedframe. He'd only met these two and wasn't about to trust the wife with something so significant, but he was willing to give her the hands, make her think she still had some level of control.

The husband had already been naked when he and Juliet came in. Sprawled out on the bed checking something on his phone instead of watching his wife undress on the opposite side of the room. Romeo had found that a little sad. Disrespectful. He'd been with Juliet going on four years now, and just the thought of her shedding her clothing was enough to send every inch of his being in a tailspin. He hadn't asked Byron or Cindy how long they'd been together, but the true answer was clearly *too long* because you don't lose interest in a soulmate, only in a partner whose time had passed. This might be the first fun they'd had in years.

Romeo shifted the heavy .44 Magnum from his left hand to his right and rested the barrel on the back of his chair, pointed loosely in Cindy's general direction. "Does Byron normally take a pill to get in the moment? Because he is clearly not in the moment."

Cindy appeared confused for a second, then looked down at her husband's penis. It had shriveled up into a nub. Looked like it was trying to climb up inside the man and hide. "He…doesn't take anything. Not that I know of."

Juliet shifted in the doorway. "I'm thinking it's us, baby. Our presence might be throwing the poor man off his game."

Romeo nodded again. "What do you think, Cindy? Can you get your man…back in the game?"

Romeo thumbed the hammer back on the Magnum. A little gesture, but enough to help him get his point across. Then he said, "Why don't you go ahead and lose the bra and panties too. We're all friends here."

Cindy's eyes darted from the gun back up to him, and at first, she didn't do anything. Sometimes they didn't and needed a bit more persuasion, but she reached around to her back and unfastened the snap on her bra, let it drop to the ground. She hesitated with the underwear, and Romeo thought he might have to get up and help her, but she slipped her thumbs on either side and eased them down too, stepped out of them. She had a decent body, not the best Romeo had seen, but not the worst either. She was certainly in far better shape than poor Byron.

Romeo waved the gun. "Get to it now, Cindy. Time to wake up Little Byron. He's got work to do."

Cindy had cried earlier, and the waterworks started up again, and that was no good. Nothing killed the mood like tears.

He waved the gun again. "Is this what's bothering you? How 'bout I put it away?" He tucked the large weapon behind his back, into the waistband of his jeans, and held up both hands. "See? No gun."

"A little tug-and-rub, Cindy," Juliet purred from the doorway. "You know what to do."

Cindy shuffled closer to the bed and reached for her husband. Her hand was shaking so bad it was a wonder she managed to get it around him, but she did. To her credit, she tried, but Little Byron had checked out.

After about a minute, Romeo cleared his throat again. "Juliet, I hate to ask, but I'm thinking you may need to do this thing."

Juliet's shadow froze in the doorway as she considered this, then she stepped into the room just far enough for the moonlight creeping in from the far window to catch her. She was wearing those cut-off jean shorts Romeo liked so much, the ones that hugged her just right. Her tan legs stretched on forever, and it took every ounce of willpower Romeo could muster to keep himself from taking her right there in the middle of the floor, showing Byron and Cindy how the dance was supposed to go.

Juliet crossed the room, gave Cindy a quick glance, and leaned over the man tied to the bed. She got down close and said softly, "Hey Byron, I want you to forget your wife for a second, forget all about Romeo down at the foot of the bed, it's only you and me now, baby, just the two of us." Her voice purred. Her breath so warm Romeo could nearly see it slipping from her lips to the man's ear. "I've been standing over there watching you, imagining your hands on my body, slipping under my shirt, down the front of my shorts… the things I bet you could do to me with one finger…just thinking of all that has got me so wet…I want you so bad…" She eased her hand down his chest, traced the edges of the ropes until her palm was resting on his thigh. "If we ask Cindy real nice, do you think she'll put it in my mouth? Let me taste you? I want my lips around you when you grow…that's my favorite part."

The words threw the room into complete silence.

Byron was staring at her.

Several seconds ticked by, and Cindy let out a soft gasp.

Her hand had still been around her husband's penis when it began to rise. She released him and took a step back, this horrified look on her face.

"Ha!" Romeo cried out. "There he is! I knew you had it in you, Byron!"

Romeo reached behind his back, grabbed hold of the Magnum, and swung back around as he jumped out of the chair. The first shot entered Cindy's left temple and sprayed the wall with her last thought. He quickly put two rounds in Byron—one in the chest, another in his forehead. He shot him again in the balls, because, why not?

It was loud.

It was fantastic.

When the echo died, he told Juliet, "I can't bring myself to respect a man who covets another man's wife above his own."

She'd jumped to the side when Romeo took out the gun, but some of Byron's blood still managed to speckle her face. She made no attempt to wipe it away. "I didn't like him much, anyway. For a second there, I thought you were gonna make me do him."

He lifted her face to his and rolled his thumb over her chin. "Never, baby. Never." He brushed his lips across hers. That was when he smelled the gasoline. "Did you get some on you?"

"A little bit," she confessed. "When I emptied the can on the floor downstairs."

5

"Can you move your elbow? That kinda hurts."

"Sorry."

Brendan was on top of Abby, his arm pinned between his chest and her breasts. Their heavy quilt had gotten tangled up in their legs. From the Alexa speaker on his nightstand, Adele was crooning about holding on and some mess she'd gotten herself into.

Sex between them had never been spontaneous. Maybe in the early days, back in college when the next day entailed nothing but classes or a shift at whatever minimum wage job they'd been working, but the second they found themselves out in the "real world," spontaneity had been shoved out the window by eighty-hour work weeks, stress, and growing responsibilities. At one point, they'd scheduled sex (every third day, unless Abby was on her period). That had gone on for the better part of the Obama administration, even into the early years of Trump, right up until the Great Snore Incident of 2020—Abby fell asleep midsession, and once Brendan had gotten over the humiliation of that and had silently debated the finish/don't finish question (he did not), he'd fallen asleep too. The schedule vanished, packed away in the same box their spontaneity had gone to storage, and they'd resorted to the occasional grab-n-go quickie brought on by a steamy scene in their latest Netflix binge. Brendan called that Maintenance Sex. Abby called it Shtupp Time. Both pretended to enjoy it even though it felt more like a task to be checked off some marital to-do list rather than something pleasurable.

The doctor had given them an assignment.

Reluctantly, they'd both agreed to convene in the bedroom and complete their assignment at 9 p.m.

The lights were out. Abby had lit a candle, but it was one of those scented ones and the smell of lilacs made Brendan want to sneeze. He knew from past experience if he sneezed once, he'd sneeze a dozen times. He needed to get away from it. "Can I go down on you?"

"Yeah."

Abby sometimes got self-conscious, so Brendan made it a point to ask. He eased down the length of her body, kissing her as he went. He did his best to kick the quilt out of the way and took a moment to rub his nose and stifle the sneeze before it got worse. He was certain she didn't notice him do that, but to be sure, he spent a little extra time kissing the back of her knee before moving to her inner thighs and the place between. Abby let out a soft moan, arched her back, and pressed into him. A minute had passed, Adele had moved on to "Easy on Me," when Brendan heard something that horrified him. He lifted his head and looked at Abby.

"Are you giggling?"

Abby froze. Her eyes went wide, and her mouth dropped open. She quickly pinched it shut before any words escaped.

"You were, weren't you?"

He got up on his elbows so he could see her better. Her cheeks were flushed.

She swallowed, embarrassed. "I'm sorry, it's just…you didn't shave, did you? Your beard…tickles."

"Seriously?"

"I'm sorry. Just do it again. Pretend that didn't happen. It was nice. Really. I liked it."

Brendan sat up further. "Do you want me to shave?"

"No. It's fine. I just wasn't ready for it."

"You weren't ready to be tickled by my beard?"

"No."

"And if you were, that would have been okay?"

She paused a beat. "Yeah. Sure."

He wasn't buying that. "I always shave in the morning. That means my beard is always this length at night. When we…you know. Does it always…tickle?"

Abby went quiet for another second, then finally nodded. "Yeah."

Brendan rolled over on his back and stared at the ceiling. "If it bothered you, why didn't you ever say anything?"

"*Bothered* is a very strong word."

"Okay, then pick another word. That's not the point. The point is if you don't tell me, I don't know. Christ, Abby, we've been together for thirteen years. It's not like this is our first time. It means it's always…you never actually enjoyed…" Brendan let out a sigh and rolled over.

Abby sat up. "That's not true. I always like it."

"Sure."

Abby reached for the quilt and covered herself up. The moment (if there had ever been one) was over. "It's not something we talk about."

"Well, maybe we should," Brendan said. "You told the doctor

we don't talk. I suppose there's some truth to that. Maybe you were right."

Abby inched closer to him and rested her head on his shoulder. "We used to. In the beginning. I guess life gets in the way sometimes."

From the speaker, Adele launched into her version of that old Garth Brooks song, the one he stole from Billy Joel.

Brendan ran his hand through Abby's hair. "Mind if I share a secret?"

Abby looked at his face. "I wish you would."

"I don't even like Adele."

This time, Abby laughed. "I thought you did. If we're being honest, I always thought she was a bit whiny."

Brendan found himself laughing too. Finally, he said, "Alexa, stop."

And she did.

The room went quiet.

Abby kissed his shoulder and stood from the bed. With the quilt draped over her shoulders, she crossed the room and ruffled through her purse on the dresser. When she returned, she was holding Brendan's phone and the scrap of paper from Dr. Donetti. "Maybe we should give it a try. Why not, right?"

"Why not." Brendan took his phone from her and went to the app store. "What's it called?"

"Sugar & Spice."

6

"Wow," Abby muttered. "How could an app have a hundred and six thousand reviews and I've never heard of it?"

"Is that a lot?"

Brendan honestly wasn't sure. He rarely downloaded anything to his phone. Abby, however, was a seasoned pro. She spent far too much time staring at that little screen lately. When Hannah started making real money posting online, Abby began studying all things Internet hoping to find some lucrative corner of her own. They'd had their share of fights about it, particularly since she quit her job. It burned him to see her bumbling around the web when she was supposed to be writing.

"It's number one in the app store." Abby rolled her thumb down the screen, quickly reading the description and glossing over several images of the app. "It's free to download and doesn't say anything about in-app purchases."

"So?"

"So I can't tell how they're making money."

"So?"

"So, nobody creates an app unless they're trying to make money."

"So?"

Abby smacked him in the shoulder. "Stop! Just download it."

Brendan clicked the download button and pressed his index finger to the reader when prompted by a security screen. Wrapped in the quilt, Abby hovered next to him, both watching the small progress bar slowly fill from left to right. When it completed, Brendan clicked OPEN. The screen locked, then went blank.

"What the hell?"

Abby frowned. "Did it freeze?"

He clicked the side buttons and tapped at the screen. Nothing happened.

"Maybe restart it?"

He did.

The phone rebooted, and when prompted, he keyed in his security code. The Sugar & Spice logo filled the screen, followed by—*Brought to you by International Entertainment Corp: Your gateway to the freedom you live!*

"That's a stupid company line," Abby said.

"It's probably written by some Chinese kid in his parents' basement. It reminds me of the instructions that came with our smart doorbell: *You will enjoy powering on the button marked D!* I still don't know what the *D* stands for. Drives me nuts whenever I think about it."

Another screen came up:

Welcome, Brendan Hollander! Would you like to simultaneously install Sugar & Spice on your partner's phone?

Although it was a question, it didn't offer him a *Yes* or *No*, only *Ok*. Brendan clicked on it, and Abby's phone let out a soft *ding!* from her vanity in the master bathroom.

"It's letting you install an app on my phone? How does it even know I'm your partner?"

"Maybe it searched my texts and assumed based on your incessant nagging?"

She smacked him again, and Brendan realized she was smiling. Not some half-assed polite grin, but smiling. It was nice and he almost told her so, but didn't, and the moment slipped away.

Would you like to log in with Facebook?

The smile left Abby's face. "Aren't you already logged in? It knew your name."

Again, it wasn't a *Yes* or *No* question; the only option to respond was *Ok*. Brendan clicked it again.

Allow Sugar & Spice to track your activity
across other companies' apps and website:
- Ask App not to track
- Allow

Brendan clicked *Ask App not to track* and nothing happened. He pressed it again, harder, as if that would make any difference. When he mashed it down a third time, the word *Allow* flashed, and the screen went away. "This thing is seriously buggy."

Another progress bar appeared on the screen. It took nearly a minute before it completed.

In the bathroom, Abby's phone dinged again. Neither of them looked at it. They were both busy reading the next message on Brendan's screen:

*I am in good physical condition. Aside from the 2.5mg dose of
Lisinopril I take daily for elevated blood pressure,
I have no other cardiovascular or underlying health issues.*

"How does it know that?"

Brendan had no idea. "Probably my health app. Or maybe my pharmacy app. I don't know."

This time there was a *Yes* or *No*, Brendan clicked *No*.

*Do you consider yourself to be adventurous
or boring when it comes to sex?*

Brendan's finger hovered over *Adventurous*, and Abby cleared her throat.

"Okay, okay." He clicked *Boring*.

The next message read:

*Which of the following best describes your partner in bed?
Frigid, timid, or frail?*

"That's not exactly a choice." Abby frowned.

"It's being buggy again; it won't let me answer. The only option is *Yes* or *No*."

Brendan clicked *No*.

Understood.

"Okay, now I'm really confused."

Does your partner enjoy pain?

They both stared at that one for a moment, then Brendan said, "Oh, I see what it's doing. The app is trying to establish a baseline."

"Well, duh. But it's not allowing you to answer yes or no on that question, either. Only *Ok*. And for the record, I *don't* enjoy pain. What kind of question is that, anyway?"

"What do you want me to do?"

"I don't want to say *Ok!*"

Brendan sighed. "It's just an app, Abby. Some game. If it tells us to do something and we don't want to, we won't." He clicked on *Ok* before Abby could object again. That brought up a follow-up question:

Do you enjoy pain?

Again, he pressed *Ok*.

Do you enjoy inflicting pain?

Ok.

Have you or your partner ever asphyxiated during sex?

Abby frowned. "Is that a thing?"

Brendan nodded slowly. "Do you remember that band INXS?"

"Sure."

"They found the lead singer in a closet with a belt around his neck. He accidentally suffocated himself while jerking off."

"Whoa."

"Yeah."

This time, the app allowed him to answer *No*.

Would you like to?

"That would be a *No*," Abby said flatly.

Like before, answering *No* wasn't an option. Only *Ok*. Brendan mashed down the button before Abby could object. "If it tells us to do something and we don't want to, we won't," he repeated.

As the remaining questions came up, he clicked *Ok*. Faster each time, until the questions flew by so quickly he barely read them—

Have you and your partner ever welcomed others into your bed?

Ok.

Do you consider yourself to be dominant?

Ok.

Do you consider yourself to be submissive?

Ok.

Have you or your partner ever considered sex with an animal?

Ok.

Have you ever had sex in a moving vehicle?

Ok.

Were you driving?

Ok.

Do you practice safe sex?

Ok.

Under the right circumstances, would you consider unsafe sex?

Ok.

Have you ever used tools or props (such as a vibrator)?

Ok.

Do you own tools or props (such as a vibrator)?

Ok.

Do you view pornography?

Ok.

Regularly?

Ok.

Have you or your partner ever created pornography?

Ok.

Do you or your partner masturbate?

Ok.

Regularly?

Ok.

Have you or your partner masturbated in front of the other?

Ok.

Have you or your partner masturbated in front of a stranger?

Ok.

Has a stranger masturbated in front of you or your partner?

Ok.

At least another dozen questions flew by. By the end, Brendan was hitting *Ok* so quickly he didn't realize the app was no longer asking simple questions but was prompting him to enter text. He stopped and read the next one aloud—

"Agree on a *safe word* with your partner and enter it here. If at any point you or your partner feel uncomfortable, simply say the safe word to bring the current activity to a stop." He glanced over at Abby. "Any suggestions?"

Her eyes were wide, still staring down at his phone. No doubt thinking about the flurry of previous text. He was about to ask her again when she said, "Magnolia. Go with that."

"Magnolia?"

"It's easy to remember, and it's not the kind of word either of us would say on accident."

Brendan couldn't argue with that.

He keyed in MAGNOLIA and hit enter.

You've granted this app access to your camera and microphone.

"Ah, no I didn't."
"Buggy, remember?" Abby said.

Please speak your safe word aloud.

Abby frowned. "So now it's listening?"

Please speak your safe word aloud.

Brendan cleared his throat. "Magnolia."

Thank you.
Abby Hollander, please speak your safe word aloud.

Abby looked over at Brendan, the surprise at seeing her name on his phone evident on her face. Then she whispered, "Magnolia."

Thank you.

There was another progress bar, then a soft triple-chime, followed by—

Welcome to Sugar & Spice!

7

In the bathroom, Abby's phone played the same melody. Three notes. Still draped in the quilt, she got up and retrieved it, brought it back to the bed, and dropped it next to Brendan's phone before sitting back down. The Sugar & Spice logo was splashed across the screen, and then both phones displayed the same message:

Welcome to Sugar & Spice!
Working with your partner, the object of the game is to earn points.
Accumulating enough points will help you graduate to the next level.
Levels are as follows:
Beginner
Bronze
Silver
Gold
Platinum
Those of a lesser level are considered
submissive to those of a greater level.

Abby hovered over the screen. "What exactly does that mean?"

"It means if I'm a *Gold* and you're a *Silver*, you have to do whatever I tell you."

"Well, that's not going to happen."

"Where's your sense of adventure, Mrs. Hollander?"

Some points are earned individually, others are earned with your partner and shared. Congratulations - you've both been awarded 100 points for installing the app and agreeing to our Terms of Service!

Both phones dinged.

100 appeared in the top right of their iPhone screens, directly below the battery indicator.

Abby said, "I wonder how many points you need to reach the next level."

You're both 4900 points away from reaching Bronze!

"I guess that answers that."

Playing the game is easy—select Sugar or Spice and complete the related task. Points are assigned based on difficulty.
Sugars tend to be tame, playful—questions meant to spur conversation with your partner while Spices lean more toward the risqué.

"So it's truth or dare for sex?" Brendan asked.

"Sounds like it."

If at any point you find yourself uncomfortable, simply utter your safe word. Would you like to begin?

Again, the only option was *Ok*.

Brendan clicked the button, and his phone went dark. The display on Abby's phone came to life with the Sugar & Spice logo followed by one simple question:

Sugar or Spice?

"I guess I'm going first," she said, then tentatively tapped on *Sugar*.

Tell your partner about the last time you touched yourself.

Abby's cheeks flushed. "I guess we're going there right out of the gate? Okay. I can do this." She drew in a deep breath. "Last night in the shower."

"Really?" Brendan felt his cheeks burn. They'd never talked about that sort of thing. He'd never seen Abby look so embarrassed. Then he remembered something and grinned. "When I got in the shower last night, the diverter was set to the handheld instead of the overhead sprayer."

A horrified expression swept over Abby, and she buried her face in the pillow. "Oh God, I'm gonna die."

"That's kinda hot," Brendan said softly. "How often do you…?"

Abby pressed deeper into the pillow. "Too much. Not enough. I don't know." Her ears were bright red. "Isn't it your turn?"

A playful melody came from Abby's phone, and Brendan glanced at the display. "Hey, that earned you 100 points!"

"So I'm winning? I get to tell you what to do now?"

"Easy, Shower Girl. We're both still Beginners. You don't get to tell me jack."

Abby's phone went dark, and Brendan's lit up with the same question—

38

Sugar or Spice?

"Time to take a commanding lead." Brendan smirked, pressing *Spice*.

Both phones came to life with identical text:

Date Night: You're going out to dinner tomorrow night!
A reservation has been made at Menton's in Boston for tomorrow night at 8 p.m. Buy a sexy outfit for your partner to wear, and leave it for them on your bed no later than 6 p.m. tomorrow. This means everything from underwear to shoes—dress them from head to toe.
Click HERE to retrieve their various sizes at any time during this Spice.
A timer appeared on both their phones, directly below their current points: **21:35:22**

"It's impossible to get a reservation at Menton's," Abby said. "They're booked out months in advance."

Brendan had scooped up his phone and tapped on the link in the message. After a few seconds, he held the phone out to her. "Are these really your sizes?"

She studied the list—everything from her shoe size to measurements—and nodded.

He looked up at her. "How do you think it knows?"

"When you installed the app, you gave it access to information stored in other apps. I order a lot of my clothes online, I guess it got it from there. Same way it knew about your blood pressure meds."

"That's a little creepy."

"I guess that depends on where you land with the whole privacy thing. Some people see it as a time-saver."

"It's fucking creepy."

"Yeah, I guess it is."

His phone dinged.

"That's an email confirmation for Menton's. 8 p.m. tomorrow, just like it says."

Abby was still draped in the quilt, but the corner had slipped from her shoulder. He could see a hint of her breast. When she caught him looking, she covered back up. "Can we even afford it?"

"No," Brendan muttered. "But I think we should do it anyway." He reached for her hand. "Look, I know we've been in a bit of a rough patch, but I love you and I think if we work at it, we'll come out the other side just fine. If we don't try. If we keep going like we have been…"

His voice trailed off, but Abby clearly knew where he was going because she was nodding her head. "We've fallen into a rut, that's all. I think we do what our therapist said—no book talk, no money talk, no work talk. Let's just go out like we used to back when we were dating. Forget everything else, and enjoy each other's company. We'll put it on our credit card and figure out how to pay for it next month. The dinner, clothes, everything."

As someone who monitors the financial downfalls of others for a living, Brendan cringed at the thought of dropping something they can't afford on their credit card, but he knew she was right. This was something they needed to do. He let out a sigh. "Okay, but maybe we should leave the tags on the clothes so we can return the glass slippers when the ball is over."

Sugar & Spice™

Sugar
*When did you first realize you wanted
to sleep with your partner?*

8

Stuckey leaned against the wall and sipped his chocolate milkshake. "If there's no God, who the hell invented yoga pants?"

Brendan had dragged him to the mall for their lunch hour. They were standing outside Victoria's Secret, looking in like patrons at a zoo exhibit. "You know, I'm thirty-three. I've been in there before. Why does this feel so weird?"

"It's designed to make you feel awkward. It helps to break down your defenses. They put all these frilly unmentionables out on full display, get you all worked up, feeling like a pedophile at Disney, and when your brain is complete mush some girl from the pages of their catalog steps out and offers to help you like a lifeline. You won't be able to say no to her. You'll buy whatever she hands you just to make it all end. When you finally escape, they've got a Sports Station Bar and Grill right across the hall." He jerked his thumb back over his shoulder and pointed. "It's like a safe haven. A beacon. A warm blanket. We stumble in, have a beer, share our war story with some dumb schmuck who went through the same thing five minutes earlier, and head out. Beer and bras. You go to any mall in America, and you'll always find them right across from each other, keeping the economy going one desperate husband at a time."

"Excuse me, gentlemen, may I help you?"

Brendan turned to find a girl of maybe nineteen or twenty standing just inside Victoria's Secret. She was wearing a short black skirt and leather high-heel boots that came to her knees. The first few buttons of her white blouse were undone, revealing a lacy pink thing beneath. The tag pinned above her breast read MANDY.

Stuckey slurped down the last of his milkshake. "Yep."

Twenty minutes later, they were perched at the bar across the hall. Brenden held a draft in one hand and the receipt from Victoria's Secret in his other. "Three hundred seventy-eight dollars. Abby's gonna kill me."

"No, she's not. She'll be thrilled you bought her something nice, something that makes her feel all womanly. Here's the part you gotta wrap your head around. She'll wear this stuff once. Tonight. That's it. After that, it will end in the back of her underwear drawer where such things go to die. It doesn't matter how sexy they look in it, they only wear it one time, then it vanishes."

Brendan took a drink of his beer. "Three hundred seventy-eight dollars."

"You're worried about that? She's out spending your bling-bling right now on something for you to wear, and you still got dinner tonight. Dinner at Menton's is gonna set you back a five-spot, easy. You're looking at a grand in spending, just for today. Maybe more. This is why married people don't date. We blow our load courting the object of our affection, then borrow up to our eyeballs so we can lock them down with a wedding and a place to live, then spend the rest of our lives paying it all off. You got real problems if she enjoys tonight, 'cause that means she'll want to do it again."

Across the wide hallway, Mandy poked her head out of Victoria's Secret, spotted Stuckey, and waved.

"I spent all that money and she's waving at you?"

Stuckey grinned and waved back. "Can't help it. I'm cuddly. Women love me."

Brendan did the math in his head; Stuckey wasn't far off. One or two nights like this, and he and Abby would be eating ramen noodles for the next month. Their bank account was surviving on fumes. "How do you and Hannah keep it together?"

"Me and Hannah are a fucking train wreck. Both of us. I think that's why it works. If I got my shit together, I think she'd get bored and leave me."

Stuckey was Black and at least thirty pounds overweight, had been since high school, but he carried it well. Somehow it softened him up, took down the defenses of those around him. Brendan had seen him use that more than once when they were on the job. They'd do their version of good cop, bad cop. Brendan would dig into someone during an interview, then Stuckey would swoop in like their best buddy, rescue them from the evil auditor, and they'd end up spilling their dirty little secrets. His Jedi mind trick seemed to work on everyone but his wife. Hannah danced to her own drum.

Brendan's phone rang, and he glanced at the screen. "Shit."

Stuckey looked over. "Why is your girlfriend calling you?"

"She's not my girlfriend. It was a misunderstanding."

Stuckey took a sip of his beer. "Whatever."

Bringing the phone to his ear, he answered the call. "Hey, Kim."

"Where are you? You didn't leave the office, did you?"

"I had to run an errand. I should be back in about thirty minutes. What's up?"

"We were supposed to compare notes on INTENT over lunch today so we're on the same page for our meeting with the assistant director at two."

Shit.

Brendan racked his hair. "Sorry, this couldn't wait."

"Is Stuckey with you?"

"Yeah."

"Put me on speaker."

Covering the phone, he told Stuckey, "She wants to talk to both of us."

"Why? What did I do?"

Brendan shrugged and set the phone down on the bar. He clicked speaker. "Kim? We're both here."

"I think INTENT might be hiding money in Laos."

Brendan and Stuckey exchanged a glance.

They'd been investigating INTENT for nearly four months now. Formerly a software development firm, they'd branched out into peer-to-peer lending, and through a combination of low prices and blitz marketing campaigns, they'd managed to grow into the number three spot, biting at the heels of Lending Club and Upstart. This was the same company Brendan and Kim Whitlock had visited in Chicago, chasing a high number of customer complaints over the previous year. Primarily failure to pay back loans in a timely manner.

Stuckey spoke first.

"Are you sure?"

"90 percent."

"That's not sure."

"No. It means I'm 90 percent sure. That's why I said ninety. If I was sure, I would have said one hundred."

Stuckey pressed mute on the phone. "I can see why you like her. She's feisty."

Rolling his eyes, Brendan unmuted the call. "What gets you to ninety? What did you find?"

"Six trips by a member of senior staff over the past year on commercial airlines."

"That's not exactly a smoking gun."

"Why fly commercial when they lease three private jets?"

"Kim, that's—"

"Not one of those trips was submitted for reimbursement."

Stuckey's eyes narrowed. "Then how did you find it?"

"Some personal credit card records somehow got copied in our initial document request."

"Who's credit card?"

"Their CFO, Isaac Alford."

"There's nothing illegal about going to Laos on his own dime. Sounds like a vacation."

"Six times in under a year? Come on. That's not pleasure, that's business. Nobody goes to Laos for pleasure."

"That's really weak," Stuckey said softly.

Kim wasn't about to be deterred. *"Six times!"*

"Putting you on hold for a second, Kim." Stuckey brought his finger down on the mute button again before she could object and gave Brendan a dismissive glance. "Laos is a red flag because the money launderers love it, I'll give her that, but if you're laundering money, you don't visit. You hide that shit. More likely Alford's a pedo and going there to dip his wick. Child prostitution is big there too."

Stuckey was probably right. He might be a smart ass, but he'd been doing this longer than Brendan, certainly longer than Kim. Criminals weren't that bright, and he'd seen it all two times over. Brendan clicked off mute. "Kim, you said you thought they might be hiding money in Laos. How are you even connecting this travel to the company?"

"Robin Church."

"Who?"

"On the credit card receipt, someone wrote the name Robin Church and circled it. I found that same name written on a few of INTENT's internal financial statements—same handwriting, circled the same way. Some with a question mark next to them, others with an exclamation mark. Like someone connecting dots. The handwriting doesn't match the samples we have for Isaac Alford, which means he didn't write it, somebody else did, and they wanted us to see it."

Brendan pursed his lips. "Stuckey's right, Kim. That's weak."

"It's something," she stated firmly.

"Does INTENT have anyone on staff named Robin Church?"

"Nobody. Whoever wrote this wants us to look at Alford. Why else would they slip his personal credit card statement into document production?"

Stuckey rolled his eyes. "Putting you on hold again, Kim. Sing along with the happy music." He clicked mute. "You take this to the assistant director, and she'll bust you down to customer service."

Brendan wasn't so sure. "It could be something. Maybe a whistleblower dropping bread crumbs."

"Sounds more like a whole lotta nothing. You dig deep enough, you'll find just what I said. Their CFO flew to Laos to diddle little boys or girls. Some fucking pervert. Nothing more."

"Then why would that name appear on internal docs, too? This wouldn't be the first time we found evidence of a company investigating something on their own before we arrived on their doorstep. Maybe Kim's got it wrong. Maybe Alford found some rogue employee and was chasing it down. At the very least, it's a loose end."

Stuckey thought that over and unmuted the call. "Kim, you need more before we can go to the AD with this."

"If you found this, you'd take it to her," Kim said. *"You know you would."*

"That's not true. I—"

She disconnected.

Stuckey whistled. "Oh, man. You got your hands full training that one. How long is she on the job?"

"Two years."

"Bet you a dollar she don't see three."

"She's got a good head on her shoulders; she just gets overzealous."

Stuckey finished off his beer and stood. He was watching Mandy across the hall again. "Maybe I should pick up something nice for Hannah."

"Why didn't you buy something when we were in there? We need to get back."

"Who said anything about buying?" His voice dropped low, eyeing Mandy. "Hannah told me last night she was open to a three-way."

Brendan dropped a twenty on the bar top and shook his head. "Why are everyone's lives so much more interesting than mine?"

9

The sun was setting, and Abby was standing at the front door when Brendan finally got home, her face burning with frustration. She held up her phone. The tiny timer in the corner had gone red, just like his had in the car nearly forty minutes ago. Before he could say a word, three chimes rang out from his Apple watch followed by a text message:

You were due home at 6 p.m. Your tardiness has cost you 30 points. Tick, tock, Mr. Hollander!

"Wonderful." He shook his head and offered Abby his most apologetic grin. "There was a wreck out on I-90. Three lanes were blocked. I managed to get off at Brownling, along with half the other cars. I'm sorry, I got home as fast as I could."

"Our reservation is in an hour and twenty-three minutes. Menton's won't hold a table more than five minutes, not with their wait list." She looked like she might explode. "It will take us at least thirty minutes to get there, more with parking. And we still need to get ready. Maybe you should have left earlier."

Before Brendan could reply, she turned and stomped up the stairs.

"Perfect start to date night," he muttered, chasing after her.

He found her standing on the far side of their room. There were two boxes and a glossy bag from Gary Percey laid out on the bed in front of her. Gary Percey was a high-end men's retailer with a shop out on Middleton in Boston. He'd driven past a million times, but had never gone in. Any place that advertised custom-tailored suits with designer names he couldn't pronounce was not exactly on his radar, not on a government salary. He'd always been more of a Men's Warehouse or Black Friday sale at Sears kind of guy.

Brendan set the bag from Victoria's Secret down on the bed opposite her, and the two of them faced off like outlaws in an old Western. He half-expected a tumbleweed to blow by when Abby slid the two boxes and bag across the bed to him along with a page printed from the Gary Percey website.

"I got you everything in that picture."

From the crinkled page, a twenty-something male model pouted at the camera wearing…what exactly was he wearing? Khaki pants with brown loafers, Argyle socks. His white button-down was open at the neck, and a dark red sweater was draped over his shoulders. The model clutched it with one hand. "Is that a belt or a piece of rope?"

"It's a belt made from rope," Abby told him. "It's stylish. I like it."

"Okay."

He slid the Victoria's Secret bags over to her.

She riffled through the contents, the color slowly leaving her face. "This is what you want me to wear?"

"It's stylish," he repeated. "I like it."

Her irritated gaze jumped from him back to her phone screen.

"We need to hurry."

Scooping up both bags, she went into the bathroom and closed the door.

She locked it.

Actually locked the door.

Brendan wanted to shave. Brush his teeth. Hell, he'd shower if he could.

None of that would happen.

He blew out a breath and began to strip off his clothes.

Ten minutes later, he was dressed, fumbling with the rope belt.

Twenty minutes later, he was standing at the full-length mirror in the corner of the room. He draped the sweater over his left shoulder, then his right, then both. He looked like a fucking idiot.

Forty minutes later, he was sitting on the corner of the bed. Abby was still in the bathroom.

"Abs?"

Silence.

"Abby, we're gonna be—"

The lock clicked, and she came out.

The red dress he'd picked plunged low in the back and was held together by a series of crisscrossing straps running down the left side from Abby's chest to her thigh. When Mandy had shown it to him and Stuckey, she explained it wasn't meant to be worn with a bra or panties and double-sided tape might be needed to ensure nothing wasn't exposed that wasn't meant to be exposed; Brendan had been sure to pick up a roll at the register. He was fairly certain the tape wasn't supposed to be visible, and when Abby moved he caught an eyeful of her left breast, so something was wrong. The matching shoes he'd gotten her dangled from her hand. "These are like five-inch heels. How do you expect me to walk? I can't—"

Her voice cut off when Brendan stood up.

She was staring at him.

"What?"

Abby clamped her mouth shut and bit her lower lip. Her eyes grew wide, and she began to giggle.

"What's wrong?"

She tried to hold back the laughter, but it only grew worse. "Oh my God, you look ridiculous…"

The sweater was still over Brendan's left shoulder, but he'd given up holding it. When he glanced back at the mirror, he realized he looked like someone had dumped the laundry basket over his head. The socks itched and the shoes pinched his toes so bad his right foot had gone numb. He shifted his weight to keep from falling over. "You don't like it?"

That only made Abby laugh harder. Brendan couldn't help but laugh too, and both fell back on the bed, the anger and frustration forgotten. Neither had the energy for it anymore.

"We're hopeless, aren't we?" Abby finally managed after nearly a minute.

"Certifiably hopeless."

Both their phones dinged with a new message telling them they had thirty-eight minutes until their reservation. Not only was the timer red, now it was blinking.

"We'll never make it."

Abby still had curlers in her hair and hadn't done her makeup. Brendan knew she was right.

"I think I need to call an audible," he said.

"A what?"

He jumped up and started stripping out of his clothes; hopping and fighting the pants as he made his way over to the closet. "I'll throw on a suit and meet you there. Just follow after me in your car.

I might be a few minutes late, but we won't lose our table. I'll stall with a drink or something until you get there."

Abby did something then that surprised him. She walked over and kissed his cheek. "Thank you. I'll be as fast as I can."

10

The lightbulb in the corner of the sauna flickered twice and died with a resounding *pop!* Joel Hayden looked up and realized only three of the six overhead lights remained working. He shook his head and went back to the financial news he'd been glossing over on his phone. He'd been coming to Back Bay Fitness for the better part of a decade and watched the place slowly fall apart. Cracked leather on the workout gear. Faded paint on the walls. Tile covered with scuffmarks so dark and plentiful they blended with the pattern. The sauna had been the only saving grace, and now that was going too. If the owners raised their rates again, he'd find someplace else to wind down after work.

It was quiet.

At least there was that.

He hadn't seen another soul for the better part of an hour.

Shuffling across the hot floor, Joel scooped up a ladle of water and poured it over the rocks. There was a sharp hiss as white-hot steam bellowed out and filled the room. He added one more scoop for good measure, then returned to his favorite corner of the bench, leaned back against the cedar wall, and closed his eyes.

He might have drifted off.

He didn't hear her enter.

When Joel opened his eyes, there was a girl stretched out on the long bench directly across from him. Her towel hung open, her naked body glistening with steam and sweat, her eyes closed.

She had a small tattoo of a butterfly on her ankle.

Joel pinched his eyes shut, opened them again; she was still there.

Not his imagination.

Not a dream.

She was real.

Was she asleep?

He couldn't tell.

Didn't think so, though.

There was a steady rise and fall to her chest, but aside from that, she wasn't moving.

Joel shifted his considerable bulk, and the bench beneath him let out a soft groan.

Her eyes opened, saw him, and she reached for the folds of her towel to quickly cover up. "I'm sorry, I thought you were off in dreamland."

Her voice sounded like warm butter, had a slight Southern accent to it. Carolinas, maybe? Alabama? Joel had no clue, but he liked it.

"You don't have to do that," he told her. "It's okay."

Her grip on the towel relaxed. "You sure? It just feels nicer without it. I don't want to make you uncomfortable, though."

"Hardly, it's fine."

She released the towel, let it fall open again, and grinned at him. "My name is Juliet."

"Joel. Joel Hayden."

"What do you do, Joel Hayden?"

"I'm an investment banker with Morgan and Hoffman."

"That sounds important."

He'd never heard it described like that. "It's…lucrative."

"Lucrative," she repeated, the word slipping off her tongue. She stretched out her right leg, then bent at the knee and began massaging her ankle, the one with the tattoo. "Do you mind pouring a little more water on the rocks? I pulled something out on my run this morning, and the heat seems to be loosening things up."

Standing wasn't exactly in the cards right now, not unless Joel wanted this girl to fully understand what she was doing to him, and he wasn't sure he wanted to go there just yet. Scratch that—he certainly wanted to go there, but she was a tough read. He couldn't tell if she was flirting or just naive. He'd always been a gambling man, that's why he worked in finance, so he decided it was time to roll the dice.

Joel got to his feet, let his towel drop to the floor, and walked over to the heater. He told himself he looked perfectly natural doing it, sexy even, and if she didn't want to look, she didn't have to.

She did look.

He made it a point of checking before dipping the ladle in the water bucket and dousing the rocks again.

"More…" she said behind him.

So he added more.

He was dumping his third scoop when he heard a gruff male voice behind him. "Them rocks are called igneous. Can't use just any kind of rock in a sauna, they need to hold the water just right or you get no steam."

Joel Hayden was a large man, not exactly built to move fast, but at the sound of that voice, he spun around quick enough. His left thigh caught on the corner of the frame housing the heater, dug in, and left a gash at least three inches long.

"Oooh," the voice said. "That's gonna leave a mark."

Joel was big, but this man was bigger, and while Joel was fat, the man standing between him and the door was built like a house, solid muscle. At least six-foot-three. His dark hair was slicked back like he'd just gotten out of the shower. A towel was wrapped around his waist, and he was holding Joel's towel in his meaty hand.

Had he been in the sauna the entire time?

Must have.

Must have come in with the girl.

On the bench, she'd covered herself up and was holding Joel's phone, thumbing at the screen. Without looking up, she said, "We're gonna need his passcode."

Joel considered trying to snatch his phone away from her, but the expression on the other man's face told him that would be a mistake. He looked like he wanted him to try. Like he would enjoy what came next if he did.

Joel didn't move. "What do you want?"

The man tossed Joel his towel and nodded at the bench. "Take a seat."

Having just added water, the air was thick with hot steam. Nearly two hundred degrees. It made it difficult to breathe. Joel covered up and sat, doing his best not to look frightened, knowing full well he was shaking, and the other man knew it.

"My wallet is in my locker—I've got nearly a thousand in there. It's yours if you want it."

Still tapping on the phone, the girl who called herself Juliet said, "That's mighty generous of you, Joel."

The large man sat down next to Joel, leaned back on the wall, and waved his hand through the steamy air. "It's hot as balls in here. You enjoy this?"

"It helps me think."

"Helps you think." He nodded at the girl. "Remember when we were in Belize, baby? Living in that box on the beach. What was that? Two summers ago? Remember how hot it got around midday? Did that help you think?"

"Not in the slightest."

The large man chewed on that for a moment, lost in some memory, then he inched closer to Joel, too close. "We're going to need your passcode."

"Why?"

"You needn't concern yourself with that. You have more pressing issues. If you don't give me your passcode, I'm gonna rip off your penis with my bare hands and make you swallow it. That's not an easy thing to do, I learned that lesson the last time I did it. But here's the thing, even when I can't tear it completely off, it hurts like a motherfucker. The worst pain you could possibly imagine. There's a lot of blood, too, even when it doesn't come off completely. So much damn blood." The man raised his hand between them, clenched his fist, then opened it again and showed Joel his palm. "You could try to scream, but what are the odds of someone getting in here and helping you before I get a solid grip? Before I twist and pull. A lot of bad things can happen in a second or two, if you let them."

"Oh-nine-six-four-three-seven," Joel blurted out. He tried to move away from the guy, but the large man's hand came down on his thigh and held him still as he looked back to the girl.

"Baby?"

Juliet keyed in the code. "I'm in."

The man released Joel's thigh. "That's good, Joel. A solid start."

"Start? What exactly do you want from me?"

The large man said nothing. His gaze was fixed on the girl. He didn't speak again until she looked up from the phone and nodded.

"Your wife is home right now, Joel. Giving your twins a bath. In twenty minutes, she'll be tucking them in bed. Then she'll shower and settle on the couch with a book to wait for you. Same routine as the last three nights. She's a predictable woman, don't you think?"

Joel didn't answer that. He wasn't sure he could say anything even if he tried.

"I'm going to give you a bit of a choice. Take that towel of yours, tie it to the rafter up top, and hang yourself here in the sauna. You do that, and your wife and kids get to continue repeating that routine for the foreseeable future. You don't do it, and I'll snap your fucking neck, go to your house and rape your wife, then I'll kill your whole goddamn family. When your kids are crying, when they're screaming the way kids do right before I end them, you know what I'll tell 'em?" He narrowed his eyes at Joel. "I'll tell 'em daddy made me do it." He winked at Juliet. "What do you think, Joel? Where's your head at?"

Sugar & Spice™
♥

Sugar
What is the one thing you always wanted to
do with your partner but didn't have the courage to ask?

11

Brendan didn't have time to park, so he left his car with the valet. He nearly tripped on the brick steps running up the walk, and by the time he made it to the hostess stand in the crowded lobby, the alarm was going off on his phone again. It had gone off at eight and every minute after. He fumbled with the buttons and managed to silence it, but not before the now-familiar triple-chime from Sugar & Spice played followed by a new message:

You're late again, Mr. Hollander! What are we going to do with you?
-10 points.

He cursed, shoved the phone in his pocket, and realized the young Asian hostess was staring at him. "Sorry. Work stuff. Hollander. We have a reservation for eight."

Running a slender finger down the calendar on her tablet, she located his name and frowned. "We have you down for two people."

"My wife is right behind me."

She made a point of leaning to the side and peering around his shoulder.

"Well, not literally. We drove in separate cars."

"Perhaps you'd prefer to wait at the bar?"

Brendan didn't have to look around to know where this was going. The restaurant was packed, and they didn't want to tie up a table waiting for people to arrive. If he went to the bar, their table would go to someone else, and who knows how long they'd have to wait for another one. Abby would kill him. "She's right behind me, I swear."

His watch vibrated. A text from Abby—*ETA seventeen minutes.* He quickly covered the small screen, hoping the girl hadn't seen it. "She's parking now."

"I'm sorry, sir. I simply can't—"

A message flashed across her tablet, and Brendan swore he heard that triple chime again. There was a quick frown before she clicked the text away and looked out over the busy dining room. "Oh, It appears we can accommodate you after all."

Retrieving two menus, she told Brendan to follow her and led him to a table at a window in the rear corner. He'd been in his seat for less than thirty seconds when the chimes rang out from his phone again—that was just about enough to push him over the edge; the last thing he needed was some automated message nagging him again, but the text surprised him:

Sit back, relax, and reconnect with your partner. Enjoy your evening, Mr. Hollander. Your date is on us. S&S.

Brendan was still processing the text when his waiter appeared, holding a bottle of red wine. "This is a 1961 Château Mouton Rothschild Pauillac, Premier Grand Cru Classé, compliments of the chef." He pulled the cork and handed it to Brendan, who wasn't exactly sure what to do with it, so he smelled the cork and handed it back.

"From the chef?" Brendan repeated.

"Yes, sir." The waiter poured a small amount in Brendan's glass and again waited.

Brendan swirled the wine around several times and drank. It tasted incredible. Approval must have been written all over his face because the waiter filled his glass, then the one across from him as another man set a basket of bread down on the table. "I understand your wife is running a few minutes late. Would you care for an appetizer while you wait? The Royal Osetra Caviar is divine."

"Sure," Brendan said, because he wasn't quite sure how to answer that. He'd never heard of an app buying dinner. He wasn't sure how that even worked. When the waiter walked away, Brendan did a quick search for the wine and learned it cost nearly seventeen hundred dollars.

Unless Abby had paid something he didn't know about, the app hadn't charged them anything. How could they justify the cost without an income stream? Maybe it was a promotional thing? Or maybe a contest? That would explain why the waiter mentioned the chef. The restaurant was somehow in on it. Brendan quickly realized his mind had shifted into full-on work mode, analyzing the balance sheet and business model for some app on his phone, and he quickly pushed the thoughts out of his head.

He wasn't working right now.

The *hows* or *whys* of all of it didn't matter.

He would enjoy it.

Abby arrived shortly after the caviar, and Brendan's heart thudded at the sight of her.

She rushed in, as he had, and paused at the far end of the dining room to look for him.

Her dark hair was partially swept up in the back, while just enough had been left down on the sides to frame her face. Her eyes sparkled nearly as much as her grandmother's diamond earrings. She was wearing a dress he'd never seen before. Black with a slit that followed the curves of her leg, it hugged her body like a second skin. When she spotted him, she smiled, and started over, there wasn't a single eye in the restaurant that didn't follow.

Brendan stood and kissed her gently on the cheek. "You look incredible."

"Thank you."

He pulled out her chair and eased it back when she sat.

She smelled faintly of vanilla.

Returning to his own seat, he took her in again. "You're absolutely stunning. I've never seen that dress."

"I bought this about two years ago for an event out in Brookline, a fundraising thing. The event fell apart, and I never got the chance to wear it. I forgot I had it." She took in the wine and caviar. "What's all this?"

Brendan showed her the latest message from Sugar & Spice.

She leaned back in her seat, her eyes filled with wonder. "Could it be some kind of mistake?"

"Probably," Brendan considered. "Maybe. I don't know. Here's what I do know." He picked up his wine glass and held it out to her. What came next was difficult, but had to be said. "Whatever this is, you and I, we need it. I didn't agree with everything that the therapist said, but she did make one thing very clear. We've drifted apart. The two of us are so caught up in our individual lives we've neglected the life we've built together. We've let silliness create a wedge between us. I'm willing to commit 100 percent to not only finding what we've lost, but building something better on the rubble of all this other nonsense." He reached across the table and rested his hand on hers. "I knew from the moment I first saw you, I wanted to spend the rest of my life with you. That hasn't changed, and it never will. I love you, Abby Hollander, with all my heart. I always will."

She'd gone silent, her eyes welling up with tears. When Abby finally spoke, her voice wavered with emotion. "How much of that wine have you had to drink?"

Brendan couldn't help but smile. "Enough to shut down my inner asshole and remind me what's important."

"Fair enough." Abby reached for her glass and clinked it against his. "To a new chapter of our lives. One I couldn't imagine writing with anyone else."

The waiter returned with a large tray and began placing plates on the table—lobster, carabinero, various sliced meats laid out over fish.

"…we didn't order yet," Brendan told him.

"Compliments of the chef," the waiter replied, glancing at the half-empty bottle of wine. "I'll have another of those brought out as well. I've been told you are to receive nothing short of our best. Enjoy!"

He was gone before either of them could say anything.

Abby simply raised her glass again. "Enjoy!"

Three minutes later, Brendan's phone let out another triple-chime followed by a new message from Sugar & Spice.

12

The first message had been a *Sugar—*

Do you remember your first date? Describe it.

Brendan remembered it vividly, because their first unofficial date began with misdemeanor theft. Both attending Northeastern. Broke. Saturday afternoon. Brendan had rounded the back of the Movico Cineplex to the emergency exit on the east end of the building with hopes of sneaking into the latest *Twilight* movie, *New Moon*; he'd found Abby holding the door open for two of her girlfriends. They'd never met, but he'd seen her around campus. He went in with them, ended up sitting next to Abby, and they spent the entire movie talking. There was a trip to the local bookstore after the movie (which they thought was far better than the first), then pizza at Milanos (which they loved, but not as much as Arlo's downtown). It was nearly midnight by the time he walked her back to her dorm, and they made plans for a real date the following night.

The memory came back to Abby too, and when they finished with that one, both were laughing and she selected another *Sugar*, that one a little more daring—what is your favorite place to be touched. Brendan went with an obvious choice; Abby told him it was her cheek, which surprised him. He had no idea. They went on like that for more than an hour, reliving fond memories and sharing secrets, taking turns pressing *Sugar* on their phones, until the dessert finally arrived and the second bottle of wine was nearly gone. It was then a mischievous grin filled Abby's face.

"You're winning, Mr. Hollander." Her finger slipped across the points at the top of both their phones. He was at 510, she had 420. "I think it's time I pull ahead."

She pressed *Spice* and was immediately told—

Take off your underwear and hand them
to your partner for safekeeping.

"I'm glad I didn't get that one," Brendan told her looking down at his suit pants. "Would have been particularly tough if I'd worn that damn rope belt."

He thought he'd get a laugh with that, but when Abby remained silent, he looked over at her. "It's not that I didn't like the rope belt, it just seemed like something geared more toward a twenty-year-old."

"Forget the rope belt." She was looking around the crowded dining room, her eyes bouncing from table to table. "If I do it, do you think anyone will see?"

Brendan was shocked. Abby could hardly be described as adventurous. Under most circumstances she was reserved, but there was something new in her face; she looked alive in a way he didn't recall ever seeing before. Whatever it was, he liked it.

Although it was getting late, at least a hundred people were still in the restaurant. Many had been there as long as they had and were well into their meals. Their table was in the corner of the room, dimly lit. There was a tablecloth, but it only dropped about four inches from the top. It didn't offer much in the way of cover. Brendan would need to improvise. He eased his chair closer, shielded her as best he could, and whispered in her ear, "You're okay, nobody can see."

He knew that was probably not totally true, but the wine had given him liquid courage, same as Abby. The real question was how much courage.

Abby answered that when she casually leaned against him and slipped her fingers through the slit in the side of her dress, pinched the corner of her panties, and slowly tugged them down. She made the move as if she'd practiced it a thousand times, but it was what she did next that really impressed him. Abby dropped her napkin from where it had been resting on her knees to the floor and somehow landed it directly on top of her feet. "Can you get that for me?"

Brendan bent over, retrieved the napkin, along with the slinky black panties resting beneath it at Abby's ankles. He had no idea how she'd gotten them past her pumps.

Abby was a beautiful woman, but she had never been the type to wear lingerie. Instead, she opted more for comfort in her day-to-day life. That was partly why he'd bought her a dress at Victoria's Secret rather than some lacy undergarment. He'd never seen the black silk panties before and could count the times Abby had worn a thong in front of him on one hand. He rolled his fingers through the soft material, then slipped them into his pocket. He leaned in close and let his warm breath wash over her ear. "You're full of surprises tonight, Mrs. Hollander."

"I'm also winning," she replied, nodding triumphantly at her phone. Her score had ticked up to 520. He was still at 510.

Brendan finished off his glass of wine and tapped *Spice* on his phone.

Touch your partner under the table.

The room was buzzing. So many people, all lost in their own conversations, their own worlds. All of them vanished as Brendan nudged his chair a little closer to Abby's. He was still holding her napkin. He met her eyes and didn't look away as he drew the napkin back over her knees. Nor did he look away when his fingers found the slit in the side of her dress and slipped beneath to her thigh. Her skin was hot to the touch, anticipating. She eased her legs apart only enough for him to move between them. His fingertips grazed her soft, moist flesh, eliciting a gasp from her lips, then he pulled away and settled back in his own seat, his heart thumping like a hammer. Only a handful of seconds had passed, but time no longer felt like it was moving.

Brendan's phone dinged, and his points ticked up by one hundred.

"Winning," he managed, turning the phone so she could see.

"Yeah," Abby said quietly. "Not for long, though. Count to twenty, and meet me in the bathroom."

13

"You fucked Brendan in the ladies' room at Menton's?" Hannah's mouth was hanging open. *"Because some app told you to?"*

They were in Abby's small office on the second floor of the house. Hannah had stopped over at a little after ten with breakfast bagels and two caramel macchiatos from Starbucks; she wanted a full download. Abby had texted her around midnight, after the Uber driver had dropped Brendan and her off. They'd both been too drunk to drive.

Abby blushed. "The men's room. Somebody was in the ladies'."

"Of course there was. And your cars are still there?"

"Mine is. Brendan picked up his car this morning on his way to work."

Hannah considered all of this, then pressed her palm to Abby's forehead. "No temperature. Who are you, and what have you done with my friend?"

"Crazy, right?"

"Crazy? That's like porno hot. Not the cheap shit they film in

California, but the import kind from Italy." She drank some of her coffee and leaned back on the corner of Abby's small desk. "I always thought I was the wild one, and you make me look like an extra on *The Handmaid's Tale*. What the fuck, Abby, what if you got caught?"

Abby was still wearing her pajamas. She twisted the drawstring from her shorts around her finger. "That's the thing, I know we were drunk, but it almost felt like the people there wanted us to do it. Like they expected it and nudged us along. One of the waitresses saw us come out of the bathroom together, and she didn't say anything."

Hannah chewed her bottom lip and thought about that. "So this app buys you dinner *and* clears the path for lewd and nefarious behavior…between two consenting adults, of course."

"Of course."

"Well, that's bullshit."

"How do you know?"

Hannah shrugged. "Because it's an app. That's like saying Candy Crush helped wash your car or Wordle paid your taxes. It was probably designed by some horny sixteen-year-old in China or some shit. It's throwing you a bunch of pre-written, canned messages based on a pre-determined schedule. As far as apps go, it's not even a complicated one. You're giving it too much credit."

"The wine alone last night was four thousand dollars."

Hannah took another sip of coffee, then suggested, "Maybe Brendan paid for all of it and lied to you."

"Why would he do that?"

"Because men are idiots. Maybe he figured it would be easier to sell you on the whole thing if he said everything was comped."

Abby was shaking her head. "We only have two credit cards, and there's no way he'd dip into our savings for something like that. I'd see it."

"Men are also sneaky little fuckers. You don't think he's got his own credit card? How does he pay for porn?"

"Brendan doesn't look at porn."

Hannah stared at her, blank-faced. The room flooded with silence.

"Oh, shit. Do you think he does?"

Don't you?" Hannah frowned. "Everybody looks at porn."

It was Abby's turn to go quiet.

"Oh my God, Abby, seriously? You don't?"

Abby's cheeks burned, and she took a long drink of her coffee.

"You write romance novels!"

"Porn and romance are hardly the same thing."

"Fucking is fucking."

Abby's eyes narrowed, and she stared at her friend. "Did you even read my book?"

"Of course I did."

"How many sex scenes were in it?"

"I didn't exactly count."

"Describe one."

Hannah took a bite of her bagel, but said nothing.

"There were exactly zero," Abby told her after several long seconds. She picked up a copy of the paperback and smacked Hannah's leg. "You didn't read it!"

"I don't have time for books! You know how crazy my schedule is. I figured I'd watch the movie or something." She snapped her fingers. "Get that on Netflix, already. Wait a minute…you wrote a best-selling romance book and it doesn't even have sex in it?"

"The sex is implied, but it happens behind closed doors. Off camera," Abby told her. "Sometimes it's better to let the reader's imagination fill in the blanks."

Hannah nodded at Abby's computer. "Well, now that you've

actually *had* sex, in a public place no less, maybe you should include it in the new book."

Abby quickly closed the lid on her MacBook. "We don't talk about the new book."

"Shouldn't we, though? Because that screen looked very blank."

Abby was about to respond to that when the doorbell chimed downstairs, followed by three hard knocks.

"Expecting someone?"

Abby shook her head.

Carrying what was left of the bagels and coffee, they went downstairs and opened the front door in time to see a UPS van pulling away. A small box was sitting on the doormat.

Hannah waved and turned to Abby. "I think I just thought of the opening to your book. You start with your female lead, she's in the shower when someone knocks at her front door. She wraps herself in a towel, runs to answer, and when the delivery guy hands her the package, she accidentally drops her towel. He could be wearing one of those cute uniforms with the brown shorts. Maybe he makes some silly comment about another delivery...better yet, maybe she dropped the towel on purpose. Maybe she does that all day long to everyone who shows up—pizza. Amazon guy. Mormons. Whoever. Like some kind of—"

"Oh, please stop."

"No good?"

"No. No good."

Hannah was nodding slowly, the gears turning. "Maybe I'll do it for real and film it. Start a new TikTok trend."

Abby picked up the box and studied the label. It was addressed to her, but the label contained no shipper information. Where shipper data would normally appear, her name and address were repeated.

She hadn't ordered anything.

A triple chime rang out from her phone. Sugar & Spice:

Put them in immediately. Only your husband is permitted to remove them. Enjoy!

"Okay," Hannah said studying the box. "Now I'm curious. If you don't open it, I will."

Abby carried the box over to the small catch-all table they kept in the hallway, cleared a space, and sliced open the lid with a spare car key. Inside, packed in tissue paper were two silver balls, heavy, about an inch in diameter, connected by a piece of black plastic with a loop on the end. She held them up to the light. Abby had no idea what they were. "Put them in where, exactly?"

Hannah was grinning. "They go in your hoo-ha."

"My..."

"Your vajayjay. Honey pot. Taco. Muff. Pretty little flower. You know, down below. Your special place."

Abby looked at her, puzzled. "You know what these are?"

Hannah looked like she'd eaten chocolate for the first time. "They're called Ben Wa balls," she friend explained.

Hannah shared in far more detail than Abby would have preferred so early in the day.

Abby could think of a million reasons to pack them back in the box and pretend she'd never seen them, but Hannah wouldn't let her. Her friend pushed her into the downstairs bathroom and closed the door. "Just give them a try."

Abby probably stood there, her back against the door, for a full minute, then finally decided, why not? Last night, the Sugar & Spice app had shown her a side of herself she didn't know existed. It gave her a glimpse of the man she married, someone she thought was long gone. She hadn't felt that excited in years, maybe ever. If she didn't like this, she could toss them in the trash, and nobody would be the wiser. Well, except for Hannah, but she'd keep quiet if Abby pressed her.

Abby pulled the string on her shorts and let them drop to the floor.

With a deep breath, she spread her legs, slipped the Ben Wa balls into herself, and pressed her back against the door. They were cold, and she wondered if she was supposed to use lubricant. "Umm. That feels…weird."

From the hallway, Hannah said, "They need to warm up. Give it a minute."

She did.

Then, "Oh…oh my."

14

"Hi, this is Cindy Messing, I'm unable to come to the phone right now, but if you leave a message, I'll get back to you shortly."

Kim Whitlock's slender finger hovered over the disconnect button. She waited for the beep and said, "This is Kim Whitlock with FCID. I've left you several messages. I need to speak with you regarding travel by several of your employees. You have my number."

She hung up, sighed, and settled back in her chair.

Brendan was doing his damnedest not to stare. She was wearing a gray skirt with a white button-down blouse, and one of her buttons had come undone. Every time she moved around, he caught a glimpse of her belly button—which was pierced with a tiny diamond stud. For some reason, seeing the piercing made the entire experience that much more intimate, voyeuristic. After what happened in Chicago, he wasn't sure if that button had come undone accidentally or—if knowing they'd be alone—she'd unfastened it herself. Some veiled attempt at flirting. He knew the latter thought was a bit self-centered, but he couldn't keep his mind from going there because surely she knew it was unbuttoned, right? She'd feel that?

Brendan forced himself to focus and studied the names on his legal pad. "Who is Cindy Messing again? I don't have her here."

"Cindy Messing is just a low-level staff accountant at INTENT corporate. Best I can tell, she slipped the credit card records for Alford into our document production. I think she also gave us this, too."

Kim handed him a sheet of paper. A phone number was written in the top corner.

"Whose phone?"

"It's a burner, not registered to anyone," Kim told him. "I pulled the call log and found twenty-six calls between numbers registered to INTENT and this phone over six days in July—the sixth through the eleventh—all of those calls taking place in Laos." She found another sheet of paper in the stack at her side and slid it across to Brendan. "That's Isaac Alford's personal cell phone records for the same period. Notice how it goes dark for those six days? Not one call out. According to his phone carrier, the phone didn't leave his house. The dates coincide with one of the trips I told you about. Whatever he was doing in Laos, it was off the books. He left his phone at home and used this one to try and cover his tracks."

"This still doesn't prove they're doing anything wrong. Do you know who he was talking to at INTENT while he was overseas?"

Kim shook her head. "He dialed the main switchboard. We'd need a warrant to track the calls internally, but you'll like this;" She positioned both call logs next to each other and tapped on a phone number she'd circled in blue ink—the same number appearing on both logs. "That number is registered to Joel Hayden."

That did get Brendan's attention. "From Morgan and Hoffman? That Joel Hayden?"

Kim nodded. "Isaac Alford and Joel Hayden have history. They graduated from DePaul together."

Morgan and Hoffman was an investment banking firm that had been on their radar for a few years now. Although they were still building a case and hadn't brought charges, it appeared they were involved in several pump-and-dump schemes, possible tax evasion, *and* money laundering. Lately he'd incorporated Bitcoin, further muddying the waters. FCID had no less than five open investigations. Joel Hayden was a real piece of work. If Isaac Alford was in contact with him on burner phones, they weren't discussing the Red Sox or the Blue Demons.

"INTENT does peer-to-peer lending," Kim went on. "My gut says Alford found a way to skim off the top, and he's working with Joel Hayden to hide it."

Brendan considered all that. "The woman who slipped you this, Cindy Messing, she's dodging your calls?"

"Not just Cindy. I can't get anyone on the phone over there anymore."

"When did that start?"

"I spoke to Alford three times last week. He picked up every time. Then I started getting his voice mail. Cindy too. Everyone on our initial contact list. It's like they had a company-wide meeting and decided to no longer take my calls."

Brendan knew where Kim was heading with this. She wanted to go back to Chicago. Ask questions face-to-face.

Kim stood, rounded the conference table, and sat on the corner. She crossed her slender legs. "You know we need to go back."

"Let me talk to Stuckey."

"And the assistant director?"

"If Stuckey thinks this is enough, then yes. I'll speak to the assistant director. In the meantime, reach out to INTERPOL. Maybe they can track the phone's position in Laos and help us piece together what Alford did while he was there."

"Good work, Kim," she mumbled softly, collecting her documents.

"Good work, Kim," Brendan replied. When he rose, his phone buzzed on the table; he'd silenced it earlier. Both his and Abby's scores were on the screen—she was leading by more than two hundred points.

How did she pull so far ahead?

The scores vanished and a new message appeared:

Would you like to try a Spice?

Brendan clicked *Yes.*

15

An address appeared on Brendan's screen along with a timer:

Go to 109 Burbury Avenue. You have ten minutes.
Await further instructions in the lobby.

It wasn't far, only a few blocks from his office on High Street, so rather than get his car out of the garage and have to deal with parking, he walked. He stepped through the glass doors into the lobby of 109 Burbury with one minute left on the timer. There was a bank on the first floor, offices on the next ten, then apartments. Twenty-seven floors in all.

When the timer hit zero, a new message appeared:

Take the third elevator from the left to the top floor.

Brendan spotted several cameras mounted in the lobby, more in the bank, and he couldn't help but wonder if someone was watching him. He assumed the app was able to determine his location with the phone's GPS—that's how they knew he was here—but these directions were a little too spot-on. The hair on the back of his neck tingled. He *felt* eyes on him. Like a puppet master pulling his strings.

The elevators lined the far wall, and he considered turning around and heading back to his office when the doors of the third elevator from the left opened.

Now, Mr. Hollander.

Several people exited the elevator, and others quickly began to stream in. It was now or never.

Brendan quickly crossed the lobby and stepped inside. The moment the doors slid shut, he regretted it. Nothing about this felt right.

What if the elevator dropped?

What if one of these people had a gun?

What if it was some kind of trap?

"What floor?"

So lost in his own head, Brendan barely heard her. The old woman standing next to the elevator's control panel stared at him, her face lined with impatience. She cradled a small Shih Tzu in her arms. The white fur around the dog's eyes was stained yellow. It stared at him, a growl rumbling from its throat.

"Uh, twenty-seven, please."

She pressed the button, and it lit up with about half a dozen others. His phone vibrated in his hand.

Do not exit the elevator under any circumstance.

They began to rise.

Brendan tried not to look at the dog.

The doors opened on four, seven, twelve…slowly the car began to empty; nobody boarded. The woman with the dog got out on twenty-one, and Brendan found himself alone with a young couple huddled in the opposite corner holding hands, both watching the display above the door with the floors ticking away.

Do not exit the elevator under any circumstance.

The message repeated on his phone a moment before the elevator jerked to a stop. According to the screen on the wall, they were somewhere between twenty-five and twenty-six.

Do not speak. Do not move.

They were stuck. No alarm sounded. Brendan fought the urge to reach for the panel and start mashing in buttons or pick up the phone. A voice in the back of his head told him if he were to pick up the emergency phone, the voice on the other end would belong to whoever had stopped the elevator in the first place, and he might not like what they had to say. He considered dialing 911 and was about to do just that when the phones of both strangers rang out with a familiar triple chime.

Both raised their phones to read the incoming texts.

She was pretty, maybe early twenties, long chestnut hair flowing over a tan sweater, nearly touching the top of her jeans. He seemed a few years older. A tattoo of a rose with a thorny stem peeked out from the sleeve of his tee shirt.

When both pocketed their phones and started to undress, a breath caught in Brendan's throat. They didn't so much as glance in his direction as they shed their clothing in a pile at their feet and began to kiss, their hands roving over each other's bodies, exploring, caressing. Tentative at first, then at a fevered pitch. It wasn't until the man hoisted the young woman up and pressed her against the far wall of the elevator that she looked at Brendan at all. She kept looking at him as she wrapped her legs around her boyfriend, as he thrust into her.

16

"Wait a minute, they fucked right there in front of you?" Stuckey dropped down onto the couch next to Hannah, careful not to spill his beer. "You just stood there?"

"What was I supposed to do?"

Thursday night was Game Night, and while the worn box for *Cards Against Humanity* was on the coffee table, nobody had bothered to open it. They were too wrapped up in Brendan's story. He'd told them everything. Stuckey knew all about the app; Brendan had filled him in on their way to Victoria's Secret the other day and he could tell by the look on Hannah's face, she knew too. He imagined Abby had told her, maybe Stuckey did; he never could keep his mouth shut. Either way, both clearly understood what was going on.

Stuckey wrapped his arm around his wife. "So they had the app too, and it told them to have sex in front of you."

"I guess so."

"And they just did it."

"Wow." Hannah had this playful grin on her face. Her hand roved over Stuckey's knee to his thigh. "Was it hot?"

Brendan couldn't help but glance at Abby. She was standing across the room, nursing a glass of white wine. Her cheeks were still flushed from earlier. "Yeah, but not the hottest thing that happened to me today."

The couple in the elevator had finished fast, and when it was over, they'd quickly gotten dressed. All three of them had avoided eye contact for the awkward minute or so before the elevator started moving again, and when the doors opened on twenty-seven, they'd rushed out, both laughing. Brendan managed to gather enough focus to press the button for the first floor, and he'd gotten out at the lobby. He didn't realize he was sweating until he stumbled out of the building to the sidewalk and the fresh air hit him. Two messages appeared on his phone simultaneously. The first was from Sugar & Spice, informing him he'd earned another one hundred points. The second was from Abby and simply said, *Come home - now* followed by a heart emoji.

He'd tried calling her, and when she didn't answer, he'd retrieved his car and made the drive in record time.

Abby had met him at the front door.

No, *met* was the wrong word. She jumped him. Damn near accosted him. It was incredible.

She opened the door wearing nothing but the skimpy drawstring shorts she liked to sleep in, and before he could ask her what was going on, her mouth was on his, hungry and burning. Brendan managed to kick the door shut as she pulled him into the living room, leaned against the back of the couch, and hooked her fingers in the top of her shorts. She gave them a gentle push, and let them fall away.

Her back against the couch, one leg straight and the other bent slightly at her knee, Abby stood there naked. Broken by the blinds, the light streaming in from the windows crept across her skin like warm fingers, tracing every curve. She eyed him with a look that was both eager and ravenous. In all their years, he'd never seen her like this. She usually insisted all lights were off during sex, she even locked the door when she showered. But this…she was so exposed. Vulnerable. Yet filled with a confidence Brendan had never known her to have.

She bit her lower lip and spread her legs ever so slightly.

He saw it then. Something inserted inside her. Just revealing it to him seemed to make her hotter. "I was told you need to take it out. Only you."

Brendan had no idea what *it* was, but he was certainly curious.

He stepped closer. His lips found hers again, but only briefly as he brushed her hair aside and left a trail of soft kisses down her cheek, her neck, and shoulders. He teased both her nipples with the tip of his tongue before moving on to her belly and below. He removed *it* with his teeth, and Abby let out a soft moan. She pressed into him, every inch of her burning. He brushed his lips over her clitoris, circled it, but only for a moment, nothing but a tease.

"I need you inside me," she managed between breaths. "Right now, right here. Just fuck me."

"Yo, buddy," Stuckey snapped his fingers. "You still with us?"

The three of them were staring at him. Abby's cheeks were bright red now, and by the look on Hannah's face, she knew all about his afternoon. She gave him a quick wink before telling her husband, "Brendan played a little ball after work today."

Stuckey shot him a look. "And you didn't tell me? Hell, I would have shot some hoops. You ain't got nothing on me. Hell, your game ain't shit."

"That's not what Abby says," Hannah said playfully.

"Oookay," Abby cut in, reaching for the cards on the table. "Whose turn is it to deal?"

Brendan woke that night at three in the morning, his throat like sandpaper. They'd made love again after Hannah and Stuckey left, going at it twice until both collapsed in exhaustion. Abby had fallen asleep naked, another first for her, and she was snoring softly. He slipped from the bed and crept downstairs to the kitchen.

He didn't see Kim Whitlock, not at first, not until the light from the refrigerator revealed her standing just inside the back door. She was no longer wearing the gray skirt from earlier, nor was she wearing the button-down blouse. Both were puddled at her feet. She stood there in a black bra, matching panties, and heels. "Is she finally out?"

"I didn't think you'd wait."

Brendan reached into the refrigerator, took out an open bottle of Fiji water, and chugged. When he was done, he held it out to her.

Kim shook her head. "I'm not here for the beverages."

"No, I don't suppose you are."

He closed the fridge, sending the room back into darkness, and waited for his eyes to adjust. Kim slowly came into focus, first only a hazy shadow, then her pale skin caught what little light came in through the window over the sink. "Why don't you take me upstairs?"

"Because Abby's upstairs."

"I know." She reached for the band of Brendan's underwear and ran her fingers along the edge. "Maybe it's time I get to know her as well as I know you. We're all friends here. Or at least we can be."

"That's not going to happen."

"She surprised you today. Maybe she'll surprise you again."

"Abby's not like that."

"No? I bet her and Hannah are closer than you think. You'd be surprised what kind of secrets girls share." Kim's hand slipped inside Brendan's underwear, her fingers wrapped around him and gave him a gentle squeeze. "Maybe that was our mistake in Chicago: not including Abby. Nobody wants to be the third wheel. We make this about her, and I think you'll find she's far more open-minded than you believe."

"I love my wife. You and I, it's…wrong."

This was clearly not what Kim wanted to hear, and Brendan regretted uttering the words the moment they slipped out. Her grip on him tightened. He was so focused on that he didn't see her remove the large knife from the block on the counter. It wasn't until she held the knife between them he saw it at all.

Brendan's body went rigid. "What are you doing?"

Her grip tightened on his penis as she pressed the flat edge of the knife against his lower stomach. "I'm confused, Brendan. I'm not sure what you want from me."

"I don't want anything from you."

"But we kissed."

"You kissed me," he fired back in a hushed whisper.

"Only after you spent an hour telling me everything that was wrong with your marriage. I saw the way you were looking at me. Don't think I didn't notice. Today at work, you looked like you wanted to fuck me right there on the conference table. And you know what? I would have let you. I think we need to. I don't think you and I will get past whatever this is between us until we do. Why do you think I'm here? Can you think of a better way to get me out of your head? Get all this tension out of your head?"

"I won't. I love my wife."

She pressed the knife tighter against his skin. "Well, that's unfortunate. Because you're not thinking straight, and I need you to think straight. We have unfinished business in Chicago, and you can't see it right now because your head's not in the game."

"I don't understand."

"I know you don't, and that's sad. You used to be so sharp."

Brendan felt the warmth of his blood a moment before the hot pain of the knife slipping into his belly registered. He looked down in time to see Kim twist the blade and force it in deeper. "It's time I take you to church."

"Brendan!"

Abby was hovering over him as he jerked up in the bed. He sat up so quick, his head cracked against her chin, but she didn't let go of him. Instead, she managed to wrap her arms around him tighter and lower him back to the pillows. "It's okay, Brendan, it's okay… you had a bad dream."

Brendan hugged her back and kept hugging her until the sun came up. Although she eventually drifted off, he didn't dare fall back asleep.

17

"Well, you two look a little happier." Dr. Donetti grinned. "I take it things are going well?"

Brendan and Abby sat on the same couch as last time, but unlike before, their bodies were pressed together, and they were holding hands. Abby was beaming. "It's been a good week."

"The app?"

"Well, the app has helped for sure," Abby replied, "but we've connected in a lot of ways. I feel like I've got the man I married back."

Donetti looked to Brendan. "And you? How are you feeling?"

Brendan squeezed Abby's hand. "I've learned some new things about my wife. I feel like we've grown closer. Discovered each other again, like she said. I didn't realize how far we'd drifted apart until this week. I think it took a slap to the face to remind us. I was skeptical, but I'm honestly not sure what would have happened to us if we hadn't come to see you, so thank you."

"Good. Very good." She scribbled something in her ever-present notepad, then studied them both again before the grin returned. "So I've gotta ask; you downloaded the app, right? Who's winning?"

Brendan retrieved his phone from beside him on the couch and held it out to her. "I didn't realize how competitive Abby was. She won't let me pull ahead."

Abby had 2170 points, he was at 2050.

"I earned every one of those points," Abby told her.

"I bet you did."

And all three laughed with that.

Abby then added, "I may have also come up with an idea for the new book."

Brendan had no idea. "You did?"

"I've got an opening chapter. Twelve pages. It's early, but it feels right. I think the story has bones."

He offered her a smile. "Good for you."

This seemed to please Donetti too. Her scribbles were happy scribbles.

"We talked about the other thing too." Brendan figured it was best to weigh in before the doctor asked.

"The woman at work?"

Brendan nodded.

"Did something else happen?"

Abby answered before Brendan could. "No, nothing like that. I just wanted Brendan to know I overreacted. I should have trusted him, and I appreciate the fact he was honest with me about the whole thing. I think last week I was still feeling hurt, and that was causing me to be defensive. I needed to get past the anger."

"And now you are?" Donetti asked. "Past the anger?"

"Brendan talked to…Kim…they had a frank conversation about what happened and agreed it was just a misunderstanding. They've moved beyond it, and I don't want to be the one dwelling."

Brendan had told Abby all that, but it was a lie. He felt it was something Abby needed to hear, and he'd been right about that. Neither he or Kim had brought up what happened in Chicago again, and he had no plans of doing so. It was clear Kim had forgotten or let it go. Either way, things at work were smooth again, and he wanted to keep them that way. The dreams were another story. He'd had two more. Last night, he'd barely slept at all.

"Brendan? Is there something else on your mind?"

Brendan glanced back at Dr. Donetti and smiled at Abby. "No. Nothing else. We're in a great place right now."

The doctor settled back in her chair. "Good. That's good. There's something I need you both to understand. You've made some strong progress in a short amount of time, and it's important we continue in the right direction, but it's also important you don't lose sight of where you were. You were in a bad place, and that wasn't something that developed overnight. It took years. Recovery can take equally as long. Patients often experience immense progress in the early weeks of treatment, it's very common. It's also common for that to be followed by one or more back-steps." She raised a hand defensively before either of them could respond. "I'm not saying that will happen, I'm only pointing it out so if it does, you both recognize it as normal and understand it's all part of the healing process. What's important is your steps forward continue to exceed your steps back. Does that make sense?"

It did, and they both nodded.

"Good." Dr. Donetti looked like a proud mama at her child's graduation. "Here's your homework for the week. Keep doing what you're doing. It's clear the app has helped you connect, but it's also important you learn to connect without the app. Maybe plan a date night where you leave your phones at home, I don't know, something like—"

The doctor's phone vibrated on the small table at her side. She glanced at the display and went quiet for a moment, the color leaving her face.

"Everything okay?" Abby asked.

Donetti didn't appear to hear her at first, only stared at her phone. Then she snapped back and placed the device back on the table, facedown. "Yes…I'm sorry. Personal stuff." The smile returned to her face. "Same time next week?"

Brendan glanced at the clock. He had a lunch meeting scheduled with Kim and Stuckey.

He and Abby rode the elevator down together.

They were alone apart from a stocky older man huddled in the opposite corner, his face buried in his phone. Brendan half-expected a *Spice* to appear on his phone instructing him to have sex with Abby in front of the stranger, but no such message came. Abby must have had the same thought, because she was fixed on her screen when he looked over at her. She blushed and they both laughed.

Sugar & Spice™

♥

Sugar

What is your partner's greatest talent?

18

"Okay, show me how this works." Hannah clicked away on Abby's phone. "There's no menu. No instructions. Nothing but these two buttons, *Sugar* and *Spice*."

"You have to go back to the home screen to see my score."

"Why can't you see it in the app? I'm confused."

They were sitting on Hannah's back porch, both nursing iced coffee. Abby had discovered some new blend called Carpe Diem, and it was incredible. The sun was out, and it was a pleasant seventy-three degrees. Fall had officially started two weeks earlier, and while the leaves hadn't turned yet, this was probably Abby's favorite time of the year.

Abby took the phone from Hannah and minimized everything. "See, I've got 2170 and Brendan is at 2050."

"And you need five thousand points to get to the next level?"

"Yeah, bronze."

"If bronze is the next level, what level are you now?"

Abby thought about that. "You know, I'm honestly not sure."

Hannah took the phone back and returned to the app. "So *Sugar* is like *truth* and *Spice* is a dare, is that it?"

"Exactly."

"Let me guess, Play-It-Safe-Abby just keeps chomping away at the sugars so you can stay ahead of Brendan?"

"Hey, I did the Ben Wa balls."

"You did, I'll give you that. But they just showed up, right? You didn't click on anything?"

That was true, but she'd gotten points for leaving them in for Brendan. What did it matter? She was having fun. And she was winning. "We've been mixing it up."

"Ah, huh," Hannah muttered. "Can I try?"

Abby took a sip of her iced coffee. "Sure."

Hannah's finger hovered over the screen, then she clicked on *Sugar*, read the message, and frowned.

"What does it say?"

"It's a little hard-core. It says, *Have you ever fantasized about being raped?*"

"Really?"

Hannah held the phone out to her.

"That is hard-core. Usually, they're sweet little things. Conversation starters, mostly."

"Well, that's a conversation starter for sure." Hannah smiled slyly. "So, have you?"

"Ever fantasized about being raped?"

"Repeating the question isn't going to get you out of answering the question, Mrs. Hollander."

Abby went quiet.

Hannah rolled her eyes. "Of course you have. Everyone has. Not raped for real, nobody wants that, but pretend? Sure. You don't need to feel ashamed about it. There's something to be said for being completely dominated or being the one doing the dominating."

Abby still didn't say anything.

Hannah's interest was piqued. She rolled off the side of her lounge chair and sat up. "Geez, Abs, have you ever even been tied up?"

Abby shook her head.

"Blindfolded?"

Again, she shook her head.

"Handcuffed? Whipped? Spanked? Slathered in whip cream and chocolate syrup?"

"Eww. That sounds very sticky."

Hannah clearly found this all fascinating. Abby was beginning to feel like a nun. "I had one serious boyfriend before Brendan, and neither of them expressed an interest in that sort of thing."

Hannah looked like her head was about to explode. "Forget their interests—what about you? Your interests? My God, Abby what am I going to do with you?"

"There's nothing wrong with a more traditional sex life."

"No, there's nothing wrong with that at all. Except it's fucking boring! Life is too short, Abby. Before you realize it, you'll be eighty years old, sitting on the porch thinking about all the things you wanted to do in life and didn't. And if I'm stuck sitting in the chair next to you, the last thing I want to hear is you bitching about what could have been. Sex is like food; you need to experiment a little. Try something new, then rule it out if you don't like it. But don't *not* try something just because you think you might not like it."

Abby's phone played the triple chime and a new message appeared—

Would you like to try a related Spice?

Both women saw the message at the same time. Abby tried to reach for her phone, but Hannah held it at arm's length. "No way, you're not weaseling out of this one, Ms. Prude. You need to live a little." She quickly tapped *Yes*.

The screen went blank for a long moment, and Abby got a strange feeling the app had crashed. Then it flashed white, came back to life, and filled with text. From her angle, Abby couldn't read it, but Hannah appeared engrossed, her eyes widening as she scanned the words. "Okay, now we're talking."

"What does it say?"

Hannah cleared her throat. "You are to dress comfortably in clothing unfamiliar to your partner along with a wig; disguise your appearance. Have fun with it. But don't take too long—you don't want to keep him waiting. Be at the Westminster Arms Hotel in downtown Boston at two. A room has been reserved for you under the name Mrs. Robinson. Proceed there and await further instructions." She looked up at Abby. "So, now what? Brendan's app tells him where to go?"

"Yeah, that's how it works." Abby glanced at the clock. With the drive into the city, she had less than an hour to get ready. "Where am I supposed to find a wig?"

Hannah lowered the phone and stared off into space. "Christ, the Westminster..."

"You know it?"

Hannah pinched her thumb and index finger together. "You know Stuckey was a little bit married when I first met him, right?"

"A little bit?"

"They'd been together since high school, and the marriage was pretty much over, but neither had been willing to rip off the bandage and walk away. We couldn't go back to his place for obvious reasons, and my apartment was an embarrassing shit hole complete with loser roommate who never left the couch. When me and Stuckey started seeing each other, we'd sometimes meet at the Westminster. It's a few blocks from his office, and they rent rooms by the hour."

"Sounds lovely."

"It's not the kind of place you'd want to fire up a black light."

"I'm not sure what that means."

Hannah handed Abby her phone. "Oh, my dear Abby. So innocent in the ways of the world." She started inside. "Let's find something for you to wear. Lucky for you, I own several wigs."

19

INTERPOL came through.

Brendan, Kim, and Stuckey had taken an outside table at Randals. A small, family-owned sandwich shop not far from the office. Stuckey had devoured a roast beef sandwich in record time. Kim had yet to touch her vegan something-or-other. Brendan had pastrami on rye.

The photographs supplied by INTERPOL were spread out between them. Isaac Alford sitting at an outdoor café in Laos with three known associates of Joel Hayden. Two of those men were well known for laundering funds worldwide for a long list of cartels, mobsters, and third-world governments. The third man was Keo Sengphet, VP at Notakopi, Laos's largest bank. The fact they were all sitting together in the open was nothing short of a giant fuck-you to authorities since all of them were under investigation by multiple agencies in a dozen countries.

Kim's laptop was open, the screen filled with spreadsheets. Printed versions cluttered the remaining space on the table. They contained every borrower and lender INTENT had paired up over the past year along with the dollar amounts. The loans were all over the place—as small as a hundred dollars and scaling up into the hundreds of thousands. They'd spent the better part of the week searching for missing money and not finding it. It wasn't until Stuckey suggested they compare the printed copies to the electronic records that they found anything, and what they found was big.

Kim slumped back in her chair. "I can't believe I didn't think of that."

Stuckey ran a French fry through a mountain of ketchup on his plate and plopped it in his mouth. "Not your fault. Usually when a company we're investigating provides printed versions of their electronic records, they do it to waste our time, right? It's silly for us to dig through boxes of paper when we can run the spreadsheets electronically."

"But you did it anyway." She frowned.

Stuckey tapped one of the spreadsheets. "Only because you told us to watch for this." The initials R.C. were written in the top corner, now highlighted by a red stain from Stuckey's ketchup. "Stands for Robin Church, right? What else could it mean? Then when I saw dots next to some of the entries, I compared them to the electronic version."

Brendan read the page upside down. Six of the loans had dots next to them and had since been highlighted in yellow. The printout listed the loans in good standing, but the electronic records had the same loans coded as defaults. Between the six, they were looking at a little over four hundred thousand dollars. "The borrowers are bogus? You confirmed that?"

Kim nodded. "Shell companies for the first four, the other two used social security numbers belonging to dead people. Joel Hayden's handiwork, I'm sure."

"So Hayden takes out the loan with some fake entity, Isaac Alford codes the loan as a default, and they pocket the cash when nobody is looking for it anymore. Then…"

Kim slid one of the photographs closer. "Then they get the money to this guy, Keo Sengphet at Notakopi Bank in Laos—he cleans it."

"Have the funds left the bank yet?" Brendan asked.

"Best INTERPOL can tell; everything is still there. Sengphet prefers to hold funds in numbered accounts for at least six months before farming them out to his network and cleaning them; none of this has been going on for very long, but they've moved a lot of money."

"How much?" Brendan asked.

Stuckey and Kim exchanged a look, then Stuckey said, "INTENT has just over $104 million in defaults on their books. Some of those are probably legit, but we're working under the assumption most are part of Alford's skimming operation."

Brendan whistled. "How is it possible nobody is looking for all that?"

"This isn't like defaulting on a bank," Kim told him. "With peer-to-peer lending, one loan may be funded by a thousand people. The losses to individuals are small so they just write it off as a bad gamble and move on. There's no real recourse. Look, these guys are ramping up." Kim's hand settled on Brendan's. "We need to get back to Chicago, try to—"

Brendan jerked his hand away, moving so quickly his elbow cracked against the back of his chair.

Kim looked horrified. "I'm sorry. I didn't mean—"

Ignoring the pain in his arm, Brendan waved her off. "My fault. I…didn't sleep well. I'm a little jumpy."

His eyes on both of them, Stuckey sucked the last of his Pepsi through his straw with a loud slurp. "Anyyywayyy…let's focus. We've got motive. We've got means. We've got the framework of a theory, now we need proof." He nodded at Kim's laptop. "Look at every default. Get a dataset together of every borrower. Compare all that to what we have on Joel Hayden. I want solid proof so that slippery fuck doesn't get away again."

Stuckey finished off the last of the French fries. "Nice work, Whitlock. You keep this up you'll have Brendan's job in no time."

"Funny," Brendan muttered.

"Will you take this to the assistant director now?" Kim pushed. "You have to, Stuckey. We need a face-to-face with Cindy Messing. I can't get her on the phone. Maybe she's panicked or worse, maybe Alford found out she's been helping us. Either way, we need to get in front of her and get her under protection. Once she's isolated, we confront Isaac Alford...*in person*. We need the AD to sign off on a return trip to Chicago."

Stuckey weaved his fingers together on the table and slumped in his seat. He cocked his head to the side and did his best Brando impersonation from *The Godfather*. "You have pleased me. I will take this information back to the family."

He sounded nothing like Brando.

On the table, Brendan's phone vibrated with an incoming message from Sugar & Spice. An address and some instructions. Something about Abby. This was quickly followed by another message:

Steal a knife from the restaurant. You'll need it.

20

From the outside, the Westminster Hotel wasn't much to look at. The inside was worse. The walls of the small lobby were covered in green felt wallpaper that looked like it went up around the turn of the twentieth century and started falling about fifty years ago. There was a couch, a few chairs, and a table. When Abby came in, the three men sitting in the lobby all looked at her like feral dogs that hadn't eaten in a week. They made no attempt at concealing their lewdness. One of them actually put his fingers to his cracked lips in the shape of a V and wiggled his tongue through the center.

Abby, dressed in the tightest jeans Hannah could squeeze her into along with a tank top and black wig, did her best to balance in the shoes Hannah had also given her; a pair of what she called her favorite *fuck-me pumps*. She stumbled to the small booth at the center of the room under a crooked sign that read: RECEPTION.

"I was told you were holding a room for me. I'm Mrs. Hol... Mrs. Robinson."

There was an old man in the booth watching an equally old

black and white movie on a television held together with duct tape. He didn't look at her, simply retrieved a key from one of the hooks on the wall and handed it to her. "Sure you are, kid. You're in 3B. Elevator's busted, so you'll need to hoof it."

Abby took the key, considered taking off the shoes, then thought better of it—a twisted ankle was probably preferable to whatever was living on the floors.

She managed the steps without dying.

3B was at the far end of the hallway, the interior as dank and dreary as the hotel lobby and hallways. Green shag carpet. Heavy orange drapes on the window. Matching bedspread. An air freshener plugged into the wall did little to mask the earthy mildew scent hanging in the air.

Abby stood at the threshold for a moment before entering, thinking, *this one's for you, Hannah*. When she closed the door, her phone chimed with new instructions:

On the bed, you'll find a pair of handcuffs and a blindfold. Set your phone on the dresser. Keep the lights off and do not open the curtains. Move to the far end of the room and face the wall. Cuff your hands (in front) and place the blindfold over your eyes. Continue facing the wall. Do not move. Do not utter a sound under any circumstances. Completion of this Spice will earn you 1000 points.

Abby stood still for a moment, rereading the message several times. Nothing she'd done so far had remotely brought in that many points. She stepped over to the bed, studied the items left on the faded orange quilt. The blindfold looked new. Soft. Black silk or something. The handcuffs were new too, still in the box. She scooped up both and went to the other side of the room, leaving her phone on the dresser as instructed. Before she could change her mind, she removed the handcuffs from the box, slipped the key into the front pocket of her borrowed jeans, and fastened the cold metal around both her wrists. When the blindfold went on, the world went dark, the room suddenly felt smaller. She was conscious of the sound of her own breathing. Her heart began to thump wildly, she felt it in her ears.

The next few minutes ticked by agonizingly slow.

Anticipation?

Excitement?

A yearning.

Abby wasn't quite sure how to describe what she was feeling other than she felt entirely alive.

When she heard the door open behind her, it took every ounce of willpower to keep from turning around. There were footsteps, then the door closed with a soft click.

The shuffle of feet crossed the room.

No words.

No sounds.

Don't move.

Brendan's hands on her.

With his first touch, Abby let out a soft gasp; she couldn't help it. He grazed her cheek with his thumb, slipped down to her neck. She didn't realize he was holding a knife until she felt the cold metal press against the skin below her chin, and somehow that heightened everything. Just a game, but still… He said nothing, there was no need. Every inch of Abby's body was afire. When he pressed against her, she felt the hardness of him, and couldn't help but push into him, wanting to get closer.

All her senses heightened; she heard him unfasten his belt. The rustle of his pants dropping to the floor. Then his free hand was on her again. He traced the fullness of her breasts through the thin tank top, brushed across her hard nipples, and edged down to her jeans. He was breathing hard as he thumbed open the snap and took down the zipper. Harder still when he tugged her jeans and underwear down to her ankles. There was no foreplay, no warning; he thrust himself into her, and while Abby thought she was ready, she wasn't. She wanted him, just not like that. "Brendan, that hurts," she whispered. "…not so rough."

He stopped.

He grew as still as she had been when he entered the room.

"Maria?"

The voice was not Brendan's.

The man yanked off Abby's wig, tossed it to the ground, and stumbled back.

"My God…"

Tearing away the blindfold, all thumbs with her bound hands, Abby faced him.

"You're not my wife…"

Thirties. Short blond hair. A thin scar ran from the corner of his nose to the top of his lip. Abby had no idea who he was.

He dropped the knife and fumbled his pants back up. "Who are you? You're not my wife!"

Words deserted her.

Abby's knees became rubber.

She fell against the wall behind her, struggling with the handcuffs, covered herself as best she could. She slid down to the floor, pushed against the wall, wanted to climb inside of it, as this man she'd never seen before backed away from her to the door, equally frightened. "I'm sorry…I didn't…" was all he got out before he managed to get the door open and disappeared down the hall.

21

"This is weird," Brendan muttered, opening the e-mail on his phone to make sure he'd read it right. A second e-mail had come in right behind the first. "Did you deposit twelve cents into our checking account today and then withdraw it?"

Abby sat across from him at the kitchen table, picking at her roast beef and mashed potatoes. She'd barely eaten her dinner.

"Abs?"

"Huh?" Her eyes were glossy, tinged red.

Had she been crying?

Her hair was still wet from a shower, and she was wearing her old Boston Red Sox pajamas. He hadn't seen those in at least five years. They used to be her favorite. She'd worn them so much there were holes in the elbows, but she swore they were extremely comfortable and refused to throw them away.

Brendan clicked off his phone and set it on the table. "Everything okay with you?"

She forced a smile. "Yeah. I'm sorry. It's just been…a day."

Her briefcase was sitting on the empty chair between them. He hadn't seen that in at least a month. Not since—

"Oh. Are you seeing your agent tomorrow? Is that it?"

Abby's forehead knit into a frown, then she followed his gaze and stared at the pages sticking out the top of her bag for several moments before she said, "Yeah, that's it."

"I know we're not supposed to talk about it, but you told Dr. Donetti the book was going well. Wasn't that true?"

"It's true. It is. I guess I'm a little nervous, that's all." Abby's lips drew into a tight line. "I haven't told Connie much yet, but she's going to want details tomorrow. A progress report. She said she just wants to check in, but I know what this really is. She needs to determine if I've got a viable plot and whether or not I'll be turning in a finished draft on time. If my cog won't be ready for its place on the machine, the publisher will need to give the slot to another title and push me back."

"I'm sure she'll love it."

"You don't even know what it's about."

"You've got at least fifty pages. Unless you're pulling a Torrance and they all say, *All work and no play makes Abby a dull girl*, I'm sure it will be okay."

Abby's face turned cold. "Is everything a fucking joke to you?"

"That's not what I meant. I'm just trying to be supportive. I'm sorry I brought it up."

Three quick knocks rattled the kitchen door, and they both looked over. Stuckey was standing on their back porch peering in. He held a six-pack of beer up to the window and nodded toward the garage.

The Red Sox were playing the Tampa Rays in thirty minutes. It was one of the last games at Fenway for the year.

Abby drew in a deep breath and let it out slowly. "Go."

Brendan didn't move. "Are you sure?"

"Go," she said again. Abby buried her face in her hands and let out a deep sigh. She raked her hand through her wet hair. "I'm just tired. I shouldn't have snapped at you. It's okay. I'll clean up."

Brendan rose slowly and started for the door, paused, then went over to her and kissed the top of her head. "If you want to talk about whatever is on your mind, text me and I'll come in, okay?"

Abby nodded, but he knew she wouldn't.

Ten minutes later, the pregame on the flatscreen in the garage, Brendan finished telling Stuckey what happened after he left the lunch meeting. He'd hoped talking about it would lift the weight on his chest, but it only made him feel worse.

Stuckey was rarely at a loss for words, but nearly a minute slipped by before he finally spoke. "That's seriously fucked up. You have no idea who this woman was?"

Brendan shook his head. "No. As soon as I realized it wasn't Abby, I panicked and got the hell out of there."

"Let me see your phone again."

Brendan had loaded the Sugar & Spice messages back up; they were still on the screen.

Stuckey read aloud, "You'll find your partner in the room. Remember, this is her rape fantasy, so play along but keep things fun. Use the knife as a prop and take her from behind. It's best she doesn't see your face. If she tells you to stop, stop. Although specifically requested by your partner, this Spice has been known to be a trigger event; be ready for your safe word. Should that occur…" He looked over at Brendan. "There's an actual disclaimer. What the fuck. Are they all like this?"

"Some…"

Stuckey took a long drink of his beer. "Must be some kind of glitch in the app. Mixed up partners or some shit."

"That's a nasty glitch."

"Yeah. That's how apps get those one-star ratings." He looked back at him. "You gonna tell Abby?"

"What do you think?"

"I think after the way she reacted with the Kim nonsense, you tell her about this, and you'll be single by next Tuesday. You want my advice, you take this to your grave, my brother."

Brendan stared him dead in the face. "That means you do too. Not a word to Hannah."

Stuckey mimicked locking his mouth with an invisible key, then thought of something else. "You said the app gave you a thousand points for today. How you gonna explain that?"

Brendan had no idea.

Abby's score had gone up by fifteen hundred. He didn't want anyone explaining that to him, either.

"We've both been playing the app alone. If she asks, I'll chalk it up to that. I'll tell her I'm trying to keep things competitive."

Stuckey clinked his beer can against Brendan's. "To lies and deception; the foundation of every solid marriage." He took a drink, then changed the subject. "...speaking of Kim."

"I'm sorry about that. I overreacted at lunch today. It was stupid."

"If things are weird between you, it's because you're making them weird. I don't know what happened in Chicago, and I don't want to know, but the two of you need to work your shit out because others are starting to take notice, and that ain't good."

"I know."

"I told the assistant director what Kim found."

"What did she say?"

Stuckey took another drink of his beer. "She wants the two of you on a plane to Chicago for an in-person with the folks at INTENT."

Fuck.

111

22

"Roomeeeo," Juliet called out from the bathroom off the master bedroom.

"Yes, my love?"

"How much do you love me, my dear Romeo?"

"More than chocolate, baby."

"And how much do you love chocolate?"

"More than air."

"That's a lot."

"Because I love you bunches."

"You're so damn sweet," she replied. "I don't deserve you."

Something had changed. Romeo no longer heard the man crying. No splashing. No whimpering. No nothing. "Hey, baby?"

"Yes, my dear?"

"Everything all good with our friend in there?"

Juliet didn't reply.

"Baby?"

"I may have done an uh oh."

Sitting on the edge of Isaac Alford's bed, Romeo closed his eyes and drew in a deep breath. He loved her, but sometimes she did get carried away. He'd been going through the man's nightstand, but aside from dirty magazines older than dirt, he hadn't found anything of interest. He replaced everything as he found it, closed the drawer, and rose.

The bathroom door was locked. "You'll need to let me in, baby." There were several seconds of quiet, then the lock clicked.

When Juliet didn't open the door, he did.

Isaac Alford was right where he'd left him—in the bathtub under a foot or so of lukewarm water. The hairdryer floating next to his head wasn't supposed to be in the tub, though.

Romeo traced the cord back to the GFI outlet in the wall. The paper clip was still jammed in the reset button. Most likely, the breaker in the panel had blown, or maybe it hadn't. Either way, enough juice had made it down the pipe to leave Alford crispy. Below the surface of the water, the man stared up at him with wide, dead eyes.

"Oh, baby, what did you do?"

"I only meant to scare him, but he made a grab for my leg, and I lost my grip on the blower. It fell in."

Isaac Alford's laptop was powered up, sitting on the vanity, a screensaver had beach photos floating lazily by. When Romeo tapped the space bar, the password box came up. "Did you get it?"

Juliet, wearing a white tank and her favorite jean shorts, leaned back against the wall next to the tub. Her head sank. "I'm sorry, baby."

Romeo had an anger in him. Always had. It lived somewhere behind his gut, and most days it was comfortable sleeping there, all curled up and warm in the dark. Sometimes, though, it stirred. Now was one of those times. Stirring was one thing, waking was another entirely. He didn't want the anger to wake. Not for Juliet. It was one thing if someone else woke it up, but not Juliet. Never Juliet. He cleared his throat. "Can you give me a minute?"

Juliet didn't move.

She'd seen his anger, and she'd have to walk by him to get to the door.

"Please."

Juliet peeled herself away from the wall and stepped around him, the back of her legs brushing the side of the bathtub as she gave him the widest berth she could. When she reached the door, she closed it behind her.

Romeo was grateful for that.

Glad she was gone.

He hadn't realized he was gripping the corner of the marble vanity top until he looked down at his hands. His knuckles were white, and he was sure if he gave his thick palms a little bit of twist, he'd snap a chunk of the marble right off. Hell, if he wasn't resting his ass on the top of the vanity, he'd probably yank the whole slab out. Maybe bash it against the wall or use it to muddle Isaac Alford into a mush.

Romeo knew he could do none of those things.

Not here.

Not now.

So instead, he worked to slow his breathing. He worked to tuck the anger back into a restful slumber. He just about had it when his phone rang.

No name appeared on the screen.

No number.

It didn't even say UNKNOWN CALLER.

He had no idea how she did that, but her calls always rang in that way. Romeo raised the phone to his ear and answered. He was never one to beat around the bush, and he was pretty sure, on some level, she appreciated that. "We had a bit of an accident. Nothing I can't clean up, but we didn't get his password."

She said nothing.

She rarely did.

Romeo waited a moment to let his words sink in before he went on. "I'll find some way to make this right with you."

He was fairly certain she hung on the line for a few seconds after he said that, but he couldn't be sure. When he looked back at the screen, he confirmed she'd disconnected.

Romeo looked around the bathroom. Granite and marble everywhere. A shower the size of a carwash and the big soaker tub. Isaac Alford face-up. Hair dryer still plugged in.

He could make it look like a suicide easy enough, he was grateful Juliet hadn't flubbed that, but they'd have to take the laptop. There was no getting around that; it was the reason they were here in the first place. Normally, they'd leave the suicide note on the laptop. He'd already searched the rest of the house and hadn't turned up any other computers, no tablets, no nothing he could leave a suicide note on other than paper, and he wasn't about to go that route. He had no idea what this man's handwriting looked like and wasn't good at faking it anyway.

So, no note.

He'd hope for a stupid cop, of which this world had plenty. Someone who wouldn't notice the laptop was missing.

He looked around the room again.

When he'd jammed the paper clip in the GFI button, he'd wrapped it in toilet paper. No prints there. He grabbed a hand towel from beside the sink and went to work wiping down the rest of the room. If the cops decided to print the room, finding it wiped down carried its own set of problems, but those fell a little further down the ladder than the problems created by them finding either his prints or Juliet's. When he was done in the bathroom, he'd have to backtrack through the house, wipe whatever else they touched.

And hell, he'd still have to get into the laptop back in the van.

He needed to make this right.

No way he'd get on that woman's bad side; not when they were this close to the finish line.

Sugar & Spice™

Sugar
*If you had to hook up with one of your partner's friends,
who would it be?*

23

"Holy hell, this is good." Connie Cormack pushed her thick, black-framed glasses back on her nose, lingered over the final page, and finally rested it facedown on the pages in front of her on her desk. She patted the top of the stack like the head of a good puppy, then settled in her chair, removed her glasses, and studied Abby. "If I saw you walking down the street, looking all first-grade-school-teachery like you do, I'd never guess something like that could come out of your head," she tsked. "It's always the quiet ones."

"I could have e-mailed it to you."

"Then I wouldn't get the opportunity to see your lovely face, and let's be honest, you weren't exactly returning my calls."

Abby did her best to smile. "I'm sorry. I had a lot of starts and stops on this one, and I was beginning to think I didn't have another book in me."

Connie's mouth fell open in an exaggerated *O*. "Abby, dear, I've been doing this for the better part of thirty years, and after reading your first book, getting to know you, I can safely tell you, you have *many* books in you. More than you'll ever be able to write. Any agent worth their salt can smell it on you. Some people are born with that storyteller gene, and you are one of them. Don't ever think that again. It's perfectly normal to have starts and stops with a new book. I'd be worried if you didn't. It simply means you're not willing to phone it in, you want to craft a good book—me and your readers thank you for that."

This time, Abby did smile. "Do you lay it on that thick for all your authors?"

"Yes. Yes, I do."

Abby's phone let out a soft triple chime. The following message flashed across her screen:

> *Your partner has initiated a Spice. Send them
> a naked photo in the next five minutes.*

A timer began counting down. She turned the phone over and set it down on the chair next to her.

"Abby? Everything okay?"

Abby blinked. "Yes. I'm sorry. It's just my husband."

"The financial crimes detective?"

"The accountant on a government salary."

"Ah." She let it go and retrieved a business card from her top desk drawer. "This is why I really wanted you to come in."

Abby looked at the card. "Who is Ryan Lewis?"

"He's a film and television agent. He works with authors to get their stories on the screen. He'd like to talk to you."

Abby swallowed. "About?"

"For starters, your first book, but more importantly, this one." Connie tapped the stack again. "He thinks he can—"

Connie's phone rang.

She raised a finger and reached for the receiver. "Hello?"

There were several seconds of silence as she listened. Then she held the phone out to Abby, a frown on her face. "It's…for you. Sounds like a robocall."

Abby didn't understand. Aside from Brendan and Hannah, nobody knew where she was.

She took the phone from Connie and pressed it to her ear. "This is Abby Hollander."

A robotic female voice said, *"Your partner has initiated a Spice. Send them a naked photo. You have two minutes and twelve seconds to comply."*

The line went dead. Abby's stomach twisted into a knot. She handed the phone back.

Connie returned the receiver to its cradle. "You know, for some-one who's writing next year's number one *New York Times* bestseller, you sure look despondent. Are you maybe coming down with some-thing? Success fever, maybe?" Connie kept a large bottle of hand sanitizer on her desk; she slowly slid it toward Abby, a grin growing on her face.

Abby pushed it back. "Funny." She nodded at the business card. "Tell me about this guy."

"When the book is ready, he'd like to shop it to the folks in Hollywood. It may go somewhere, it may not, but if it does…being able to talk about a potential film deal at release can go a long way when it comes to the press. Talking about two film deals is even better. I've got another author who—"

Connie's iPhone was set to silent, and it vibrated across her desk with an incoming text. She quickly read it and appeared confused. "Okay, that's weird."

She showed the message to Abby. It was from an unknown caller and simply said: *One minute, eighteen seconds. DO NOT allow time to expire. Bad things happen when time expires.*

Abby's heart thumped.

What the hell was this? How the hell was that even possible? This had to be Brendan messing with her somehow. Or maybe Hannah.

Bad things happen when time expires??!

What the actual fuck.

This meeting was important.

Her phone dinged, and the countdown timer went red as it ticked below a minute.

59.

58.

57.

"I'm sorry. Can I use your restroom?" Abby asked.

Connie gestured toward the door to her private bathroom. "Sure." She only seemed to half-hear her, she was busy clicking around her phone, no doubt trying to find the source of the strange message.

Abby stepped into the bathroom and locked the door.

As bathrooms went, Connie's was large, particularly for one in someone's office. There was even a shower twice the size of the one she had at home. The entire room was gray marble and smelled like wildflowers.

Abby studied herself in the mirror and didn't like what she saw. There were dark circles under her eyes. Her cheeks looked pale and sallow. She'd put on makeup before leaving the house, but it had been a half-assed job at best. She was digging through her purse looking for lipstick when a thought struck her—

Fuck Brendan.

If he was behind this, who gave a shit if she looked good or not?

Her phone was still counting down:

38.

37.

Abby quickly stripped out of her clothes, snapped a few photos from different angles, and texted them to Brendan, adding the message: *I am NOT in the mood for this right now. You're an ass.*

A new message appeared from Sugar & Spice:

Congratulations! You've reached 5,000 points.
Welcome to bronze level!

"Lovely," Abby muttered. "I feel honored."

She quickly dressed and remembered to flush the toilet before leaving the room. She hadn't used it, but figured some semblance of normalcy might help Connie believe she was a little less crazy than she currently felt.

24

Brendan was operating on little to no sleep.

Whenever he closed his eyes, he saw the woman who wasn't his wife in that hotel room, standing against the far wall with her back to him.

Waiting for him.

The room was dark.

She was clearly wearing a wig and he'd been told Abby wouldn't be in her own clothes—all part of the game—all part of the fantasy she wanted to act out. He'd be lying if he said the thought of it all hadn't excited him. Prior to Sugar & Spice, his and Abby's sex life had been running on autopilot. Lately, it had been dialed up to eleven. Abby had completely come out of her shell, he had too. Their sex life was incredible. *She was incredible.* Walking into that hotel room, he'd wanted her more than ever, only it hadn't been her. It had been someone else.

Nothing had happened, not really. The woman's perfume was all wrong. This strong, flowery scent Abby would never wear. When

Brendan spoke, the woman had turned, saw the knife in Brendan's hand, and screamed. That's when he ran.

The app gave him a thousand points.

The app gave Abby fifteen hundred.

No matter what he did, he couldn't silence the little voice in the back of his head that kept asking why she got more.

He should have said something last night, she was obviously upset. But he hadn't. Deep down, he didn't want the answer. They'd spent the night physically next to each other, but in reality, they were a million miles apart.

This morning, he got up early, kissed her cheek, and went to work.

He was pretty sure she was only pretending to be asleep.

Brendan arrived in the office at a little after seven and downloaded all of INTENT's defaulted loans going back two years. When he couldn't wrap his brain around them, he'd chugged a cup of coffee and printed them out, hoping the caffeine and physical pages might help. Instead, it made him jittery, and his desk was littered with paper.

He got up, shut his door, and dropped into his chair.

Closed his eyes.

Five minutes.

Maybe ten.

Just a little shut-eye to help him get back in the game.

His phone vibrated.

When Brendan woke, his head was on his desk in a puddle of drool. The time on his phone read nineteen after ten.

Abby had sent him a photo.

Groggy, it took a moment for Brendan to wrap his head around it.

A selfie in some bathroom he didn't recognize.

She wasn't wearing a stitch of clothing.

The first photo was quickly followed by several more at different angles.

Oh man, she looked hot.

Was this her trying to make up for last night?

Two more came in, then a text message he probably read ten times:

If I asked you to fuck me in the ass tonight, would you?
I think I want you to.

Whatever sleepiness lingered quickly vanished. Brendan sat up straight in his chair and scrolled back through the images. Where the hell was she? Oh, wait. Hadn't she gone to see her agent this morning? Did she take these there? Somehow, that made them even hotter. The thought of her doing this in some semi-public place.

Abby sent another message:

Are you hard? Can you send me a picture?
I want to see it. Right now.

Brendan *was* hard. Hell, if he tried to stand right now, he'd be doubled over. He looked around his office. His blinds were closed, same with the door. Most of the staff was out on audits and wouldn't be back until Friday. The office was a ghost town.

Before he could change his mind, he unfastened the buckle on his belt, fumbled open the snap and zipper on his pants, and tugged them down along with his underwear. He quickly took several photographs and sent them to Abby.

Two quick knocks on his door, and it swung open.

Kim looked in through the gap. "I just got a notification from Reuters—Isaac Alford, the CFO of INTENT, was found dead in his bathtub! Sounds like a suicide. His wife called police last night and—" Kim frowned and stepped through the door. "Are you okay? You look pale."

Brendan froze. His pants were still down. He inched deeper under his desk, not sure what she could see, if anything. "Yeah...I...didn't sleep well last night."

Kim took another step into his office and placed her hand on the door, began to close it behind her.

No! No! No! He couldn't let her in. If she saw. If she told someone. Worse, if it led to something happening—

Brendan's heart was racing. He felt sweat break out across his brow. "Did you tell Stuckey?"

The words came out far faster than Brendan wanted them to, and he knew how odd he sounded, but he could think of nothing else.

Kim's voice dropped lower. "I figured I'd tell you first. There's something else you need to know, it's about—"

"You should go tell Stuckey. I'll be right there."

She drew closer, spotted the drool on his desk, but was far more interested in the printouts. "You're digging through defaults? I thought Stuckey wanted me to do that?"

"Kim. Go tell Stuckey. I need a minute."

Oh, and that came out all wrong.

Angry.

Hostile, even.

Kim froze. Her eyes fixed on him.

She was so close, there was no way she couldn't see, but if she did, she didn't say anything. "Okay, Brendan. I'll be in Stuckey's office. Join us when you're ready."

"Okay."

126

"Okay."

She turned and left, closing the door so softly you'd think she just put a baby down to sleep.

Brendan's heart was beating with a fierceness, it might burst through his chest. His palms, his forehead, his chest—all were covered in sweat.

He quickly pulled his pants and underwear back up, tucked his shirt in. When he looked at his hands, both were shaking, shaking violently.

His phone buzzed with another text from Abby—a heart emoji, nothing else. He was still looking at that, trying to calm himself down, when his desk phone beeped. The assistant director's voice came through the speaker.

"Brendan, my office. Now."

25

Brendan took the time to visit the bathroom and splash some cold water on his face and check himself in the mirror. He stood at the sink for at least a minute before drawing in a deep breath and forcing himself to continue to the assistant director's office.

It felt like some kind of death march.

Unlike his office blinds, Mary Dubin's were kept wide open. She preferred to see her staff through the large glass windows that looked out on the bullpen of cubicles and the conference room on the other side of the large office space. More importantly, she wanted the staff to see her. And she was always there. She'd been in her office when Brendan arrived at a little after seven that morning, and she would no doubt still be in there when he left at the end of the day. Rumors of her sleeping at the office had circulated more than once.

Brendan's office was two doors down from the conference room, across the bullpen from the AD, and when he circled the cubicles, he spotted both Kim and Stuckey already in there. They sat in the two chairs in front of Dubin's desk, their backs to him.

Neither turned when he came in.

Assistant Director Dubin, sitting in the cracked leather chair she refused to replace, barely glanced at him. "Close the door behind you, Brendan."

Kim saw.

She must have.

She literally caught him with his pants down and either went straight to the AD or told Stuckey and he took her to the AD. Either way, they were all in there and he was fucked. His career was over. If there was some kind of disciplinary action, if word got out, his life would be over. Press. The Internet. Hell, if you Google Congressman Anthony Weiner, the first thing that comes up is his Wikipedia page which begins with *Anthony David Weiner (born September 4, 1964) is an American former politician and convicted sex offender.* The Internet was forever.

Dubin took off her glasses and shook her head before finally saying, "Kim told you about Isaac Alford, right?"

Brendan forced a nod.

Oh, thank you, baby Jesus.

This wasn't about him. This was something else. The AD confirmed that with what she said next.

"Joel Hayden is dead too."

A knot formed in Brendan's stomach. "How?"

"Apparently, he hanged himself in a sauna at some health club downtown almost a week ago. Nobody thought to tell us until now."

"Joel Hayden and Isaac Alford both killed themselves?" Brendan managed.

Assistant Director Dubin didn't answer that. Instead, she nodded at Stuckey. Stuckey didn't turn around. He held his arm up over his head, a sheet of paper clasped between his fingers.

Brendan took the page. It was a printout from a newspaper

article that ran in some paper he'd never heard of in Woodstock, Illinois. The headline read: "Home Invasion/Arson Leaves Two Dead." That was bad, but it was the names that got him. "Cindy and Byron Messing?" He looked at Kim. "Is this *your* Cindy Messing?"

Kim nodded bleakly.

Nearly a minute of silence hung over the room, broken by AD Dubin. "I've spoken with a colleague at the FBI. This can't be a coincidence. We either have two suicides connected to a potential money laundering operation, or…"

Or, Brendan's mind muttered. *Or, we have three murders connected to a potential money laundering operation, with two made to look like suicide.*

Neither of those options was good.

Again, the room went quiet.

Finally, Stuckey cleared his throat. "I filled in the AD on everything. She agrees we need to act fast."

Assistant Director Dubin leaned back in her tattered chair and absentmindedly tapped a pen on the corner of her desk. "You and Kim are booked on the 7 a.m. to Chicago. You'll be staying in the same hotel as last time, but with the feds. At this point, the FBI doesn't want the folks at INTENT to know they're under the microscope so the two of you will go in first, do some quick recon, then the feds will organize a raid. They want everything Isaac Alford touched."

"Maybe…me and Stuckey should go."

Kim's face turned red. "Why? I've done all the legwork on this. I connected the dots. If I hadn't—"

Dubin raised a hand and silenced her. "The people at INTENT know the two of you. We send someone else, it could raise suspicions before we're ready to move."

"This could be dangerous and—"

There was no holding Kim back now. "Oh, and because I'm a woman I can't handle myself? You chauvinistic piece of—"

"Kim, enough," Dubin interrupted. "The FBI doesn't believe you'll be in any danger. In fact, they've assured me of that. They *do* believe it's important we keep up appearances and not tip our hand. They don't know what we know. Suicide or not, they'll expect you to look at Alford. They will be too, and we need to get in there before they have time to scrub evidence."

Brendan held both hands up defensively. "Kim, I didn't mean to imply you can't handle yourself. That's not it at all. Stuckey's been doing this longer than both of us. He's more likely to spot something. That's what I was getting at. And let's be honest, he's a better people person than either of us. He can get someone to confess to damn near anything, they talk like they're doing him a favor. If this escalates, and it sounds like it will, this might be our last opportunity behind their doors. Hell, they might already be destroying evidence." He looked back to the AD. "Maybe send Kim and Stuckey instead of me?"

Stuckey leaned back in his seat. "Can't, buddy, I'm heading to Laos. I'm on the red-eye tonight. We've been granted an emergency order to seize the assets connected to Alford, Hayden, and Keo Sengphet at Notakopi Bank. I need to meet up with INTERPOL."

Brendan took a moment to process that.

Stuckey was good at reading people, but Assistant Director Dubin was better; she knew exactly what he was thinking.

"FBI has no jurisdiction outside the US, but we do," she said. "It would take them a week or longer to arrange something with another agency; much faster for us to send someone. Stuckey leaves in a few hours, serves the subpoena, authenticates the asset seizure, and turns back around."

"With the layover, the flight's seventeen hours and change. I'm home day after tomorrow."

Dubin said to Brendan, "Authentication requires two senior staff members, and I'll be in and out of closed-door meetings. I don't want to risk Stuckey not being able to reach me. Can you keep your computer close so you can enter your ID and a password when Stuckey is on site?"

Brendan nodded. "Okay."

Dubin scribbled a name and number on a piece of paper and slid it across her desk to Kim. "When you arrive at the hotel tomorrow, call that number and ask for Special Agent Marcus Bellows. He'll coordinate the INTENT visit with you."

26

Brendan, Kim, and Stuckey spent the remainder of the day organizing their data, determining who they would need to speak to and in what order, knowing full well that would become more difficult as the day went on. Particularly if senior staff at INTENT felt they were sniffing around something they didn't want sniffed. Legally, they had full rein of the office; they could open any drawer, copy any document—that was threatening enough. If they discovered Alford wasn't acting alone, things would get ugly.

He and Kim kept it cordial, but he'd be lying if he said it didn't feel awkward. If Stuckey picked up on the tension, he didn't say anything.

As the day progressed, Abby sent more photos. All taken in the same bathroom. Some were accompanied by teasing and taunting messages, all these things she wanted him to do to her and things she said she wanted to do to him. By the time Brendan pulled into the driveway at half past six, he wanted her so bad if she greeted him in the driveway, they might not make it back inside the house.

Abby didn't greet him in the driveway. She wasn't in the living room, either. He stepped inside the empty room and called out her name.

"Abs?"

The lights were dim, and Elle Fitzgerald singing "Someone to Watch Over Me" played softly through all the smart speakers around the house. When his eyes adjusted, he noticed the dining room table—normally covered in clutter, it had been cleared and set for dinner. Several candles burned at the center.

Abby appeared in the kitchen doorway.

White silk blouse, black skirt, matching heels. Her hair was swept back from her face in a way that looked perfectly happenstance but probably took her an hour at the mirror to perfect. She looked lovely. She stepped over to him and handed him one of two glasses of red wine. "We're going to try something a little different tonight."

Abby's words were slurred. Not bad, but Brendan could tell she'd started without him.

"What do you have in mind, Mrs. Hollander?"

Abby held out her palm. "Give me your phone."

"My phone, why?"

She didn't answer, nor did she lower her hand.

Brendan took his phone from his back pocket and handed it to her. She keyed in his passcode (he knew hers, too) and loaded up the Sugar & Spice app, tapped through several screens, then held it out to him so he could read. It was a service message dated earlier in the day:

Your app has been updated to the latest release.
Among other issues, this patch corrects problems that led to
a system-wide processing error yesterday. We apologize for any
confusion or inconvenience this may have caused you.

As a thank-you for putting up with our growing pains, you will be permitted to keep the related points awarded to you yesterday.

Sugar & Spice™

When Brendan finished reading, she powered off his phone and set it on the table near the door. Her phone was already there.

"I turned mine off too. You and I are going to spend tonight unplugged. No phones. No computers. No television. We need a break from all that." She clinked her glass gently against his and took a small sip, then said softly, "We're not going to talk about what happened yesterday. Not now, not ever. In fact, it *didn't* happen, so wipe it from your mind. Instead, we're picking up where we left off. We were in a good place, and I don't want to backstep. I imagine you don't want to, either."

There was nothing Brendan wanted to do more than forget, but even as she said it his mind reminded him Abby had been awarded more points than him. He hadn't touched the woman in the hotel room, and he got fewer points than Abby. *What exactly did* she *do?*

He shook it away.

All of it.

She was right. If something did happen, he didn't want to know. And more importantly, it wasn't her fault. He had to let it go.

Brendan brushed her cheek. "I've been thinking about you all day. I couldn't get you out of my head if my life depended on it. Wow, those pictures, Abby..."

She kissed him.

Tenderly at first, then with a growing hunger, this intensity, but when Brendan tried to pull her closer she peeled from his grasp. "Not yet. Dinner first. Take a seat, Mr. Hollander."

He tasted the wine on her breath, her lips.

"There's something I need to tell you, it's about work."

She gave him a gentle peck on the cheek. "No shop talk, that can wait too. Tonight's about us. Just us. Take a seat. I'll get dinner."

"How about I help?"

"Sit."

Abby disappeared into the kitchen. She'd left the wine bottle on the table. There was less than an inch at the bottom. Both their glasses were half-full, which meant she had drunk at least two more glasses before he got home. She rarely drank alone.

Brendan sat in one of the empty seats. Abby returned a moment later with two Caesar salads and took the seat across from him. She sipped her wine, then topped off her glass with the remains of the bottle.

"Maybe you should slow down a little?"

She smirked and reached for the glass again. "Why? It's just the two of us, right?"

There was a shine to her eyes, her words a little more fumbled as she slipped past buzzed and moved into tipsy territory.

"Sure. Just us." He took a bite of the salad. "This is delicious."

"I'm glad you like it."

Brendan knew she met with her agent today, and she hadn't said a word about it. He wanted to ask how it went, but she said no shop talk and he assumed that meant her work, too. Was that what this was about? Had her meeting gone poorly? Maybe her agent didn't like the new pages. That had to be it. If she had good news, surely she'd tell him. Abby threw him with what she said next.

"You and I are enough, right?"

"What do you mean?"

"We're okay, right?"

"Sure. Of course."

Abby took another drink, a long one this time, nearly polished off her glass. "I always thought we were enough…"

"I don't understand."

Abby kept going. "…I'm sure if I asked Hannah, she'd do it, but…no matter what…I don't want it to be that woman from your office. That would be too much. If not Hannah, then maybe we can find someone on Tinder or something."

"Abs, what are you talking about?"

"Your message from earlier. You said you wanted to try a three-way tonight."

Now he was really confused. "No, I didn't."

She rolled her glossy eyes. "Seriously? Now you're gonna deny it?"

"Abs, I didn't…"

She stood on wobbly legs and retrieved her phone from the table at the front door, powered it on, and began tapping through screens. After about a minute, she cursed under her breath. "I don't understand."

"What?"

"Our entire conversation is gone. All our text messages. I don't even see you in here as a contact anymore. It's like you've been deleted."

"What? Like you canceled me?" he joked.

"This isn't funny."

"I didn't send you anything like that," Brendan reiterated. "I'll show you."

He went and got his own phone, turned it on, and loaded up his text conversation with Abby. "You've been flirting with me all day. I only responded one time with the picture of my…well, you know."

A puzzled look filled her face. "I don't know." She reached for his phone. "Let me see that."

137

Abby scrolled through all the messages today, clearly growing more and more confused with each one. "I sent you those pictures from the bathroom, but that's it. All this stuff after wasn't me." Her thumb froze the screen on the message right after the photographs—

If I asked you to fuck me in the ass tonight, would you?
I think I want you to.

"Well, I certainly didn't send that."

Then she found Brendan's dick pic, and her eyes went wide. "And I didn't get that."

"Are you sure? How much did you drink today?"

Abby lowered the phone and glared at him. "Oh, that's not fair."

"All I'm saying is maybe you deleted the conversation on accident. Or maybe you changed your mind and thought this was the best way…" He lowered his voice. "Look Abs, if you don't want to do it, it's fine, we don't have to."

"Oh, we're certainly not doing *that*."

"Okay."

"Or the other thing."

"Okay."

"Fine." She glanced back at the table; her mood had gone sour. "You know, I'm not that hungry anymore. There's steak in the oven, help yourself. I'm going to bed."

"Abs, let's talk about this."

"Why? You clearly think I'm some blackout drunk lush who can't remember what she does and doesn't do. What's the point in talking to me when I'll just forget?" She swiveled and started up the steps.

She was halfway up when Brendan said, "Abs, I have to go back to Chicago tomorrow."

Abby didn't look back at him, didn't slow. He heard her stomp around on the second floor for a moment, then his pillow came sailing down followed by a quilt. The bedroom door slammed, and all went quiet.

27

"This isn't going to be weird, is it?" Kim asked. "I really don't want it to be weird."

Their plane had just pulled away from the gate and was taxiing to a runway. Brendan had a knot in his shoulder from sleeping on the sofa and the little leg room in coach wasn't helping, he couldn't stretch.

He'd crept into his bedroom at a little after five to pack. If Abby heard him, she hadn't stirred. He didn't want to leave her alone, not after last night. He'd considered calling Hannah, telling her what happened, and maybe asking her to keep an eye on her, but he knew that would only embarrass Abby further and that would make things worse. Hopefully, she'd wake, remember what happened when she sobered, and apologize. Hell, he didn't even care if she apologized, he just wanted her to remember the truth so they could move past it. It wasn't worth fighting over.

Brendan quickly tapped out *I love you* in a text to her—he always did before taking off in a plane, then he added, *I'm sorry about last night*, because he didn't care if she blamed him, he only wanted to put it behind them.

He switched his phone into airplane mode and told Kim, "No weirdness, I promise."

Kim donned a pair of headphones, settled back in her seat, and closed her eyes.

Brendan was about to do the same when his phone vibrated.

Please take a moment to complete this brief survey.

There was no *Yes* or *No*, only *Ok* and that wasn't okay. Brendan was getting tired of that. He checked the settings on his phone and confirmed it was on airplane mode, then he held his thumb on the Sugar & Spice app logo until it began to vibrate, he selected *Remove this app* from the menu. The logo vanished for a second, then reappeared.

We're sorry to see you go! Because your account is linked with your partner, consent to remove the app must be received by both parties. We have sent your partner a request. While we wait for your partner to respond, please take a moment to complete this brief survey.

Brendan let out a frustrated sigh and clicked on *Ok*. He had three hours to kill.

Do you feel closer to your partner since discovering Sugar & Spice?

He hesitated for a moment and thumbed *Yes*. Which was the truth, even if they had fought last night.

*Glad to hear it! Would you recommend
Sugar & Spice to a friend or co-worker?*

This time, he clicked *No*. Did they miss the part where he tried to uninstall? No way he'd recommend them. Not after what happened at that hotel.

We're sorry to hear that. How would you rate your partner's
performance during your last sexual encounter?
Poor, Adequate, or Exceptional?

Brendan clicked on *Exceptional*.

That's wonderful news! Do you feel you are more
attracted to your partner since first joining Sugar & Spice?

Brendan clicked *Yes*.

Wow! We're thrilled! Too bad you're leaving. Our experts have taken
a moment to evaluate your partner's physical appearance.
Would you care to review their findings?

Brendan read that message twice. *What the hell??!* Before he could respond, one of the photos Abby had sent him yesterday appeared on the screen, silhouetted behind the text. He quickly glanced over at Kim; her eyes were closed, and if she wasn't sleeping, she was well on her way. He turned slightly anyway to ensure she couldn't see his screen and clicked *Ok*, because, as usual, the app didn't give him a choice.

While your partner is attractive, she is only thirty-two. As she ages,
it will become increasingly difficult to maintain her current physique.
In fact, her recent changes in employment from a career that kept her
active as an event planner to her current profession as a writer, which

is sedentary, will quickly prove to be detrimental.
Signs of this change are already visible:

Brendan could only stare as the photograph moved to the side and another appeared next to it. Another naked picture of Abby he'd never seen before. Another selfie, this one taken at the full-length mirror in their bedroom.

This comparison photograph is dated four years ago. As you can see, there is a noticeable sag in your partner's breasts as well as your partner's buttocks. Under your partner's chin as well.

Yellow lines appeared on both images, highlighting various portions of Abby's body.

Your partner has put on four pounds in the last two months alone. We strongly suggest your partner take up running or join a fitness center. Because we understand this may be an awkward conversation for you to initiate, we've taken the liberty of sending your partner several coupons for local gyms. A healthy body is an attractive body!

The two images faded out, replaced by two others. This continued for nearly a minute, cycling through pictures of Abby at different angles, pointing out what it considered flaws. He vaguely remembered granting the app access to his camera and photos during the installation process. Abby did the same. They must have pulled them from there.

Would you care to see your personal evaluation?

A lump quickly formed in his throat. Again, the app didn't give him a choice. He clicked on *Ok*.

While our records indicate you have a monthly membership at Core Fitness, you haven't gone in nearly two months.

Brendan wasn't in the habit of taking naked pictures of himself, but the app managed to find several photographs of him shirtless during a vacation two years ago to the Bahamas. It compared that to one in which he was sleeping dated two weeks earlier. Had Abby taken that for some reason? While he was sleeping? The app quickly highlighted flaws in his body as it did with Abby, which was embarrassing, but that wasn't the worst of it. The picture he'd taken at his desk yesterday came up.

Microphallus or Micropenis is a condition typically diagnosed at birth. The condition can be caused by irregular hormone levels during the third trimester of pregnancy. An adult penis is considered abnormally small only if it measures less than three inches (about eight centimeters) when erect. Treatment might involve hormone therapy or surgery. While you do not have Micropenis, it's important you have a candid conversation with your partner to ensure your partner is satisfied not only with your length, but your girth. Both can be corrected through surgery. Supplements may also prove helpful. If your partner is unable to reach orgasm during intercourse, it may be because—

Brendan closed the app. He was done with this bullshit. The second he got back home, he'd get with Abby, and it was coming off both their phones.

28

The box had been on the front stoop when Abby opened the door to get the newspaper.

A small box wrapped in plain brown paper. No return address. Inside was a silver chain with a small charm. A square piece of bronze with the number 73 stamped on it about a half inch long on each side. There was no note, nothing else inside, but Abby knew it came from Sugar & Spice. Some trinket for reaching the bronze level. She had no idea what the number meant, though.

She'd brought it up to her office and set it on the corner of her desk. Then she went in search of Advil.

Yes, Abby had a hangover.

No, she didn't care.

She'd written nine pages since rolling out of bed. It was crazy. She'd never been struck with the bug this bad. Nine pages, barely a pause. The words were coming out of her so fast her fingers couldn't keep up. She was seriously considering dictating—something she'd never tried before. She was always self-conscious someone would hear her, which was silly since Brendan was usually at work when she wrote. Sillier to consider now, since he was halfway to Chicago.

Chicago.

Fuck.

That did it.

Full stop.

Fuck. Fuck. Fuck.

Abby settled back in her chair and tried to gather her thoughts.

She hadn't drunk that much last night; it had been the pill that sent her over the edge, and she had Hannah to thank for that. Small. Pink. Round. Abby had no idea what it was. Hannah had called it her *Happy Happy* and said Abby had earned one after her ordeal at the hotel the night before last. Abby had told her what happened, she told Hannah everything, good and bad, and while recounting everything had been horrible, it also lit a spark. More like a fuss. There was no way she could sleep the night it happened, and after wandering the house, she'd found herself at her computer.

Brendan had no clue. She was pretty sure he didn't even realize she hadn't spent the night in bed.

By the time morning came around, she had the first fifty pages of her new book.

The pages her agent had loved.

She'd forgotten all about Hannah's *Happy Happy* pill and decided she'd save it for what she hoped would be a special night with Brendan. A celebration. A reunion.

Instead, last night had been a colossal clusterfuck.

Okay. She needed to get that word out of her head before it started finding its way into her pages. No more f-bombs. She didn't need them. The story was that damn good.

It was the app.

She'd taken the general idea of the app, added a *what if?*, and threw in a character who wasn't altogether different from her (Emily). A husband not far off from Brendan (name undecided, but David for now). Marital problems. A therapist. From there, she was off to the races. Abby had heard of stories writing themselves and considered them to be nothing but a mythical beast, until now.

The fog she'd been experiencing for months vanished.

Her brain was dialed to eleven.

After last night, she'd even worked in the whole three-way thing. In her story, the wife, Emily, had made it all up—told her husband he'd sent it to her in a text when he didn't. She'd made it all up because she wanted to gauge his reaction when she brought up the idea of inviting her best friend into their bedroom. In her story, the wife and best friend had secretly been having an affair. One originally meant to counter the husband's affair with a co-worker (New Yorker in the book, no name as of yet). The wife and best friend had fallen in love, though. They'd fallen in love and were plotting revenge against the husband for his indiscretions. Abby had no trouble blurring the lines between fact and fiction, pulling moments from real life, and embellishing for the story. That's where the best material came from. And when she did get stuck, there was the real app. She'd click a Sugar or a Spice and use the result like a writing prompt. Fuel for her fire.

After the Westminster, she'd been ready to delete the app, erase it from her life, but now it had become as integral to her storytelling process as her MacBook. Each idea the app gave her was better than the last.

Chicago.

Yes, that put on the brakes every time it popped into Abby's head. The idea of Brendan traveling with *her.* Spending days and nights away with *her.*

That was a hard stop.

But she'd gotten past it the last two times it wormed into her thoughts, and she'd beat it down again.

Reaching for her phone, Abby loaded up the app. She expected the main screen asking her to select a Sugar or Spice, but instead, there was a message asking if she wanted to remove the app. Apparently, something initiated by Brendan. Long-distance fuckery.

Ugh, that word again.

Abby clicked *No*, dismissing the message. He wasn't going to ruin this for her. The app wasn't going anywhere until she was done with this book. The screen defaulted back to the main menu, and she clicked on Spice.

Wearing nothing under your coat, visit your partner at work.

Well, that wasn't going to happen. Not while she was mad at him. Not while he was traveling. But her character certainly could do it. Abby read over the last few pages she'd written, took a sip of her coffee, and worked that into the next scene. When she looked back up, thirty-eight minutes had slipped by, and she had four more pages.

Three more Sugars.

Two more Spices.

Nearly three and a half solid hours of writing.

Abby had amassed nine hundred points just this morning, and those nine hundred points had garnered eleven more pages. At this pace, she'd have a completed novel in less than a month. Maybe sooner.

On the flip side, she hadn't eaten, showered, brushed her teeth, combed her hair, or changed out of her jam-jams. Artistry sometimes required sacrifice. Abby was considering doing all those things when the app played its little triple chime and flashed a new message on her screen:

Wow, you're on a roll! As a Bronze member, you can unlock special features currently in beta and not available to members of lesser stature. Would you like to unlock those features now?

Abby read the message and realized this was the first time it asked her a question and actually gave her the ability to answer *Yes* or *No*. Usually, there was only a single *Ok* button. Maybe that was one of the glitches they'd fixed with yesterday's patch. She tapped *Yes*.

The app closed, and a small hourglass appeared on her screen as it downloaded some type of update. When the hourglass vanished, the app's logo appeared with v1.1 in the bottom corner.

Would you like to try a Sugar or a Spice?

The font was slightly different, but otherwise everything looked the same. Abby had been sitting with her feet curled up under her on the chair, and her legs had fallen asleep. She stretched out beneath her desk, let out a yawn, and clicked on *Sugar*.

Would you kill a total stranger to save your partner's life?

Beneath the single sentence, there was a map and two buttons. *Yes* or *No*.

"Holy shit," Abby muttered, nearly falling from her chair.

Sugar & Spice™

Sugar
*If your best friend called you in the middle of the night
and asked for your help hiding a body, would you?*

29

"It can't be for real." Hannah plopped down into a bean bag next to Abby's desk, the phone in her hand.

Abby called her right after the message appeared.

Unlike Abby, Hannah was fully dressed; her hair and makeup were both flawless. She'd been trying to get the "perfect" recording of some dance for a TikTok video. Something involving that old song, "Iko Iko," a bucket of whipped cream, and a two-foot length of rope. Abby hadn't asked beyond that. She didn't want to know.

Hannah tried to enlarge the map, but pinch and zoom didn't seem to work. "Who do you think it is?"

"Does it matter?"

"No. Of course not. It's crazy." Hannah looked up at her, her eyes going wide. "You should totally click *Yes*."

"I can't."

"Why not? It's just a game, right?"

"Like the hotel was just a game?"

"Good point."

Abby realized she was chewing on one of her cuticles. She wiped her hand on her shorts and tucked her fingers under her thigh to keep from doing it again.

Hannah had gone quiet, absentmindedly twisting Abby's phone in her fingers, clearly thinking. Finally, she said, "Would you?"

"Would I what?"

"Kill someone to save Brendan's life." Suddenly Hannah became very serious. "Truth, Abs. No bullshit."

Abby wasn't one to hurt anything. She didn't even kill insects in the house. She had a bug-sucker, like a little vacuum. Brendan had bought it for her. If she found a fly in the house, she sucked it up, trapped it, and released it outside. She'd once caught a mouse in a no-kill trap. The little guy had been in there for several days before she realized it, and when she tried to set him free, he couldn't move. Malnourished and dehydrated, he only lay there. Using an eyedropper, she fed him milk and nursed him back to health before finally releasing him in their backyard. She was no pacifist, there was a line, but what would it take to get her to cross it? "I guess it depends on the circumstances, right? I mean, if someone broke into the house and they were going to hurt Brendan and I had to kill them to keep that from happening, sure. I'd do that."

"You think you have that in you? You wouldn't freeze?"

"If it's self-defense or I'm being protective, it's reactionary, right? Heat of the moment stuff. Adrenaline goes a long way. In a situation like that, I think you act on an instinctual level. Yes. I think I could if I had no other choice."

"Okay, but yeah, that's reactionary. I don't think that's what this question is asking. If I'm reading this correctly, it's more of a preemptive strike. *Would you kill someone to save your partner's life?* So, I point to some guy in the street, tell you that man is going to shoot Brendan in a week. Would you be able to kill that man?"

Abby grinned. "Now you're Tom Cruise in *Minority Report?*"

"Let's say I have a good crystal ball. Not a knock-off from one of those stores off Bourbon Street in New Orleans, but the real deal from some old gypsy in Romania."

"Like forged from the eyes of virgins and polished with the tears of orphans?"

"Exactly."

"In that case, if it was an absolute certainty, then yes. I think I could do it," Abby told her. "But that's the real problem, right? How would you know? You couldn't. Not knowing for sure creates doubt. Doubt leads to hesitation. You'd be killing someone on faith, and you'd have to live with the uncertainty. The guilt of it. That's where I'd draw the line. I couldn't do that. What about you?"

Hannah laughed. "Stuckey gets himself into some life-or-death situation, he's on his own. I've got a fat life insurance policy on his ass. He gets himself killed, I'm buying a condo in Barbados."

"Your love is inspiring." Abby reached for this morning's pages on her printer and added them to the growing stack in the corner of her desk.

"You wrote all that in the past week?"

Abby realized the last time Hannah had been in her office, she'd had nothing. "Since the hotel."

"Two days? All that?"

Abby's face flushed with embarrassment. She had no reason to be embarrassed, but she was anyway. She told Hannah how she'd been using the app to get inspiration. She gave her the broad strokes on the story, too.

"Well, then you clearly have to click *Yes.*"

"Why?"

"Why? Are you kidding me? Plot twist for the book, Abby!" Hannah rolled to her side on the bean bag and began ticking off points on her fingers. "You've got a marriage on the rocks. Not one, but two affairs—I'm flattered, by the way."

Abby's cheeks burned.

"Now the husband in your story is off in some distant city with his paramour, your wife is home alone with her doughnut bumper, and the app throws something like this into the mix??! Of course, you have to click *Yes*."

"I'm not comfortable with—"

Hannah tapped the screen. "Too late."

"You didn't."

"I most certainly did."

Abby tried to get a look at the phone, but Hannah twisted it away from her. "Hold on a second."

"What's it doing?"

"It's thinking. There's an hourglass thingy."

"Cancel it before it finishes! Close the app or something!" Abby grabbed for the phone.

Hannah held it at arm's length for several seconds, then smiled triumphantly when the triple chime played from the speakers. "Too late!"

"Hannah!" Abby finally snatched the phone from her, but she was right, it was too late. The question was gone, replaced with something far worse. A timer. It was ticking down from forty-one hours.

Abby quickly recalled the last timer the app had thrown at her, back at her agent's office. It had called. Texted. There'd been no getting out of that *Spice*.

"According to this, I have less than two days."

Hannah stood and looked over Abby's shoulder. "Seriously? It's actually giving you some kind of target? Like a real person? Does the map work now?"

Abby tapped on the map. It expanded and brought up an address about thirty minutes away in Brookline.

Hannah reached for Abby's coffee mug and chugged what was left. "Rinse the stink off yourself and get dressed. We're going for a ride."

30

"Is that it?"

"No, that's 27." Abby double-checked her phone. "It's the white one next door. 29 Belfer Drive."

"With the guy mowing the lawn?"

"Yeah, with the Lexus in the drive."

Hannah drove so Abby could follow the map in the Sugar & Spice app. The map worked in much the same way as the one she used for navigation, providing turn-by-turn directions, but it also asked her something she hadn't expected when they first started driving—

Would you like to disable location services on your phone?
This will prevent others from tracking you.

Abby and Brendan both used the Find My app to help keep track of each other, but she had never considered other people could access the same information.

"Well, we are on our way to kill someone," Hannah pointed out. "Probably best not to leave an electronic trail of bread crumbs."

Hannah had told the app, *Yes*, and that had brought up a second window that also contained a map but showed them traveling in the opposite direction they were. As they drove, Abby watched in amazement; it matched their speed and distance mile per mile, but placed them far from their actual location. When they reached the house on Belfer, the app had them across town parked at the mall.

"That's some crazy spy shit, Double-oh-Hollander."

The man mowing the lawn didn't live there. When he finished with 29 Belfer, he gassed up at a blue pickup truck and trailer with Mac's Landscaping plastered on all sides, then moved on to another house two doors down.

Hannah drove a BMW 3-series, candy-apple red. Not the most discreet car on the road. Although the windows were tinted far darker than the state of Massachusetts allowed, they'd both put on sunglasses. Hannah had even plucked a pink Red Sox cap from the floor in the back at a stoplight a few miles back. Her blonde hair was tucked neatly inside with a thin wisp hanging down the side and a ponytail out the back. She made a very fashionable assassin as she slowed the car to a stop at the curb across the street from the house and peered over Abby through the passenger-side window. "Do you see anyone inside?"

Abby tried not to appear too conspicuous as she looked too. "No, nothing."

Hannah keyed the address into her phone. "According to Zillow, whoever lives there bought that house in 2019 for $1.9 million, and they pay $20,700 annually in taxes. Whoever they are, they're doing okay."

"You are way more into this than you should be."

"Open the glove box."

"Why?"

Hannah was busy typing on her phone again and didn't hear her. Instead of answering, she mumbled, "Rats."

"What?"

"I'm looking at the tax records. The house is owned by an LLC rather than a person, so I can't find the real owner's name."

"You can see all that on your phone?"

"They're either worried about getting sued or hiding from someone, maybe both."

Brendan would know how to dig deeper, Abby thought. Half his job was unraveling twisty financial records. She couldn't call him, though. Not after last night. How would she even explain this? He'd tried to uninstall the app. He'd tell her to turn back around and go home.

Hannah's fingers were a blur as she typed. "Somebody's in there. There's a car in the driveway. Can you see now?"

"We're too far."

Hannah frowned at her and leaned across the car. "I told you to open the glove box."

She popped it open. Inside was a pair of obscenely large binoculars.

"Do I want to know why you have those in your car?"

"No. You probably do not. Let me see 'em."

Abby handed them over and caught a whiff of Hannah's lilac perfume as she leaned across the car and dialed in the focus. "Oh, there we go…"

"You see someone?"

"A woman. Maybe fifty or sixty. Hard to tell. She has short gray hair, glasses. Dressed professional, dark slacks and a button-down. Looks like she either came home from an office somewhere for lunch or is about to head out. Nobody dresses like that around the house unless they have to."

"What's she doing?"

Abby's phone dinged with a triple chime.

Congratulations! You've located your target
and earned three hundred points!

"She's looking at her phone," Hannah told her.

Abby frowned. "She looked at her phone when mine chimed, or she was already looking at her phone?"

"When yours chimed, I think. Or maybe right before. Hard to tell. She picked it up from the kitchen counter about the same time. She's still looking at it."

When the timer was about to go off at her agent's office, the desk phone had rung. Her agent started getting text messages…what if she had the app too and it told this person they were out there?

"We need to go."

"Why?"

"I just…I've got a bad feeling about all this."

Hannah lowered the binoculars, raised her phone, and took several pictures of the Lexus in the driveway. "We can run the plates when we get back home. That should give us a name."

"Hannah, I want to leave."

"In a second, I—"

The knock on Hannah's window seemed to rattle the entire car. Two hard bangs.

The landscaping guy.

He wore an old AC/DC tee shirt, soaked through with sweat, and motioned for Hannah to roll down her window with an arm bulging with muscles.

"Just go, Hannah…"

"He might be able to tell us something."

"Hannah…"

Her finger was already on the button, lowering the window. Her face filled with her go-to Instagram smile. Hannah tilted her head a little to the side. "Hey."

If Hannah had been wearing a tee shirt that said *Flirt* across her ample chest, she wouldn't be more obvious, but it worked. It was like she had some sort of influencer-hot mind control power. The scowl melted from the man's face. He bent and peered through the open window. "You two lost? You look a little lost."

Hannah was still holding her phone. She showed him the Zillow app. "We're real estate agents." She gestured toward the house. "We were told this one was for sale and wanted to get a better look, but I think it's some kind of mistake. There's no sign out front. That is 39 Belfer, right?"

"That's *29* Belfer, not 39. Looks like you've got the wrong house." He nodded at the binoculars. "Guess those don't work too well."

"Guess not." Hannah let out a sigh and shifted slightly in her seat. "I don't suppose you know who lives in this one, do you? It's *exactly* what our client is looking for."

The man's gaze had drifted to Hannah's legs. He made no attempt to hide it. Then he winked at Abby. Honest-to-God winked like Sweaty Lawn Guy thought he'd stepped into some cheesy porno. "Those two will never sell. They've been there forever. My buddy lives two doors down, the place I just mowed. He ain't home, but if you want to come in for a minute, we can call him and see if he'd be open to selling."

"Do they have names?"

"They do."

He didn't elaborate. Instead, he leaned a little deeper into the car. "I got a bottle of Red Tail in the truck; I picked it up for later. Wouldn't mind opening it now."

Hannah licked her lips. "Which house again?"

He leaned back and pointed. "That one there. The yellow one."

Hannah slammed her foot down on the gas.

Sweaty Lawn Guy wasn't completely out of the window, and the sudden acceleration sent him stumbling back with a twist. He shouted something, but Abby couldn't make it out over the scream of the engine. Hannah nearly sideswiped an old red van at the corner. She didn't slow until they were two blocks over and she had to make a right on Beacon.

"That went well," Abby managed, gripping the handle on the door with one hand and holding her seat belt with the other.

"Oh, come on, Abs. Sometimes you've got to live a little to learn a little."

31

After a quick strategy meeting with the feds in a conference room downstairs, Brendan and Kim went up to their adjoining rooms on eighteen to drop their bags. Brendan tossed his suitcase on the bed, unlocked the door to Kim's room, and knocked. Her lock clicked and the door opened. Her room was the mirror image of his.

"How about we take ten minutes to freshen up, then call Dubin?"

She nodded. "Maybe find something to eat before heading over to INTENT? I'm starving."

"If she still wants us to go."

"If she still wants us to go," Kim repeated.

Brendan's phone rang.

Stuckey.

Glancing at his watch, Brendan realized it was only one in the afternoon. Stuckey wasn't scheduled to arrive in Laos until late tonight. "Stuckey? Everything okay? Where are you?"

"I'm at my layover in Athens. You alone? We need to talk."

"Umm, give me a second." Brendan looked over at Kim. "Ten minutes, then we'll call Dubin, okay?"

"Okay," she raised her voice. "Hey, Stuckey!"

"Hey, Kim."

She smiled and gently closed the door between them.

Brendan closed his side and crossed over to the window. "What's up?"

"You know I like me some porn, right?"

"Ah, okay."

"I got a few go-to sites. About three hours into the flight I figured, why not, right? Nobody's looking. I got like a full day in the air to kill."

"You're on a plane," Brendan pointed out. "*Everybody* is looking."

"I used some of the miles on my credit card and upgraded to one of those private pods. Got me some leg room. A little Stuckey treat. I use a VPN too, so none of my shit is visible on the network. I'm a professional porn ghost. That's not the point. I fired up my gear and I'm rolling through my regular sites and found something you need to see."

Brendan didn't have time for this. He needed to use the bathroom. Brush his teeth. Organize his thoughts for the call with Dubin. "Can this wait until we all get home?"

His phone dinged.

"Click that link."

Brendan let out a sigh, put the call on speaker, and clicked on the link. It was to some video. When he clicked play, his stomach twisted into a tight knot.

It was Abby.

"What the hell is this?"

Stuckey didn't reply.

Abby was standing in a bathroom, undressing. The video was

shot from multiple angles and looked like it had been slowed down.

"Stuckey, what the fuck? Where did you find this?"

Brendan recognized the bathroom from the naked pictures Abby had sent him yesterday. He watched dumbstruck as Abby stripped out of her clothes and began taking pictures of herself in the mirror, the same shots she'd sent him.

"I'm guessing the video cameras were hidden somewhere in that room, but then she starts taking photos of herself so...well, you know her better than anyone. Fake hidden cameras are a thing in porn. Like acting or role-playing. Would she do something like this on purpose? Hannah, sure, but Abby? She never struck me as..."

As the blood coursing through Brendan's ears increased, it drowned out Stuckey's voice. Abby was at her agent's office, right? Would her agent have hidden cameras? Would she post video taken with those hidden cameras? It occurred to Brendan he'd never met Abby's agent before; he knew nothing about her.

Stuckey's voice faded back in. "...this isn't the only site where I found the video. I ran a quick search using the file name and found it on three others."

Three sites in one day. How many by this time tomorrow? This time next week?

"How do we shut it down?"

"I don't think you can. These sites aren't even hosted in the U.S. One is in Estonia, another is in the Ukraine. I think the third one is out of China, but I can't tell for sure. Not without doing more digging." Stuckey's voice fell away again, then, "I'm sorry, man."

Brendan dragged his fingers through his hair. His forehead was sticky with sweat.

You couldn't stop this sort of thing. Files were copied, shared, reposted. Some of these companies owned dozens of websites. With international laws being what they were, there was no legal way to take down something like this. Threats amounted to nothing. All you could really do is ask nicely. Beg and plead when that didn't work. Offer money they didn't have. Abby was an adult. Even if they could prove the video was taken without her consent, that wouldn't be enough to force any kind of action, other than maybe sue her agent, maybe her publisher, and would Abby even be willing to do that? Doubtful. Her writing career would come to a hard stop.

Brendan clicked pause on the video and scrolled through the accompanying text. The headline just said *Hidden Camera Striptease!* They didn't mention Abby by name. No location, nothing identifying.

Stuckey found it, though.

Fuck.

"Don't tell anyone."

"I won't."

"Definitely not Hannah."

"I'll see what else I can dig up. Maybe find a way to get it taken down or stop whoever is distributing it, or something. I've got a lot of time in the air."

"Thanks, man."

Half in a daze, Brendan disconnected and knocked on Kim's door. He heard the muffled sound of her speaking to someone. When she opened the door, she was on the phone. She held a finger up to Brendan and mouthed, *It's AD Dubin,* before turning her back and returning to the call. She had this oversize pink phone case with a knob on the back to make it easier to hold. He always thought it looked obnoxiously large.

"...thanks, Mary. I'll let you know what we find."

Brendan's gut clenched. *Mary?* She was on a first-name basis with the assistant director now? Why was she even talking to her without him?

32

Abby and Hannah pulled into a Five Guys a few miles from the house in Brookline to regroup. They took a booth near the window. Abby's phone sat between them, the countdown ticking away. The GPS map provided by Sugar & Spice also had them at a Five Guys, but this one was across town.

"In all seriousness, it's never given you a message like this before, right?"

Abby began dissecting her burger and didn't look up. "Kill someone? No. Of course not."

"Some of these companies are pretty big, and they have a bunch of games. You said the app recently updated. I'm wondering if the code for your app got crossed with some other one, like maybe they have a spy game or something too, and some programmer mixed it up on accident."

Abby removed the bun from her burger, placed it off to the side, and scraped off the pickles and sauces from the beef with a plastic knife. "I guess that makes sense. But I think she had the app too."

"Because she was on her phone?" Hannah waved around the

small dining room. "Everyone is on their phone. All the time."

Abby set the sauce-covered knife off to the side, removed a fresh one from its plastic wrapper, and began cutting up her burger.

Hannah narrowed her eyes. "What the hell are you doing?"

"The bread is all carbs, and I don't want to know what they put in the toppings. Beef is okay, though."

Taking a large bite of her own burger, sauce dripping from the corner of her mouth, Hannah chewed and swallowed.

"Don't get me started on the fries."

"We could have gone somewhere else."

"I love Five Guys." Abby speared a small piece of burger with a plastic fork and plopped it in her mouth.

"You're so fucking weird sometimes." Twisting Abby's phone around, Hannah tapped on the timer, which brought up the main app. "Can you cancel a *Spice* after you've accepted it?"

"Not that I know of."

"What about uninstalling the app?" Hannah knew Abby wanted to keep the app for her story, so she quickly added, "We can uninstall it and put it right back on. Force the latest version to your phone. See if that fixes it."

"I guess you can try."

She watched as Hannah held down the app's icon and selected *Remove* from the menu.

"Oh, shit."

"What?"

"It says, *A pending removal request is already in the system. 1000 points have been deducted from your profile.*"

Abby quickly turned the phone back around and checked her score. She was now at 5200, Brendan was at 3910. "Okay, let's not do that again. I don't want to slip back below *Bronze*; the prompts weren't as good."

"Abs, I don't know if this is healthy. I probably shouldn't have clicked *Yes*, and you're getting a little clingy with this app."

"You don't understand, *I need the app for my book*. I've never written this fast or this good before. Without the app, I'll never hit my deadline." She knew how defensive she sounded and didn't care. "I don't know if I can even finish this story without the app feeding me prompts."

"You're a good writer."

"I didn't have a single word until this app. I can't go back to a blank screen."

"You're letting an app run your life." Hannah made a show of shoving five French fries in her mouth, moaning softly with each chew. "Oh, you don't know what you're missing."

Scooping up her phone, Abby took a picture of Hannah. Hannah's eyes were half closed, her mouth partially open, and there was ketchup on her cheek. Hunched over the table, she looked twenty pounds heavier. One of those rare moments where she looked terrible. Abby held the phone up to her. "What if that went up on your Instagram account? No filters, no airbrushing, nothing but the real you. How would your followers react?"

When Hannah didn't answer, Abby continued.

"It would go viral, you know it would. Imagine the comments you'd get. The bottom-feeder press might even pick it up. Your sponsors would vanish. Your income would vanish. *Your career* would vanish…all because of an app, so don't get all high-and-mighty with me. We're exactly the same."

Hannah remained silent. She took three more fries, ran them through a glob of ketchup on her plate, and slowly ate them. Finally, she said, "Wow, Abs, I didn't realize you had balls. I think I like this you. How 'bout we delete that pic?"

When she reached for Abby's phone, Abby slid it to the side.

"Okay. Not funny."

"The sick feeling in your stomach right now, that's how I feel at the thought of losing the app before I finish this book."

"Point taken."

Abby gave it a few more seconds to sink in, then deleted the photo. The tension melted from Hannah's face.

"Maybe we look at it this way, then…what's the name of the wife in your book?"

"Emily."

"Okay. What would Emily do? You put her in this exact situation, what would she do next? Hypothetically, would she kill this person to save her husband?"

Abby hadn't considered that. "Her husband's a bit of a bastard."

"Brendan can be a shit, but he loves you. I don't think he's crossed into bastard territory."

"The story in my book isn't following my life. Not exactly. I borrowed little bits and embellished, twisted things into something far worse. The husband *is* having an affair in the book."

"And you don't think Brendan is?"

Abby gave it one final thought, then shook her head. "I think something happened between him and that girl, it could have gone further, but he shut it down. I don't think he lied to me. If he'd cheated, he would have hidden it, not told me. Telling me makes no sense."

"Unless he told you because he knew you'd believe telling you made no sense." Hannah ate another fry. "Makes it seem like it couldn't possibly be true."

Again, Abby shook her head. "My character is a cheater, Brendan is not."

"So that brings us back to my original question. What would Emily do? Does she want her husband to die?"

"I haven't decided yet, but I certainly don't want anything to happen to Brendan."

The timer on Abby's lock screen silently ticked away: 39 hours, 41 minutes, 12 seconds, remaining.

"If my math is right, the clock will hit zero just before five in the morning the day after tomorrow. When does Brendan get back?"

"Tomorrow, around dinnertime, I think."

"So he'll be home. That's how we solve this. We wait it out. Lock his ass in the house and not let him out until it's over."

"You think it's that simple?"

"If you'd rather paint a target on his back and set him loose in Boston Commons, I'm game, as long as you let me post it."

Abby was about to respond when she caught something from the corner of her eye. "Don't turn around."

"Why?"

"The van you almost hit back at the house. I think it just parked next to your car."

33

To her credit, Hannah didn't turn around. Instead, she reached for her soda and casually took a sip. "Are you sure it's the same van?"

"I think so," Abby replied. "I only caught a quick look at it. This one is red and old. It's got rust around the fenders like the other one."

Hannah picked up her phone, turned on the camera, and switched to the forward-facing lens so she could see over her shoulder. "I can't tell. Anybody get out?"

"Not yet."

"Excuse me, are you Abby Hollander?"

Abby jerked in her seat and Hannah nearly dropped her phone. They'd been so busy studying the van, neither had heard the girl walk up. She was wearing cut-off jean shorts and a white tank top. Her dark hair fell loosely over her shoulders. She was holding a paperback copy of Abby's book, *Understanding Ella*.

Across the table, Hannah quickly recovered, checked her face with her phone camera, and set her iPhone down next to the remains of her lunch.

The girl shifted her weight to her right leg and bent her left, standing in what Abby always thought of as the stork pose. Her pink sandal dangled precariously from her big toe. "I'm halfway, and it's sooooo good. I might just be your biggest fan."

"Well, thank you."

"No, I'm serious. I haven't crushed on a book this hard since Harry Potter!"

Hannah tried to stifle a laugh and nearly choked on it.

Abby kicked her under the table and smiled at the girl. "That's very flattering."

"Hey, do you think you could sign it for me?"

She said this like the idea just occurred to her. Like it was the most off-the-wall suggestion someone could ask of a writer. As she said it, she set the book on the table and thrust it over toward Abby.

As Abby looked down at the book, a strange thought popped into her head. More of an observation. The girl said she was halfway through the story, but none of the pages were folded. There was no bookmark sticking out the top. No creases in the paperback spine. The book looked new. Something about this felt wrong. She didn't want to sign the book. She didn't want to *touch* it.

"I'm afraid I don't have a pen."

"Oh, I have a pen," Hannah chimed in, somehow still amused by all this. She reached into her purse, produced an old ballpoint with a chewed cap, and handed it to Abby.

Reluctantly, Abby took the pen and peeled back the cover of the book. She half-expected to find a fresh receipt, but there was none. She turned to the title page and glanced back at the girl. "Who should I make it out to?"

"Cordelia. C-O-R-D-E-L-I-A. Maybe write, 'to your biggest fan' or 'to *my* biggest fan' oh, you know what I mean!" She twisted a loose strand of her hair between her fingers, rolled it around her knuckle.

"Cordelia, like in *King Lear?*"

"Sure, just like that," the girl replied, although Abby was fairly certain she had no idea what she was talking about. Abby quickly scribbled out the words, added her signature, and slid the book back over to the girl, realizing a little too late it probably seemed weird she didn't hand it to her.

The girl scooped it up and pressed it to her chest. "Thank you so much! I will treasure this forever!" She turned on her heel and bounced off toward the opposite side of the restaurant, disappearing around the corner.

"Geez, *Misery*, much?" Hannah frowned. "That happen to you a lot? I didn't know author-stalking was a thing."

"I think we should go."

Hannah started to twist around and caught herself. "What about the van? Is it still out there?"

The van hadn't moved.

Abby hadn't seen anyone get out, but it's possible they did when the girl was at the table. Either way, sitting around waiting for them to leave didn't seem like much of an option, either. She needed to get home and keep going on the new book. Reaching into her purse, she took out the small can of pepper spray she'd bought a few months back at the army surplus store and showed it to Hannah. "They try something, and we get to learn if this stuff really works."

Hannah's eyes grew wide. "I have no idea who you are."

They cleared away their trash and tossed it in the bin on their way out the door. The October air had taken on a crispness. Abby told herself it was the icy breeze that caused goose bumps to dance across her arms, not the growing anxiety as they approached Hannah's car and the red van next to it.

The two small square windows in the back doors were tinted and offered no view of the interior. Hannah had backed into her space while the van had pulled straight in—right at the white line—leaving very little room for Abby to squeeze between and get to the passenger door. When she did, she had to twist sideways to fit through the narrow opening. As she turned, she managed a glance through the van's passenger window.

A man was sitting behind the steering wheel, slumped slightly in the driver's seat. He wasn't looking at Abby. Instead, he faced forward, his eyes hidden behind dark sunglasses. He drummed his fingers across the top of the wheel. His arms were as thick as Abby's thighs, and even that slight movement caused the muscles to roll and ripple against the thin material of his tee shirt, like they were trying to escape.

Abby dropped into her seat, slammed the door, and jabbed down the lock. She'd forgotten she was holding the small can of pepper spray, and it fell from her grasp, landing down near her feet.

Hannah got behind the wheel, closed her door, and started the engine. "I guess whoever's driving that thing got one look at you and decided they didn't want to die today. Good job dialing up the Terminator vibe, Abs."

"Just drive, okay?"

Hannah pulled out of the lot and headed east toward the interstate.

Had they been watching, they would have seen the girl who asked for the autograph climb into the passenger-side of the van. Had they been able to hear, they would have caught Romeo asking, *Was that the wife?* They would have also heard Juliet reply with an emphatic, *Sure was*, as she discarded the book with a loose toss into the back of the van.

Sugar & Spice™

Sugar
How well do you know your partner?
Ask them something you wouldn't normally dare.

34

The van at the forefront, Abby's head was swimming with thoughts as Hannah pulled into her driveway, so many thoughts when the nagging feeling she may have forgotten something started to silently shout at her from somewhere in that noise she nearly missed it, then it got louder, and it was all she could think about. Then it hit her.

"Oh, shit."

Hannah switched off the motor. "What?"

"Today's Thursday. I completely forgot, Brendan and I had an appointment with our therapist this morning."

Climbing out of the car, Hannah shrugged. "Worst case, she'll ding you for the cost of the appointment. I'm sure you're not the first. No biggie."

"I kinda wanted to talk to her without Brendan, though. I should call her."

"Then you should just show up," Hannah countered. "Trust me, I'm a therapy pro. You call her, and she'll put you on the books for some time next week. You show up on her doorstep, and she'll squeeze you in today between appointments."

"You sure?"

Hannah rounded the car and gave Abby a big hug. "Go. Keep me posted on everything. I'm going to knock out a little grocery shopping, then maybe do some day-drinking around three. I found this expensive bottle of bourbon hidden away in Stuckey's office. You're welcome to join me. It's less sad when there are two."

Traffic was light, and Abby made it to Dr. Donetti's office in less than twenty minutes. The doctor's two o'clock appointment was sitting in the small waiting area. An elderly woman picking at her fingernails. When Abby entered, she looked up at her, embarrassed. "I was working in my garden this morning, never seem to get all of it out."

Abby offered her a smile and dropped into the seat across from her. She was shuffling through a stack of old magazines when the doctor's door opened, a short pudgy man in a sweater stepped out, and another man's deep voice boomed from behind him. "You're doing great, Harry. Not many make it through the first month without a single smoke, I'm proud of you."

The pudgy man waved back over his shoulder on his way out the door. His clothing stunk of cigarettes.

One month, my ass, Abby thought.

The man with the deep voice appeared in the open doorway and smiled at the elderly woman. "Delores, I'll be with you in a few minutes. I just need to make a quick phone call." Then he eyed Abby curiously. "May I help you?"

Abby had never seen the man before. He seemed a little older than Donetti. If Abby had to guess, she'd put him around forty-five.

His eyes were dark, but kind. This brown that reminded her of melted chocolate. She had no idea Dr. Donetti shared the office space with someone else. That's what she gets for listening to Hannah and not bothering to call. "I was hoping to speak with Dr. Donetti. I missed my appointment with her this morning. I didn't realize she wouldn't be here." She stood, suddenly feeling embarrassed. "I'm sorry, I'll call and schedule something. It was silly of me to just show up."

She had one hand on the door when he spoke.

"Perhaps we should talk in my office?" He glanced at the other woman. "Delores, you don't mind, do you? It will just take a moment."

"Not at all. I need to use the little girl's room, anyway."

He started back into the office and gestured for Abby to follow. "Close the door behind you?"

Abby did.

He settled into the leather chair and nodded at the couch across from him. "Please."

Although Abby was alone, she slipped into what she considered to be her side of the couch, leaving the place where Brendan typically sat empty.

"I'm sorry, I didn't catch your name," he said.

"Abby, Abby Hollander."

"Pleasure to meet you. I'm Dr. Bixby. How long have you been seeing…Dr. Donetti?"

"About two weeks," she told him. "I didn't realize she shared the space."

"It's common in our business. I use this one, and I have another on the west side. Makes it easier for clients like Delores out there who no longer drive and don't like to navigate public transportation. The elderly makes up a large portion of my practice." He shifted his weight and crossed his legs. "Mind if I ask how you found Dr. Donetti?"

"I was at the mall, and when I came out her business card was on my car, under the windshield wiper. My husband and I were…I… we thought it would be good for the two of us to talk to someone." Abby's cheeks flushed with embarrassment. "I know, it's probably not the best way to find a therapist, but I figured if she wasn't good, we'd find someone else. Seemed kinda like destiny, finding her card when I needed it. We all need a little destiny every now and then."

"I see. What type of work do you do?"

"I'm a novelist."

Saying that aloud still felt weird to Abby, like it wasn't a real job. Like she should say she was an event planner and writing was still a hobby. He reacted as most people did.

"Oh, that must be exciting."

She got the distinct impression he was making small talk, dancing around some bigger issue he hadn't worked up the courage to bring up. Then it dawned on her. "Oh no, did something happen to her?"

He let out a soft sigh and pursed his lips before lowering his voice. "I'm afraid there's no easy way to say this, so I'll just come right out with it. The woman you know as Dr. Donetti is not a doctor."

The words hit Abby like a punch to the gut. "I'm sorry?"

"Not a licensed doctor, anyway. There are assorted online degrees you can get in this profession, but she's not registered with the state or any of the local medical boards, so if she went to an accredited school, she didn't follow procedure when establishing a practice."

Abby's gaze went to the framed license hanging on the wall behind the desk. While it was difficult to read from the couch, she could make out the name, Harlan Bixby. She remembered there being a framed license hanging in that same spot each time she and Brendan had come here, but she'd never studied it close enough to see the name. It might have been Donetti, might have been Bixby. Hell, it might have said Bugs Bunny. *How could she be so stupid?* Brendan obviously hadn't noticed either or he would have said something.

"I imagine this must be quite jarring."

Jarring? They had shared personal things with this woman, opened up to her. "Do you know where she is now?"

"I'm afraid I don't. I only just learned of all this yesterday when the leasing company contacted me trying to find her. Apparently, she paid her first month's rent along with a security deposit, but paid nothing toward October; it was late as of the fifth. I made a few phone calls and learned the rest." He retrieved a notepad and pen from the desk behind him. The same place Donetti had kept hers. "If you'd like to leave your number with me, I can contact you if I hear more. I can't recommend seeing her again, though, not unless you can establish she is in fact licensed and this is some sort of oversight."

In a daze, Abby rattled off her number.

A briefcase was open on the corner of the desk. He reached inside and took out a stack of business cards held together with a rubber band. He removed the band, shuffled through the cards, and found the one he was looking for. He handed it to Abby. "I personally don't practice couples therapy, but this is a colleague of mine who does. He has an office two floors up in this very building. I've known him since university." He paused for a moment, then added, "If my husband and I were having…had the need to talk to someone, this man would be my first call."

Abby didn't realize her hand was shaking until she reached for the card.

She was still shaking when she climbed back into her car.

35

Home.

Blank screen.

When Abby sat back down at her desk, her novel was dead in its tracks again.

Abby tried every trick she knew.

First, she typed random words, hoping something would click.

Then she typed whatever entered her head, stream of consciousness stuff, and that went nowhere.

Delete.

Delete.

Delete.

It wasn't until she wrote about Hannah and her driving out to that house, spying on the woman who lived there, when she allowed those words to come out, the story started to flow again. The deeper she got, the more she thought—why not? Why the hell not? Nobody would ever believe it was true, so she wrote it all up—from the *Spice—Would you kill a total stranger to save your partner's life?*—to the moment she learned her therapist had been some sort of fraud.

Every last word.

And that felt good.

It felt right.

It was twelve more pages.

She twisted it into the existing narrative, changing the names, of course, defaulted to all her existing characters, and made up a few new ones for the various walk-ons. Enough to get it all down.

But now she was stumped again.

Normally when she wrote a story, she saw it play out in her head, like watching a mental movie, and she documented it. This was different. Because the events hadn't come from her imagination but had come from the app, her imagination wasn't exactly sure where to take it next.

That brought her back to another blank page.

Abby considered stopping for the day. After all, twelve pages was a respectable number. She knew Hannah was home (probably halfway through Stuckey's bourbon by now) and would be all in when she told her about the therapist, but was that where the story needed to go? To Abby, that seemed like a dead end.

The app was out, at least for now.

Not because she didn't want to use it (she tried) but because it was caught up in the latest *Spice*. The app wouldn't allow her to select a new *Sugar* or *Spice* until the latest was complete, and since Abby had no intention of killing anyone, the app had gone from an inspiration powerhouse to useless.

Black screen.

Again.

Hannah's words from earlier came into her head so clear, for a second she thought her friend was standing behind her—*What would Emily do? You put her in this exact situation, what would she do next?*

Abby may not be a killer, but the wife in her story? That was still undecided. In the writing world, there were two camps—plotters and pantsers—those who plotted out their stories in advance, and those who wrote by the seat of their pants, made it up as they went. Abby fell into the second camp. She firmly believed if she didn't know where the story was going, her readers wouldn't figure it out, either. That meant she had no idea if her lead character was a killer. She did know she was smart, intuitive, resourceful. She wasn't spontaneous or reactionary, she was cautious.

So, what would Emily do?

WWED.

She'd research her target, that's what she'd do. She'd learn what she could about this person, maybe figure out why they were a target in the first place.

Abby opened a browser window and typed in 29 Belfer Drive, Brookline MA, and pressed enter. Her Mac hummed for a moment, but instead of returning results, the Sugar & Spice logo appeared—

Thank you for installing the Sugar & Spice browser extension! Congratulations! As a Bronze member, you have been automatically enrolled in a two-week trial of our Privacy Enhancement Package! During this trial period, all data transferred to and from this device will be encrypted, and enjoy the use of our VPN network ensuring your activity cannot be tracked, traced, or monitored by a third party! Should you wish to discontinue this service, simply decline at the end of your trial period!

Abby had two thoughts after reading the message. First, that was a shit-ton of exclamation marks. Second, this was probably a good thing. She should have opened a private browsing window before typing in the address. She knew it was intrusive, but it wasn't the first time an app installed on her phone found its way to her Mac. All her Apple products worked in sync. Honestly, she was surprised Sugar & Spice hadn't made an appearance on her watch yet to complete the Holy Apple trinity.

Abby's original browser window closed and reopened. She spotted a tiny S&S in the top right corner along with a picture of a lock to indicate she was now secure. She keyed in the address again. This time her screen flooded with results—there was a map and several photos up top, numerous listings from real estate companies. A few of those *Who lives at* type services that will provide personal information for a fee…at the bottom of the page was something she didn't expect. The definition of a stranger:

> *Stranger (noun) a person whom one does not*
> *know or with whom one is not familiar.*

An obvious, not-too-subtle call back to the original *Spice*—would she kill a stranger—and if she researched that person, would it mean they were no longer a stranger? She wasn't sure exactly what that meant. Would the app pick someone else? Would she fail the *Spice?* Why exactly wouldn't the app want her to know who this person was?

Abby would never kill anyone.

Her character might, but not Abby. That meant it didn't matter if she learned more about this person, because she'd never actually go through with it. If that meant the target was no longer a stranger or the app changed the rules by replacing the target because she did a little digging, so be it, it wouldn't matter, because Abby wouldn't kill anyone.

Her character might.

But her character wouldn't do a damn thing until she knew exactly who her target was, why they were a target, and what the possible repercussions were. Her character would learn everything about that person she possibly could. There was something else her character would do that Abby hadn't done yet and probably should. She quickly typed out a text to Brendan—*Should I be worried about whatever you're doing?*—but before hitting SEND, she deleted it, then replaced it with *I'm sorry about yesterday. I trust you. Get home soon.* This time, she did send it. It was a message both she and her character would send, one because it was true, the other to cover her bases in case someone went back through her texts at some later date.

Abby wouldn't kill anyone, but her character might. The thought kept circling like a shark.

Abby needed to figure out where this story was going next.

She transferred the search results from her Mac to her phone and scooped up her keys. Before she even started her car, the app had directions to 29 Belfer loaded up. It asked if it should disguise her actual travel again as it did earlier.

"Yes, please," Abby said softly, tapping the button.

36

"What do you mean, they're gone?" Stuckey's distant voice crackled from Brendan's speaker phone.

They were standing in Kim's hotel room, the door leading back to Brendan's room open behind them. The last of the sun dipped beneath the horizon outside, and both spaces were cast in dull yellow light.

Kim leaned in closer. "INTENT completely cleared out. No furniture. No files. No computers. We didn't find so much as a paper clip. The whole place smells like cleaning products. Every surface scrubbed and vacuumed. A new tenant could move in tomorrow."

"A company that size can't just vanish."

"Building security said they moved last Friday. They didn't provide any forwarding information."

"That's before Isaac Alford was killed..."

"Correct."

"How many people did they have working there?"

"Two hundred and nine."

Jesus. This is bigger than we thought.

No shit, Brendan thought. "The feds have a list of employee addresses. They're working with the local PD knocking on doors, but so far they haven't located anyone. Cars are gone. Houses are dark. It's like they had a company-wide meeting and told everyone to leave town."

"Yeah, well maybe they're all with Keo Sengphet, because he's MIA too."

"He's not at the bank?"

"Nobody has seen him since last week. He hasn't called in. INTERPOL has a car heading to his house now."

"Somebody's cleaning up…" Brendan said softly. "Is the bank cooperating?"

"So far, but you know how that goes." Stuckey replied. *"We've taken over one of their conference rooms. INTERPOL positioned people around the bank, watching senior staff. They've been after Sengphet for a while, so they're jumping all over this. We've got access to their systems, and we're working from a list of numbered accounts under Sengphet's control to isolate the ones involving INTENT. It's slow going, but we'll get it done. Once we identify an account, it goes into the wrapper."*

The electronic wrapper was like a protective bubble maintained by the international banking authority. Once placed inside, funds could only be accessed through a dual authentication system by the agency that locked them away. Brendan retrieved his USB fingerprint reader from his pocket. "Do you want to set up authentication now while we're both on the phone?"

"Yeah, probably should. Phone service here can get sketchy."

Brendan's laptop was on a small table near the window. He leaned over the screen, plugged in the USB reader, and logged into FinCap. "What's the wrapper code?"

"652-2301BT7-GR509."

As Brendan typed, Kim came up behind him and watched over his shoulder. When the screen populated with the wrapper information, she let out a slow whistle. "You're over one hundred and nine million already?"

"Like I said, this is bigger than we thought."

Stuckey was already set up as the first authorized party, so Brendan clicked through and registered as the second, watched it populate with his name, user ID, and clearance information. When prompted, he keyed in a password, repeated it in the second box, then pressed his index finger to the USB reader. The reader asked him to repeat several times from different angles, then flashed green when complete. "Okay," he said. "All good from my end."

Kim had turned away when Brendan entered his password, but she was looking back again. "I've never seen this before. How does it work?"

"Anything Stuckey moves into the wrapper will be frozen and can only be removed if both of us sign in and authenticate together. It's a failsafe to ensure people like Stuckey don't run off to some beach in Belize with other people's money."

"What keeps you and Stuckey from running off together?"

"My complete lack of desire to see Stuckey in a G-string."

"I would totally rock a Speedo." There were several voices from Stuckey's end of the call, then he said, *"INTERPOL is at Sengphet's house. I've got to go. Talk soon."*

When he hung up, the room went oddly quiet. Brendan's stomach gurgled, and he looked at his watch. It was a few minutes after five, and they'd skipped lunch.

"I've got us on the 7 a.m. flight back to Boston," Kim said. "Do you want to get something to eat downstairs?"

Brendan agreed to dinner, he was jonesing for a NY strip, but he ordered a Coke to go with it. He was relieved when Kim ordered an iced tea.

"I wanted to apologize for what happened last time we were in Chicago," Kim said halfway through their meal. "I misread the signals and I overstepped. I appreciate the fact you didn't report it."

"That was hardly only on you," he replied. "We both acted inappropriately. And for the record, it's not that I don't find you attractive, I do, but…"

"You're married."

"I'm married."

Kim hesitated for a second, a glint of nervousness in her eye. She looked like she was about to say something, then changed her mind.

Brendan tried to lighten the mood. "What about you? I can't imagine you're not seeing someone."

Kim grinned and tossed her blonde hair back over her shoulder. "Can't imagine, huh?"

"Come on, you're smart, pretty, funny. You can't possibly be single."

"My supervisor is a bit of a tyrant. I work a lot," she joked. "All the travel can be a bear, too. It can be hard to hold a relationship together."

"So there's no one?"

"Oh, there's someone. It's just…complicated."

"The ones worth holding onto always are." Brendan speared a piece of his steak and popped it in his mouth.

Kim seemed to consider that, consider *him*, then reached for her phone. She swiped through several screens, settled on a photo, and set the phone down next to Brendan's plate.

The photograph was of a beautiful woman with long brown hair, deep, dark eyes. Young, early twenties at best.

"Her name is Ana. We've been seeing each other on and off for about a year now."

Brendan did his best to hide his surprise and must have failed miserably, because Kim burst out laughing.

He couldn't help but laugh too. "Okay, so I gotta ask. If you're... Why me?"

"Honestly?"

"Yeah, let's start there."

Kim's cheeks flushed again. "Because I'm not sure..."

"Not sure about her?"

"...not sure I'm a lesbian."

"Oh."

"It's not only that. She's almost seven years younger than me, so as a couple, we have a few disconnects. I'll be thirty in two months, and I feel like I'm at the point where I want to settle down and start a family. I can't do any of those things until I'm sure of who I am."

Brendan rolled his Coke glass between his fingers, wiped a line through the condensation. He tried to think of something constructive to say, but came up blank.

"Most guys are jerks. I wasn't interested in dating anyone. I knew you wouldn't leave your wife... Married guys know how to keep a secret. You seemed safe..." She let the last word hang for a moment. "So again, I apologize for what happened the last time we were in Chicago. And I apologize for what I said in the AD's office before we left. Both were knee-jerk reactions, and I was wrong."

"Let's chalk it up to water under the bridge and move on."

Kim raised her glass and clinked it against his. "Deal."

Brendan's phone began to vibrate.

Abby.

Brendan's finger hovered over the screen for a moment, then he sent the call to voice mail. He'd call her back from upstairs.

The remainder of the dinner went smooth, until the waitress returned with Brendan's credit card. "Sir, I'm afraid this has been declined. Do you have another?"

"Declined? I don't understand."

"I ran it twice. Maybe the chip is bad? That happens sometimes with those newer ones."

Kim quickly fished her card from a pocket on her purse. "It's okay, I've got it."

37

Brendan was back in his room and had just gotten out of the shower when the laptop he'd left running on the bed began to whir and ding with incoming e-mails.

He quickly toweled off and stepped from the bathroom to look at the screen.

Nine messages from Stuckey, no, ten, with more on the way judging by the spinning hourglass in the center of the screen. He'd caught a direct flight back and was sending data from the air. Photographs of Keo Sengphet's house. Apparently INTERPOL had breached and found the place deserted. In the bedroom, drawers and closets were open. Clothing was all over the floor. No suitcases. The man had clearly left in a hurry. An earlier e-mail from Stuckey said they'd seized over $230 million.

Stuckey had copied Kim and the AD on the messages, but not the FBI. Brendan considered forwarding them, then decided he'd leave that with the AD. He was on the seventh e-mail when a message box popped up:

You have received a wink from a Sugar & Spice member.
Would you like to wink back?

Shit.

Abby.

He'd forgotten to call her back.

He clicked *Yes* on the message, found his phone, and dialed her. She answered on the third ring.

"Hey."

"You okay? What are you up to?"

"Just working on the book."

Brendan glanced at the clock next to the bed. "At nine o'clock? That's late, even for you."

"I knocked out two chapters earlier. Now I'm doing a little research so I can hit the ground running tomorrow."

"Sounds like it's going well."

"Better than expected."

Her answers were short, clipped. Her voice was flat. Nothing like her usual self. She was clearly still upset.

Brendan let out a soft breath. "I don't like it when we fight, Abs."

"I don't either."

"So why do we do it?"

"I don't know the answer to that, either."

"I guess that's why we're in therapy."

Abby let out a soft laugh. *"About that…"* She told him about Dr. Donetti.

When she finished, he ran his hand through his wet hair. "I thought something seemed off about her."

"You never said anything."

He thought he had, but with everything going on it was very possible he'd only thought about it. "It doesn't matter, we'll find someone better, okay?"

"Okay."

Her voice dropped off again. Something still wasn't right. Maybe she'd found those pictures of herself on the web. He hoped that wasn't it. He knew she'd learn about them eventually, but he wanted to be there with her when she did. Nobody should have to go through that alone.

"What's going on, Abs? What's bothering you?"

What she said next surprised him.

"You're not doing anything dangerous, right? This isn't like the thing in Florida?"

Three years ago. A real estate investment firm based out of Palm Beach, Florida. They'd bought off several local appraisers and had been inflating the values of their properties in order to leverage them and buy more, then they'd inflate those too, and buy more, and on and on. Brendan had been part of the coordinated raid on both the real estate holding company and the appraisers' office. Someone had tipped off both, and they'd had people up all night shredding documents, erasing hard drives, destroying whatever evidence might be on-site. When Brendan's team breached the real estate office, a security guard came at them waving a gun. Just a kid, no more than twenty, but he'd clearly been up all night, wired on something to stay awake, and to say he was edgy would be an understatement. He didn't speak English, and Brendan had no idea what he'd been told, but he pointed the gun in a wobbly grip at the first man through the door and fired. The shot went wide, but he managed to get two more off before agents subdued him. One agent got clipped in the leg, another in her forearm. While he was firing, someone deeper in the office lit a match, setting the building on fire. The sprinkler system had been disabled at some point earlier. There'd been a push to arm FCID agents after that, but it was voted down.

"Abs, no, nothing like that." He felt like that was a lie, even though it wasn't. Maybe it was because the FBI was involved. "The company we're here to audit, they cleared out. Shut the office down. There's been a lot of crazy, but nothing dangerous. I'll fill you in when I get home. We're booked on the 7 a.m. I've got to stop in the office to debrief, but I should be able to cut out early."

Abby's voice became so distant she might have been in a tunnel. *"How's...Kim."*

He considered what to tell her and decided it was best to hold the big stuff until they were face-to-face. *"We had a chance to talk earlier. I'll tell you all about that too. I was completely off-base. There's nothing to worry about there, either."*

Abby said nothing.

"Abs?"

"I guess I'll hear all about it tomorrow."

Brendan pressed the phone tighter against his ear. "Are you sure you're okay? You sound...I don't know, like you've got something on your mind."

"Just tired, I guess."

"Well, get some rest. I'll see you soon. I love you."

"Love you, too."

Brendan disconnected and nearly called her back. Something about their conversation felt unfinished. He was about to dial when another message from Sugar & Spice appeared on his laptop screen—

You've received a wink back. Would you like to open a dialog with this member on your laptop rather than your default device?

Brendan had a sinking feeling in his gut. Apparently whatever Abby needed to tell him couldn't be said over the phone and she wanted to do it through some messaging system. She'd told him long ago she sometimes preferred to put her thoughts in writing. She found it easier to get her point across. He hated when she did that, because it felt like this one-sided lecture rather than a conversation. Paragraph after paragraph of her talking at him rather than with him. He couldn't ignore her, though. That would only lead to a larger argument. He clicked *Yes*.

A browser window opened and began to fill with images.

Brendan's mouth fell open. What came up had nothing to do with Abby.

His screen flooded with naked photographs of Kim.

Unlike the pictures of Abby, taken with some sort of hidden camera, there was no doubt Kim knew she was being photographed. She smiled coyly at the camera as she posed, her hands exploring her body, touching herself. In some, she was lying on a bed, sheets rumpled around her. In others, she was on the floor, on all fours, looking back over her shoulder with this hunger in her eyes. A new message appeared:

Would you like to respond?

Brendan stared at the screen. Every muscle in his body had gone tight, stone-like. He couldn't move if he had to. He didn't touch the keyboard, but the message box vanished anyway, replaced with another—

Done! Photo sent!

Directly below, in a small thumbnail, was the picture he'd taken of his penis the other day for Abby.

"Oh no...oh no!"

He searched for some kind of recall button or cancel, but there was none.

Brendan's eyes jumped to the adjoining door.

He'd meant to lock it before getting in the shower but forgot.

38

When Abby hung up with Brendan, she assumed he might use the Find My app to check her location. She certainly did—Abby had received notifications throughout the day as Brendan arrived in Chicago, went to the airport Hilton, then to some office building downtown she assumed belonged to the firm he was investigating, then returned to the airport Hilton where he was when they spoke. When she set up the notifications, Abby told herself she wasn't tracking his activity because of some trust issue, she was tracking his activity because she was worried about him. Every time one of those notification boxes popped up, she reminded herself of that.

The affirmations did little to calm her guilt.

Spying was spying. The means didn't justify the end, or the method.

The Find My app was a double-edged sword. In order for Abby to keep tabs on her husband, he was able to keep tabs on her. There was no one without the other. So, when she hung up with Brendan, she immediately checked her location on her phone and felt relieved when the pin showed her in the center of their own house. If the app had X-ray vision, it might show her planted on the couch awash in the glow of the television, six minutes into some black and white movie on TMC. Better yet, at her desk, hands poised over her keyboard.

Right where Brendan expected her to be.

That wasn't where she was, though. She hadn't been home for nearly five hours, but somehow the Sugar & Spice app had made it so.

Abby was parked at the Walmart in Brookline. Two rows back from the grocery entrance where she had watched the woman from 29 Belfer go in twelve minutes ago pushing a cart she found in the lot. Prior to Walmart, she'd followed her to Westminster Bank & Trust, a dry cleaner off I-9, and a Rite Aid pharmacy where she'd sat in the drive-thru for nearly twenty minutes.

Abby had taken to calling this woman Sue.

She had no idea what the woman's real name was, but she looked like a Sue.

Sue was married to a man Abby had dubbed Stanford. He'd arrived home (presumably from work) at a little after six, promptly removed his tie before he even entered the house, then put on a sweater vest in the twelve minutes Abby couldn't see him through the windows. She was going to call him Bob until he broke out the sweater vest. Only someone named Stanford would slip into a sweater vest when settling in for the evening, so Stanford he was. Both Sue and Stanford had become characters in the story unfolding in Abby's mind, what would become tomorrow's pages. The two of them had settled in for a quick dinner of something Abby couldn't make out from the street, something reheated in the microwave and spooned out onto plates, then eaten on stools at the kitchen counter.

Best Abby could tell, Sue and Stanford had no pets. No children.

And didn't enjoy each other's company much, because they didn't seem to talk while they ate. Sue was busy studying a stack of documents while Stanford was glued to a small television set on the kitchen counter.

Stanford drove a black BMW. Sue drove a white Prius. The Prius was parked three cars over from Abby at Walmart, diligently waiting for Sue to return.

Tonight, Abby wasn't Abby, she was Emily, the main character in her story. Emily was following Sue, trying to determine why this woman was meant to die. Surely the app didn't pick her at random. Both Sue and Stanford spent a lot of time on their phones, not exactly a red flag in today's society, but Abby pictured them both responding to various *Sugars*, maybe settling on a *Spice*, because it made sense they were users of the app. How else would the app find them? But why them? That was the real question. Of the two, which was the actual target? The app hadn't told her that. Her gut told her it was Sue, but that might only be because she'd spotted her first. Maybe if Stanford had been home when she approached the house with Hannah, she'd be following him right now instead of Sue.

"Fucking sweater vest is reason enough," Abby muttered to herself, then laughed softly. Her voice sounded much louder than she expected alone in the confines of her car.

She should have taken their mail.

She'd been parked halfway down the block when the mailman appeared (the lawn guy long gone) and stuffed their box with circular ads and several envelopes. Abby easily could have snatched it all. You can learn a lot about a person from the mail they receive. Magazines were gold because they communicated hobbies and interests. At the very least, that would have gotten her actual names.

Sue emerged from Walmart pushing a full cart.

She walked right by the red van on her way to the Prius.

Didn't give it a second glance.

Abby did, though. Her eyes locked on it.

The red van was parked at the curb and had been concealed behind a motorhome with its flashers on. Abby had no idea how long the van had been there. The motorhome had been illegally parked in the loading zone when she pulled into the lot behind Sue. The van hadn't been there then, she would have noticed. It arrived sometime after them.

The van also had its flashers on, and although Abby couldn't see inside, she was sure the driver was the large man from earlier. The one Hannah nearly hit. The one who followed them to Five Guys. How the hell had he found her? Had he been following her all day? Surely she would have spotted him sooner. Maybe he somehow ran Hannah's license plate and learned where she lived. With Hannah's house across the street, he would have seen Abby leaving her home. She'd been so busy following Sue around, she hadn't thought to look in her own rearview mirror.

Abby found herself sinking deeper into her seat.

Three cars over, Sue opened the trunk of her Prius and began loading her groceries.

A small cloud of white smoke drifted from the tailpipe of the van.

The trunk of the Prius came down and Sue got behind the wheel.

When the Prius backed out of the parking space and started to pull away, Abby's hand went to her keys, hesitated. She was still trying to decide if she should continue following Sue, head home, or even drive to the nearest police station, when the red van pulled away from the curb and fell into traffic behind the Prius.

He wasn't following Abby.

He was following Sue.

39

Brendan stared at the unlocked door, unable to move, his heart thumping wildly. On his laptop, more images came in—Kim in the shower. Kim sleeping. Kim laughing from across the table, a half-finished breakfast in front of her. Brendan caught glimpses of new windows opening over the old from the corner of his eye as he glared at that adjoining door. When the onslaught finally ended, at least a hundred pictures had come in, maybe more. That wasn't the worst of it. As Brendan minimized windows, closing box after box until nothing was left but the photograph of his penis, he realized that wasn't the only picture of him that transferred. There were several dozen more—some taken by Abby, others he'd taken in mirrors. Aside from the penis shot, there was nothing sexual about the others, he was either shirtless or in his underwear, but it appeared any picture where he showed even a minimal amount of skin had gone to Kim.

Brendan had several apps on his phone linked to cloud storage, set up to create backups of his camera roll and documents online as well as with his laptop in case something ever happened to his phone—the images had to come from there, although he had no idea how.

A soft thud came from the room next door.

A moment later, Brendan heard Kim's hesitant voice at the door. "Brendan?"

Not much more than a whisper. As if she'd started to speak and pulled back the word at the last moment.

Brendan's eyes jumped from the unsecured dead bolt to the doorknob, to the twist lock on the knob, also unlocked.

He didn't remember standing, but somehow he was off the bed and halfway to the door when he saw the knob begin to turn—not all the way, just a tentative twist, as if checking to see if it was locked or not.

Brendan moved fast, closed the remaining few feet. His fingers were sweating when he gripped the dead bolt's thumb latch. He fought the urge to twist quickly and instead turned the latch as slowly and quietly as he could manage. There was a soft *click* when it reached the end. Not loud. Hopefully not loud enough for—

"Brendan? Are you there?"

He didn't speak.

Couldn't.

"We need to talk about this, Brendan. If you changed your mind, or something, well… we should talk."

She was just opposite him, on the other side of the door, he was sure of that.

Pressing his palm against the wood, he felt the warmth of her on the other side, and had he turned off the lights, he'd surely see her shadow in the small crack beneath.

"Let me in, Brendan."

Brendan swallowed.

Sugar & Spice™

Sugar

Do you trust your partner? If your partner found themselves in a situation where they could cheat without any chance of getting caught, would they?

40

When she got home, Abby had tried to sleep, but she was too wired. After an hour of staring at the ceiling, she'd gotten up around one and went to her office where she let the story out. Typing had been a release, like opening a pressure valve—her lead character, Emily, following Sue. The red van. She used it all. This mad rush to get it all down on paper.

Abby was still typing when the sun began to rise. She didn't look up for another three hours.

Nineteen pages.

Her longest run yet.

Last night, she hadn't followed the red van. Oh, she wanted to—every cell in her body screamed danger for Sue, for Stanford, maybe even for herself if she followed. But to what end? Ring their doorbell? Tell them to peek outside? Check the doors? The locks? Abby considered calling the police, but she had no idea what she would report. She certainly couldn't tell them how she'd been following Sue and spotted the van. Even worse, there was no way to explain why she recognized the van in the first place, not without coming off like some crazy stalker.

Ultimately, she'd returned home. Cursing herself for some form of self-preservation over doing what was probably right. She told herself whatever danger those people were in wasn't coming yet, not until the timer hit zero.

There'd been some wine.

Abby needed that to steady her nerves, then shower, and her failed attempt at sleep.

On the desk to the right of her Mac, the timer clicked down on her phone:

19 hours, 45 minutes, and 18 seconds.

This morning, she'd drive back out to the house on Belfer, Abby had decided that much, if only to make sure everyone was all right. See if the van was there. See if it wasn't. See something. Then more writing this afternoon.

Abby needed to eat something, too.

She was about to get up when an e-mail came in from her agent. A PDF document with the subject line, *Read Me!*

Abby hadn't talked to Connie in two days, and she made a mental note to give the woman a call later today to fill her in on the book's progress, then clicked on the attachment.

The document didn't open. Instead, an hourglass appeared on her screen and began to turn. Abby closed a few of her open programs, expecting that to speed things up—her Mac was older and sometimes ran slowly when she asked too much of it, but nothing changed. Instead, the icon for her mouse stopped moving, it was frozen near the top right of the screen. The hourglass kept spinning, though. Her hard drive started churning too, loud. Same with the fan.

Abby cursed softly and reached for the power button. She was about to reset the Mac when the hourglass vanished, and a large red text box appeared. She read it twice and was on her third before the words sunk in:

The contents of your computer's hard drive have been encrypted within a locked file. This file will be deleted if you do not pay $10,000 in bitcoins to us, the new owners of your data. Should you notify authorities, your data will be deleted immediately. We are not located within your country. You have no recourse. Failure to comply will result in the deletion of your data. Do not turn off your computer or reboot. Doing so will result in the deletion of your data. Do not attempt to back up. Your backup will be infected as well, and all data will be deleted. We will provide payment instructions shortly. Say hello to your friends for us - you just infected them too.

There was a skull and crossbones below the text.

Abby was reading the message a fourth time when her phone rang.

Her agent.

Connie didn't give Abby a chance to say anything. She frantically blurted out, *"You didn't click it, did you? The file?"*

"I…I clicked on it."

"Did it…?"

"Yeah."

"Shit. I'm so sorry," Connie managed. She sounded as if she'd just run a marathon.

Abby slumped in her chair. "Please tell me it's not real. Just some kind of joke."

"Our IT guys are all over it. It's on our company server and hit every computer in the office this morning when we logged in. I pulled the network cable from the computer box thing-a-ma-jig under my desk, but

not before that e-mail snuck out to you," Connie quickly explained before covering the receiver and yelling at someone in her office. She returned a few seconds later. "*You took your computer offline, right? Before it could send itself to everyone in your contact list? That's ransomware 101.*"

Abby looked back down at her Mac and tried to move the cursor again. It was still frozen. "I think it's locked up…"

"*It's not locked up! It's sending!*" Connie shouted loud enough to rattle Abby's iPhone. "*Unplug the network cable!*"

"It's a laptop. I'm on Wi-Fi. There is no network cable."

"*Turn it off!*"

"But the message says if I—"

"*Fuck the message! Take out the battery! Turn it off!*"

Abby quickly flipped over the Mac and realized there was no way to remove the battery. It was inside the aluminum housing somewhere. The whole thing screwed tight. Without the use of her mouse, she couldn't turn off Wi-Fi. She flipped the Mac back over and mashed down the power button. Held it down. When nothing happened, she thought maybe the software had overridden the power switch too, but after about ten seconds the screen blinked out and went black. Abby hadn't realized she'd been holding her breath; she let it out. "Okay, I got it."

"*I hate to do this to you, Abby, but you need to call all your contacts right away. Tell them not to open that attachment if they got it, or this thing will keep spreading.*"

"But my contacts are on my computer. How do I get to them?"

"*You don't have them synced with your phone?*"

"Some, I guess."

Connie clucked her tongue. "*Well, call whoever you can, I guess. Jesus, you have no idea how sorry I am. Please tell me you have a hard copy of your book?*"

Abby glanced at the stack of pages next to her printer and felt her gut sink. "Shit."

"You haven't been printing as you go?"

"I…I have most of it. Just not what I wrote last night. Or this morning. I'm missing the last twenty pages or so."

"You wrote twenty pages since yesterday? Wow, you are a machine! You're a lot better off than the last two authors I talked to. Bob Wentworth doesn't print at all, and Lindsey O'Dell backs up to the cloud; she may have lost everything unless she pays. And you know Lindsey, she can be a bit emotional."

Abby didn't know Lindsey. She'd never met or spoken to the woman, but she couldn't fault Connie for mixing up things like that, not right now.

Connie rattled on about what her IT people were doing, then told her, *"Call as many contacts as you can. When you're done with that, try to rewrite those lost pages while they're still fresh in your mind. I know it's rough, but it could be worse. Think of Lindsey. Can you imagine? She'll have to pay, she has no choice, and there's no guarantee she'll even get her book back!"*

"Who are these people?"

"Probably some twelve-year-old hacker kid in Russia somewhere. I don't—"

An incoming call from Hannah cut her off.

Abby told Connie she'd call her back and picked up on Hannah.

"Abs, what the fuck did you just send me? I need to get all my sponsored social media posts out by 10 a.m. or I don't get paid today. Please tell me this is some sort of joke."

41

"What do you mean Kim didn't make the flight?" Special Agent Marcus Bellows asked from the speakerphone on Assistant Director Dubin's desk.

Dubin crossed behind Brendan to close her office door and nearly tripped over Stuckey's outstretched foot on her way back to her desk. He was sprawled out in one of her chairs, doing his best to keep his eyes open after the long return flight. Unlike the luxury seat he enjoyed on the trip over, he'd had to sit in coach for the nonstop return and hadn't been able to sleep.

Brendan scratched at the stubble on his face. He'd forgotten to shave. "Honestly, I'm worried. We were supposed to meet in the hotel lobby at five-thirty to catch the Uber to the airport. I texted her a couple of times, and she didn't respond. When the car showed, I ran back up to the rooms and knocked on her door. She didn't answer. I figured she forgot and went to the airport on her own. I tried calling her from security, called again when I got to the gate…I hoped she'd be in her seat, but she wasn't on the plane…" His voice trailed off.

Stuckey had his phone out. "She has read receipts turned on for me, so I can usually tell when she reads my texts. When I send her something, it doesn't even say DELIVERED. It's like her phone is off. Maybe she turned it off before going to bed and overslept?"

"No way," Brendan added. "I knocked on her door loud enough for the person across the hall to shout at me. She didn't sleep through that. She wasn't in there."

Back in her chair, AD Dubin leaned over the phone. "Agent, do you think this could be related to the deaths at INTENT? We had three deaths before you sent my people in, now one of my team is missing. That can't be a coincidence."

A long silence hung over the room.

Brendan's heart was beating like a jackhammer. If he didn't get out of Dubin's office soon, he'd surely start sweating. He refused to look at Stuckey. His friend could read him like a book. One glance, and he'd know there was more to this.

"*Brendan,*" Bellows asked. "*Are you sure you didn't see anyone strange around the hotel?*"

"Not that I noticed."

A knock at Dubin's door.

"Yes?"

Dubin's assistant poked her head into the room. "I checked with the airline. Ms. Whitlock didn't board her flight, and there's no record of her booking another. She didn't check out of the hotel. Her bags are still in the room. No phone or computer, though. She's not answering her cell. All calls are going straight to voice mail."

"Thanks, Carmen. Keep trying." Dubin blew out a breath and looked back down at the speakerphone. "Did you hear that, Agent? Kim's laptop is missing too."

"*I did. My people should be at the hotel within ten minutes. They'll lock the room down. Brendan's too. See what we can find on the security*" *camera. Hopefully, she'll turn up, but if she doesn't, I don't want risk evidence contamination."* Bellows went quiet for a second. *"Brendan, when did you say you last saw your laptop?"*

"Airport bathroom. I set my laptop case on top of my luggage just inside the bathroom door. I took my eyes off it for maybe a second or two, and when I went to wash my hands I noticed it was gone."

"Taken at the airport, though. Not the hotel? You're sure?"

"Yes."

The images of Kim flashed through Brendan's mind.

Naked.

Exposed.

All of them, still on that laptop.

The pictures of him, too.

What was on her laptop? On her missing phone?

What would these people think if they found it all?

Brendan's face flashed red. He tried not to think about any of that.

He couldn't.

Not right now.

"How secure are your laptops?"

Dubin cleared her throat. "We use Avox, probably the same as you."

"So three bad password attempts and the drive auto wipes?"

"Yeah."

"Good. Let's keep the communication open on this. I'll let you know what my people find at the hotel. I'll run a trace on Kim's phone too; maybe we'll get lucky. You call me if you hear anything on your end."

"Understood." Dubin hung up.

When the call disconnected, Stuckey let out a sigh. "You know that's bullshit. How long before they pull the entire thing out from under us and take over?"

Dubin looked out across the bullpen at Kim's empty cubicle.

"My best guess is that depends on what happens with Kim. We're not equipped to deal with…"

Kidnapping.

Murder.

"…an investigation beyond the financial aspects. They need us for that."

"They have their own people for that too."

"Not as good as our people." She let that hang for a second. "Until we get pulled, I want everyone on this. Take INTENT apart from every angle. Look at every document we have, every file, every person. We need to connect the dots. The answer is there. I don't want it slipping through on our watch."

Stuckey cocked his thumb toward Brendan. "Are you okay with us working on this from home? All things considered, I don't think we should leave our wives alone."

Dubin nodded. "Okay, but let's reconvene back here in the morning for a quick in-person to compare notes. I know tomorrow is Saturday, but I think we can all agree this won't hit pause over the weekend. Call me the moment you find anything." To Brendan, she said, "Stop by IT on your way out. Requisition a new laptop, and file a report on the missing machine."

In the hallway outside Dubin's office, Stuckey gripped Brendan's shoulder and lowered his voice. "Hey, you want to tell me what the hell is really going on?"

Before Brendan could answer, Stuckey showed him a text message from Kim on his phone. It was time-stamped yesterday, minutes before they went to dinner—

Going to get some food with him. If my body turns up in a ditch, tell the police it was Brendan! Ha! Kidding. (Sort of kidding 👀)

42

"Oh, come on," Brendan told Stuckey. "You don't believe that, do you? We ate, actually had a good conversation, and sort of aired things out." He lowered his voice. "Did you know she is a lesbian?"

Still holding Brendan's shoulder, Stuckey steered him through an emergency exit into the stairwell. "Of course I knew. I know everything. Who do you think told her it was okay to tell Dubin? Who do you think told her you were a good guy and not to push a sexual harassment claim through after the bullshit in Chicago last time? Who the fuck do you think told her you were a happily married man, and you only kissed her because you were loaded?"

"She kissed me."

"I don't give a fuck. Where the hell is she, Brendan?" Stuckey shoved the phone back in his face, the text still on the screen.

"That's a joke. She was clearly kidding."

"Was she?"

"You show that message to someone like Bellows—someone who doesn't know us—and you'll steer him down some bullshit rabbit hole. He'll be looking at me when he should be looking at INTENT. What if she didn't run off? What if they have her? If he's wasting time looking at me, because of you, you might get her killed." Brendan looked him square in the eyes. "Kim and I had a quiet dinner. No drinking. I told her about Abby, she told me about her girlfriend, Ana. We joked about what happened last time. Finished dinner and went back to our rooms. That was it."

Brendan knew that was a lie, but if he told Stuckey what happened later with the app, there'd be no walking it back. Now wasn't the time.

"I didn't hurt her, Stuckey. I'd never do that."

Stuckey shoved the phone into his pocket. "Look, Brendan, we're friends, but I can't get wrapped up in something. I've got a career to think about, too. I can give this until tomorrow, but if she doesn't turn up, I gotta show that text to someone. You understand what I'm saying? Covering for you with Abby for some silly nonsense is one thing, but this is something else entirely."

"What do we tell them? Hannah and Abby?"

Stuckey sighed. "Nothing yet. Let's see how this looks tomorrow. We got the wives for Game Night tonight. No point in getting them all worried until we have a better idea of what's going on." He started down the steps. "Did you tell Abby I found her on those websites?"

Brendan shook his head. "Not yet."

"Wonderful. So we gotta tap dance around that too."

Brendan stood there, gripping the metal railing, and listened to Stuckey's footfalls, then the sound of the parking garage door opening and closing. He didn't release the railing for nearly another minute. He just stood there, his mind reeling.

His laptop hadn't been stolen, he'd ditched it at the airport. But not before entering his password incorrectly three times and letting Avox do its work.

Allowing someone to find those pictures on his computer wasn't an option.

He wasn't going down for this.

No way.

43

Game Night.

The mood was anything but festive.

Kim hadn't turned up.

The phone trace went nowhere.

Even though they agreed not to say anything, they told Hannah and Abby what was going on. They knew something was wrong, there was no hiding it. Abby had already been distracted, quiet and distant since the moment he got home. Learning about Kim didn't help.

Brendan was on his third rum and Coke, and while that would have normally taken his nerves well past settled, his skin felt like it was on fire. If someone told him ants had taken up residence in his bones, he would have believed them. There was this itch deep down he couldn't scratch, and the only thing that satiated it was constant movement. That was the adrenaline, his racing blood pressure. He expected his phone to ring any second. Maybe Stuckey's. Maybe a knock on the door. AD Dubin, the police, someone with news. Someone with worse.

It seemed every time he glanced Stuckey's way, the man was staring at him from the other couch. And thinking what? Brendan tried not to let his mind go there, no good came of it. Instead, he sucked down half his drink.

All of them were spread out around the room. Tension so thick you could taste it in the air. Abby was at one of the kitchen island stools nursing a glass of red wine. Hannah was sitting cross-legged on the floor blabbering about some virus she and Abby picked up on their computers earlier. Made it sound like it was the end of the world. Brendan had caught enough to follow, not enough to really care, not with more pressing issues on his mind.

"…so, when I got to the library," Hannah droned on, "I still couldn't log into my accounts." She waved her hand through the air. "I use this password management program called SecureAll, and somehow this ransomware garbage locked me out of that too. I managed to get something posted on Instagram and TikTok from my phone, but without my computer, I missed a dozen other platforms. I couldn't schedule anything, had to message in real-time. And my posts were *so* amateur. Normally I edit, run some filters, add music, you know, take them all pro, and I couldn't do any of that."

"So, your computer is still locked up?" Stuckey asked.

Stuckey had gone straight home from Dubin's office and gotten a few hours of sleep before cracking the files on INTENT. The red was gone from his eyes, but he was still sluggish from the jet lag. Every twenty minutes or so he took out his phone, dialed a number, then hung up when it went to voice mail. Brendan didn't have to see the screen to know he was calling Kim. Although they all watched him dial, nobody said anything.

Hannah played it off like it wasn't happening and told him, "Well unless you're willing to give me ten grand in Bitcoin, Sugarloaf, we're going to be a one-income household until I can get set up on a new computer."

"Ah-huh," he muttered and pointed his beer bottle toward Abby. "What are you gonna do?"

When she didn't answer, Brendan said, "Abs?"

She looked up. "What?"

Abby had this deer-in-the-headlights look on her face. Her thoughts lost in God-knows-what. He caught the quick glances between her and Hannah. Stuckey probably showed that text to Hannah. Who knows what Hannah told Abby. And Abby was off in Conspiracy Land with the other two. His own wife, somehow afraid of him, believing he did something bad. Brendan took a sip of his drink and tried to shake it off.

"Stuckey asked what you plan to do about the ransomware on your Mac."

She'd already told Brendan, but he wasn't sure she was serious. Apparently she was, because she said it again.

"I'm writing the rest of the book by hand."

Stuckey set his phone back down on the coffee table and gave her this confused look. "Can you do that?"

Abby nodded. "I talked to my agent about it. The virus came from her office, so she feels horrible. She said she doesn't care if I write the book out on candy bar wrappers as long as I finish it. She'll have someone on her end transcribe everything."

"That seems so..."

"Old school?"

Stuckey shook his head. "I was going to say archaic. Who the hell hand-writes anything these days?"

Abby finished off her glass of wine, reached for the bottle, and generously refilled her glass. "I did it today. I rewrote the twenty pages I lost and added seven more, and honestly, I think it's better.

Something about using pen and a notebook makes it more…I don't know…more personal. I guess that's the best way to describe it. I feel closer to the story."

"What's this one about?"

Abby glanced at Hannah again, drifted over to Brendan, and quickly looked away when she realized he'd been watching her. "I'd rather not say just yet."

"It's fantastic," Hannah beamed. "Way better than the first one. Way steamier."

Stuckey pointed his thumb at his wife and tried to lighten the mood. "You let this one read it, but not me? Hell, if you need someone to fact-check the sexy-time parts, I'm your man. I got me a dog-eared copy of 50 Shades back at the house. That shit is sex gospel."

Hannah rolled her eyes. "That fucking book. Stuckey used to moan in his sleep—*Oh, Christian, the things you do to me! My inner goddess is doing handstands!*"

"The hell I did."

Hannah stood, clasped her hands together, and lowered her voice. "*Ana, let me demonstrate my love for you by beating you with this stick and covering your perfect ass with welts!*"

Ana.

The name of Kim's girlfriend.

Stuckey shook his head and reached for his phone again, began to dial.

Brendan had had enough. "I didn't hurt Kim."

The words were out before he could stop them. A quiet voice. One he didn't recognize as his own.

Nobody moved.

The room went silent.

Finally, Stuckey said, "I don't think we should talk about that, buddy. Not here."

Brendan set his glass down on the side table a little harder than he wanted to. It sloshed over the side. "No? I'm pretty sure there's already been talk about it, just not with me."

Stuckey eyed the puddle from Brendan's drink. "Maybe you should lay off that a little bit. We're all just a little concerned, that's all."

"Sure, we're all very concerned," Brendan fired back. "And we should be. Because she either ran off for some reason or worse, but I can assure you, if it's something worse, it had nothing to do with me."

Stuckey said nothing.

Both women stared.

"You don't seriously think I'd hurt her, do you?"

"I don't know what to think right now. I'm just hoping she's okay."

Abby, who had remained quiet through all of this, drank the rest of her wine, grabbed a bottle of vodka from the counter, and slammed it down on the coffee table in front of the couch. "It's Game Night, right? Let's play. Enough of this tip-toe bullshit. Let's fucking play."

44

The three of them stared at her.

Brendan had never heard Abby speak like that. Even Hannah looked shocked, and nothing surprised Hannah. There was no denying Abby was drunk—hell, they all were—but she wasn't so far gone she didn't have control of her faculties. The alcohol had only loosened her up, put a door in the normally solid wall in her mind between her thoughts and her mouth.

Abby sat on the floor in front of the coffee table and motioned for Hannah to sit beside her. She looked at Brendan, then at the empty place on the couch next to Stuckey. "You sit there. All four of us, nice and cozy."

Brendan knew better than to question her, not when she was like this. He shifted over to the other couch and sat across from her.

She twisted off the cap from the vodka and slid the bottle to the center of the table. "We're going with a classic tonight." She thought for a second, then said, "Never have I ever...eaten pizza for breakfast.

If you have, you have to drink. If not, you don't. We're all friends here, I think we can forgo the shot glass, right?"

Hannah's face filled with confusion. "Are you being serious right now?"

Abby ignored the question. "I've seen you eat two-day-old lobster rolls for breakfast, I know you've done pizza. Drink."

For a second, Hannah looked like she might argue, then she shrugged, took a swig from the bottle, and handed it to her husband. "I'm pretty sure you ate pizza for breakfast last Saturday."

Stuckey seemed as confused by Abby's behavior as the rest of them, but he drank from the bottle and handed it to Brendan. "You lived off that shit in college."

Brendan drank too.

When he finished, Abby took the bottle back, drank, and set it on the table. "Okay, now that we got the practice round out of the way, let's start for real." She looked around at the others, studied each of their faces, and spoke in a clear voice suggesting she wasn't as drunk as Brendan thought. "Never have I ever cheated on my partner."

Brendan felt a lump form in his throat.

Again, Abby studied their faces. "Keep in mind, I already know the answer."

Seconds ticked by, and nobody reached for the bottle.

Brendan swallowed. "I told you, nothing happened between me and Kim. Only the kiss. Nothing more."

She didn't look at him. Instead, her eyes remained fixed on the bottle. "And this trip?"

She knew.

He didn't know how she knew, but she did.

While he was fumbling for the right words, she opened a drawer on the coffee table and took out his old iPad. He hadn't used it for years.

"When my computer locked up," Abby said, "I remembered we had this in the kitchen junk drawer. I charged it up, figured it would be better than nothing until I got my Mac working again. All the accounts are under your name, too, so I didn't have to worry about the ransomware somehow transferring over. I plugged it in so it could charge, clicked *Yes* on a few software updates over the next hour or so, then went out to run some errands. When I got home, there was a message about a photo sync." Abby tapped the screen to life and entered Brendan's passcode. She spun the screen around so everyone could see.

Stuckey's eyes grew so wide they looked like they might burst from his head. "Is that Kim?"

Brendan's throat felt like sandpaper. "I can…"

"I don't need you to explain. The *Sugar & Spice* app is on here too. I went through your history. I saw the wink from her, your wink back. The photos back and forth after that. It's all there in the log. Nice, neat, and timestamped. Hell, you earned points for sharing your favorite dick pic. Yay for you."

"All that happened before I could stop it, Abs, I swear."

Her face was unreadable. "The app did it."

"Yes!" Brendan said a little louder than he wanted to. "Right after all that, Kim tried to come into my room, but I locked the door. I pretended I wasn't there. She gave up after a minute or so, and that was the last time I heard from her. In the morning, when she didn't show for the Uber, when she wasn't at the airport, I—"

"You destroyed your laptop. That's what really happened, right? It wasn't stolen."

That came from Stuckey.

"You destroyed evidence."

"I… I protected myself."

Abby reached for the bottle again. "Never have I ever cheated on my partner."

"I didn't cheat!" Brendan shot back. "I have no idea what happened to her after all that, I swear, but I didn't see her, and I certainly
didn't touch her!"

"Well, I have. I cheated on you, Brendan." Abby twisted the
bottle between her fingers, then raised it to her lips, and drank.
When she sat it back down, the others had gone deathly quiet.

Abby told him about the encounter at the hotel. "I thought he
was you."

"That's not cheating, Abs," Hannah whispered. "It was a terrible
mistake, but it wasn't cheating."

Brendan struggled to find words. He felt like he'd been punched
in the gut. "The app sent me to a hotel the same day, and there was
a woman in the room. We didn't…we stopped when we realized…"
He turned to Abby. "Hannah's right, that wasn't cheating. You didn't
know."

Abby slid the bottle first toward Stuckey, then Hannah. "Anyone
else?"

Neither drank.

"Not cheaters. That's nice. At least you got that going for you. I
suppose it's because when you fuck others, you do it together, right?
Both figuratively and literally?" Abby sighed and looked up. "Shall
we continue?"

Hannah's face had gone this ashy white and when she spoke,
her voice was thin. "Are we going clockwise or counterclockwise?"

A grin flashed at the corner of Abby's mouth, gone as quick as
it appeared. "You know, I think I'll go again."

"That's not how it works."

"My game, my rules. I think it's best you shut the fuck up."

Hannah looked like she'd been slapped. "Okay, Abs. Okay."

Abby licked her lips. "Never have I ever used my best friend to
get ahead."

Brendan had no idea where she was going with this and, while he wanted to blame the alcohol, Abby sounded stone-cold sober.

Hannah's eyes grew glossy. When a tear fell, she made no effort to wipe it away. She swallowed. "How did you find out?"

"It was that stupid triple chime," Abby said. "I heard it when you were in the bathroom. I thought it was my phone, but it wasn't, it was yours." She turned to Hannah. "I checked your log, too. You got a thousand points for recruiting Brendan and me as new Sugar & Spice members. Yay for you. Everybody's racking up the points, it seems."

Brendan was confused. "I don't understand. Dr. Donetti told us about the app. Not Hannah or Stuckey."

Abby glared at Stuckey. "Yeah, funny how that worked."

45

Stuckey took a drink of the vodka not as part of the game, but because he clearly needed a drink. He took a good, hard swig before setting the bottle down and wiping his mouth with the back of his hand. "Abby, I—"

"Never have I ever..." Abby interrupted, her voice taking on this hard edge. "...put a business card for a bogus doctor under the windshield of my best friend's wife's car."

Now Brendan was really confused. "What?"

"Those errands I ran today," Abby explained. "I went to the mall and asked to see the parking lot security footage for the day the card appeared. I told them someone broke into my car and was curious if the cameras caught anything. Doesn't take much to get a mall cop to spring into action. Anything to liven up their day. Stuckey parked two cars down from me that day." She glanced at him. "Followed me, I guess? He placed the card and took off. Honestly, Stuckey, you could have worn a baseball cap or something. I had no trouble identifying you."

Hannah stood from her place on the floor and sat on the arm of the couch. She put her arm around Stuckey's shoulders. "I made him do it."

"You didn't make me do anything."

"I don't care about any of that," Abby shot back. "I want to know who told the two of you to do it."

Hannah said, "I think you already know."

"I want you to say it."

"The app," Hannah told her. "It was a *Spice*. Recruit a new member."

"Not any new member, though, right?"

Hannah shook her head. "It gave me a map and a countdown. The app wanted you."

"And you got more than just points when you handed us to them, didn't you?"

Hannah's mouth dropped open. "How did you—"

"Forget how I figured it out. It doesn't matter. I want to hear you say it."

Stuckey reached over and squeezed Hannah's hand. Gave her a nod.

"The app sponsored my feeds. All my social media sites. They started to outbid everyone else until there was nobody else."

"They gave you a shit-ton of money."

Hannah nodded.

"You didn't think that was weird? You didn't question why some app decided to pour on the cash?"

"Oh, like you did when they paid for that expensive dinner?" Hannah shot back. "Did you pick up the phone and start digging? Did you search for some way to pay them back or right whatever atrocious wrong was committed? No. You. Did. Not. You want to call me out, Abby, go right ahead. But don't be a fucking hypocrite."

Brendan stared at Stuckey. "Where did you get the business card for Donetti?"

"It came in our mail, addressed to me," Stuckey said. "My *Spice* said *Refer a friend*. I didn't know it meant Abby until I got to the mall. The map took me to Abby's car." His face creased with lines. "It's a fucking app. A game. What's the harm? The two of you have never seemed happier. It was a good thing."

"I got raped," Abby replied, her voice cold. "Some guy I never met before put his dick in me because of your harmless app. Your *good* thing. Your wife even pushed me to go."

Hannah looked horrified. "Abby, that's not fair. I didn't know. How could I?"

Abby glared at her.

Brendan thought she might hit her.

Lunge at her.

Worse.

Instead, Abby settled back on her heels, closed her eyes, and drew in a long breath. When she spoke again, somehow she managed to calm herself. "This app is playing all of us. The money. The sex stuff. Hell, even the way I've been using it for my book. I don't think any of that has happened by chance. There's something bigger going on here."

"What? Like a puppet master or something?" Hannah bit the inside of her cheek. "That's crazy. I don't see how that's possible. Do you know how many people use this thing? Why would they give a shit about us?"

"Kim had the app, too," Brendan reminded them. "It sent me that wink, remember? This isn't only about us." He looked at each of them again. "Look, I swear I don't know where she is. I don't. She either left the room on her own or someone took her, but whatever happened, it happened right after the bullshit with the wink and all those photos syncing up." He closed his eyes, tried to recall the events exactly. "I could hear her moving around in her room, through the adjoining door. Then she was quiet. I didn't hear her leave, but that doesn't mean she didn't."

"If someone knocked on her room door or came in, do you think you would have heard it?" Stuckey asked.

"I'm not sure. Maybe?"

"No struggle, though? You didn't hear any other voices?"

"Definitely not."

Stuckey glanced at Hannah, then Abby.

When Hannah spoke, her voice was soft, childlike. "Never have I ever been asked to kill someone."

Brendan frowned at her. "What the hell is that supposed to mean?"

Hannah bit her lower lip, then looked at Abby. "Did you tell him?"

"Tell me what?"

Abby took out her phone and set it in the center of the table, next to the vodka bottle. When she tapped on the screen, the countdown appeared:

7 hours, 3 minutes, and 28 seconds.

Abby clicked on the timer, bringing up the related *Spice—Would you kill a total stranger to save your partner's life?*

Brendan read the message along with Stuckey, then slowly pulled Abby's phone closer and clicked through several more screens. He brought up the map, zoomed in. "I doubt Kim's in Brookline," he said tentatively, "and she's not a stranger."

"It's not Kim," Abby told him. "I don't know who it is. Just some woman or her husband. The app hasn't said which one is the target. The point is, if the app sent a message like this to me, it might have sent one to someone else… a message leading to Kim."

"Wait, back up. *You went there?*" he tapped on the map. "To some stranger's house?"

"I went with her," Hannah quickly added. As if that would make it better.

"I went back," Abby told them all. "A few times. I followed the woman."

Brendan shook his head.

Tried to process everything.

He reached for the vodka and took a drink. Stuckey snatched the bottle from him before he could put it back on the table, drank too. "It's a fucking app. A game," he said again. "Nobody's killing anybody." Although, this time he didn't sound as convinced.

Brendan's fingers were shaking as he minimized everything and clicked back to the countdown. He checked his watch and did the math. "That works out to 4:51 tomorrow morning. That's either very specific or very random."

Hannah took the bottle from Stuckey and cradled it in her hands. "Kim might be dead. And these people are next."

Like a toddler firmly planting his feet, Stuckey grunted, "Nobody is going to kill someone because an app tells them to."

Abby's phone let out the triple chime, startling all of them. A message appeared:

You could use your best friend's gun to do it, Brendan.

Brendan's heart thumped at the sight of his name. "What the fuck."

This was Abby's phone, not his.

"We don't have a gun," Hannah mumbled, her face glued to the phone. "I hate guns."

Stuckey went quiet. His expression sallow.

She turned on him. "We don't have a gun, right?"

He said nothing.

"You brought a gun into our house?"

"I bought it after the bullshit in Florida a few years back." Stuckey licked his lips. "It's just a .38. A little snub nose. That's all."

"Oh, it's just a little killing machine. I guess that makes it okay. As long as it's cute and cuddly." She smacked his arm. "You're an asshat. I want it gone."

Stuckey took another drink of vodka. "How does the app know I have a gun?" He looked at Brendan. "More importantly, why does it want you to use my gun? Is it trying to set me up? Kill some random white person, blame it on the nearest Black man? That's some bullshit." He turned back to Hannah. "I told you we should have never moved to the suburbs. Fuck this."

"This isn't a joke," Abby countered.

"You sure about that? Nobody's twisting anyone's arm to kill someone. Nobody twisted anyone's arm to do any of the things the app suggested. It's thrown some garbage at Hannah and me too, doesn't mean we got to do it all. We *chose* to do it all. There's a difference."

"Bad things happen when time expires," Abby mumbled.

They all looked at her.

"When I was in my agent's office and the app wanted me to take…pictures…it sent a text with that message. Like it knew I wasn't going to do it and needed to push me along."

"We're not killing anyone," Brendan told Stuckey. "You don't have to worry about that."

"No? You're not gonna take my gun and frame me for murder? Thanks for that, buddy."

"Where exactly is it?" Hannah prodded. "Your cute gun?"

"It's in the pantry. I hid it in a box of Granola Whip-Its."

"I hate those fucking things."

"Exactly."

Brendan was staring at the phone. "It knows what we're talking about."

"Okay, now who's being paranoid?" Hannah replied.

Abby leaned closer. "Can an app do that? Listen? It would explain a lot."

Stuckey thought about that for a second and nodded. "Can I look at your privacy settings?"

She pushed her phone toward him. "Go ahead."

It took a moment for Stuckey to find what he was looking for. When he did, he flipped the phone back around so Abby could read the screen. "You granted access to your phone's microphone when you installed the app. Your camera too."

They watched as he turned both of those off.

It was far worse than that.

"App tracking is also on. That means it can see what you're doing in other apps. Every keystroke. With Bluetooth and Wi-Fi, it can see and connect to other devices nearby. Things on your network."

"I never agreed to that."

"It's probably buried in the Terms of Service. Most apps default to *On* unless you specifically tell them not to. And who reads that shit?"

Stuckey toggled those settings off too.

A moment later, the Amazon Echo on the shelf behind Brendan's shoulder beeped and said, *"The Sugar & Spice app is having trouble connecting to this device. Please check your network connections and app settings. You have six hours, fifty-three minutes, and nine seconds remaining on your current Spice."*

46

"What the actual fuck." Hannah's grip on the vodka bottle tightened.

Brendan stood, crossed the room, and pulled the device's plug from the wall.

From the hallway, their smart thermostat dinged. *"You have six hours, fifty-two minutes, and forty-three seconds remaining on your current Spice."*

In the kitchen, the familiar triple chime rang out.

"I think that was the microwave," Abby whispered.

They heard it again, this time from the laundry room.

Again from something upstairs.

All their connected devices.

The triple chime, over and over, growing louder. This cacophony of muted tones. Some spoke, others did not.

Brendan forced his legs to work and ran to the garage. He fumbled with the latch on the electric panel, got it open, and switched off the main breaker at the top. There was a loud click, then silence. A blanket of black fell over the house as all the lights went out. He was halfway back to the living room, feeling his way along the wall, when he heard the chime from his Apple watch. The screen lit up:

6:50:13 Remaining
Sugar & Spice™
♥

Unsure of exactly how to turn it off, Brendan mashed down the crown and the button on the side. He held them down until a slider appeared with the words *Power Off*. He struck it twice with a sweaty index finger before it finally took and the screen went dark. When he returned to the living room, he found the others removing their various smart devices, pulling batteries, switching them off, and piling them on the coffee table.

Abby retrieved a candle and lighter from the drawer in the end table and lit the wick. She set it down as Brendan returned to his place on the couch.

They sat in silence for nearly a minute, all of them waiting for the chime again, the voice counting down, but nothing came. There was only quiet.

Finally, Hannah said, "I'm not ready to go Amish, so how do we work through this?"

Abby shuffled in the dim light. Flickering yellow playing across her face. "It's my *Spice*. I don't think it wants you."

Brendan removed his smart watch and set it on the table. Someone had powered off his cell phone; it was in a pile with the others. "Do you have a name or anything for the people in Brookline?"

Abby shook her head. "They live at 29 Belfer Drive. A husband and wife, I haven't seen any children. I've got pictures of their license plates, but they're all on there." She nodded at her dark phone.

"Hannah found info on their house, but no names. Doesn't matter anyway. When I tried to figure out who they were, the app sent me the definition of a stranger, like it didn't want me to dig."

"What, like a threat?"

Abby nodded.

"We learn their names, what good will it do?" Hannah asked.

Brendan had no idea. He just felt like he needed to do something.

He picked up the iPad, then realized it was useless. Without power, the Wi-Fi router was down and the tablet couldn't connect to the Internet.

"*Sugar & Spice* is on that tablet," Abby said. "It's on our phones, our computers. You use any of those devices, and whoever is watching us will know."

Stuckey let out a chuff and reached for the vodka bottle. "Do you have any idea how paranoid you all sound right now? It's just a game. That app had its fun moments, but it always felt like it had fingers everywhere. I bet all of this is just part of the game. What you need to do is open up a Google search and ask the question 'has *Sugar & Spice* ever asked you to kill someone?' You do that and I bet you get a gazillion results from people who got played just like you. Pawns who bought into all this bullshit. For all you know, the people who live at that house are on the app too. They're playing the game. Hell, maybe they're expecting you to show up on their doorstep."

Abby and Hannah exchanged a look, but neither said anything. Stuckey didn't miss it, though. "What?"

"When Abby and I got to the house, the app gave her some points for 'finding her target.' The woman in the house looked at her phone around the same time the message came in."

"Not around the same time," Abby corrected. "The *exact* same time."

Stuckey clapped his hands together. "There you have it. They're players too. Mystery solved."

"That doesn't mean much of anything," Brendan told him. "And it doesn't explain what happened to Kim."

"It doesn't explain it because the two things aren't related." Stuckey frowned. "Look, up until a few minutes ago, that app had access to everything on your phones. Probably everything on your laptops, tablets, and who knows what else. You gather all that intel, it's easy to start pushing buttons. The app knows you better than you do. That's all I'm saying. It's still only a game." He nodded at Brendan's bare wrist. "When did you say the timer would hit zero?"

"4:51 in the morning."

"Stand up. Off the sofa."

Brendan got up. "Why?"

Reaching for a pillow, Stuckey placed it on Hannah's lap and spread out on the couch. "We keep the power off and have ourselves a sleepover. Wait this thing out. Nobody leaves, that means nobody is off killing anyone."

Hannah looked down at him. "Comfy?"

"Yeah, baby." Stuckey reached for the bottle again. "Things will look different tomorrow, you'll see. Daylight does that. The world ain't so scary when the boogeyman has to hide."

Brendan slipped his hand into Abby's. She was cold, trembling. She allowed his touch for only a second before pulling away.

47

"Brendan? Are you there?"

He didn't speak.

Couldn't.

"We need to talk about this, Brendan."

Kim was just opposite him, on the other side of the adjoining door, he was sure of that.

Pressing his palm against the wood, he felt the warmth of her on the other side, and had he turned off the lights, he'd surely see her shadow in the small crack beneath.

"Let me in, Brendan."

Brendan swallowed.

"Why'd you lock the door?"

Brendan's heart was thumping so loud he could hear it. This jackhammer in his chest.

"Is it because I said I was a lesbian? Did that turn you on? The idea of me with Ana?"

Brendan didn't speak.

Couldn't.

Wouldn't.

"I told you I was confused, Brendan. That's all it was."

Shouldn't speak.

But he did.

"Why did you send me those pictures, Kim? Everything was okay between us. Why would you do that?"

"I didn't send you anything, Brendan."

"I've got dozens of photos of you. Explicit stuff. Why did you send it to me? I'll have to take it to HR. This needs to stop."

Brendan regretted the words. They came out far more confrontational than he had hoped. But he couldn't take them back.

"You're my boss, Brendan. You have complete access to my work papers. My computer. You were alone with my phone when I went to the restroom earlier during dinner. If you accessed any of those devices, if you downloaded private images of me without my knowledge... I prefer to think you wouldn't do that, but if you did, *if I told HR you did*, who do you think they'd believe? This is the kind of thing that ends careers. We involve them, *anyone else*, that's what happens. Careers end. Unlock the door, Brendan. Let me in. We can still work this out on our own. Nobody will ever know."

Somebody always knew.

Somebody always—

"Brendan, wake up. It's almost time."

His eyes opened on Abby, sitting up in bed with her grandmother's watch in her hand. On her nightstand, a candle had burned down to the nub.

She leaned closer to the light and studied the watch face. "Less than two minutes to go."

Brendan had slept in his clothes and was covered in sweat. His mouth and throat were gritty, like he'd swallowed a handful of sand. It took him a moment to understand where he was, what was happening. Why the power was out. Finally, he got his bearings and said, "Are Hannah and Stuckey still here?"

Her face buried in the ticking hand of the watch, Abby got off the bed and started for the door. "Downstairs."

Brendan sat up.

Most dreams vanished within moments of waking. Dissolved like the frame of a film caught on a projector and melting with the heat. Not this one. This dream stuck. This dream had teeth. Even as he navigated the hallway and stairs in the dark, Brendan felt like his fingers were still entwined in the carpet of that hotel room floor.

Stuckey and Hannah were on the couch, Abby across from them, all three looking down at the small watch as Brendan stepped into the living room.

"Ten seconds," Abby whispered.

Hannah, who normally didn't rise for a few more hours, watched glassy-eyed, too tired to comment. If Stuckey slept, it hadn't been much. Coupled with his jetlag, he looked as tired as his wife. He gave Brendan a subtle nod as he stepped into the room and sidled up next to Abby.

"Five."

He leaned over and watched the second hand sweep past the eleven, the twelve.

Time.

"That's it," Brendan said softly. "4:51."

"And the world didn't implode," Stuckey managed, his voice full of morning gravel.

Abby stared at the watch for several more seconds, then set it on the table and picked up her iPhone. "Should I turn it on?"

Stuckey let out a sigh. "Can't live like this forever."

She held the power button down, and a moment later the Apple logo appeared.

The boot-up sequence seemed to take forever, but when it completed, there was no sign of the countdown on Abby's display. She entered her passcode and swept through the various screens. "The app is gone."

Brendan leaned closer. "Are you sure? Maybe it moved to another screen with the reboot."

"It's not here. Check yours."

Hannah reached for her phone and powered up. "Mine's gone too."

It wasn't on Brendan's or Stuckey's phone anymore either.

"Maybe that's that," Stuckey said. "You didn't complete a *Spice*, so they sacked you."

At some point, Abby had brought her MacBook down and put it with the phones. She booted that up too, then frowned. "The ransomware is still on this thing. I think part of me hoped they were related."

"The Internet is still down," Brendan reminded them. "Maybe it will update once it's back on the web. Should I turn the power back on?"

"Power is needed for Internet *and for coffee*," Hannah muttered. "Coffee is needed for *me* to boot up."

Brendan went to the garage and flipped the master breaker. The lights flickered on around him, followed by the hum of the old refrigerator they kept in the corner. The sounds of the house coming back to life.

Back in the living room, he watched as Abby waited for the Wi-Fi indicator to appear in the corner of her Mac, then she rebooted. When the laptop came back online, she shook her head.

"Still locked. I guess that was too much to hope for."

"Still waiting on that coffee." Hannah yawned.

Stuckey put his hands on her shoulders. "How about we grab that for you at our house? Give these two a chance for a little more rest." He eyed Brendan. "We told AD Dubin we'd go in this morning."

Hannah frowned. "On a Saturday?"

Stuckey pulled her close and kissed her on the cheek. "There's a lot going on, but I'll try and have us out by lunchtime." Looking back at Abby and Brendan, he said, "I hope there are no hard feelings here. The last thing we'd ever want to do is hurt the two of you. You know that, right?"

Brendan nodded. "We're all good." When Abby didn't say anything, he reached over and gave her hand a gentle squeeze. "Right, Abs?"

"Yeah," she said quietly, still looking at her phone. "All good."

She didn't sound good, though.

Stuckey steered Hannah toward the door. "Try to get in the office by eight. I'll get us out by eleven."

Brendan wanted to lighten the mood. "Maybe we could hit some balls over at Fairlane?"

"Let's see how things go."

Then they were gone, and Abby and Brendan were alone.

"Are you going to stay up or try and get more sleep?" he asked her.

Abby finally lowered her phone and faced the staircase. "I can't sleep. Not now. I think I'll try and get some pages done."

He tried to take her hand, but she pulled away from him.

"Abs, are we okay?"

Her back to him, she said nothing for the longest time. "I think we can be."

Abby left her MacBook on the coffee table as she vanished up the steps.

Sugar & Spice™

Sugar
If you lost everything but each other, would it be enough?

48

The police were waiting for Brendan when he arrived at the office.

Well, that's what he thought when he saw them—two uniformed officers and a woman in a rumpled suit. Brendan caught a glimpse of their backsides as they stepped into AD Dubin's office and closed the door.

Rather than walk by her office, he skirted the opposite side of the cubicle bullpen, slipped into his office, and silently closed the door. He stood there for a moment, his back against the wall, before crossing the small room, dropping into his chair, and dialing Stuckey's extension.

Stuckey's voice came from the small speaker. "Hey, you made it."

"Are they here about Kim?"

"I think so. Probably."

"She hasn't turned up yet?"

The question hung between them.

If Kim had been found, and that prompted the police to come to the office, it wasn't good.

If Kim was still missing, and the police were at the office, that wasn't good either.

"Any word from the FBI?"

"Not that I've heard."

Brendan's replacement laptop was sitting on the corner of his desk. He pulled it closer and powered it on. "She'll turn up."

On the laptop screen, Brendan entered his username and password. A message appeared:

To restore your previous desktop, please select a disk image.

The IT department used some type of software that took snapshots of everything on their computers on a regular basis. This made it easy to restore everything as of a specific date. Normally, he'd select the most recent snapshot, but instead he scrolled back more than a month, long before all this started, and selected *Restore*.

Thinking aloud, Brendan said, "I shouldn't have destroyed the computer."

"I get why you did, but yeah, that was a dumbass move."

"What would you have done?"

"I probably would have made some other dumbass move. But not that."

A progress bar crawled across the screen as the laptop whined, both the fan and hard drive churning as the software restored all his data.

A lump formed in Brendan's throat. "Do you know if our laptops back up while we're on the road?"

"As far as I know, they back up 24/7, as long as they're connected to the Internet. Why?" The answer came to him a moment after he asked the question. "Oh. You're wondering when Kim's laptop last backed up."

Brendan swallowed. "The wrong person sees all that, and it would look really bad for me."

"Maybe you should call George Keegan."

Hearing that suggestion, *that name*, come from Stuckey's mouth felt like a sucker punch to the gut.

George Keegan was a criminal defense attorney they'd come up against more times than Brendan could count. Keegan wore these glossy Italian suits that shimmered when he walked, fostering a glow only outdone by the large amounts of product in his hair. He billed at a thousand per hour and rarely lost. In the decade Brendan had known of the man, he was only aware of two clients who actually went to prison, and both got the minimum sentence at low-security facilities.

"You hate George Keegan," Brendan told him.

"Yeah, because he's good."

"I didn't do anything wrong, Stuckey."

"That doesn't mean you don't need an attorney. Keegan would have told you not to destroy the laptop."

Several minutes went by, the drive screaming, then it finally went quiet. A dialog box with *Completed!* popped up. Brendan clicked the message away and his familiar desktop appeared, albeit altered slightly from what he remembered since it was a month old. No sign of the app, photos of Kim, none of that.

A beep came over the line.

Stuckey said, "That's Dubin. Stay put. I'll call you right back."

He disconnected before Brendan could reply.

Brendan opened a browser window.

It took him a moment to recall the Brookline address Abby had mentioned yesterday. When it came to him, he keyed it in and clicked *Search*.

Dozens of results appeared, all of them reporting the same story.

Brendan's heart began to race.

He clicked on the first link—a report from the local NBC affiliate:

Two Believed Dead in Brookline Gas Explosion - Possible Arson
The usual quiet neighborhood of Brookline, Massachusetts, awoke to a loud blast just before 5 a.m. this morning as what is believed to be a gas explosion detonated in the home located at 29 Belfer Drive. The cause of the explosion is yet to be determined. The residents of the home, Douglas and Mary Dubin, were believed to have been inside. Much to the credit of the Brookline Fire Department, firefighters were able to contain the blaze to the single residence. Authorities would like to speak to this woman. She appears on several neighborhood security cameras, observing the Dubin home in the days preceding the explosion. Police are looking for either a red BMW 3-series or a charcoal Nissan Ultima. Should you recognize this woman, please alert authorities.

This story is developing. Check back for additional information.

While the photographs were grainy, it was clearly Abby. In one she was watching the house through a pair of binoculars, in the other she was sunk low in her seat, staring out at the house.

AD Dubin's house.

Holy shit.

Holy fucking shit.

Brendan's head jerked up, and he stared at Dubin's office across the bullpen. Although they'd partially closed Dubin's blinds, he could see the police officers and that woman shuffling around inside—opening drawers, cabinets, inspecting documents on Dubin's desk.

This was insane.

Dubin was dead?

Police thought Abby...

Brendan keyed in Stuckey's extension, but he didn't pick up.

Fumbling his phone, Brendan located one of the news stories and forwarded it to Abby.

His phone dinged with a reply a moment later.

A screenshot from Abby's phone—

> *You have violated our terms of service.*
> *Your membership is hereby revoked.*
> **Sugar & Spice™**

A second later, she texted:

> *You need to come home – now!*

Brendan dialed her number, but the call went straight to voice mail.

"Pick up, dammit." He dialed a second time, and again got voice mail. He hung up without leaving a message and tried Stuckey's office again. He didn't pick up either.

Rising from his desk, Brendan went to the door and opened it a crack, just enough to see Dubin's office. The police officers were still in there, Stuckey too. Her door was closed. Shit! That kid from IT was in there too, leaning over a laptop on Dubin's desk. He jerked a thumb toward Brendan's office. Had they restored Kim's data? Found the pictures? Something else?

A new text on his phone.

Abby again:

> *Are you coming?! Please hurry!*

He heard the triple chime. Not from his phone, but from his new laptop. When he looked back at the screen, the Sugar & Spice logo was at the center with an installation progress bar. He watched in horror as it completed, and the company's ridiculous tagline appeared:

Brought to you by International Entertainment Corp:
Your gateway to the freedom you live!

Brendan's eyes grew so wide they might have popped from his skull. His legs turned to rubber. Why hadn't he seen it before?

International Entertainment
INTernational ENTertainment
INTENT

His desk phone rang.

Brendan picked up the receiver, expecting it to be Stuckey.

It wasn't.

It was a female voice.

Robotic.

"Listen to me carefully, Brendan. You are to leave your office immediately and return home. Under no circumstance are you to speak to anyone as you do."

The Sugar & Spice logo vanished, and pictures filled the screen. All of Abby, taken through various windows of their home.

"Take this laptop. Take your phone. Do not use either device to contact anyone. We will know. We'll kill your wife."

"Who the hell is this?"

"Prepare to leave in five, four, three, two, one…"

The call dropped.

249

Brendan heard a distant line ring. When he looked back out the crack in his office door, the detective was reaching for Dubin's desk phone. Stuckey was looking down at the cell in his hand, and the officers were reaching for theirs, the IT guy too. It sounded like all their phones were ringing at once.

Brendan didn't understand the hows or whys, but he recognized a distraction when he saw one—he needed to get to Abby—

Grabbing the laptop and his phone, Brendan hunched low—he used the cubicles for cover on his way to the elevator.

49

Brendan was racing down I-90 when a text came in from Stuckey—

Did you go somewhere? The police want to talk to you. Dubin's dead. They have pictures of Abby. Brendan- Abby didn't leave last night, did she? Would she...you know?

He didn't respond.

Instead, he tossed the phone to the passenger seat and ignored the calls and texts that followed. None were from Abby. She had her own ringtone and text chime, he'd know.

How the fuck had whoever this was called not only AD Dubin's office line, but Stuckey, multiple police officers, and the kid from IT all at the same time? How would they have all the numbers? Could they all be on that app?

International Entertainment.

INTENT.

Fuck.

Fuck.

How the hell did he miss that?

Distracted, Brendan nearly missed Exit 127. He swerved across three lanes of traffic, cut off an Amazon delivery van, and skidded as his wheels caught the gravel at the edge of the breakdown lane before finding purchase on the blacktop. He didn't slow until he reached the turn for Washington.

Right on Centre.

Left on Marcuslin.

A green Ford was parked in front of his house, and when he skidded to a stop in the driveway, it sped off. Brendan didn't recognize it.

The front door of the house opened, and Abby appeared. "Hurry, get inside!"

Brendan rounded his car and ran up the walk. He threw his arms around her and squeezed. "Jesus, Abs. That house…they think you… Abby, that was my boss!" He showed her the message from Stuckey on his phone.

Abby only stared at him, horrified. "I didn't go…I would never…"

Brendan squeezed her tighter. "I know. I know. It will be okay."

Pulling from Brendan's arms, she slammed the door, twisted the dead bolt, and put the chain in place. Abby inched the curtain covering the sidelight aside and peered out. She was trembling. Anxious. Nervous. Scared. Maybe all of the above. Finally, she managed, "You saw that car, right?"

"The Ford?"

Abby nodded.

"Yeah, why?"

"People have been stopping out front for the last few hours. Just parking and watching the house. They leave when they notice me watching them."

"What people?"

"I don't know. People."

"The same car?"

"No. Different cars. And there's this—"

Abby showed him her phone. She was holding it not like she wanted to, but like she had to. Like it was some diseased thing she'd been forced to carry. There was the *Sugar & Spice* logo, a map, and a pin directly over their house.

A silver pickup jerked to a stop outside.

"There!" Abby pointed.

Although the windows were tinted, Brendan could make out at least two people sitting inside. Both appeared to be studying their house. A moment later, a yellow hatchback lumbered up the street and stopped behind the pickup. Nobody got out. They just sat there.

Brendan's blood began to boil. He removed the safety chain, disengaged the lock, and yanked the door open. He'd only taken a couple of steps onto the sidewalk when both vehicles quickly drove away.

What the fuck was this?

Abby's phone rang.

When he looked back at her, her face had gone pale. "It says UNKNOWN CALLER."

Brendan stepped back inside and closed the door. "Answer on speaker."

Abby was shaking as she held the phone between them and clicked on *Accept*. She didn't say anything.

They heard someone breathing, followed by a woman's voice. *"Abby? Are you there? It's me—Connie."*

To Brendan, Abby mouthed, *Connie Cormack. My agent.*

"Call her back," Brendan muttered, looking out the window.

Before Abby could say anything, Connie spoke in this low voice. Rushed. An urgent whisper.

"You need to listen to me carefully. Grab whatever you can and leave that house. Leave your phones behind. Computers. Anything that can be

tracked. Do you understand? It's in everything. Go someplace nobody will find you. You need to hide. You need to disappear."

Brendan's breath caught in his throat. He turned from the window and glared at the phone. Abby looked confused, but he knew exactly what her agent was talking about. "You planted those cameras, didn't you? What the hell is wrong with you?"

Abby didn't understand. "What cameras?"

"Are you listening to me? You don't have much time. They made me do it. You need to know that. They made me do it! They have a—"

Crack!

Both Abby and Brendan jumped. Although it hadn't been very loud over the phone, they both recognized the sound for what it was—a gunshot. That was followed by what sounded like the phone clattering to the ground.

"Are you there?" Abby managed. "Connie? Are you there? Connie!"

The call hadn't disconnected.

There was a shuffling, then someone picked up the phone.

Breathing.

Deeper this time.

A female voice. Older. *"Ain't love grand?"*

Abby nearly dropped the phone, and Brendan snatched it from her hand. "Who the fuck is this?" he shouted. "What happened to Connie?"

"Abby Hollander? You there? You still with me, honey?"

Wide-eyed, Abby glanced at Brendan, then back down at the phone. "What do you want?"

"Abby Hollander, you should have done it. Oh, you should have done it. Now it's on you, too. Hard to believe you value a stranger's life over your man, but that's the way you let the cookie crumble. I guess when your husband is a lying piece-of-shit, the choice is a bit easier. Sugar and

Spice and everything nice, till your husband sticks his dick in someone else's slice. I—"

Brendan hung up and found himself staring at the screen.

It's in everything.

Abby must have had the same thought, because she slapped the phone from Brendan's hand and stomped it. Crushed it. She ground the pieces under her shoe until nothing was left but bits of glass, plastic, and mangled circuitry. "Pack a bag," she said in a wobbly voice. "We're not waiting around here."

"We can't just leave," Brendan told her. "The police are looking for you. They think I hurt Kim. I'm sure of it."

"If you didn't, she'll turn up. We can't stay here." Abby jerked her thumb toward the street. "I don't know what that's about, and I don't want to know. Stay. Go. I don't care. I'm leaving."

If you didn't.

She didn't believe him, either.

Christ, was she leaving him?

"Abs, please. I swear I didn't cheat on you. I didn't hurt her. I don't want to lose you, I—"

Abby pressed a finger over Brendan's mouth, shut him up, and pointed at the Amazon Echo on the table across from them. It was still unplugged, but when she pointed around the room—at the smart thermostat, smart switches, smoke and fire detectors, all their connected devices, he understood. If the right person or persons wanted to listen, they could.

Hell, they were. They must be.

Looking him in the eyes, she carefully mouthed, *I believe you.*

Brendan felt the air slip from his lips, this relieved sigh he couldn't hold back.

Abby raised her voice. "Pack a bag or don't. I really don't give a shit what you do."

Real or not, that stung.

Abby then mouthed, *How much cash do you have?*

Taking out his wallet, he showed her. A little under three hundred dollars.

She produced another eighty in crumpled bills from her pocket. Not much.

Not enough.

The look on her face said she was thinking the same thing.

"Five minutes," she told him. "I'm going to the lake house until this blows over."

They didn't own a lake house.

Abby pointed at Brendan's phone. He'd set it down next to the door with his laptop. "They told me to bring them both here," he said as softly as he could manage.

They destroyed them both together.

50

Brendan hadn't unpacked from the latest trip to Chicago, so he pulled his dirty laundry from the bag, replaced it, and was at the door in under three minutes. Abby came down the steps right behind him with her tattered red backpack. The same one she'd used a few years back when she went on the book tour for *Understanding Ella*.

Brendan pulled back the curtain and looked out the sidelight at the front door again. "Fuck."

"What?"

"There's some van blocking us in."

"A van?" She pushed in next to him and looked for herself.

Abby had already been tense, but at the sight of the red van, every muscle in her body turn to stone and the color left her face.

"Do you know who that is?"

Abby kept her voice low, barely a whisper. "They followed Hannah and me a few days ago. They were watching the people on Belfer, too."

A young woman with long dark hair rounded the side of the van and leaned against the front fender. She was wearing cut-off jean shorts and a blue-striped bikini top. She eyed Brendan's car, the front of the house, then absentmindedly twisted a length of her hair between her fingers as she chewed gum.

"Stay behind me," Brendan told Abby.

Hefting up his bag, he unlocked the door and stepped out onto the sidewalk.

The woman gave him a flirtatious wave and grinned at him. "Hi, I'm Juliet. You must be Mr. Hollander."

Abby clearly had no intention of staying behind him. She set her bag in the grass and took a few steps toward the girl. "I thought you said your name was Cordelia? What's next, Macbeth? Portia? Cleopatra?"

She twirled her hair again and grinned. "I don't know them, but they sound lovely. How's the new book coming, Ms. Hollander? I just can't get enough of the other one. Been reading it nonstop."

Brendan inched next to Abby. "You know her?"

"She asked me for my autograph when I was with Hannah the other day."

"Your lovely wife was kind enough to give it to me. She's a peach."

Brendan took a step toward her. "You need to move your van."

"I'm afraid I don't have the keys." Her lips drooped into a pout. "Romeo *never* lets me drive."

"Romeo and Juliet, that's cute."

Abby drew closer. "Where is...Romeo?"

The young woman who called herself Juliet waved a dismissive hand through the air. "You know...around."

"I was checking for a back door!" a gruff voice called out from the corner of the house. "Figured you might make a run for it that way. Didn't think you'd chat up my little lady. She keeping you entertained?"

The largest man Brendan had ever seen rounded the side of their house and crossed the grass toward them.

Sauntered.

That was the word that popped into Brendan's head.

That's what the man did. He sauntered.

He was at least six-three, maybe six-four. Two hundred plus pounds. A beat-up cowboy hat rested on his head, and it had been several days since he'd shaved. A few since he'd bathed, too. Brendan caught a whiff of him in the air. His jeans were stained, as was his faded black tee-shirt, the logo for the band Boston cracked and barely readable. He held up a cell phone. "I'm glad you trashed yours, tracking with GPS takes all the fun out of it. Now we got ourselves some real sport."

"Get your van out of our way."

"Or what, you gonna hurt me, Abercrombie? Beat me with your man purse? If I was even the least bit concerned, I'd ask Juliet over there to tell you what happens to people who throw threats at me all willy-nilly. I ain't concerned, though. I kinda respect the fact you're willing to do it. Better than cryin' and beggin' and the like. I hate that about as much as I hate GPS."

"We called the police," Abby told him.

This brought on a grin.

The man's teeth were yellow and crooked.

He crossed the rest of the lawn in that lazy gait of his and got within inches of them. His eyes locked with Abby's, breath foul. Like day-old meat. "No, you didn't. The cops want you in a bad way, and your hubby there is on the lam for disappearin' some girl. The last thing you'd do is run to the cops." He leaned over her and gave a loud sniff. "Ah, that's nice."

"Back the fuck off," Brendan growled, his blood burning.

Romeo licked his chapped lips, his eyes never leaving Abby. "You're our ticket to platinum, but that don't mean we can't have a little fun first. How 'bout you and me go back inside? Juliet don't much mind, as long as she gets to watch. Your hubby can come too. Maybe he'll learn something."

Abby brought her knee up, swift and hard. She put all one hundred and eight pounds of herself into the blow and caught Romeo square in the balls. The muscles of his lined face went tight, and he tumbled back several steps, like a large tree trying to remain upright in the howling winter wind.

"Come on!"

Grabbing Brendan by the hand, Abby dragged him toward the street, toward Hannah and Stuckey's house.

Behind them, Romeo shouted out, "Oh, I love it when they're feisty!"

51

Brendan stumbled and nearly tripped on the steps leading up to Hannah and Stuckey's front porch. Abby beat him and was frantically digging through the dirt in some long-dead potted plant, looking for their spare key.

"Isn't Hannah home?"

"She dropped Stuckey at the office and went to the bank," Abby told him. "She told him she was paying the ransom."

Brendan admittedly knew very little about how Hannah earned her income, but the idea of paying some stranger ten grand in Bitcoin just to gain access to social media accounts seemed absurd to him.

"A blow like that will leave a man singing soprano!" Romeo shouted out from behind them. He was halfway across the street, taking his time.

Juliet hadn't followed. Instead, she was back at their house, crouching near the front door. "Bitch forgot her bag! Got some nice stuff in here!"

Abby's backpack was open, and the girl was busy pulling out Abby's clothes, throwing everything around the lawn.

"Found it!" Abby got up, brushed the dirt off the key, and fumbled it into the lock. The moment she opened the door, the alarm panel off to the side started to chirp. Abby ignored it and ran for the kitchen.

Brendan shut the door and twisted the dead bolt as Romeo slammed into the other side. His considerable bulk and size shook the entire house, rattled the pictures on the walls.

"I'll huff and I'll puff, and I'll blow your house down," he sang in a low voice as he struck the door a second, then a third time.

The heavy bangs were bad.

The silence that followed when he stopped was worse. There was only the chirp of the alarm panel, then that stopped too. A moment later, the shrill alarm began to scream.

Brendan backed up slowly, then found Abby in the kitchen.

The pantry door was open, and half the contents were on the floor. Abby appeared to be grabbing boxes at random, dumping them, and throwing them aside. "Where did he say he—"

"Granola Whip-Its!"

"I don't see any Granola—"

In the living room, a window shattered. Another after that. Then a louder, deeper crash as Romeo kicked open the French doors. A harsh thud. The crack of plastic. The alarm went silent.

Brendan ran to Abby, grabbed her around the waist, and pulled her into the pantry. He closed the flimsy louvered door behind them. Abby kept looking as he peered out through the thin slots. He saw Romeo's shadow first, growing on the kitchen floor like some monster waking in a child's nightmare.

"Gee, Juliet. Where do you think those two could possibly be hiding?"

He kicked a box of Cheerios, sending cereal skitting across the tile. When he turned toward the pantry door, he made no effort to hide each crunch of his feet. He wanted them to hear.

Brendan didn't know when Juliet entered the house, but when she spoke, she sounded like she was either in the living room or standing at the kitchen door. "I don't know, Romeo. Maybe they snuck out the back and they're long gone. They're awfully smart. Got a leg up on us for sure. Maybe we should just give up and go home."

Romeo drew closer to the pantry door, his large frame blocking out the light.

Brendan didn't realize Abby had found the gun until she pulled the trigger.

Stuckey had said it was only a .38, played it off like it was some small gun, but the explosion in that confined space was anything but small. There was a hefty bang, followed by a ringing in Brendan's ears. That was followed by three more shots as Abby emptied the gun into the pantry door. Brendan had no idea how many shots a .38 held, but he thought it was more than four, which meant Stuckey had hidden the weapon away without ensuring it was fully loaded.

The shots ripped through the thin wood of the door.

One moment it was solid, then there were four holes, each about the size of a dime.

"Goddamn it!" Romeo cried out from the other side. "You clipped me!"

Brendan twisted the knob and threw all his weight against the pantry door. It swung open and slammed into Romeo even as he was staggering back. Romeo slipped on the cereal, lost his footing, and dropped. He cracked hard on the floor and Brendan saw a growing red stain in the man's shirt above his left flank where at least one bullet had found him. He jumped on Romeo's chest and began punching wildly at his face.

Brendan had never hit anyone before. The man's jaw felt like steel. Like Brendan was hitting concrete. There was a satisfying crunch as Romeo's nose cracked to the side. His lip opened. Brendan kept hitting. Even when two of his knuckles split, when his blood mixed with Romeo's, he kept hitting.

Romeo was barely phased.

He laughed. "Oh, it's good to be alive!"

With a sharp scream, Juliet jumped on Brendan's back. She wrapped her legs around him, grabbed a handful of his hair, and yanked. "*WHAT YOU DOING TO MY ROMEO'S FACE!* Get off him, you shit!"

Her free hand reached around Brendan's head, and he only caught a glimpse of her long, sharp nails as she went for his eyes.

Brendan slammed his head back and connected with her bony chin.

He didn't notice Abby exit the pantry, nor did he see her reverse the gun in her grip and bring the butt down on the girl's skull, he only heard it. Juliet went stiff and tumbled from his back. She landed in a heap next to Romeo on the floor.

Abby grabbed Brendan's shirt and pulled him to his feet. Together, they ran for the garage.

52

Stuckey's Tesla was in the garage.

Stuckey had purchased the car, a black Model S, a few months earlier, telling Hannah it was necessary to help him through his second midlife crisis. They'd installed a charging station at home, but it died last week, and Stuckey hadn't gotten it fixed yet. Their office building only had two, so the odds of beating the other EV owners were slim, and not one Stuckey was willing to take, so the car was gathering dust.

"I'm driving!" Abby called out, jumping into the driver's seat.

Brendan rounded the car and got in beside her. He tapped the garage door opener on the visor, and the door started to lumber up.

Abby was staring at the unfamiliar dashboard. "How do you start this thing?"

The key fob had been left in the center console; it looked like a computer mouse. The only buttons were for the door locks and front and rear trunks. No start button. Abby rolled it between her fingers and dropped it into the cup holder.

Brendan tried to remember what Stuckey had told him. It was something strange. Then it came to him. "Hold the brake pedal down for three seconds."

Abby jammed her foot down on the pedal.

The dashboard came to life, and when she pressed the accelerator, they shot forward, the car moving in near silence.

Romeo appeared at the door leading back into the house, his hulking frame so large he looked like he might get stuck walking through. His face was a bloody mess, his yellow teeth lined with crimson as he grinned like a toddler standing at the entrance to Disney. "Leaving already? That's a shame!"

There was a hole in his shirt where the bullet struck him, and although he'd lost some blood, he seemed unfazed. The cowboy hat was gone, his dark hair hung in greasy tangles. He reached for a hammer from Stuckey's workbench and lobbed it at them as they shot past—it crashed through the back passenger window and thumped down on the seat.

Romeo stepped out to the driveway and watched them as Abby turned left at the street and jammed down the accelerator. The car shot forward like a rocket with nearly no sound. As they passed their house, Brendan eyed all of Abby's things spread out on the lawn, the entire contents of her backpack. Then he realized his suitcase was still out there somewhere too. He couldn't remember when or where he'd dropped it. Probably in Stuckey's house.

"Damn," Abby muttered, looking up at the rearview mirror.

"Now what?" Brendan managed, twisting around in his seat to get a look out the back of the car.

Juliet was behind the wheel of the red van. She stopped in front of Stuckey's house only long enough for Romeo to climb in, then she accelerated too. A cloud of black smoke sputtered from the back, and they began to pick up speed.

Although she was already going nearly twice the posted limit, Abby sped up.

"There's no way they can catch us in that piece of shit."

The sentence had barely left Brendan's mouth when the display in the center of the dashboard went red. A message appeared in all caps:

TWO-FACTOR AUTHENTICATION FAILED.
AUTHORIZED MOBILE PHONE NOT DETECTED.
ENTER SECURITY CODE TO AVOID
VEHICLE SHUTDOWN.

53

Abby took her eyes off the road only long enough to read the message. "Did Stuckey give you the code? Any idea what it is?"

"He never told me." Brendan stared at the screen. "I never saw him enter anything either."

The code was six digits.

There was a timer. It had started counting down from sixty and only had thirty-seven seconds left.

Brendan instinctively reached for the phone in his back pocket and remembered his mobile was in pieces back at their house. Abby's too. "Don't these cars have some kind of built-in phone? Check the steering wheel!"

Abby found a button on the right back side of the wheel. That caused the timer to minimize as the center screen cycled through various options with each press. She landed on the phone screen when Stuckey's picture appeared—he was calling them.

Twenty-two seconds.

Brendan clicked *Accept*. "Stuckey, we're—"

"What the hell you doing in my ride?"

"It's me, Brendan. Abby's with me!"

"No shit. You're on camera. Want to explain why my phone is lighting up with pictures of you stealing my car? Why the fuck did you leave the office? Do you have any idea how much trouble you're in?"

Twelve seconds.

"I need your override code!"

"What override code?"

"For the car!"

"Why?"

Brendan glanced out the back. Piece-of-shit or not, the van was gaining. "No time to explain! What is it?"

"I don't know. Hannah set all that stuff up." He went quiet for a moment. *"Is my back window broken? It's hard to see from this angle."*

Five seconds.

"Forget the goddamn window, Stuckey. Somebody is trying to kill us!"

"What?"

They didn't have time for this. "It's the app! It's made by International Entertainment—that's INTENT!"

One second.

The screen flashed red. All four doors locked, and the vehicle began to slow.

Abby frantically jammed her foot down on the pedal. "Everything shut down! Nothing's working!" Then her eyes went wide as the steering wheel twisted in her hands, moved on its own—the car pulled itself to the curb and rolled to a gentle stop.

The red van came up behind them so fast Brendan thought for sure they'd hit. When Juliet realized they'd stopped, they were close enough for Brendan to see the panic in her face. She jammed down the brakes—the back tires locked with a loud squeal. They fishtailed and came to a halt within a foot or two of the Tesla.

"Shit, Stuckey, the code!"

"Try Bourbon1 with a capital B. Hannah and me use that for everything."

"That's not it! It's six digits, all numbers!"

Romeo climbed out of the van.

His shirt and jeans were covered in blood. His face was a mess, yet he'd found his cowboy hat and put it back on. He spied Brendan watching him, gave him a wink, and reached back inside the van. He retrieved a baseball bat. Spinning the wooden bat in his large hand, he started toward them. The fucker was whistling.

Juliet rolled the driver-side window down, climbed halfway out, and perched on the opening. "You teach, 'em, Romeo! Messing up your face like that. Bust his skull wide like a pumpkin the day after Halloween!"

"Stuckey…what's the code? Think!"

"Hmm. Maybe try 696969?"

Brendan mashed the buttons. Another buzz. "That's not it!"

Romeo swung the bat. He smashed the taillights on the right, then shuffled a few steps and destroyed the ones on the left.

"Hannah would have used your birthday!" Abby shouted. "It's her combo at the gym!"

"Really? That's sweet."

"WHAT THE HELL IS IT, STUCKEY!"

"012482."

Romeo brought the bat down on the rear window, shattering the glass.

"Oh, hell no!" Stuckey cried out over the car's speaker.

Brendan entered the code.

The screen flashed green, and the message vanished, replaced by a map of their current location and info on the active phone call.

Abby wasted no time.

She threw the Tesla in reverse, stomped down on the accelerator, and hit Romeo with enough force to knock him down. Brendan thought she'd run him over—part of him wished for it, wanted to feel the satisfying bump, hear the crunch—but instead, she put the car back in drive and raced off.

Brendan didn't see Romeo get up, but he had no doubt the big man had.

54

"You still there?"

Stuckey's disembodied voice came from the speakers all around them.

With no sign of the van, Abby left the residential roads and took the ramp to I-90.

Brendan finally faced forward and melted into the seat. The adrenaline fled him as quickly as it had come, leaving his body feeling like an empty, tired husk. Every inch of him began to hurt— arms, legs, back—he looked down at his hands, his split knuckles. Swollen. Dripping onto Stuckey's leather seat. "We're still here," he managed.

"How bad is my car?"

As Abby maneuvered them onto the highway and gained speed, wind whistled through the missing windows. The back seat was covered in glass. With the taillights gone, they'd surely get pulled over if a state trooper got anywhere near them.

"We need another car," he told Abby.

Without taking her eyes off the road, she said, "We need money. We're not doing much of anything with $380."

Stuckey cleared his throat. *"Why exactly do you need a new car? What did you do to my baby?"*

"Stuckey, forget the car, did you hear what I said? INTENT owns the app."

"INTENT is a lending facilitator. Why would they own a sex app? Hold on a second—" Stuckey's voice went muffled as he covered the phone and spoke to someone else. He came back a moment later. *"You're on I-90, right? You need to come back to the office. It's not too late to try and fix all this, but you need to come in now. Both of you."*

Brendan gave Abby a nervous glance. "Who are you talking to? How do you know where we are?"

"You're in my car. I can see where you are on the Tesla app. I can also do this—"

The car jerked softly.

"We're slowing down." Abby stomped the accelerator, but nothing happened. "Stuckey, knock it off!"

The car jerked again, and they began to pick up speed.

"Are you watching the battery level? You're almost out of juice. You've got enough to make it to the office, but you try to run, and you'll be dead on the side of the road in under thirty minutes."

Brendan leaned over and studied the various electronic gauges. Abby pointed at the battery indicator. It was at seven percent.

Stuckey's voice dropped low. *"Brendan, I'm not gonna lie to you. They restored Kim's laptop from one of the backup images. They have all the photos and the back and forth between the two of you. If you come in, you still have time to explain it all. They don't know how Abby fits in, but none of the theories are good. I'll help you explain, get in front of all this. But you need to come in now."*

Brendan glanced over at Abby, who was staring ahead worriedly, weaving them through traffic. "Maybe we should. Where else are we going to go?"

Abby's gaze remained fixed on the road.

She said nothing.

Stuckey cleared his throat. *"You don't come in, you run, you know how that will look. Brendan, we—"*

His voice cut off. The center screen flashed, and the *Sugar & Spice* logo appeared:

App successfully updated!

The car jerked forward, accelerated.

"Brendan, that's not me!" Abby looked down at the pedals, then back at the road again. "I'm not doing that!"

Their speed began to climb.

75

83

92

98

Text began flying across the screen, random sugars and spices:

What is the craziest thing you've ever done with your partner?
What color underwear is your partner wearing today?
Would you sacrifice your own life for your partner's?
Would you die for your partner?
Would you die for your partner, <u>right now</u>?

The messages began flying by so fast, Brendan couldn't read them.

Abby yanked hard on the wheel, maneuvered around the back of a slow-moving semi, and nearly hit a Chevy pickup when she came around the right side. She swerved to their flank, cut into the breakdown lane, and somehow managed to claw back on the pavement, coming within inches of the bumper. "The car's fighting me! It won't let me steer! We're going to wreck!"

They were still picking up speed.

104

107

Brendan reached for the wheel, and when his fingers wrapped around the hard plastic, he felt it vibrating under his hand, fighting Abby, fighting him. When Abby tried to pull to the left, get in front of the semi, the wheel jerked in that direction, tried to run them into the truck's cab. It took all their strength to keep the car from ramming the truck. The force increased, like the Tesla was attempting to overpower them. If the key fob hadn't slipped in the cupholder when they swerved, Brendan wouldn't have noticed it, wouldn't have remembered it was there. It was pure luck. Like a fucking sign.

Brendan grabbed the key fob and threw it out the missing back window.

The screen flashed red, *Key Fob Not Detected,* appeared in the center, and the car immediately began to slow. He didn't know if Abby managed to navigate them to the shoulder and off the pavement or if that was the car again. He didn't much care. The moment they stopped, he yanked off his seat belt and tumbled out the door to the wet grass.

A moment later, Abby dropped down next to him.

Brendan put his arm around her shoulder and pulled her close. He buried his face in her hair.

They sat there for the longest time.

Sugar & Spice™

Sugar
Share your darkest secret with your partner.

55

Abby and Brendan walked along the edge of the highway, followed it about two-thirds of a mile to the next exit, then trudged down the off-ramp until it intersected with Linden Street near Allston. They held hands the entire time, their fingers intertwined, squeezing, grappling for a closeness they both desired but couldn't quite find, even in each other.

At the base of the ramp was an old Gas 'N' Go. Run down, but serviceable. Signs out front boasted spectacular sales on cigarettes by the carton and twelve-packs of Michelob Ultra. People buzzed around the pumps. A baby cried from one vehicle; a golden retriever watched them from the open window of a GMC pickup. Some woman pushed through the double glass doors, furiously scratching the first of many lottery tickets in her hand with the edge of a quarter. She crossed the parking lot to an old, double-parked Chevy Malibu next to the Dumpster, oblivious to her surroundings.

Standing there, still holding Abby's hand, Brendan watched all of this, the ordinary nature of it all, and began to doubt all the events of the past hour. It hadn't been real. It had been some kind of dream, vision, hallucination. Anything but real, because the things that happened in the past hour, those things didn't happen to real people. Those things only happened in the movies. Streaming shows. Books. Not in real life. He'd been to this gas station before, about six months ago. The GPS had routed him off the highway to avoid some accident, so he'd stopped to fill up and grab a can of Coke. He'd been ordinary then. An ordinary moment. He so desperately wanted to be ordinary again, and for one brief second, he was. Then Abby's finger twitched across one of his bruised knuckles, and he looked down at their hands folded together. Some of his blood stained her skin. More stained her jeans. Then he saw the gun. Stuckey's gun. She was holding it in her free hand, dangling openly at her side.

"Jesus, Abby—" He snatched the gun from her, stuffed it in his waistband behind his back, and untucked his shirt to help cover it up. "You've been carrying that the whole time?"

She looked at him, but said nothing.

Her face was expressionless.

She was in some sort of shock.

For all Brendan knew, he was too.

He pulled her close and brushed some loose hair from her eyes. "Listen. We're going to go inside and get cleaned up. If there's an ATM, I'll take out whatever I can. Then—"

"You take out money, and they'll know." Abby sounded nothing like herself. Her voice was flat, hypnotic.

"We don't have a choice. Besides, if they're watching us that close, they'll know where we left the Tesla. They'll know we walked to here. So we hurry—we get some cash and use it to get some-where safe. We get all the money we can and go off-grid—we stay off-grid—until we figure this out. Does that make sense?"

Abby nodded. "Brendan?"

"Yeah?"

"Is Connie dead?"

Yes.

"I don't know. Let's hope not. Come on."

He led her through the double doors into the gas station's small convenience store. He spotted an ATM to his right and a sign for the bathroom near the back. "You go first. I'll get the cash."

She didn't move.

He pulled her close and nuzzled his face in her hair, spoke quietly, "We'll figure this out. I promise. It will all be over soon. We need to stay strong."

With a soft nod, her hand slipped from his and she made her way around the narrow aisles to the back corner.

At the ATM, Brendan took out his bank card and keyed in his security code. He clicked withdrawal and entered $3000. A message came up and told him the maximum withdrawal permitted was $500.

He swore under his breath.

Even with the $380 they already had, that wouldn't be enough. Hotels, food—they needed a car. How the hell could they go off-grid with less than a thousand dollars? They'd have to hit more than one machine. From here, they'd walk down the street until they found a used car dealer. They'd hit every ATM along the way. Whoever was tracking them would certainly figure that out, but once they had a car, they could vanish. They just needed to move fast. Not give anyone enough time to get here.

Brendan changed his withdrawal amount to $500 and pressed the enter button. *Authorizing* appeared on the dirty screen.

A moment later, *Funds Not Available* appeared.

Frowning, he changed the amount to $300 and got the same message.

Sweat broke out on his brow as he clicked back through the screens until he found the option for a balance inquiry. He selected it and waited.

The machine spit out a receipt.

When Brendan found the available balance on the thin paper, he could only stare.

.12

He found the same amount in their joint savings account.

"No. No. No. No. No!"

"Everything okay over there?" the cashier asked. An older man wearing a Patriot's sweatshirt. "It can be slow sometimes. I think it still uses dial-up."

Brendan waved a dismissive hand at him and tried one of his credit cards. It came back as *Declined*.

He smacked the side of the machine.

"Hey!" the cashier shouted. "Do that again, and I'm calling the cops!"

"Sorry," Brendan managed. "It's been a tough morning, and my card isn't working."

The cashier got a better look at him, saw the blood on Brendan's hands. A tear in his shirt. "Maybe I should call the cops. What you been into?"

Abby came out of the bathroom. She'd pulled her hair back into a ponytail and washed her face. She untucked her shirt, too, covering the blood on her jeans. When she sided up next to Brendan, he handed her the receipt with their balance, his hand shaking.

She studied the number and blew out a breath.

Something about her was different.

Somehow, in that short amount of time, she'd regrouped.

Gone was the look of shock, replaced with a look Brendan knew all too well. It was the same look she had when she painted herself into some corner while writing, the look she had when she'd placed a character in some impossible situation and needed to come up with a way out to continue. Her brain was running on overdrive. Working the problem.

Abby patted Brendan on the butt.

When she spoke, there was a twang to her voice, some accent. She spoke loud enough for the cashier to hear. "That's my fault, honey. I went shopping yesterday and cleaned out our checking. My paycheck should hit tomorrow, no worries. Do you want something?"

Brendan watched as she crossed the small store, went to the register, and put a pack of gum on the counter. She pulled a couple of crumpled bills from her pocket and called back to him over her shoulder. "Last chance, baby-cup."

"I'm fine."

Abby scratched her cheek. "Suit yourself." To the cashier, she said, "Can I get a pack of Marlboro Lights and one of those cheapo throwaway phones you got there?"

The cashier gave Brendan another quick glance, then turned and plucked a pack of cigarettes from the overhead rack at his back and put them on the counter. Then he removed a burner phone from a display to his right and set it down next to the gum. "Your man's got a bit of an attitude problem."

"Oh, he don't mean no harm. How much?"

"$26.58. Need a bag?"

"No, thanks." Abby handed him thirty dollars. "Keep the difference, for your trouble."

Scooping up the phone, gum, and cigarettes, she went to the door and hollered back at Brendan, "You coming?"

He followed after her, dumbstruck.

On the sidewalk outside the store, he said, "What the hell was all that? You don't smoke."

"When the police ask him who he thinks stole his car, we don't want him describing us. We want him to describe someone else." Abby held out a small ring of keys and pressed the button on the attached key fob.

A rusty Honda Civic chirped to their left.

56

"Hold still, baby." Juliet hovered over Romeo, an alcohol-soaked cloth in her hand. She'd set his nose and was wiping away the blood. "It ain't so bad. You'll be pretty again in no time." She kissed his forehead. "You're still my cuddly teddy bear."

They were in the back of the van, parked two blocks down from the Hollander place. He'd cranked the AC before they climbed in the back, and now he wished he hadn't done that. Chills kept running through him, made his whole body quake. He tried to will them away, but they kept coming. Goddamn adrenaline wearing off.

The gunshot hurt like a son-a-bitch, but that beanpole of a woman couldn't shoot for shit, and the bullet had gone straight through his love handle. Wasn't much of nothing compared to other times he'd been shot. Most of the bleeding had stopped by the time Juliet got his shirt off and cleaned up the wound. Truth be told, he was more pissed about the shirt. He loved Boston, and as far as he knew, they weren't touring no more. The tee shirt was priceless, and she'd fucked it up. He'd rain down a special kind of hell on her for that. He'd make Abercrombie watch.

Romeo's phone rang from someplace up front.

Juliet froze mid-wipe, her head slowly swiveling toward the sound. "It's her, ain't it?"

It would be her, all right. Nobody else had that number. Only her.

She wouldn't like any of this.

Not one bit.

"Hand it to me."

Juliet didn't move. "Maybe you shouldn't answer. Let her think you're busy or something."

You don't *not answer*. Not for her.

"Hand it to me," he repeated.

Juliet let out the breath she'd been holding and retrieved the phone, gave it to Romeo.

The caller ID name was blank, and the number that appeared below made no sense—there were too many digits, and it started with a four. Some country code, probably. It didn't matter, she was bouncing the call, always did. She could be right outside the van, for all he knew.

Romeo cleared his throat and answered the call on speaker. "We had a bit of a situation at the Hollander place, but we got it under control."

She didn't speak. Rarely did.

He glanced to the corner of the van, at the pile of laptops, tablets, and pieces of cell phones they'd retrieved from inside both houses. "We have all their hardware. I had to blaze both houses. The second one had an alarm, and those shitknockers set it off. We had no time for cleanup."

In the Hollander house, Romeo had used the gasoline he'd found in the garage next to their lawnmower. With the house across the street, he'd had to get a little more creative. He'd turned on the gas burners, blew out the flame, and lit up a tub of Crisco oil on the counter. Both houses had gone up nicely.

"The bitch shot me. I couldn't leave blood behind, you know that. Stuff we touched. Figured the alarm would bring the cops. We only had a few minutes. Not enough time to clean the place, so I made a call. A good one, 'cause the cops *did* show. We barely had time to do what we did, but we got things contained."

"Sloppy."

She spoke low, almost a whisper. Or maybe it was some kind of electronic voice-garbler—she'd used those before. Either way, hearing any kind of response from her side of the call caught him off guard. Another chill rolled through him, crawled over his bones, and clawed at his skin. He told himself that was still the adrenaline.

"The police won't buy any of that as an accident. They'll circle back to the gas explosion at Dubin's house. Maybe the Messings' place too. They'll tie them all together and know they weren't accidental either. You're compromised. And you let them go. You lost them."

Romeo swallowed. "Ain't nobody compromised, and we didn't lose no one. I know where they're going even if they haven't figured it out yet. We got this. Don't you worry your"—he almost said *pretty little head* and realized that might be just enough to paint a target on his back—"Don't you worry one bit."

The woman hung up.

No good-bye, no click, the call simply dropped.

Romeo should have felt relieved by that, but he didn't. He looked over at Juliet. "We may need an exit plan. Something sooner over later."

Juliet let out a soft *tsk* and went back to work on his wounds. "Ain't no running from her, you know that. We best finish the job. We're close. We get it done for her, we're set for life. That's our exit plan. Ain't no other way out."

Juliet dabbed at a cut next to his right eye. The alcohol-soaked rag felt like a hot knife. Romeo sucked some air from between clenched teeth, then willed the pain away. Told himself he felt nothing until there was nothing to be felt.

He was pretty sure he knew where they were going, but that hinged on one simple question that was out of his control. *Were they smart enough to figure it out?*

Romeo was pretty sure they were.

He'd put dollars on the Skinny Bitch before Abercrombie, but together they'd piece it together. The real question was, how long would it take them?

"How much time we got?"

Juliet fumbled around her feet, found her phone, and held it out to him so he could read the display. The timer said—

57 hours, 36 minutes, and 19 seconds.

Come on, Skinny Bitch. Connect the dots.
Come to daddy. Daddy needs a payday.

57

The Civic smelled like old pizza. The back seat was piled high with dirty laundry. The brakes squealed whenever Brendan applied pressure. Water dripped from the rotted rubber around the sunroof even though it hadn't rained in more than a week.

Never have I ever stolen a car.

"Drink," Brendan muttered under his breath.

"What?"

He shook his head dismissively.

Abby had been busy searching the car for anything useful—under the seats, the glove box—she even crawled in back and picked through the laundry, then checked the hatchback where she found nothing but a rusty tire iron, a flat donut spare, and an assortment of trash from various fast-food restaurants.

She climbed back into the passenger seat, tried to fasten the safety belt, then gave up when the latch wouldn't work. "Hopefully this guy is working a double and won't notice his car is gone until late."

"I think we did him a favor by stealing it."

After leaving the gas station, Brendan took a right at the first traffic light, then a left at the next. He had no destination in mind, but every bone in his body told him they needed to keep moving.

"You told Stuckey this was INTENT. What is INTENT?"

The word seemed foreign coming from Abby's mouth, and hearing it threw him for a second. "It's the peer-to-peer lending firm we've been investigating at work. Their CFO has been stealing funds from the company and laundering them in Laos. We seized it all, over two hundred million. He wasn't acting alone. Their offices in Chicago are empty, the entire staff is in the wind. At least three people are dead. Now Dubin and probably…"

"Kim."

Brendan nodded.

"Could this be some kind of retaliation?"

"For seizing the money?" he considered that. "I don't know. Maybe. I'm not sure what any of this means."

"It means," Abby said, "someone is using the app to silence people. That *Spice* I received said *Would you kill a total stranger to save your partner's life?* I didn't follow through, and someone else killed those people in Brookline anyway." Her eyes went wide. "The guy in the van, Romeo, he said we were his ticket to platinum."

Brendan made another random right turn. "Come on, Abs, nobody is going to kill someone to get points in a game."

Abby had no response to that. She went quiet. A moment later, she pointed to the right. "Turn in there."

A Walmart parking lot.

"Why? We should keep moving."

"We'll be quick."

He thought she meant to buy something, but instead Abby directed him to a crowded corner of the parking lot and told him to park. He found an empty space. When he switched off the engine, it sputtered a few times before finally going silent.

Abby plucked two dimes from a pile of random coins in the ashtray and handed one to Brendan. "Use this to take off our license plate. Don't let anyone see you."

She left the car before he could say anything.

Brendan climbed out and rounded the Civic. He was on the last screw when Abby returned with another license plate. She handed it to him and took his when he got it off.

"I'll put this back on the other car," she quickly explained. "They're less likely to notice that way."

Brendan found himself staring at her. "Where is all this coming from? Hell, you stole this car like you spent your youth in and out of juvie instead of private school."

Abby licked her lips. "I just keep asking myself if this were my book, what would my lead character do. WWED. What would Emily do."

"Emily seems to know her shit."

"That she does."

"I don't suppose you know how the book ends, do you?"

"Not yet."

Brendan tried not to sound overwhelmed, but he was. "Abby, they emptied our bank accounts. Our credit cards aren't working... These people have reach."

"I think we gave them permission to do that."

"How?"

"Remember what Stuckey showed us? How the app was using the camera on our phones, the microphones. I think we gave the app permission to view data from other apps. There's no way to know for sure, but if that's true, anything we had on our phones was compromised. Usernames, passwords, anything we typed or said near enough for our phones to pick up."

"Everything was on our phones. Our entire lives."

"We have to assume they know all our friends, all our contacts. They could use our GPS data to figure out every place we've ever been. Every place we could possibly go."

"How do we hide from that? It's like they're in our heads."

Abby shook her head softly. "I don't know."

When he finished and stood, Abby took both his hands in hers. The blood was dry, but they were bruised and swollen. "Does it hurt?"

Not as bad as it did," he lied. "I'll live."

Reaching into the back of the car, Abby took out a plaid button-down shirt and a Red Sox ball cap. She put the hat on his head and handed him the shirt. "Go inside and wash up. Change into that. Bring the bloody shirt back out with you, don't throw it away. Things like that always get found. We'll get rid of it somewhere else."

The hint of a smile caught the corner of his lip. "What would Emily do?"

"WWED." She nodded. "Emily would go somewhere she could think and figure out how to stay alive. Then she'd solve this."

58

An hour later, Brendan shifted the car into park.

"Are you sure about this?"

"No," Abby replied softly. "But it's all we've got."

"What did you say his name was?"

"Harlan. Dr. Harlan Bixby."

They'd gotten to Donetti's office building as Bixby, the psychologist who shared Donetti's office, was walking out the door. He climbed into a late-model gray Saab and drove downtown to a popular fifties-style diner off Legacy Boulevard. He made a quick call from the car, then went inside.

Brendan eyed the .38 in Abby's hand. "I don't know if you should bring that."

"If he's part of this, I don't want to go in there without it."

"It's empty."

"He won't know that. What if he has one?"

"If he has a gun, I doubt it will be empty." Brendan chewed the inside of his cheek for a second. "Maybe I should carry it."

"Why? Because you're a man, or because of your extensive training and background with firearms?" she replied. "How many shots have you actually fired?"

"Well, none but—"

"I've fired four in self-defense. That's four more than you. Recent experience, I might add. That means I win."

Before Brendan could object, she was out the door and halfway to the diner's entrance, the gun hidden under the folds of her shirt. He swore softly and chased after her.

Pushing through the doors, they stepped back in time.

The walls were teal and white, lit by an assortment of neon signs. Red leather booths, black-and-white checkered floor, an old Wurlitzer jukebox against the far wall belting out Elvis from honest-to-God records. The place was packed for lunch.

A red-haired hostess appeared wearing a white uniform and plucked two menus from a stand on her left. "Got a couple spots at the counter if you want to sit now. It will be about twenty minutes for a table or booth."

When she glanced down at Brendan's scabbed knuckles, he shoved his hands in his pockets.

"We're meeting someone," Abby told her, scanning the crowd. When she spotted Bixby sitting alone in a booth about two-thirds of the way down the window-covered wall, she stepped around the woman and started toward him.

Brendan took the menus from the hostess, thanked her, and followed.

Abby slid into the booth opposite Bixby, Brendan beside her.

Bixby appeared startled, stared at them both, his face filled with confusion. When he recognized Abby, he grew tense. "This is a... coincidence."

"It is not," Abby said flatly. "We followed you."

He glanced briefly at Brendan and started to rise.

"Sit. I don't want to shoot you."

"Shoot me?"

Both Abby's hands were under the table. She raised them just enough for him to see the top of the gun, then eased the weapon down and out of sight.

Bixby settled back in his seat, his face pale. "I don't know what this is about, but I'm meeting someone, and they'll be here any minute."

"We won't be long. Slide your phone across the table."

He stared at her for a moment, like she spoke in some foreign tongue, then took his phone from the front pocket of the leather briefcase on the seat beside him and did as she asked.

Abby nudged Brendan with her elbow. "Check if the app is on there."

Brendan picked up the phone, tapped the screen to wake it, and looked at Bixby. "What's your passcode?"

His eyes dropped to the table, like he could see the gun through the wood. "Seven-three-two-five-eight-one."

Brendan keyed that in and swiped through the various screens. "I don't see it."

"That's good."

The color started to return to Bixby's face. "See what? What is this about?"

Abby licked her lips. "We need to find Dr. Laura Donetti."

He appeared puzzled. "I left you a voice mail, didn't you get it?"

Abby shook her head.

"About an hour after you left."

"I've had phone trouble the last few days."

Bixby let out a frustrated sigh. "Look, it's probably nothing, but—"

When he reached for his briefcase again, Abby raised the gun. More of a reflex move. Her hands thumped against the bottom of the table.

To his credit, Bixby didn't jump at the sound. Brendan knew the gun wasn't loaded, and he still jerked in his seat.

Bixby held both his palms out to her. "I'm just getting something out of my briefcase."

"Slow," she told him.

He reached inside and produced a prescription pill bottle. Handed it to Abby.

Brendan was nervous.

And when Brendan was nervous, he had a hard time sitting still. A harder time keeping his gaze on the man across from him in the booth. Instead, his eyes wandered. Normally that was a bad thing, but if his eyes hadn't been wandering, he might not have noticed the older couple at the far end of the counter staring at them, nor would he have noticed the way they quickly looked away when he caught them looking. Both were holding their phones.

"Abby, I think we have a problem."

The absurdity of that statement hit him right after he said it. His wife was sitting next to him, pointing a gun at some man he'd never met. Their bank accounts were empty. And someone tried to kill them only a few hours earlier.

"Can I get you something?"

None of them had noticed the waitress approach. She was hovering over the table, holding a small pad and pen.

"No thanks, we're leaving in a second," Brendan managed.

When she walked away, he spotted the old couple watching them again. It wasn't just them, there was a large man in a red flannel shirt and a Patriots cap two stools over, also watching them. Unlike the older pair, he made no effort to hide the fact he was staring.

Even when he glanced at his phone, he looked right back up. Met Brendan's eyes. Like he was confirming something. Like he was looking at a photograph and confirming—

"Abs, we seriously need to go."

Ignoring Brendan, Abby studied the pill bottle. It was orange. About half were gone.

"She left that behind," Bixby said. "I found it in the top desk drawer. Lamotrigine. That's usually prescribed for seizures."

Abby turned the bottle to the side and studied the label. The name read Lois Donatelli, not Laura Donetti. "How do you know it's hers?"

"Nobody else used the office. Similarity in the name. Who else could it be? I couldn't find any record of a Laura Donetti in the area, but I did find a Lois Donatelli near Fenway." From the same pocket of his briefcase, he produced a small piece of paper with an address written in neat script.

"Did you Google it?"

"I didn't Google. I checked Zillow, that real estate app. It's a duplex." He looked nervously at the door. "Look, just take it and go. My patient will be here any minute. It's only our second meeting. She's in a delicate place. I don't want her to get spooked."

A woman two booths down was watching them now too.

Five people.

No, six.

A cook had come out of the kitchen, his phone in a greasy hand, staring right at them.

"Abby, they know we're here."

That finally got her attention.

Abby looked back up. When she did, they both noticed at least four other people turn away and go back to their meals. Neither saw the young girl approach their booth.

She came down the aisle. Dark hair, large silver hoop earrings. Torn jeans. She studied Abby and Brendan nervously as she stopped next to the doctor. "Sorry I'm late. Do you need me to come back?"

Bixby gently shook his head and leaned closer to Abby and Brendan. "I won't tell anyone. Just go. Walk out and leave. As far as I'm concerned, I didn't see a..." He nodded at the table. "I didn't see anything."

The young girl seemed to sense something was wrong. She shifted her weight slightly, back on her heels, her body growing tense. For the first time, Brendan noticed her left eye. It was dark, the remnants of a bruise concealed under heavy makeup. She couldn't be more than fourteen.

Bixby reached into his briefcase and took out a pamphlet. Although he covered it with his hand when he set it on the table, Brendan caught a glimpse of the title: *Hampton House - You're Safe Now.*

"Abs..." Brendan said softly, reaching for her hand. "He's right. Let's go."

She saw the pamphlet too, the girl's eye. The way the girl was looking at the door like she was having second thoughts.

Bixby mouthed, *Please.*

"I saw you on the news," the girl said, her voice timid. "It's on all the channels."

Abby was halfway out of the booth.

She froze. Stayed where she was.

Brendan felt her press the gun into his hand. He quickly slipped it under the band of his jeans and concealed it under his shirt.

Abby reached for Bixby's phone, which was still on the table. She tapped on the browser app, then clicked on *News.* When the headlines appeared, her face lost all color.

59

Back in the Honda Civic.

Racing down I-90.

"We need to call Stuckey," Brendan said from behind the wheel. "Warn him. Maybe that FBI agent I worked with in Chicago, Bellows. Maybe he can get us all into protection."

Abby had her finger on the radio's scan button, jumping from station to station in search of the news. She'd wanted to take Bixby's phone, but Brendan told her they couldn't. It was too easy to track. They had the burner.

The radio landed on a Britney Spears song, and Abby mashed the button in again. She flipped past three more stations before finding another news broadcast:

"...although the fire is contained, both houses are gone. Brendan Hollander is wanted in connection with the disappearance of this woman, Kim Whitlock. His wife, Abby Hollander, is a person of interest in an arson case in Brookline earlier today. Authorities believe

the Hollanders started the fire in their own home to conceal evidence before stealing the vehicle of a co-worker who happened to live across the street and setting a fire there, too. The stolen Tesla was recovered on I-90 approximately three hours ago near mile-marker 102. It is believed Brendan and Abby Hollander proceeded from there on foot to a nearby service station where they attempted to withdraw funds from an ATM. Their whereabouts beyond that are unknown, but they are most likely still in the greater Boston area. Again, if you see this man or this woman, do not approach them, contact the authorities immediately. Detective, do you have anything to add?"

There was a soft shuffling.

Movement of the microphone.

"Through a joint effort with the FBI, information here is coming together quickly. Brendan Hollander may be connected to several other deaths in Chicago. There is a very good chance the pair is armed. I can't stress this enough—people like that are no different than an animal backed into a corner. Their only thoughts at this point are escape and self-preservation—do not get in their way. If you spot them, dial 911." A familiar triple chime rang out from the speakers—from the phone of someone attending the press conference. The detective paused for a second, then continued, *"They are believed—"*

Abby clicked off the radio. "You heard that, right? The chime?"

Brendan nodded.

"Who are these people? Why are they doing this to us? My God, they burned our house down..."

Her voice trailed off as that last part sank in.

His head was buzzing with thoughts, but nothing made sense.

"We can replace the house. At least we're okay," he told her, because he could think of nothing else.

They weren't okay, though.

They were so far from okay.

They were driving to an address tied to a pill bottle found in the desk drawer of some man he didn't know because they had nothing else.

No place to go.

No one to turn to.

Nothing.

Abby's voice had gone so quiet. "Were those people in the diner staring because of the news, or did they all have the app?"

"I don't know."

"When we first downloaded it, it was the number-one app in the store. What does that mean, people-wise? How many people have it?"

"I don't know."

"Could they all be helping them find us?"

"I don't know."

"Brendan, who do you think—"

"I DON'T FUCKING KNOW, OKAY?!"

The second he shouted it out, he wanted to take it back, but there was no taking it back. Abby eased to the opposite side of her seat and slumped against the door, like she wanted to get away from him and that was as far as she could go without jumping from the car.

Brendan ran his fingers through his matted hair. "I'm sorry, Abs. I just…I'm sorry."

They rode in silence for nearly a minute, then Abby said, "I feel it too, but we can't take it out on each other, we do that, and we're done. I know Donetti wasn't a real doctor, but something she said was true. We need to be each other's champion. We work together, we can get through this, but if we back away into our own corners, we isolate from each other, it's over. We can't let this tear us apart. Doesn't matter how hard it gets."

Signs for Fenway Park appeared, and Brendan took the Charlesgate exit.

"Isn't Beacon faster?"

Brendan said, "It's too public. We should stick to back roads in case someone saw the car at the diner. WWED."

"Emily would probably get another car."

"I'm sure she would."

Brendan wanted to change the subject, maybe ask her about her book, but couldn't bring himself to do it. Her computer had been locked up with that ransomware. The printed copy on her desk would be gone. Anything she wrote in her notebook would be gone. Her agent was dead. Instead, he reached over and took her hand in his. "There's something else we need to consider. You're not going to like it." He chewed his bottom lip for a second. "Maybe you should turn yourself in, tell them I took off on my own and you don't know where I am. I could drop you somewhere. Just give me thirty minutes or so, enough time to—"

"Did you miss my little speech about sticking together?"

He shook his head. "I can't drag you deeper into this, Abs. Not if there's a way to get you out. If it's really about INTENT, that means I brought it all on us. Even the mess with Kim. You deserve better than me, Abs. All the garbage I've put you through…"

Abby squeezed his fingers and went quiet for a long time. When she finally spoke, her voice was hesitant. "When you first told me what happened with Kim on that trip, you know what really frightened me? It wasn't that you may have cheated on me, it was the idea of going on without you. Up until that moment, every thought of the future I had included you, the two of us, together. But you told me what happened, and I suddenly saw a very different future. I'd never felt so alone in my life. Uncertainty. Fear. If I left you, I knew I'd eventually be okay, I'd land on my feet, that's not the part that scared me. It was thinking about all the moments we wouldn't have. I know what our children will look like. I know their names. I can see them playing in the yard, tumbling through piles of leaves… with you. I see me on book tours. Calling you from every stop, hearing your voice. I can see us both old, surrounded by family. All the laughter. The warmth of it. I see it all like this quilt patched together with everything we have and will accomplish together. I saw all those things the first time we met at the movie theater back in college. I saw it again the day you proposed. And if I close my eyes, I'm sure I'd see it all now. Without you, there's nothing. Nothing I want, anyway." She wiped the moisture from her glassy eyes. "So no, you're not dropping me off anywhere, we'll finish this together."

Brendan swallowed. "Wow."

Abby's face flushed red. "Too much?"

"Just enough." He reached up and stroked the side of her cheek. "I love you, Abs. There's never been anyone else for me, and there never will be. When I told you about Kim, I should have told you that, too. I don't say it enough. You deserve to hear it more. Thank you for being you."

They were quiet then as the conversation settled over them. Not an awkward silence, but the kind of quiet that can only be found with someone who truly understands you, someone who can hear the things spoken between the words.

They were still holding hands when Brendan made the turn on Peterborough Street.

He pulled to a stop at the mouth of an alley, across the street from the address Bixby had given them.

"That can't be right," Abby said softly, studying the house. "Can it?"

60

A colorful sign near the street read LITTLE TIKES DAYCARE.

The house behind it was large. Older. A duplex, like Bixby had said. Red brick with two bright blue doors. The daycare appeared to occupy the space on the right with a residence on the left. The side yard was fenced in. Six or seven children were busy running and climbing around a well-kept playground—two slides, a swing set, a large plastic pirate ship, a pink plastic house beside it, seesaw—all housed on islands of brown mulch in a sea of green grass trimmed neat and short. An elderly man wearing a Patriots sweatshirt stood in the corner looking over everything like some father hen. When Brendan shut off the motor, the children's laughter and voices filled the Civic's interior. Considering everything that happened over the past few hours, it felt like they'd entered another world.

Abby took the gun from the center console. "Loaded or not, we can't bring this into a daycare."

Before Brendan could point out they might be walking into the kind of situation that desperately warranted a gun, she opened the glove box and shoved the small weapon inside, concealing it behind the mess of papers and trash. She had to slam the rickety plastic door three times before the lock caught.

"No gun," she said, reading his thoughts in that way only wives could.

Brendan dropped it and looked at himself in the mirror.

His cheek was bruised and darkening, there was no hiding that. Anything to make himself less recognizable was worthwhile, though, so he tucked his hair into the ball cap as best he could and smoothed out the wrinkles in his shirt. He wiped his palms on his jeans and swiveled the mirror back. "If this is wrong, we get out fast. I'm guessing that's what Emily would do."

Abby let out a nervous laugh as she straightened her own clothing. "Maybe you should let me do the talking. I know *exactly* what Emily would do *and* say."

They locked the car—guns may not enter daycares, but they sure as shit wanted it to be there when they got back.

Crossing the street hand-in-hand, Brendan opened the door for Abby. A small bell chimed as they stepped inside.

Like the sign and playground, the small lobby was awash in color. Murals of children covered all the walls, and the ceiling was painted a light blue, filled with puffy clouds made of cotton, lit by strands of LED twinkle lights. There were two purple couches and several bean bags in the center of the room. A short counter lined the wall just inside the door. On a stool behind it, a young woman of maybe twenty looked up from a dog-eared paperback of *Where the Crawdads Sing*. Her blonde hair was cut in a short bob, and she wore blue denim overalls over a loose white tank top. She marked her page with her thumb and smiled. "Hello. May I help you?"

"Oh, I hope so," Abby told her. "We just moved to the area, only about two blocks from here, and our little one is three. With both of us working, we're hoping to find a nice place for her to spend the day. Are you currently accepting new children?"

"As luck would have it, we have an opening as of yesterday." She shuffled through some paperwork behind the counter and produced a clipboard and pen. "If you could fill this out. I'll also need to make copies of your driver's license. You said you have a girl?"

Abby was about to answer when an approaching voice called out from the hallway behind them. "Sally, I'm gonna hit the store and get some watermelon for the kids, it's such a nice—"

Brendan and Abby turned to find Donetti standing there, frozen, car keys dangling from her fingers.

61

Donetti's mouth fell open, and her eyes shimmered with something that couldn't be mistaken for anything but fear. "You can't be here," she finally managed. "They'll find you here." She glanced at an open window. "The children…you need to go."

Brendan took a step toward her. "We're not going anywhere. You owe us some answers."

"I don't owe you anything."

The girl Donetti had called Sally was still holding the clipboard. She gently set it on the counter, took a step back, and reached for her phone. "Lois, do you want me to call the police?"

Lois.

Abby held out her palms. "We just want to talk. Give us a few minutes, that's it, then we'll go. I promise."

"I've got nothing to say to you."

"Five minutes," Abby insisted.

She looked them both up and down. The tattered clothing. Bruises and cuts. Brendan had his hands in his pockets again, hiding his battered knuckles, little good that did with the blood on his jeans. Not much, but she didn't miss it. She took it all in. Donetti narrowed her lips and looked at the girl behind the counter. "No police, Sally. It's okay. I know them. Go outside and tell Mark to take the kids down the street to Sparkles for some ice cream. Clear everyone out for a little bit. We'll be fine."

"Are you sure?"

Donetti nodded.

Their eyes locked, and Brendan could only imagine some unspoken message passing between them. *Call the police the second you get out of here. Tell them they're here. Brendan and Abby Hollander. The ones from the news. Arsonists. Killers. You know the ones, right? The ones I'm talking about? Everybody probably does by now.*

Abby said five minutes, he was thinking more like three.

Moving slowly, Sally put her phone in her back pocket and rounded the counter. She gave Donetti one last worried glance before heading outside.

Donetti dropped her keys and cell phone on the counter and started back the way she'd come. "Let's talk in my office."

Brendan and Abby followed her down the narrow hallway past a large playroom on the right and a dark room on the left housing several cribs and a bassinet. Both rooms were empty. At the end of the hall were a storage room and a cluttered office with an old wooden desk, the paint faded and chipped, scratched with years of use. The computer in the corner looked like an antique, all boxy beige plastic, loud fan, with a giant CRT monitor. Donetti reached around the back of the tower and pulled out the power cord and network cable. Dropped them both to the floor. The room went oddly quiet.

"Do either of you have any electronics?"

They both shook their heads.

"Good." She settled into an old leather chair held together in several spots with duct tape. "How'd you find me?"

Abby took the pill bottle from her pocket and placed it on the desk.

Donetti stared at the bottle for a moment before picking it up and rolling it between her fingers. "Well, fuck me. I thought I left them in my car."

Brendan waved his hands around the room. "What is all this? Who the hell are you?"

Abby placed her hand on Brendan's arm to silence him and asked Donetti, "Please tell me that girl isn't calling the police."

"She won't call anyone unless I tell her to. She's fine." Donetti sat the pill bottle down on the corner of the desk next to a pack of cigarettes and a lighter. Her hand hovered over them for a second, then she must have decided now wasn't the time for a smoke. Instead, she frowned at Brendan. "Business is hard enough. The last thing I need is the police storming in here and arresting wanted killers on live television. Sally knows that." She turned back to Abby and let out a rough sigh. "Look, it was a *Spice*, that's all. No different than half the shit that app has probably thrown at you. One *Spice* of many. It gave me an address, told me to dress conservatively, and pretend to be a relationship therapist." She gestured around the small office. "This is who I really am. I opened the daycare twelve years ago with my husband. He ran off with his secretary eight years ago. Dede. All tits and ass, with nothing but a hollow echo between her ears. Apparently, they'd been balling in his shit hole of an office at the insurance company while I was putting in eighteen-hour days trying to get this place off the ground. Fuckers. The both of them. Now, it's only me and a handful of part-timers. Business is good, but my sex life has been shit since Lou left so I downloaded the app. Heard about it at my hair salon and figured, what the hell, a girl's got needs…" She got lost in her thoughts for a moment. "Honestly, I get off on role-playing. Always have. When the two of you came into that office, I thought the whole thing would turn into some sort of three-way. That's the kind of thing that usually happened with the app, so I played my part and waited for one of you to make a move. We got a few minutes into the *session*"—she did air quotes around the word—"and I got the feeling that wasn't what you were there for, or you weren't into me, whatever, so I played along. I played the part. That's all it was for me. I collected my reward from the app, and that was that."

"That was that," Brendan muttered, flashing back to that initial conversation. "Are you fucking kidding me? Do you have any idea what you got us into?"

Donetti narrowed her eyes at Abby and jerked her thumb back at Brendan. "Can you keep this one in check? I don't need to tell you any of this. I probably shouldn't anyway."

There was an electric pencil sharpener on her desk. She glanced at it, then pulled the cord from the wall, twisted it in a ball, and put the entire contraption in a drawer.

Abby squeezed Brendan's arm. "Please? Let her talk?"

Brendan pinched his eyes shut and nodded. "Sorry."

Donetti gave it a second before going on. "Look, you do what the app tells you. Bad things happen when you don't. They tell you that early on, and it's no joke. I guess the two of you have figured out that much for yourselves. What did it ask you to do? Or I guess the real question is *what didn't you do?*"

Abby went quiet for a second. No doubt trying to decide if she should tell her. The words came out with a cautious hesitancy. "It wanted me to kill someone. Someone I didn't know."

If Donetti was surprised by this, she didn't show it. She gave them a soft shrug of her shoulders. "Whoever it was probably had it coming. If you're gonna sweat the small stuff, good luck getting to the next level."

This was Donetti, yet it wasn't. Brendan felt like he was listening to some alter ego or Donetti's twin sister. It wasn't only the shabby/comfortable clothing—so different from the office attire he'd grown accustomed to seeing her in, but her voice, her persona. The similarities this woman had with the one they'd shared their lives with were dropping fast, like a costume falling away, piece-by-piece, revealing the true person beneath. She'd always appeared cold, but in a clinical way Brendan had assumed was part of her profession—don't get emotionally attached to the clients—but it had nothing to do with that. There was ice in this woman's eyes, warmed only by greed.

"The...small stuff?" he finally managed.

This actually amused her. "Look, there are eight billion people on this rock of ours. Maybe a tenth of those are worth a shit. If someone is going to pay me to thin the herd, who am I to bitch about it? I took out some worthless crack-whore a year back, made enough to buy a minivan to transport the kids around town. If that's not trading up, I don't know what is."

Brendan did his best to keep his voice in check. "Made enough? So they paid you?"

Donetti settled back in her squeaky chair. "Has anyone explained the point system to you?"

Both Abby and Brendan shook their heads.

Her eyes grew wide at that. A grin formed at the edge of her mouth. "So you don't know..."

They'd already been there far too long, and Brendan wasn't in the mood for games. It took all his willpower to keep from jumping across the desk and throttling the woman. Instead, he stared at her until she continued. Abby too.

Donetti licked her lips. "What level are you?"

Abby glanced at Brendan, then said, "I'm bronze. Brendan is still…"

Donetti waved her hand through the air. "He's still a nobody. How many points do *you* have? His are meaningless if he's still a newbie."

"The last time I looked, around 6200. It might be more, though."

"What level again?"

"Bronze."

This time, Donetti looked directly at Brendan. "You work in finance, right? Is it clicking yet, Mister-Big-Shot-Moneyman?"

It wasn't *clicking*. The only thing *clicking* was the clock in the back of Brendan's head, the amount of time they'd been here. When he didn't answer, Donetti asked him another question. When she did, it did *click*. It clicked right into place.

Donetti asked him, "What is the going rate for one ounce of bronze?"

"About sixty cents."

She tilted her head. "Okay, do the math."

He tried to hide the surprise in his voice. "You're saying she doesn't have 6200 points, *she has 6200 ounces of bronze?*"

"Bingo!" She beamed like he'd just cracked the genetic code. "About four thousand dollars' worth. Not much, but it's something. The real money doesn't kick in until the higher levels—silver, gold, platinum—there's even one called elite. I've got no clue how that works. Thanks to the two of you, I'm a silver member knocking on the door to gold."

"How could they…How many users do they have?" Brendan was trying to work it all out. When he and Abby had downloaded it, *Sugar & Spice* was the number-one app in the store. What had Abby asked him? How many users did that equate to? A lot. "How can they afford that?"

Abby spoke the answer about the same time it popped into his head. "Brendan, you said they emptied our bank accounts. Maxed out our credit cards…"

"Wealth redistribution," Donetti said emphatically. "That's all it is. Robin Hood shit. The second someone hits bronze, they pull all their funds, put the money god-knows-where, and the exchange system kicks in. You begin earning precious metals. Each point is worth one ounce of whatever level you're on." She tilted her head toward Brendan. "I'm guessing all your accounts were in both your names, right? That made them fair game when wifey moved up to the big leagues. Fair game for the game." She said that last bit proudly, impressed by her rhyme. "It's all spelled out when you sign up."

"Who's running it?" Brendan prodded.

Donetti's face went smug. "How the hell should I know? I'm just a player. Same as you."

"You must know who's paying you."

She shook her head. "If I need money, I liquidate in the app and funds drop into my checking account. I don't know who is on the other end of that. Don't really care. The name is different every time, anyway."

"Does the name INTENT mean anything to you?"

Again, she shook her head.

Abby was staring at Donetti's charm bracelet.

When Donetti caught her, she held up her wrist and flicked the two small metal squares. "What? You got one, too, right?"

"Mine only has one charm."

Brendan got a closer look. There was a bronze charm with 73 on it and a silver one with the number 9. "This is from the app? What does it mean?"

She gave a dismissive grunt. "Without all four, it doesn't mean much of anything. I was told you get all four and type the numbers on the Internet and you'll learn how to find the Fall Ball. It's like a game within the game."

Brendan exchanged a look with Abby, then asked, "What's the Fall Ball?"

She rolled her eyes. "Christ, didn't you read any of the fine print? It's an annual thing where all the high rollers get together." She ticked off her fingers, "Bronze, silver, gold, platinum. If you're platinum, you've got all four numbers. That gives you the location. The rest of us bottom-feeders only get to speculate on the debauchery that takes place there. I'd sure as shit like to know."

"Four numbers typed into the Internet," Brendan muttered. "Are you saying it's an IP address?"

Donetti only smiled.

He didn't need her to answer. He knew. He'd taken a training class on this exact thing two years ago. Although people used words—domain names—to visit various websites, the Internet converted those words to numbers, and those numbers told your browser where to go, what to load. All IP addresses were assigned to local service providers in large blocks. Because of that, the address could be tied to a physical location.

"Where is 73.9?" Brendan asked her. "I bet you figured out that much."

The smile on Donetti's face went sly. "I'm sure you could hazard a guess."

He didn't have to. Abby said it first.

"Chicago."

There was a landline phone on her desk. It began ringing. When Donetti reached for the receiver, Brendan grabbed her hand.

"I have to answer," she told him. "You've seen what happens when you try to ignore them."

"Okay, but on speaker," he told her.

She gave him another shrug, then pressed the speaker button. It was the same female robotic voice Brendan had heard back at his office—

"Congratulations! You've earned five hundred points!"

"Five hundred points for what?" Abby asked.

"Well, that's obvious. For keeping you here long enough for Sally to get the shotgun from my place next door."

Behind them came the sound of a shotgun slide raking back, followed by the *ker-chunk* of a round being chambered.

62

Sally stood at the mouth of the hallway, just outside the office door, the butt of the shotgun resting low against her waist, the barrel aligned loosely with Brendan's head. "Stay put."

From the phone on Donetti's desk, the robotic voice continued—

"Press one for Sugar or press two for Spice."

"Don't," Abby said softly, no doubt knowing this woman would do it anyway.

Donetti's hand hovered over the buttons as she calmly asked Sally, "Did Mark get the kids out?"

"They're down at Sparkles, probably knee deep in sugar. I told him to call me before coming back."

The robotic voice repeated:

"Press one for Sugar or press two for Spice."

Donetti eyed the phone curiously. "They asked me to detain you. Don't ask me why, but the app wants you alive. Or maybe they just don't want you to die here. Who knows. I guess I should be grateful for that. Honestly, you'd be better off if I put a bullet in your head. Got it over quick. The two they got coming for you...wow...what a piece of work they are. If they're supposed to take you alive, that means you've got something they want. God help you. I've seen what they do to people who have something they need. I'd swallow rat poison before I'd let them get me, that's for damn sure."

"Press one for Sugar or press two for Spice."

"Gotta admit, I am a bit curious. How about you?"

Brendan watched her finger drop and press the two button. The triple chime played from the phone.

"You've selected Spice. *Congratulations! Please sit perfectly still."*

That only confused her. "Why? That doesn't make any sense."

"They must know I'm not a very good shot," Sally offered.

She jerked the barrel of the shotgun up and pulled the trigger. A fiery blast burst out with a deep explosion, catching Donetti in the chest. She slammed back into her chair, rolled, and smacked the wall behind her. Her head slumped. Dead eyes stared at the ground.

As the deafening rumble faded, replaced by a high-pitched ringing in Brendan's ears, he heard the triple chime again. This time, from the phone in Sally's back pocket.

Sally chambered another shell and leveled the shotgun at Brendan's chest. "She really should have read the terms of service. Revealing the app's payment structure without prior approval is a violation of the rules. These people are sticklers for the rules."

315

Brendan dropped to his left, drawing Sally away from Abby. He hit the ground hard and rolled, somehow managing to catch the shotgun barrel with the corner of his right foot.

Sally fired again, more of a reflex—she pulled the trigger as Brendan's foot connected with the barrel—the shot sailed high and to the side, blasting a hole the size of a bowling ball in the wall behind Donetti's lifeless body.

Abby jumped from her chair and slammed into Sally's gut. The air left Sally with a grunt, and both women crashed to the floor in the hallway as Brendan scrambled to his feet. He'd never seen Abby hit anyone, couldn't recall a single moment where she'd ever gotten violent, but she tapped into something primal. Her right fist came down hard on Sally's chin followed quickly by her left. A sharp edge on Abby's wedding ring opened a cut nearly two inches long. Sally managed to pull the shotgun trigger again, but without having chambered a new round, it only clicked.

Brendan stepped on the shotgun, crushing Sally's fingers between the trigger guard and the hardwood floor. She howled.

When Abby rolled off her, Brendan wrenched the weapon away. He grabbed both Sally's wrists. "Get me something to tie her up with!"

Looking around the office, Abby grabbed the power cord from the computer and the lighter from Donetti's desk. As Brendan held the girl still, she wrapped the cord around the girl's wrists as tight as she could, then used the lighter to melt the plastic together.

"WWED," Brendan said softly.

"Exactly."

Sally coughed. A trickle of blood dripped from the corner of her mouth. "You are so dead."

Her phone let out the triple chime again.

Abby took it from her pocket.

The screen had cracked during the scuffle, but the message was still readable:

Spice completed?

As usual, the only available response was *Ok.*

"Should we click it?"

"They'll know it's not me," Sally managed.

Brendan grabbed the girl under the chin. "Who's coming? Is it the two in the van? How far away are they?"

Sally seemed to revel in the fear and frustration Brendan's voice held. When she grinned, blood outlined her white teeth. "Do you have any idea how many people are looking for you? There are players everywhere. On the streets. In the supermarket. School teachers. Police. Rumor is the bounty they have on your heads is one of the largest they've ever offered. You think Romeo and Juliet are scary? At least you can see them coming. Try hiding from a kid looking to make a name for himself. Or some homeless man who wants to line his pockets. Hell, the leader of the local PTA. A gangbanger. The whole gang."

Brendan shook her. "What do they want from us?"

Sally only smiled.

"I'm pushing it," Abby told him.

She tapped on *Ok.*

Sally's phone chimed again and said—

Congratulations! You've earned 1000 points and graduated from Bronze to Silver! Would you like to try a related Spice?

Before either of them could stop her, Sally shouted, "Yes!"

Brendan Hollander has a .38 stolen from Stewart Morland. Use it to shoot at least three of the children in your care, then wound yourself. When the authorities arrive, tell them: "Prior to fleeing, Hollander killed my boss, the children, and shot me." Be sure to wipe your prints from the .38. They may test you for gunshot residue, this is fine. Tell them the shotgun belonged to your boss. You retrieved it when he started shooting, and you managed to fire a single shot in defense before he wrestled the weapon away from you and used it on her. You will earn an additional 3,000 points.

"Oh my god," Abby muttered.

"We need to go," Brendan said.

"We can't. If we leave and she tells the police this, they won't be looking to arrest you, they'll kill you."

"Then we take her with us. Get her to talk."

Abby was already shaking her head. "We do that, and these people make one phone call telling the same story, and they still blame you for Donetti. Donetti and kidnapping."

"At least nobody is shooting children."

Abby's mind was reeling. Playing chess. Trying to get three moves ahead. "All that means is *she's* not shooting children. They could get someone else to do it." She glanced over at Sally. "If what Donetti said about the levels is right, this girl just went from bronze to silver, she doesn't know anything. She's just a pawn. We need someone higher up if we want to figure out what's going on."

Sally's phone dinged again.

The cracked screen began to fill with video taken only moments earlier. Images of Brendan securing Sally, holding the shotgun. Only Brendan was visible.

The next video was far worse. A camera in the hallway, a long view of Donetti's office at the far end. Sally standing there with the shotgun, pulling the trigger. Donetti getting hit, visible over Sally's shoulder. Only none of it was Sally, somehow it was Brendan. Brendan's body. The back of Brendan's head. Brendan holding the shotgun. Brendan pulling the trigger.

"Hannah told me about this," Abby edged closer. "It's called Deep Fake. There are websites and apps that allow you to stitch one person over another. They can replicate voices too."

"This gets out, I'm fucked." Brendan frantically looked around the room, finding the cameras. There were four in the main room. One in the hallway. Probably more in those other rooms they passed. Outside too. There was no telling what they had on video or what they were doing with it. Particularly if they could edit on the fly so fast.

"Oh no." Abby pointed out the front window. To the red van parking at the curb. "They're here."

Brendan was still thinking about the cameras. "I've got an idea."

"You are so fucked," Sally repeated through a blood-stained grin.

"You too." Brendan grabbed the shotgun, swung it around, and brought the butt down hard on the side of Sally's head.

63

Romeo's gut hurt like a motherfucker. Like some asshole was twisting a rusty railroad spike around his innards and thumping the spike's backside whenever said asshole thought Romeo was getting a little too comfortable with the pain. The bullet had gone straight through. They'd been sure of that. Juliet had done a bang-up job patching him, it shouldn't hurt this bad. He'd taken some antibiotics—all they had on hand—should have been enough to hold back infection, so it probably wasn't that.

Probably.

They needed to score more, just in case.

Now wasn't the time to get sent to the bench.

They pulled this off. They were looking at the payday to end all paydays.

This was end game.

This wasn't life on the beach.

This was owning the beach.

She wanted these two in a bad way.

Romeo shifted slightly in the passenger seat, winced, and shook it off. Fuck the pain. Use it. They had a bottle of Oxy in the glove box, but he hadn't touched it, couldn't risk going sloppy. He told himself he'd take one when Skinny Bitch and Abercrombie were hog-tied in the back of the van. Maybe he'd take a handful followed by a nice, long nap. Maybe he'd have some fun with Skinny Bitch, then take a handful of Oxy, *then* take a nice long nap.

Propped up on her knees, Juliet hovered over the steering wheel looking at the duplex across the street with the blue doors. "Seems awfully quiet in there. What kind of daycare ain't got no kids? You sure about this?"

"I'm sure. They're here." Romeo knew the woman would have had the common sense to clear out the little shit factories, but he wasn't in the mood to explain things to Juliet, she'd piece it together soon enough. He'd be lying if he said things seemed right, though. "How 'bout you stay in the van, sugar-cup," Romeo told her instead. "Let me take care if this by my lonesome. I got a feelin'."

She looked at him only long enough to give him a cursory once-over before turning back to the window. "I can tell by your sweats you got a fever. You're as pale as a damn vampire. Probably got infection crawling all up in ya. The last thing I should do is stay in the van and let you go in alone."

"You're best behind the wheel. We may need to leave fast."

An H&K .9mm sat in the center console between them. Juliet picked it up and pulled back the slide to ensure a round was chambered, then checked the clip. "How 'bout I go in and you stay here?"

Romeo loved Juliet to death and beyond, but there were some things he wasn't comfortable with her doing on her own, and this fell smack in the middle of that list. He held out his palm and kept it there until she handed him the gun.

"I'm not out in five, you come in after me." He nodded at the wooden trunk in the back. "Bring one of the big guns. Something with kick. That work?"

He didn't give her a chance to answer. Sometimes with Juliet, it was better not to. Instead, he sucked in a breath, clenched his teeth in anticipation of the pain to come, and opened the door. He dropped his feet to the pavement and got himself standing. The hurt washed over him like a white cap in a hurricane—it started in his gut and radiated out until his vision went cloudy. He stayed still long enough for the worst of it to go away, then he took the pain and twisted it into something useful—motivation. Fuel. He sucked the pain back in and swallowed every bit of it, felt the burn of it in his throat like a nice shot of whiskey.

"Be right back, snuggle-bun." He blew her a kiss. "Love you bunches."

Juliet pretended to catch the kiss and brought it to her cheek.

He ignored the worry in her eyes as he turned and crossed the street to the daycare.

A bell above the door chimed as he stepped inside.

The smell of recent gunplay hung faintly in the air. Not much. Maybe three or four shots. Big shots, though. Not some peashooter, something with bite.

Some blonde girl was propped up against the wall. Unconscious, but alive. He knew that because the dead don't bleed, and blood was dripping steadily from a nasty scrape on her cheek. Her chest was rising and falling too, not much, but some. She had an ugly bump growing on her head.

He'd get to her in a moment.

Romeo tightened his sweaty grip on the .9mm and moved his index finger off the guard to the trigger before starting down the hallway at the far side of the small lobby. The smell intensified, and when he got to the office in the back—he understood why. What looked like a shotgun blast had made a nasty mess of some woman's stomach. Part of it was in her lap, the rest was on the wall behind her along with the back of her chair. There was another hole in the plaster above her head. At the sight of it, Romeo's gut-grazer shot didn't seem quite so bad no more.

An old landline phone was off the hook on her desk, making the buzzing sound they were prone to do when not hung up properly. Romeo's brain jogged back—he hadn't heard that sound since he was a kid. The hall phone back at the boarding house, not the one in Poughkeepsie, no phone in that shit hole, the one in Biloxi. The sound seemed so foreign in today's world of mobile phones, video calls, and general big-brother surveillance bullshit. Busy signals had gone the way of the dinosaur, cassette tapes, and good bands like CCR.

It was clear Skinny Bitch and Abercrombie were in the wind. He couldn't help but feel a twinge of respect for those two, not for the first time today. They were survivors. Romeo went back out to the lobby, and ignoring the pain it brought, he knelt beside the unconscious girl. When he saw the plastic power cord tied around her wrists, how it was melted together, he found himself smiling.

Fucking respect.

He'd have to add that one to his own box of tricks.

He stroked her cheek, making a lazy trail in the warm blood. "Hey sleepy-head, time to wake up."

When she didn't move, Romeo smacked her across the face. Gave her a good, hard blow. Her eyes snapped open, quickly filled with confusion at the sight of him, then ran through a whole gambit of emotions until there was nothing behind them but full-blown fear as recognition set in.

It was good she knew who he was, that would save some time. "What's your name, blondie?"

She swallowed, wincing as the pain from the bump on her noggin set in. "Sally. Sally Durham."

"Looks like things got away from you a little bit. That's a shame. Want to tell me where our friends are?"

Her head swiveled around the room like it rested on a loose hinge, like the weight of it had doubled. Her eyes trailed, wanting to follow along but unable to quite keep up.

Concussion.

No doubt.

"Eyes front." Romeo hit her again. Not as hard as the first time, but hard enough.

Her gaze snapped back to him, sharper this time. She licked away some of the blood from the corner of her lip. "Sorry."

"It's okay," he told her softly. "I've had my share of rough days too. I get it. Tell me what happened, don't leave nothing out, then we'll get you cleaned up."

She did.

The words came hard at first. They'd done a number on her jaw, and it was getting good and swollen, making it difficult to talk, but she did. To her credit, she got it all out. She even told him how they'd tackled her and taken the shotgun. She might have been ashamed, but she told him. She finished with, "I've got a new *Spice* on my phone. I think we should do it. They want us to shoot some of the kids and pin all this on Hollander. They're backing us with video. There are copies on my phone if you want to see. That's how we get out clean."

"They take the shotgun?"

Blondie nodded. "Must have."

Romeo settled back on his heels and studied her. She couldn't be more than what—twenty-two, twenty-three? She seemed to have a good head on her shoulders, even if she did royally fuck this all up.

She was trying hard not to let her emotions get the better of her. Another ten years or so, and she might turn into the kind of person he could work with. He brushed some of her hair back, tucked it behind her ear. "Got us a solid frame up? Video too, huh? You think that's what we should do? That make the most sense to you?"

"Yeah, if we—"

One hand under her chin, the other still on the side of her face, Romeo snapped her neck.

He loved the satisfying sound of it, like a thick branch wrapped in a warm, wet blanket.

There was also something in the way a body went limp. All tense and hard one second, then *snap!* and they go all rag doll. There was power in that, like the life left them and went into him every time he did it. So much better than a gun. Almost as satisfying as a knife. For the seconds that followed, his gut didn't even hurt.

Romeo had no trouble killing kids—he'd perfected that particular skill set when he still was one—but killing a kid only made sense when it made sense, and right now it did not. First off, there were none here and this didn't seem like a good place to hang around and wait for one. Not with shots fired and a dead body—scratch that— *two* dead bodies. They'd finger Hollander for this mess either way. A story like this was best told by the evidence, not a witness. Blondie would have only mucked it up.

Romeo realized he was still holding her limp head. He let her go and wiped his bloody fingers on her overalls and stood. That damn white vision came back, but only for a few seconds. He waited it out, then rounded the corner of the front counter.

The security system recorder was on the bottom shelf. Some fancy doohickey that stored footage on SD cards rather than tape or a hard drive. Normally, that would have been well and fine, but both SD cards were gone. Next to the recorder was a rack clearly meant to hold spare cards or previously recorded cards—that was empty too.

Although his brain was running a little sluggish, he didn't need all cylinders to figure this one out. If they had video to back up Hollander shot up the daycare, that meant they'd doctored the footage. The real question was, did they doctor the original or some copy? Hollander could start a fuck-load of trouble if he took the real footage, and it looked like he did.

Blondie had said, *"There are copies on my phone if you want to see."* Romeo sure as shit wanted to see.

He found Blondie's phone on the floor next to her.

When he picked it up. When he looked at the cracked screen, his heart thumped hard in his chest. Jackhammer hard.

There were no videos on the display; someone had dialed a number.

Someone was on the line right now.

Romeo brought the phone close to his lips and did his best to keep his voice calm. "Who do I have the pleasure of speaking with?"

He heard a soft inhale, then the call disconnected.

Whoever it was had heard everything since he arrived. His entire conversation with Blondie.

His heart thumped again.

Romeo took out his phone and dialed a number from memory. His brain was working just fine right now. Fear had a habit of kicking everything up a notch. Someone picked up but didn't speak. Like the woman, they rarely did. Romeo said, "I need you to run a number for me." He read off the last number dialed from Blondie's phone.

A soft male voice came back a moment later. *"The phone is owned by FCID. That's the financial investigative arm of the SEC. The registered user is an investigator called Stewart Morland. He's a silver member. Would you like his current location?"*

"Yeah. I think I would. Thank you kindly." He thought about

that, then changed his mind. "Better yet, send someone to pick him up. I got my hands full."

"*Understood,*" the voice replied, then hung up.

Romeo knew that name, Stewart Morland, but couldn't quite remember from where. He was trying to figure that one out when he heard an engine start up.

Across from the daycare, his red van pulled away from the curb and shot down the street.

Juliet was driving, but he also spotted Skinny Bitch in the passenger seat, and it looked like she had the barrel of the missing shotgun buried deep in Juliet's beautiful hair.

64

"*What the hell was that?*" Stuckey said on speaker after recounting what he just heard. "*Whose phone you using now?*"

Brendan crouched in the back of the van, holding a rusty metal bracket welded in the wall to keep from falling over as the red van rocketed down the road. "Donetti's, or whatever the hell her name is. *Was.*"

"*The therapist?*"

"Yeah."

"*She really dead?*"

"Please tell me you recorded all that. The whole call. Everything you heard."

From the driver's seat, Juliet let out a nervous laugh. "Romeo is going to fuck the two of you up real good for this. You best let me pull over so you can get out. Your only shot of seeing tomorrow is getting far from me and our van."

Abby pressed the barrel of the shotgun into Juliet's side. "We're already wanted for murder. What's one more?"

"Didn't take you long to go all Bonnie and Clyde, did it Karen?"

"Shut up and drive."

"It'd be nice if you told me where I'm supposed to drive to. Specially with the price of gas and all. I'd hate to knowingly harm the environment. This van ain't exactly eco-friendly."

Abby pointed out the window at an exit lane peeling off to the right. "There. Take Boylston to Ipswich Street."

"Brendan, you still there?"

Brendan turned back to Donetti's phone. "Stuckey, come on, tell me you recorded that call!"

"Yeah, yeah. I got it. What am I supposed to do with it?"

Reaching into his pocket, Brendan felt the SD cards. "Get it to that FBI agent, Marcus Bellows. Tell him any footage he might see of me killing Donetti is bullshit. It's doctored. I can prove it. I have the real video files with me."

"They'll say the files you have are fake!" Juliet called out from the front.

"Who is that?"

"It doesn't matter."

"What if she's right? Do you think Bellows will believe they're real? Why would he?"

"Because I have no clue how to fake something like that!"

"Look. Drive to the nearest police station. Walk in the door with your hands on your head. Drop to your knees. Give them zero reasons to shoot. Let them take you into custody. Nobody can touch you in a police station. They'll take the video files in as evidence, secure them. Maybe authenticate them somehow. You'll be safe. Abby will be safe. Then we can get all this sorted out."

Juliet laughed. "They'll stick you in a cell with a six-foot-four Aryan and tell him you shot up a daycare. He'll tear you apart and shit down your neck. Then they'll pay his buddies in the brotherhood and the cops who put you there with the app. Clean it all up neat and tidy by dinnertime. Don't think they won't."

"Will you shut up?" Abby jabbed the shotgun deeper into Juliet's side. "Turn on Mountfort. Right there. Then a left on Carlton."

"Turn yourself in, Brendan."

Brendan knew he couldn't do that. He and Abby had both heard the app's chime at the police press conference. Heard what Donetti said. Sally, too.

There are players everywhere. On the streets. In the supermarket. School teachers. Police. Rumor is the bounty they have on your heads is the largest they've ever offered… you've got something they want. I've seen what they do to people who have something they need.

The triple chime rattled from the phone speaker followed by the message:

Sugar and Spice and everything nice, that's what your future could be made of. Snips, snails, and puppy-dog tails… Give me what I want, or you'll soon hear the hollow clink of a coffin nail.

Abby heard it. "We need to lose that phone!"

Brendan quickly told Stuckey, "This is about INTENT. We must have picked up something when we were in their offices the first time. A photograph. A copied file. Something. Whatever it was, they're willing to kill for it. You're the best investigator I know. Dig. Tell Bellows I'll be in touch." Brendan disconnected before Stuckey could reply and began toggling through the screens until he found the Sugar & Spice app. He clicked it open. "Christ."

"What?"

"She's a silver member with 10,860 points," he explained. "If what she said was true, that's over two hundred thousand dollars."

From the driver seat, Juliet huffed. "Piker."

Brendan glared at her. "What the hell is that supposed to mean?"

"It means she's a small fish. A piker. Me and Romeo, we're gold. Haven't been no silver in maybe two years."

At the mention of silver, his eyes met Abby's. She knew exactly what he was thinking. There was nothing on the girl's wrists, but she was wearing an ankle bracelet. Abby reached down and yanked it from her leg.

"Hey, what the fuck?"

Flicking through the small metal trinkets, Abby found the one made of silver. "149!"

Brendan loaded the Safari browser on Donetti's phone and keyed in:

Where is IP 73.9.149?

When the results filled the screen, Brendan cursed softly. "Without the fourth digit, it's not enough. It's Chicago for sure, but I can't narrow it down any more than that."

Another message appeared on the screen. This one wasn't from Sugar & Spice; it was a security message from Apple:

Warning! An Apple AirTag not registered with this phone has been detected in your immediate vicinity and may be tracking your location via this phone and other Bluetooth devices.

Brendan felt deflated. That had to be Romeo. He quickly showed Abby.

She chewed her lower lip, took the phone from him, and threw it from her open window. To Brendan, she mouthed, *Find it!* When she turned back to Juliet, her face betrayed nothing. "Get off at Commonwealth. Watch for Chester and turn there." She jabbed her again with the shotgun. "Where's your phone? Give it to me."

"I ain't got no phone. I need one, I use Romeo's."

She was a horrible liar.

Brendan turned around and got a better look at the dingy van. At the sleeping bags bunched up in the corner, the small propane-fueled cooktop covered in rust and grease. AirTags were only about the size of a quarter. It could be hidden anywhere in the mess. He wanted her talking, distracted, so he asked, "If you have money, why do live like this?"

"I don't need nothing except Romeo, and he wants for nothing but me. You sit all nice and cozy in your big house surrounded by random stuff and think you got it so much better. Well, you don't. Ain't nothing better about that. Possessions bring headaches. Every last one of them is more weight on your back. It hurts until you can't carry no more. That big house of yours. Everything inside. Did that really make you a better person?"

Brendan wasn't about to get lectured by some homeless hippie hit woman. He tuned her out and started going through some wooden boxes someone had secured to the bump created by the wheel well. He found clothing, toiletries, some food. It wasn't until he opened the third box that he found the guns. At least a dozen of them. Everything from pistols to assault rifles. Cans of lighter fluid. "Abs, we got an arsenal back here."

He fished out a small .380, probably meant for concealed carry. It fit perfectly in his back pocket. He grabbed some ammunition too. A pack of zip ties. He almost missed a scrap of paper on the floor near his shoe. If he hadn't spotted his name written in scribbled cursive, he probably wouldn't have noticed it at all. When he studied it closer, he realized exactly what it was.

"Abs, I found some kind of hit list. Cindy Messing. Joel Hayden. Isaac Alford. AD Dubin. Me. Stuckey. We're all on here." Beside each name were numbers.

Points.

"Jesus," Brendan muttered.

From the front, Abby instructed Juliet. "Make a right on Ashford, then a left on Sawyer Terrace, then another left on the first gravel road. Follow it to the end."

Brendan shoved the list into his pocket.

Juliet did as Abby told her, although far slower than Brendan would have preferred. No doubt buying time for her boyfriend to catch up. Brendan was under no illusion they'd lost him. He could be tracking this van in any one of a million ways, and they only had a few minutes' jump on him.

They came to a crawl when the road narrowed due to cars parked tight on both sides.

"Where the hell we going?" Juliet was short. Half-standing to see over the steering while.

"Find a space," Brendan told her. "Park."

"There, that one." Abby pointed out the window. "Between the Audi and the green Toyota."

"That's a parallel space. I can't parallel park this thing. Romeo always does that."

"Park." Abby jabbed her again with the shotgun.

"You ain't gonna shoot me, so how 'bout you drop the pretense?"

"Like I wouldn't shoot your boyfriend? How many holes did I put in him?" Abby replied.

Maybe Juliet forgot it was Abby who shot Romeo, or maybe she'd just been so distracted she hadn't considered it since they grabbed her and the van, but the reminder brought it back. Front and center. Her eyes turned to beady little black pinpricks. "I should bite out your throat for that. Maybe I still will."

Angry or not, Juliet managed to get the van in the tight space. She bumped and nudged the Audi and the Toyota, but she got it in there and grumbled, "What is this place?"

"Put it in park. Shut off the engine."

Juliet did.

WWED, Brendan thought. It's now or never. He hadn't found the AirTag. In a minute, it wouldn't matter.

Brendan slung the backpack over his shoulder and opened the can of lighter fluid. He gave it a squeeze and doused the sleeping bags in the corner. The shelves. The box of remaining weapons and ammunition. He saturated the back of Juliet's seat.

When the scent reached her, Juliet twisted around to try and get a better look at what Brendan was doing. Horror filled her face. "You best not be thinking what I think you are."

"You burned down our house," Abby told her in a voice much colder than Brendan could have imagined coming from his wife's mouth. "Seems only fair we return the favor. I guess the real question is, will you be in the van when he lights the match?"

Brendan emptied the last of the cans on Juliet, then tossed it aside and got right up in her face with the lighter they'd taken from Donetti. "Where's your fucking phone? Don't lie to us again."

65

After Romeo hung up, he found a set of car keys sitting atop the counter at the daycare. He imagined they either belonged to Blondie or the woman with the basketball-size hole in her stomach down the hall. Either way, whoever owned it wouldn't need it no more and most certainly wouldn't be reporting it stolen anytime soon. While standing on the front stoop, he'd pressed the key fob a few times and followed the chirps to a white BMW parked at the curb. The car was older than dirt, but despite the faded paint and small pockets of rust, appeared to be well-maintained. It grumbled slightly when he started the motor, then fell into a steady rhythm.

When Romeo looked at his phone, he didn't have to waste time clicking through menus and typing this or that. The app had already loaded up a map and set two flashing pins—one for Juliet's location, another for the van. Now, both pins were on top of each other, indicating they were together.

He'd gone half a mile when two police cruisers rocketed by him heading in the opposite direction, no doubt heading to the daycare.

Aside from wiping his prints from anything he'd touched, he'd left the place as is. Blondie's plan to frame Hollander was sound—all but waiting for the kids, anyway. He knew he'd made the right call when he turned on Commonwealth and nearly got clipped by a Channel Seven news van racing after the cruisers. The app no doubt tipped them off and probably sent them the footage Blondie mentioned.

That was all about ten minutes ago, and Romeo was feeling pretty good about himself until he saw the smoke.

A thin black line rising from a half mile or so away.

Romeo knew what it was long before he saw the van. He'd started so many fires in his day; you got to know the different types based on their color and smell. Vehicle fires (especially those started with an accelerant) always went up black. It was all the plastic and rubber, the oil and grease. His van was no different.

He left the BMW in the middle of the gravel road, door open, engine running, and got as close to the van as he could, shielding his eyes from the heat.

The windows were gone, blown out. The thick toxic smoke belched out from the various openings like it was fleeing something far worse inside, and his mind immediately went to Juliet.

Had they killed her?

Left her to burn?

Did those two have it in them?

His gut twisted at the thought, and with that came the roiling pain from the infected hole in his gut.

Roles reversed, he would have killed Juliet.

She'd be in there right now, the fire eating the flesh from her bones.

That's what he would do.

You back even the most timid animal into a corner, and it will strike to survive. Skinny Bitch sure as shit had it in her, and

Abercrombie would follow like a lost puppy.

Romeo's legs didn't want to work, didn't want to get closer, but he knew he had to. He needed to know. His limbs heavy, he forced each step. When he couldn't take the heat, he rounded the side, came around to where the windshield had been. The black smoke rolled across his exposed skin like molten sandpaper. It seared his lungs with each gasp, each forced inhale. Yet he drew closer.

Through the heavy smoke, he only glimpsed the place where the driver's seat once was. The leather and padding were long gone, nothing but a jagged metal frame left. If Juliet had still been sitting there, she was there no more. While that offered him a little relief, it didn't mean she wasn't in the van.

Romeo turned his back to it all, tried to suck in a clean breath from the air behind him, but only managed to fill his lungs with more smoke. Either from the pain, the smoke, or lack of oxygen, his vision grew white again, and he found himself falling forward, dropping to the ground. He slapped hard against the gravel, felt it dig into his palms.

Without clean air, he wouldn't be able to help Juliet. He wouldn't be able to help himself. Without clean air, he'd pass out right there. This was where they'd find his body right before they pulled hers from the ashes.

He crawled.

Grabbing handfuls of gravel and dirt, he crawled until he reached the row of parked cars on the opposite side of the unpaved road. He was hauling himself back to his feet on the bumper of an old pickup when the van exploded.

The blast hit him like a Mack truck to the back, threw him forward and over the parked cars, into the grass, the ditch beyond.

Romeo blacked out.

When he managed to open his eyes, he didn't know if he'd been out for ten seconds or ten minutes. Time was lost on him. The van was still burning hot, though. The van was a funeral pyre.

He fumbled his phone from his pocket and managed to get the map back up. Both pins were gone—the one for Juliet's phone and the other for the Apple AirTag he placed under the driver's seat of the van last year. Both had vanished with the explosion. Romeo screamed out Juliet's name, but the only thing that escaped his lips was a charred, hoarse whisper.

He laid there in the dirt for maybe ten minutes. Would have laid there longer if his phone hadn't rung.

No caller ID, not even unknown caller.

Romeo swallowed.

He didn't want to talk to her.

Not now.

He also knew he didn't have a choice.

He brought the phone to his ear and answered. "Yeah."

"You've let things go too far. They're smarter than you."

"I got this."

"They're running circles around you. You look like a fool. We're exposed because of your idiocy."

"You've seen the news. They're putting all of this on him. Ain't nobody exposed."

She said nothing.

That was a mistake. He knew better than to contradict her. Romeo couldn't help it, though. Watching the van burn. Knowing Juliet…he'd cut the Hollander woman from cunt to her pretty little mouth while her man watched. He'd film it and play it over and over, listening to her screams like a goddamn lullaby. Then he'd go to work on Abercrombie. He'd make that last. Romeo licked his lips, tasted blood. "They kicked the wrong fucking hornet's nest."

Despite the pain, he got to his feet, stumbled across the gravel road, and rounded what was left of the van, giving it a wide berth to avoid the heat. He began climbing the hill behind it. There was no place else they could have gone, and they couldn't be far. "They're on foot. Close. Gotta be. You telling me to back off? Let 'em go?"

Again, she said nothing.

Romeo reached the top of the hill and looked down the other side at the largest train yard he'd ever seen. A giant knot of tracks lined with trains crawling away like mile-long snakes that just ate their fill. A dozen cargo trains. Hundreds of cars. They'd had enough time to board any one of them.

His phone let out a soft chirp, and when he glanced at the screen he realized one of Juliet's AirTag pins had returned. It was moving. Romeo resisted the urge to thank the Lord Almighty even though he didn't believe in none of that shit. "You gotta let me work."

The familiar triple chime played, and when he glanced back at his screen, a new *Spice* had appeared:

Would you kill another player to become an instant Platinum member and obtain automatic admittance to the Fall Ball?

Below the *Spice* was a map with a pin. It took Romeo a moment to realize the pin was marking his location, was marking *him*.

"If this business hasn't concluded soon, that Spice will go out to all members."

"Now, wait a minute, I—"

She hung up.

He damn near threw his phone but managed to keep his wits about him. The bullet hole in his gut burned hot, roiled with infection, and that was mucking up his thoughts, but he couldn't let it rule him.

He'd get Juliet.

He'd get them.

They'd get paid.

All this bullshit came down to those simple facts.

Fuck all the rest.

Peering down the hill at all the trains, he loaded up the location of Juliet's AirTag again. She was slowly moving away from him. Heading west. He eyed one of the trains; a long son-of-a-bitch—a hundred cars, maybe more—with an engine on each end, leaving the yard…also heading west.

They were breaking for Chicago, that's what he would do. Riding the rails left no record. That's what he would do, too.

He could wrap up this business in an hour.

One hand pressed against the wound in this side, Romeo started down the hill.

The train wasn't moving fast—it hurt like a son-a-bitch, but he managed to haul his broken ass inside.

Sugar & Spice™

Sugar
Would you recommend this app to a friend?

66

"There!" Brendan ordered, pointing to a narrow alcove between two pallets stacked with wooden crates at the back of the boxcar. "Sit in the corner and keep your mouth shut."

"Romeo's gonna fuck your world up!"

They'd zip-tied Juliet's hands behind her back and when she went to sit, she lost her balance and dropped down on the planked floor. That brought on a pain-filled grunt and an impressive string of curse words. Brendan waited for that to die down before he took the list of names from his pocket and held it out to her. "Tell me about this."

"Ain't nothing to tell."

Aside from the names Brendan recognized, there were nearly a dozen more. From what he could gather, most were INTENT employees but not all. Even Agent Bellows was on there. More than half the names had lines drawn through them. "Did you kill all these people?"

"I've never been much for killin', that's Romeo's thing. I love watching him do it, though. He's a artist. I can't wait to see what he does to you. I'm sure he's thinkin' up something real special."

"All the names you crossed off—the two of you killed those people, and the app paid you. That's what these numbers are?"

With that she only smiled.

In the van she said she was a gold member. Brendan added the numbers in his head and multiplied by the price of gold—it had been around $1,800 an ounce the last time he looked. When he came to a total, he second-guessed himself and ran the math again. Just the names on the list came to nearly $12 million and those were the ones crossed out. If he included the rest, that number more than doubled.

Like a cat chewing on the remains of a mouse, she smiled wider. "It's a lot of scratch, right?"

"Why them? What did they do?"

When Juliet didn't answer, Brendan took the lighter from his back pocket, grabbed a handful of the girl's hair, and lit the flame less than an inch away. "Let me be clear about something. If you think I won't hurt you, you're very wrong. After what you did to us, you're lucky to still be alive." He nodded toward the open door of the freight car. "We toss you out, do you think anyone would give a shit?"

"You don't got it in you."

Abby had saddled up beside him. She wrapped her hand around his, the one holding the lighter, and raised it until the flame caught the girl's hair in his other hand. The hair sizzled. Black fetid smoke drifted up stinking of sulfur. Abby pinched it out before it did much damage, but Juliet got the point.

"Why them?" Brendan repeated.

"Them are the ones she wanted dead, so we made them that way. An honest day's work for an honest day's pay," Juliet spat out. "She never told us why, just told us who."

"She?" Brendan glanced at Abby. "Do you mean Robin Church?"

"Who's Robin Church?" Abby asked.

"It's a name Kim stumbled into. It turned up on some of the paperwork we found."

"I don't know no Robin Church," Juliet said. "But that could be her. She never gave us no name. She's one pissed-off bitch, though, I'll give you that. They wronged her somehow, and she got no problem going for her pound of flesh."

Brendan took another look at the list. "Does the name Keo Sengphet mean anything to you? He's not on here."

"None of them mean anything to me."

Brendan lit the lighter again.

"No! I don't know no Keo Sengphet!"

Abby scanned the names too. "Who is he?"

"This guy," Brendan pointed, "Isaac Alford was stealing money from INTENT's client base. He worked with Joel Hayden to get the funds overseas, to Keo Sengphet at a bank in Laos. Sengphet is a known money launderer."

"So who are all these others?"

"Cindy Messing was a low-level accountant. We think she figured out what was going on or was part of it and turned on the others. The other crossed out names worked at INTENT too. Alford couldn't pull off something like that on his own. If we dig deep enough, we'll probably find all these people were involved. This woman is silencing them."

"Robin Church."

"Yeah."

"What about this one? Roland Ludlow."

His name was circled. "He's the head of their software development division."

"Software. Like apps?"

Juliet whistled softly, the same notes as the app's triple chime. "Would you like to select a *Sugar* or a *Spice?*"

"He's still alive?" Brendan asked Juliet.

"No more alive than you."

"One thousand points. That's almost two million dollars just for him."

"He's a sandy beach," Juliet muttered more to herself than to him.

"He'd know what's going on," Abby said. "Wouldn't he?"

"He might."

That's when Juliet screamed.

Juliet twisted her head toward the open freight car door and let out an ear-tearing screech. "Romeo!"

Brendan scooped up the shotgun and cracked the butt against the side of her head. It was only a glancing blow, but it stunned her into silence.

Abby nervously glanced out the open door at the train yard beyond. "We need to gag her. We don't want her attracting attention. Let me see the tape."

Brendan reached into the bag with his free hand and fished out the duct tape and a black sack he'd pilfered from the van. He handed both to Abby and turned to get a better look outside. The train was moving, but barely. So damn slow he wanted to jump back out the open door of the freight car and push. Every inch of his skin was crawling—some weird lizard-brain thing. His instincts were telling him Romeo was probably right behind them. He easily could have boarded any one of the cars and begun a systematic search.

Off in the distance, black smoke filled the sky, a thin stream still rising from the van.

"Stay away from the door, Brendan. Most of this place is

automated, but there are still a few people around. Probably cameras everywhere, too."

When he looked back, Abby was smoothing out a second piece of tape. The girl was still grumbling but barely audible now. When finished with the tape, she slipped the bag over the girl's head so she could no longer watch them. Then Abby leaned back on her heels to admire her handiwork.

WWED.

Brendan told himself never again to get on his wife's bad side.

He handed the shotgun back to her. "I thought this place was closed."

"Technically it is," Abby explained. "But until they reroute all the tracks, most of the trains in and out of Boston have to pass through here. I stumbled into it researching the new book."

Brendan had seen numerous stories on the news about Beacon Park Yard over the years, going back at least a decade. He vaguely remembered Harvard bought it at one point, but nothing came of it. They faced too much opposition. Too many politicians and wish lists. Too many deaf ears unwilling to listen to each other. The land sat. Forgotten. For an abandoned train yard, it was bustling. Trains everywhere, all moving at glacial speed as they navigate the maze around each other. Some switching tracks, others passing through. A million places to hide, nearly all on the move.

Brendan was under no illusion they'd lost Romeo, but he felt they'd bought some time.

He led Abby around several pallets stacked to the ceiling with boxes, all secured beneath a thick layer of shrink wrap, and found a place to sit on the opposite end of the freight car, as far from Juliet as they could get.

Although it had been less than a day, it felt as if they hadn't stopped moving in a month, and the moment they settled into that dark corner the rush of energy that had been driving them seeped away, replaced with something that wasn't quite calm but held a meager hint of relief.

Abby's head settled against his shoulder.

Brendan wanted to tell her everything would be ok. He wanted to tell her they would find a way out of all this, but he didn't, he couldn't. Because he saw no way out. When his eyes drifted shut, the darkness brought demons, the darkness brought fear. There was no rest, there was just that incessant triple chime rattling through all else like a death march.

67

Christ, Romeo's gut hurt.

The goddamn infection wasn't happy living where it started and decided to branch out. Expand. His entire flank felt hot to the touch. Swollen and heavy. Like he'd put on weight but only on the left side of his body. Nothing was bleeding no more, thank God for that, but there was this yellowish-green pus tinged with brown seeping out from under Juliet's bandage, and it stunk like roadkill. In no world was that a good thing. It all hurt to high hell, too. The slightest bit of pressure felt like a thousand needle jabs.

Romeo cursed himself for not taking the bottle of painkillers from the van glove box when he had the chance, and he was cursing himself for not keeping more antibiotics on hand, and he was cursing himself because he didn't normally make mistakes and today he'd chalked up a metric shit-ton of them. Nothing was going his way and that's why, when he hopped from the first freight car to the second and found about a dozen cases of Tennessee whiskey he knew his round of bad luck had finally took a turn.

The crates were nailed shut, but when a man like Romeo was determined, a couple of nails and pine boards weren't going to slow him down. This was war. A few of the bottles made the ultimate sacrifice when he kicked his way through the side of the crate, but enough of their comrades survived the assault, and the second the hole was big enough, Romeo reached inside and snagged a half pint. He then dropped down next to the battered crate, twisted off the bottle top, and took a good, long swig. The heat of it burned his throat, his belly, and he could almost picture the whiskey running into the infection on some new battle line deep in his flesh. Unlike the previous skirmish, this was where the war would be fought, and Tennessee soldiers were strong. He had faith. He also understood in any campaign it was best to surround your enemy from all sides. That in mind, he took another swig, then went to work peeling the clothing away from his angry skin. While that was nasty business, the bandages were far worse. The pus had all but fused them to his skin, and peeling back the layers felt no different than taking a paring knife to his own meaty parts and slicing them off. He didn't realize he was yelling until maybe a minute or two in, and when he did, he shouted louder. Somehow it helped, like a kettle needing to release steam.

When the last of the bandages were off and piled to the side, Romeo sucked in a deep breath and got himself a good look at the mess Skinny Bitch had made of him.

The entry wound had puckered up, swollen, and nearly closed. When he managed to twist and get a look at the exit, he found it was no different. The movement brought more pus, though. When he touched it, gave just the smallest bit of pressure, it oozed over his fingers, dripped down his side, and puddled on the plank floor. Hot and sticky.

That wasn't good.

That was so far from good.

And why was it so fucking cold in here?

Fever, you dumb fuck. You're covered in sweat. The fever is trying to burn away the bad parts and failing miserably. You need to get those bad parts out of you. Cut 'em out if you got to, but rid yourself of them.

"Shut up. It ain't that bad," he grumbled.

If it ain't that bad, who the fuck are you talking to?

Romeo took another drink, shivered.

He thought of the mattress in the back of the van.

How nice that would be. Curling up in the corner above the muffler where it was always nice and warm.

Gone now.

He thought of Skinny Bitch and Abercrombie. "Every ounce of flesh I lose over this, I'm taking two from each of you."

And that felt good, saying it out loud.

Empowering.

Romeo sucked in a breath. He'd never been one to procrastinate, and now wasn't the time to start. If he didn't clean the wound, it would only get worse. Before he could change his mind, he grabbed a handful of his love handle and gave it a solid squeeze. White-hot pain shot out, crossed every inch of his body, and took leave through a shout loud enough to rattle the bottles in the crate at his side. Before the pain had a chance to subside, Romeo moved his hand a little further and squeezed again. Pus poured out of him, flowed from both ends of the wound. Romeo squeezed again.

Again.

Again.

He kept going until the pain was unbearable, then he squeezed harder. He didn't stop until the last of the pus was out. Then he twisted to his side, spread the entry hole as wide as he could with two trembling fingers, and poured the whiskey.

Romeo passed out.

Not for long, only a few seconds. No more than a minute for sure. Maybe five. The moment he had some semblance of his wits back, he rolled to his belly, found the exit wound with those same two fingers, opened it up, and poured again.

Holy hell, he wished to pass out again, but he didn't. Instead, he was wide awake for every fun-loving second of the whiskey inching through him like acid across a baby's tender bottom.

At some point, he'd stopped screaming, he had no more of that in him. Romeo just lay there. A good ten minutes went by before he was able to sit.

He took another drink.

Done.

For now.

In the same crate were several bottles of premium whiskey in blue velvet bags. Romeo removed two of them and tore the bags into strips which he then used as makeshift bandages. He patched himself up as best he could and tentatively got to his feet.

His vision went all white again, but it cleared faster than last time.

He was still cold, still shaking, but that would break if he kept moving. "You'll be right as rain, hoss, if you just keep moving. That's the key."

Yeah, plenty of time to rest when you're—

"Fuck that. I ain't dying today."

What he was going to do was find Juliet, find them. Extract his pounds of flesh.

Lumbering past the open door of the freight car, Romeo realized they were finally picking up speed. Whoever was driving this thing would probably put the hammer down when they were outside of Boston. He had no idea how long it would take to get to Chicago, but Juliet would. He looked forward to asking her, because then he'd know how much playtime he'd have with the other two.

As with the previous doors, the one at the front of the freight car wasn't locked. Romeo tugged it open, looked down at the ground moving below him, and reached for the handle of the next car. When he swung across the chasm to the adjoining platform, the move didn't flow as elegantly as he would have hoped, but he got there, and that was all that mattered.

Romeo searched the car, didn't find them, and worked his way forward to the next.

He'd find them.

They had no place to go.

According to the FindMy app on his phone, he was damn near on top of them.

68

"Brendan?"

The room was dark, black as pitch. The air thick and musky with heat. Brendan didn't remember unlocking the door between their adjoining rooms, nor did he remember opening that door—in fact, he was certain he hadn't—but it was open now. He could tell that much by the faint outlines he managed to string together with his limited vision. When Kim's fingertips brushed his arm, he wanted to shy away but found himself unable to move.

The triple chime.

The sound seemed to play all around him.

Then there was a small screen, so bright he had to look away, but not before reading the words. It was a *Spice*:

> *For the next sixty seconds, kiss your partner.*
> *You're not allowed to kiss the same place twice.*

The phone screen blinked out as quickly as it came to life, and somehow that made the room even darker.

"Kim, don't," Brendan heard himself say.

"I have to, Brendan," she said in barely a whisper. "Bad things happen when you don't."

"I don't want to hurt Abby."

"Maybe she deserves to get hurt more than anyone. Have you ever considered that?"

Her lips brushed the tender spot behind his ear then, then the nape of his neck. He caught a whiff of her vanilla perfume, the same scent Abby wore. She kissed his chest. Lower. "They're killing people, Kim. Did you know that? They'll kill me too. Stuckey, Hannah, Abs…"

"Shhh. No shop talk. Play the game."

"How long have *you* played the game?"

"Longer than you, not as long as some others."

"Who is Robin Church? Do you know?"

"Shhhh…" Her lips drifted over his stomach, his right thigh. "You think too much."

The phone chimed again. The light flashed across the hotel room as Kim brought it back to her face and let out a sigh. "Well, that's not very nice."

"What does it say?"

She brought the phone closer so he could read it.

Sugar

Does he think too much, though? Does he think enough?
Maybe if he did, you'd still be alive. What would you
be doing right now…if you were still alive?

Kim eased closer, crawled up beside him, and rolled onto his chest, her naked body cold and moist. In the light of the phone,

Brendan saw the bullet hole in her left temple. The surrounding skin was black and puckered. She reached up and brushed her hair aside, moved it from her eyes. The tips of her fingers glistened with dark blood and bits of her skull. "You and Abby were dead the moment you downloaded the app. It's not so bad. You'll see."

A horn beeped.

Brendan's eyes opened on the freight car. His fingers digging into the cold wood floor, Abby slumped against him, nestled in the crook of his arm, sleeping. He was dripping in sweat. Brendan didn't remember drifting off, nor did he know how long they'd been asleep. Outside, the sun had begun dipping toward the horizon.

"Abs?" He shook her gently. When her eyes fluttered open, he quickly told her, "It's time."

69

Freight car number seventeen. Or was it eighteen? Romeo wasn't exactly sure, but they weren't in it just like they weren't in all the others he'd walked through. Sure, he'd found plenty of stuff. Crates and boxes of all kinds of nonsense moving from Point A to Point B. He'd even encountered a few rail-riders—hobos, bums, whatever the fuck. Not one of them had seen Skinny Bitch or Abercrombie. Not one had seen his Juliet. And he had been fairly persuasive when he asked. This latest guy, he said his name was Chuck, he wanted nothing but to help. He made that perfectly clear as Romeo held him by the shirt collar at the edge of the open freight car door with nothing but the man's curled toes gripping the ground. What was left of his greasy hair flapping in the wind.

"I ain't seen nobody! I swear!"

This was particularly troubling to Romeo because Chuck had come from the forward cars, and when Romeo found him, Chuck was holding Juliet's panties in his filthy fist.

Of course, Romeo couldn't be 100 percent sure they were

Juliet's, but how many red-and-white striped panties with *Daddy's Girl* stamped across the bum could there possibly be on this train? Romeo wasn't much of a betting man, but he was certain Vegas would put the odds against just such a coincidence. He was sure none of those bet-makers would fault him for getting just the littlest bit upset at finding them with Chuck. Chuck wasn't exactly Juliet's type, and Juliet wasn't one to hand out such a prize to just anyone, which brought into question how he got them.

"They're mine! I swear!"

Spittle flew from Chuck's mouth with each word, spraying across Romeo's cheek and neck. If there was anything Romeo hated more than a liar, it was a sloppy liar.

"Now, Chuck, I thought we had ourselves an understanding." He tightened his grip on Chuck's shirt, enough to turn each of the man's breaths into a papery rasp, and held him further out the door. They still weren't moving fast, but if Romeo got the angle right, he was pretty sure he could drop Chuck under the train. At least part of him.

Chuck must have been thinking along the same lines, because he quickly gasped, "I found 'em! That makes them mine. Rules of the rail. How 'bout I show you where and you let me keep them, friend?"

Romeo took a little longer to answer than was required, partly because he wanted Chuck to sweat it out, and partly because his brain was having trouble pulling words together. The wound in his side felt a little better, but not much. "How 'bout this, *friend?* You show me where you found them, and I won't tear out your spleen and feed it to you? How 'bout that? Maybe I won't strangle you with your own intestines. That's my rule of the rail."

"Yeah, yeah…" Chuck nodded furiously. "I'll show you."

Romeo pulled him back into the freight car and gave him a push toward the front. "Let's be quick about it."

Chuck landed with a grunt against a stack of boxed lawnmower parts, scrambled to his feet, and held out his hand. "First you give me those back."

The balls on this guy.

He weighed maybe a hundred pounds, and half of that was unkempt hair and layers of grungy clothes. He didn't know if this guy planned to wear them, spend his day smelling them, or make soup, and none of those things created the kind of visual Romeo wanted in his head. He only wanted his Juliet back. He could buy her new underwear. "You show me where, and I'll give them to you."

"Scout's honor?"

"Scout's honor."

Chuck wiped his mouth on the back of his jacket sleeve, leaving a dirty smear across the side of his face, then he turned toward the front of the car and tugged open the door leading forward to the next car. "Let's be quick about it, then, I ain't got all day."

Romeo had no idea how far west the train was going or how long it would take to get there, but he was pretty sure they not only had all day, they had themselves a few days and a night or two. He kept that to himself because it made no sense to engage this jackass in any kind of unnecessary banter. He followed Chuck through the narrow access door, stepped over the coupler and into the next car. He half-expected Chuck to make some sort of move at that point, either turn on him or run, but he did neither. Instead, he weaved his way through the crowded car and on to the next. Romeo followed him through six more before the man spoke again. "It's this next one up here," he muttered, crossing over another coupler into another crowded freight car. How Chuck knew that, Romeo had no idea. All the freight cars looked the same to him—musty big boxes filled with smaller boxes. Lots of eyes, too. That wasn't lost on him. There were far more people on the train than he expected, all of them damn good at keeping to the shadows. Two cars back, some woman kept pace with them and got Romeo's wallet out of his back pocket before he realized she was there. He would have broke her arm, but he gave her props for going all stealthy. Instead, he only snapped her wrist before taking his wallet back.

From the gloom ahead, Chuck stopped and scratched the side of his chin. He was staring down between two large pallets of computer printers. "Right here, just like I said."

Although Romeo's eyes had adjusted to the dark, he went ahead and turned on his phone's flashlight to get a better look.

Juliet's clothing was bunched together in a ball and crammed halfway under one of the pallets. Shorts, shoes, top, and bra. Even her hair tie. Everything she'd been wearing the last time he saw her.

Fucking Skinny Bitch.

This had to be her again.

Abercrombie didn't have the smarts.

When Romeo bent to pick up Juliet's shoe, the wound in his side howled in protest.

"You all right, friend? You're looking a little light in the face."

Romeo grabbed Chuck by the scruff of his beard and slammed the man's head into a metal support pole. There was this sickening crunch. He hauled back and did it again. Chuck made a couple of odd noises after Romeo tossed him off to the side, but he went quiet fast enough. When Romeo bent for Juliet's shoe again, he moved a little slower. She had tiny feet, size seven on a good day. These were her favorite Vans. He brought the shoe into the light and peeled back the padding. The Apple AirTag was right there where he'd planted it all those months ago.

How the hell had Skinny Bitch known?

Another thought popped into his head.

They weren't on this train. Never had been.

Only him.

Skinny Bitch fucking conned him.

The large door in the side of this particular freight car was closed, but the vibrations alone were enough to tell him they were still picking up speed.

How long had *he* been on this train?

An hour?

More?

Fuck if he knew.

How far had it gone in that time?

Too far, his mind muttered through the syrup coating his thoughts. *Way too fucking far.*

Chuck's bowels must have opened up when he died, because the air suddenly stunk of shit.

They never left the train yard.

This was all some bullshit ruse.

He needed to end this.

Now.

Romeo quickly scooped up Juliet's clothing, balled everything up under his shoulder, then went to the freight car door and yanked it open.

The train was moving much faster now and still picking up speed.

He pocketed the AirTag and tossed out the rest, watched the clothing scatter in the weeds and brush along the sides of the track. Leaning out, Romeo tried to get a look at what was coming. He was no longer in Boston proper. Civilization had shrunk from tall buildings to old tenements, shotgun homes, and strip malls. Before he could change his mind, he sucked in a breath and jumped, praying not so silently to hit the ground on his good side.

70

The horn beeped again.

Frantic.

Cut short.

Brendan looked toward the open door of the freight car.

Another beep.

He reached for Abby and squeezed her hand. "Are you sure about this?"

She let out a soft chuff. "No. But I keep asking myself—"

"What would Emily do."

She nodded. "Yeah. What would Emily do. And Emily is sure."

Together, they went to the door, pausing at the opening to look back at Juliet, secured and quiet in the corner of the old freight car, a bag still over her head. They'd made Juliet strip out of her clothes and change right after they blew up the van, assuming if one AirTag had been planted, there were more. It was Abby's idea to put her old clothes on the train heading west when they found the small transmitter in her shoe. That insanely long train was finally gone, the last of the cars having vanished from view. The freight car they'd been hiding in looked like it hadn't moved in years. No longer on tracks, it rested in the dirt, surrounded by weeds. There was a hole in the roof where the wood had rotten away. The door was rusted open. Some discarded relic from a time past.

"Brendan, are *you* sure?"

He nodded. "Let me see the phone."

He dialed the number from memory.

"This is Agent Bellows."

"This is Brendan Hollander."

There was a silence on the other end of the line, and Brendan could picture Bellows signaling someone, soundlessly instructing them to trace the call. Something they could do in seconds, even with a burner phone.

"Brendan, a lot of people are trying to find you. You and your wife. You need to come in so I can protect you."

Brendan thought about the triple chime he'd heard on the news broadcast, possibly coming from a member of law enforcement. Possibly coming from Bellows if he had been there.

"We have proof INTENT is behind everything. Do you know Beacon Park Yard in Boston?"

"The old train yard?"

"Yeah, the old train yard. Send someone. Tell them to find the freight car with ID number…" He leaned out the door to get a better look at the side. "53-AFT792. The woman behind the murders, the one who burned down my house, is tied up inside. She said her name is Juliet, but that's probably fake. Repeat the number to me."

"53-AFT792. Brendan, if you have proof, you need to—"

"Her boyfriend, her accomplice, is on a westbound train that left the yard about an hour ago. Big guy with a gunshot wound in his abdomen. You need to pick him up. Both of them. They had a hit list, Bellows—I've got a copy. You, Stuckey…anyone investigating all this is a target. You need to watch your back."

Silence.

"Bellows?"

"Stuckey and his wife were taken from a safehouse near Boston harbor at a little after two today. I've got four agents down."

The call wasn't on speaker, but the volume was loud enough for Abby to hear. She gripped his arm. "Taken how?"

Bellows didn't hold back. *"I haven't seen the full report, but from what I was told, they slit the throats of the two agents we had positioned outside, then took out the remaining agents when they answered the door."*

"Why would they let them in?"

"The assailants were dressed as Boston PD."

There are players everywhere. On the streets. In the supermarket. School teachers. Police.

That's what that girl, Sally, had told them.

They weren't dressed as Boston PD, they probably *were* Boston PD, and their points had gone up.

"How's he supposed to protect us?" Abby said in a childlike voice.

The truth was, he couldn't.

Kim. Dubin. Now Stuckey and Hannah. These people wouldn't stop. Not until they got what they wanted. Not until Brendan and Abby were dead too.

"Beacon Park Yard, Bellows. 53-AFT792. Get someone here. Fast." Brendan disconnected and tossed the burner phone back into the freight car.

The horn beeped again.

A gray Saab was parked in the gravel next to the freight car. The window rolled down, and Dr. Bixby eyed them nervously. "You two better get in before I change my mind."

They jumped down from the opening and quickly scrambled into the Saab.

"Thank you," Abby told Bixby. "You might be the only person we trust."

Bixby seemed to consider that for a moment, then handed Abby a folded sheet of paper containing Roland Ludlow's address. "He wasn't difficult to find. Not with such a unique name."

The address was in Chicago.

Bixby's face was lined with anxiety as he watched them both in the rearview mirror. He finally said, "Are we ready for a road trip?"

Abby handed the address back to him. "As fast as you're willing to drive."

71

Jumping from the moving train.

Landing on the asphalt.

That had been a bad idea.

In hindsight, Romeo knew it had been his only play, but he was already banged up, and shooting for grass or brush would have been smarter had he bothered to think things through before going all Superman out the open door of the freight car.

He hit the pavement on his left shoulder with his arm pinned under him, the ball of his fist in the perfect position to jab right into the gunshot wound like some ultimate fuck-you from Karma. He rolled for a bit and when he came to a stop he was in the middle of an intersection that (lucky for him, if any of this could be considered lucky) had stopped as the train went by. A heavyset man behind the wheel of an old Cadillac had been first in the long line of waiting cars, and when Romeo finally stopped rolling, the man had climbed out (no easy feat, considering his bulk) and shuffled over to see what was doing. He somehow got himself down on his knees and pressed two sausage fingers against Romeo's neck, his breaths coming in wheezing gasps from the exertion.

"Mister, you alive?"

Romeo let out a grunt that must have passed for *yes*, because the man pulled his fingers away.

"Try not to move. You're bleeding. I'll call for an ambulance. Just stay still."

The fact that Romeo was bleeding wasn't exactly news to him. The good news was the large man was looking down at Romeo's tee shirt when he said it, at the gunshot wound, not something new. Romeo managed to sit up, blotted at a couple of fresh scratches on his cheek, and pulled the Bowie knife from the sheath on his right ankle. He pressed the tip of the blade into the middle of the large man's three chins. "I'm gonna take your car now, and you're gonna let me. We understand each other, hoss?"

The man blinked, then gave a nod. "Keys are in it. You go right ahead."

Romeo got himself standing, every inch of his body screaming in protest. His damn thumb was pointing in the wrong direction.

Back when Romeo did his first stint in juvie, he busted his left thumb on some kid who's face was all chin. The staff nurse set it but did a piss-poor job and the joint never did heal right. It hurt like a mother in cold weather and would sometimes dislocate at the most inopportune times.

Romeo gripped his thumb with his other hand and jerked the bone back in place.

There was fresh wetness coming from Romeo's gunshot wound, but it wasn't blood. When he touched it, his fingers came away sticky with more yellow pus.

The fat man looked like he might throw up.

"I'm taking your damn car," Romeo told him. He thought that

was the end of it, this man looked like no fighter. He was still on a knee when Romeo started for the Caddy, but from behind him came a hollowed grasp at a mouthful of air, the man lunged, and slammed into Romeo's back with all his bulk. Got him low, like a wrestler, or like he was pulling from some ancient memory of playing high school ball—the kind of tackle that cost you fifteen yards if the refs caught it. Romeo was big too. Not fat, big but sturdy big, and that simple fact kept him on his feet. He stumbled forward, caught his balance, then looked behind him to see the man drop from his waist to the pavement in a tumble best described as the opposite of elegant.

His face buried in the blacktop, he shouted, "You're not taking my car!"

Romeo turned, raised his size twelve, and brought it down on the man's neck.

That was the end of that, but when Romeo looked back up he realized several of the people who had been parked behind the fat man and his Caddy had gotten out of their cars. Most were holding up their phones either calling someone or filming, neither of which was good.

Romeo took out his own phone and dialed the third number down in his favorites.

As always, there was no hello. Romeo simply said, "I got lookie-loos, my location. I need a disconnect and wipe."

"Understood."

They'd charge him. He'd lose big points for something like this, but it was the cost of doing business.

By the time he lowered his phone, all those people were staring at their mobiles, frantically swiping, tapping, and whatnot. Romeo wasn't going to pretend he understood the specifics of how it worked, but he got the gist—if someone had the app installed (and most people did these days) the folks in tech had full access to their phones. Dropping calls, wiping images, that was all easy-peasy. Those same phones had Bluetooth which gave them access to all other phones with Bluetooth on (which was everyone) within a thirty-foot radius. It was like they left the front door open. Hacking those devices wasn't much harder. By the time Romeo reached the Caddy and settled into the white leather driver's seat, all electronic evidence he'd been there was gone.

He threw the car in reverse, backed into the bumper of the Honda behind him, and pushed the car back until it reached the pickup behind it and got stuck. Romeo got himself the few extra feet he needed to turn the Caddy and get into the lane heading back toward Boston.

The fat man had been listening to Waylon Jennings, and that sat just right with Romeo.

Nothing like a little outlaw country to set the mood for what was coming.

72

They'd driven in silence for nearly an hour, not because there wasn't anything to say, but simply because Abby and Brendan were too tired to talk. The sleep they'd caught in the freight car had been brief and brought no more rest than a fox cornered in a tree by a pack of rabid wolves might find. The second they fell into Bixby's back seat and started moving, the weight of everything seemed to lift slightly, if only temporarily. Brendan felt like they were standing in the eye of a hurricane. The worst was yet to come, but quiet for now. Blissfully quiet. Abby settled in the crook of his arm and drifted off. While Brendan thought he might never sleep again, he was out in under ten minutes.

Dreamless.

When Brendan's eyes snapped open, full dark had settled.

He caught Bixby's gaze in the rearview mirror.

Although the man had remained quiet, it was clear he had a heated inner dialog going. Brendan could nearly picture a miniature Devil-Bixby sitting on one of the man's shoulders, an angel on the other, both arguing the merits of their case.

Brendan smoothed Abby's hair, and when he spoke, he kept his voice down so he wouldn't wake her. "You didn't have to do this. The two of us seriously owe you."

"I'm not very good at turning a blind eye. It gets me in far more trouble than I'm willing to admit."

"Most people would walk away. I wouldn't fault you if you had."

"I won't lie. When your wife called me, I intended to say no. I'd just seen the news report about the daycare for the umpteenth time and was prepping to march myself down to the nearest police station to tell them about our lunch meeting. Well, more like cursing myself for not going sooner."

"What stopped you?"

"The girl you met at the diner. My patient, Elsa. She called me about an hour after we left and said she saw something strange in the video. Although the shooter looked exactly like you, he held the shotgun in his left hand. When you were at the diner, you kept fidgeting. Picking things up, putting them back down. Your wife handed you…she handed you the gun. It was clear you were a righty, not a lefty. She wouldn't let it go. Elsa texted me a shorter version of the video, one she'd enlarged. There was this slight shimmer around your jawline, your face didn't seem to move correctly, it looked… off. She then sent me a video of Tom Cruise singing some Queen song only it wasn't Tom Cruise, it was some guy who lives in Idaho. Elsa gave me a crash course on deep fakes, and by the time she was done, I was certain the video was bogus."

Brendan couldn't help but smile. Probably the first genuine smile all day. "Sounds like she's a smart girl living under rough circumstances."

"She's at Hampton House now. They'll take care of her. Her grades are solid, and she's determined to get herself a scholarship. I'm working on an emergency order to emancipate her from her parents."

Brendan recalled the bruising around the girl's eye. "They hit her, don't they? Her parents?"

The doctor nearly answered that, then must have remembered he couldn't go into that kind of detail about a patient. "I think she's going to land on her feet."

There was a map spread out on the passenger seat. Bixby gave it a quick glance, shot a look at one of the highway signs, and swore softly. He jerked the wheel to the right, just making the exit that would take them to I-97. Behind them, a semi horn honked noisily. Bixby raised his hand and waved, then repositioned the map, which had slid halfway off the seat.

Abby stirred, but didn't wake.

"I'm spoiled by GPS, I'm not sure I could even read a map anymore," Brendan told him. "All this tech is meant to make our lives easier. What it's really doing is thinking for us. Makes me wonder what will happen to our minds in a hundred years' time."

"Like muscle atrophy?" Bixby replied. "Maybe our brains will shrink? The unused part will get absorbed and repurposed by the body. Our brains will go the way of the appendix and wisdom teeth, and we'll become these mindless beasts."

"You think?"

"No." He smirked. "Nothing that drastic. There is something to be said for regularly exercising the brain, challenging yourself, to keep it healthy. But the general thinking in my community comes down to one simple fact—the human mind is anything but lazy. If you free up some thought real estate with modern technology, the brain will utilize that space for something else. Instead of thinking about a map, I might be composing a sonata, that sort of thing. Fringe theories suggest this might lead to our next big evolutionary jump as our brains go in directions they never did before."

"We're dependent, though," Brendan pointed out. "If the tech went away, we'd have to relearn basic skills just to survive."

"But we would *relearn*. I haven't read a map in years, but I'm doing it now. Maybe a little clunky, but I'll have it down by the time we reach Chicago. That doesn't mean I don't miss GPS, but I can get by without it."

"What did you do with your phone?"

"Per your wife's instructions, it's on my kitchen counter along with my smartwatch, my Fitbit, even my earbuds."

"So you have no electronics with you?"

He shook his head. "She told me if it must be charged, leave it behind. I feel oddly…naked."

Brendan understood what he meant. He'd grown so accustomed to carrying his phone, he kept glancing down at his empty palm to check e-mail, messages, news, notifications…a million things that normally filled his day. It was both unnerving and refreshing to be without those things. Even with his wife sleeping in his arms and Bixby in the front seat, he felt alone.

At the base of the exit ramp, Bixby managed to merge onto I-87 without a single person beeping at him. He settled into the middle lane and set the cruise control at nine miles per hour over the limit. "You should try to rest. Who knows when you'll get another chance. I'll wake you when we get close."

As if in agreement, Abby let out a soft snort and snuggled deeper under Brendan's shoulder. She mumbled something softly, then was out again. He couldn't make it out.

Sugar & Spice™

Sugar
If you were about to lose your partner forever, would you rather text them a thousand words or speak only three?

73

The return trip to the Beacon Park Yard took Romeo less time than he expected it would, not because traffic was light, but because he fell in line with three Boston Police cruisers clearly heading to the same place, and everyone else got out of their way.

The flashing lights and sirens of those three cars drew attention, but were nothing compared to the circus awaiting them at the train yard.

Someone had tipped off the po-po, and they'd wasted no time coming out en masse. There were SWAT vehicles, ambulances, Boston PD, county cars. Anyone and everyone with a badge and gun made the trip. The TV crews were there too, four network vans so far, and probably more coming. But to their credit, the police held them outside the yard gate. Romeo fought the urge to wave as he drove right by the cameras, riding the tail of the same three cruisers he'd followed from the highway: just another pig on his way to the roast. When the cruisers pulled into the tangled mess of law enforcement cars, Romeo steered the Caddy off to the left, rounded a row of abandoned box cars, and shifted into park in a field littered with decades-old trash. He was up on a slight hill, and it gave him a great view of the happenings below. Behind him and up to the left, the fire department appeared to be finishing with the remains of his van. Seeing them lingering around the smoldering mess that had been his home going on three years now lit a new spark under his hatred for Skinny Bitch and Abercrombie.

Romeo twisted back around in the seat, and the pain quickly reminded him he wasn't operating at 100 percent. He needed to think this through.

Down below, the ants crawled.

"Juliet, oh Juliet, where for art thou, Juliet?" he grunted. "Where in the fuck art thou?"

Taking out his phone, he dialed the same number as earlier.

There was a soft click.

Romeo said, "I need a twenty on my lady."

A moment ticked by.

"She's offline."

"I know that. Why the hell do you think I can't find her?"

The call disconnected.

Romeo stared at the phone. "Goddamn pansy snowflake." He drew in a breath, calmed himself, and dialed again. "Sorry. I apologize. I'm a tad frustrated." He paused a moment and let the silence cleanse the air before he spoke again. "I think she's close. Got a lot of phones here. Probably a few users, right? Can you…"

"Stand by."

He half expected to be put on hold with some godawful music like the elevator version of Rush or something, but instead, he heard the soft click of fingers moving swiftly across a keyboard, a pause, and more typing. In under thirty seconds, the voice returned:

"Nineteen vehicles present. Twenty-three app users, twenty-nine others. Facial recognition has identified your query in an ambulance,

375

SID number 323423-192-9046."

Romeo felt his heart sink. "Ambulance? Is she injured?"

"Unknown."

"Is she alone?"

"Negative. At least one other person present."

Romeo's phone dinged, and when he glanced down there was a photo of Juliet taken with some fisheye wide lens. Most ambulances were wired with cameras for insurance purposes. She was lying down on a gurney, zip-tied to the frame. The arms and shoulders of someone hovering over her were visible, but little more. Looking through the Caddy's windshield, he counted three ambulances on site. The SID was some Internet network identifier. It may be relevant to the little geek-boy hacking away on the other end of the line, but it did Romeo little good in the real world. "Are you able to give me the ambulance's unit number? I see three down there. Their numbers are painted on their roofs."

"Negative."

Romeo fought the urge to swear. He didn't want this guy hanging up again. "How do I identify the ambulance?"

Silence. Then—

"Watch for brake lights."

Romeo was about to ask what he meant by that when the brake lights on the ambulance in the far right corner blinked twice, paused, then blinked again.

"Well, that's a neat trick."

"May I be of further service?"

"Naw, I got things from here, hoss."

Disconnect.

Fucker.

Romeo studied the ambulance down below. There may only be one person inside, but the surrounding area was littered with uniforms, all of them itching to plug someone. He didn't need to look in the mirror to understand he wouldn't blend if he were to go down there. He'd be lucky to get ten feet before they pounced on him—tasers, cuffs, batons, and who-knew-what flying about. No, that would not work. He wasn't exactly up to his usual physical snuff, either. The fever was back, and every inch of his flesh ached with it.

She was right there.

He couldn't exactly leave her.

Right there.

Then an idea came to him, and to be perfectly honest, the fever might have put it there. It wasn't the kind of thing he'd normally come up with when his head was on straight. The world looked a little different from behind a temperature, thoughts got muddy. It was like the fisheye lens, all distorted. Those pigs below, they were in their own fisheye, their own bubble. He only needed to pop it.

Romeo shifted the Caddy into reverse and backed up as far as he could, until the bumper was kissing an old tractor of some sort. A rusty pile of long-forgotten maintenance equipment. He shifted back into park, climbed out, and fought his cloudy vision as he scanned the ground and found himself a length of pipe a little shy of three feet long. He tested the weight, decided it would do nicely, and jammed one end against the driver's seat, the other down on the accelerator, pinning it to the floor. The Caddy's large V8 roared, seemed excited, ready to leap. Romeo closed the door, and through the open window, slapped the gearshift into drive. He barely managed to get his head out of the opening when the Caddy shot forward. The car was doing maybe fifty, possibly more, when it clipped the corner of an old flatbed rail car on the opposite side of the hill and launched over the edge. Romeo glimpsed the car do a partial corkscrew in the air before it vanished from view. That was followed a moment later by one hell of a bang and a whole lotta screaming.

74

Romeo scrambled down the hill as quickly as he could, every inch of his wrecked body screaming. He had no gun, wasn't sure exactly where he lost that. He still had the Bowie knife, but he left it in the sheath on his ankle. None of that really mattered. Brandishing a weapon of any sort in this crowd would get you a one-way ticket to Endsville.

Turns out, he didn't need it. These people had their hands full.

Covered in flames, the Caddy had landed ass-up on top of the SWAT van after clipping a few of the cruisers and at least one unfortunate gentleman in a Boston PD uniform who no longer had a head. Someone or multiple someones must have been in the SWAT van, because a dozen first responders were scrambling, trying to get the back door open as the fire spread.

Romeo reached the bottom of the hill and walked right by everyone. With his bloodstained clothes, pronounced limp, holding his left side, he fit right in. Well, not quite, but he certainly blended a bit better than he would have a few minutes ago, pre-airborne Caddy.

He crossed over to Juliet's ambulance without a single question asked, and that was good because getting down that hill had taken a lot out of him, and he was wheezing like a son-a-bitch.

When he opened the back door, the paramedic hovering over Juliet barely looked at him. He was busy picking through a cabinet. "Tell them I'm coming, I just need to find—" That's when he saw Romeo. Took in the bloodstained clothes, his scratched and battered face, arms. The burning car and chaos behind him. "Jesus. How bad is—"

In a move far more fluid than he should have been able to muster in his current state, Romeo grabbed the frame of the ambulance, hoisted himself up, and throttled the paramedic in one of his large hands. He gripped him by the throat and squeezed with a strength he knew he shouldn't possess but was grateful to have found. He squeezed until his fingers nearly touched. The man's windpipe collapsed, flattened. He made this gurgling noise, his eyes nearly left his head, then he was still. The life gone from him.

Romeo cast him from the opening to the dirt below and pulled the doors shut.

Juliet beamed. "I knew you'd come for me, baby!"

He had no words; his vision was going white.

He spotted a pair of scissors on a shelf to his left and managed to pass them to Juliet before the world went all swimmy and he passed out.

When Romeo woke, *he* was zip-tied to the gurney, belted down, too. He couldn't move, but the ambulance certainly was. Moving fast. The siren wasn't on, but the lights were, flashing red and blue. The world outside the small windows in the back doors was black beyond those flashing lights, much darker than earlier, and he knew he'd lost a few hours. Maybe half the night. Maybe more. He twisted his head around just enough to catch Juliet in the driver's seat. She was singing softly to herself, tapping out a rhythm on the steering wheel. The movement was nearly enough to send him to la-la-land again, and he turned back around, licked his lips, and managed, "Baby doll?"

He must have startled her. Juliet's singing stopped, the ambulance jerked to the left, then righted itself. "Romeo, you had me so worried!"

He tugged weakly at the bindings around his arms. "Why you got me tied up?"

"I had no choice. You wouldn't keep still on account of the fever dreams. I thought you might hurt yourself."

"How long…" His throat was full of sand. Voice didn't want to work. He realized he had an IV in his arm. The half-empty bag of saline was hanging from the ceiling.

"How long were you out?"

He nodded and realized how stupid that was. She couldn't see him.

"It's almost four in the morning. You've been sleeping about ten hours."

On the floor off to his side were the remains of his tee shirt and a pile of red-stained bandages. There were a few empty IV bags too, along with some glass vials.

"I patched you up proper this time," Juliet told him. "Cleaned the wound with saline and antibiotics. Got you on an antibiotic drip along with some choice pain meds. I guess that might be partly why you slept so long, but truth be told you needed it and I knew I could do the driving, so I figured best to let you get your rest."

Romeo licked his lips. They were dry and cracked. "Chicago?"

"Yeah, baby. Chicago. Making good time, too. Ain't nobody messes with an ambulance. Even the staties get out of the way. Not that there's many out this time of night. Romeo, I ain't gonna lie. It's bad. They got a jump on us. *She* knows too. She ain't outright come out and said it, but she knows."

This time, he turned his head. He needed to see Juliet's face. "You...you talked to her?"

She bobbed her head. "She called you twice. I couldn't *not* answer. I do that, and you know what her next move would be."

She'd do what Romeo would do. She'd order a hit on the two of them and clear him and Juliet off the board. Triage. Cleanup. She'd told him as much the last time he'd talked to her. She'd kill them and let some other player take care of Skinny Bitch and Abercrombie.

She called you *twice.*

Juliet had answered his phone. That meant the woman knew he was down. She might just be stringing Juliet along.

"Where exactly did you tell her I was?" Romeo managed. He felt the strength coming back to him and that was good. The antibiotics were working.

"Oh, you'll love this. I covered for you. I told her you stole a car and were a few hours ahead of me. I told her you left me your phone but would be in touch as soon as you got to Chicago."

Romeo looked up at the ceiling. It didn't take him long to find the fisheye lens that had captured the image of Juliet earlier. There was no red light, nothing to tell him whether or not it was on, but he knew at some point they'd got a good look at him. *She* knew exactly what kind of shape he was in and where he was. Hell, there might be a target on this bus right now.

75

When Brendan opened his eyes again, the car was slowing. Bixby had exited the highway and was following signs to a service plaza. "The car needs gas; I need coffee and a bathroom."

With a soft nod, Brendan yawned and wiped the sleep from his eyes.

Abby had spread out on the seat, her legs curled under her body beside him. She stirred, sat up, and looked out the window. A hint of morning sun had splintered the horizon. "Where are we?"

"Coming up on Cleveland." Bixby glanced down at his wrist and realized he wasn't wearing his watch. "I think it's a little after four in the morning."

The service plaza was nearly deserted, only two other cars. He parked next to an empty pump and shut off the engine. "I don't want to risk using a credit card. I'll go inside and pre-pay with cash. Do either of you want anything?"

At the idea of food, Brendan's stomach gurgled. He couldn't

remember the last time they'd eaten anything. He was starving. They both were.

"I'd love something hot," Abby told him. "Maybe a burrito? Coffee too."

Reaching into her pocket, she pulled out some of their remaining cash and tried to hand it to him.

Bixby quickly waved her off as he started toward the store at the center of the plaza. "I got it. You're on pumping duty."

He vanished inside.

A moment later, the pump's display flashed and reset to zero. Brendan removed the nozzle and began filling the Saab. A small television screen on the pump came to life with the news.

"Brendan, that's the train yard."

She was right, of course, but Brendan barely recognized it. Several images flashed behind the anchor's head—multiple fires, a large car upside down and engulfed in flames, the remains of the van, still smoldering, an insane number of first responders and emergency vehicles. All the shots were shaky, taken from a distance. The broadcast was muted, and Brendan saw no way to turn up the sound. It didn't matter. After a lingering view of the freight car where they had left Juliet, both his and Abby's pictures appeared along with the caption—*murderous spree continues…*

Abby looked toward the store, then back at Brendan. "We need to talk about Bixby. It's not fair to pull him deeper into this."

Brendan had been thinking the same thing. Bixby had gotten them out of Boston, for that they were both eternally grateful, but to bring him to Chicago, to whatever came next, he didn't deserve that.

Abby said, "Let me see those SD cards. Tell me if he comes out."

Brendan fished the cards from his pocket and handed them to her. She tore off a corner of the map and scribbled out a quick note instructing him to get the cards to Bellows at the FBI. Below that, she added, *Thank you for everything! We need to finish this on our own.* She folded the card inside the note and placed it on the top of the gas pump just as the nozzle clicked off.

Brendan was replacing the nozzle in the cradle when he spotted a state trooper pull up and come to a stop at the double glass doors leading into the plaza store. "Abs…"

She saw it too. "We need to go."

Trying not to draw attention, Brendan got behind the wheel while Abby rounded the car to the passenger side and got in too. As he started the car, the trooper climbed out of his cruiser and surveyed the cars in the plaza, of which there were few. It only took a moment for his gaze to land on the Saab, and he did not look away. Instead, he looked down at the phone in his hand, then back at them.

"He sees us," Abby breathed.

The double glass doors behind the trooper slid open, and Bixby appeared. In one hand he held a tray with three cups of coffee, in the other was a bag. He froze at the sight of the police cruiser in his path, the officer standing just beyond it, then his eyes met theirs—Brendan behind the wheel, Abby in the passenger seat—and he silently mouthed the word, *Go.*

Trying not to look conspicuous and failing miserably, Brendan slipped the Saab into drive and pulled away from the pump.

Back on the sidewalk, Bixby appeared to lose his footing. He stumbled forward and smacked into the side of the police car. The tray with the three cups left his hand, skittered across the roof, and opened in the air, peppering the trooper and the car with hot coffee. He spun around, his arms flailing, unintelligible shouts filled the parking lot as Brendan quickly followed the signs back to the highway, leaving the plaza behind them.

"We seriously owe that man," Abby finally said.

76

From the front of the ambulance, Romeo's phone let out a triple chime. He twisted his head and caught a glimpse of Juliet picking it up from the passenger seat and reading the message. She frowned and tossed the phone back down on the seat. "That's some bullshit. I thought we were making good time."

"What does it say?"

"Says they're in a Saab outside Cleveland. That puts them at least two hours ahead of us."

"Let me see my phone."

"I'm driving, baby. Not safe to be handing stuff 'round like that."

Romeo jerked his arm, but the zip ties held firm. "Then pull over and cut me loose."

"I do, and we lose another ten minutes. That puts them ten more minutes ahead of us."

"Not if you're quick about it."

"Well, I'd rather not lose the time," Juliet huffed. "Besides," she added, "you didn't see the way you were trashing around earlier. I cut you loose, you fall asleep with that fever of yours, and you might hurt yourself."

She said *trashing* instead of *thrashing*, but Romeo wasn't about to correct her on something like that. There was something bigger going on here. This wasn't about his fever or keeping him safe. He wasn't sure he wanted the truth. "Juliet, you holding something back on me?"

"No way, sugar bear."

"I get the feeling you're keeping me tied up for a reason, and it's not the one you're giving me. Don't lie now, baby, you know how I feel about people who lie to me."

Juliet said nothing.

"Baby doll?"

She let out a soft sigh, changed lanes, and sped up a little bit. "Well, there is one little thing."

"And what's that?"

"You promise you won't get mad at me? I hate to think you're angry with me."

Romeo did his best to stay calm. "You know I could never be angry with you, baby doll."

"They took away our points."

"They..." It sunk in before he could get all the words out.

When Juliet spoke again, she sounded like a small child caught with their hand in the cookie jar. "I thought it was some mistake, so I rebooted your phone, but nope, still came back at zero points. Not even a bronze member no more. Like we installed the app and started new. That ain't right, not after what we'd done, so when I called her, I said—"

"Wait a minute," Romeo interrupted. "You called *her*? I thought she called me—called *my* phone."

"Why does it matter, who called who?"

Oh, it fucking mattered, all right.

You didn't call her.

Not unless you had to.

And you certainly didn't call her with some problem. *How the hell had she even gotten a number?*

"When I *talked* to her," Juliet corrected herself, "I reminded her how we were first to get to Cindy Messing, Joel Hayden, Isaac Alford...I reminded her how we collected all their hardware, cleaned up *her* mess for her. I reminded her how we did all that and she had no business touching our points. Hell, she should be giving us more points, not taking 'em, and if she wants us to fix the rest of her mess she best stop screwing around because we need those points."

As Romeo listened to her rattle on, a lump began to grow in the pit of his stomach. This hot, festering thing dripping with acid just growing there choking him from the inside. He didn't realize he was yanking on the zip ties again until they started to bite into the flesh around his wrists.

"She said we were sloppy. Said you were a sledgehammer when she shoulda used a scalpel. Said we were doing more damage than good." Juliet smashed the steering wheel with her palm. "Well, I told her she could shut the fuck up right there because ain't nobody could have gotten things done better than us, and just 'cause we got thrown a curve ball didn't mean we were out of the game. I stood up to her, Romeo, 'cause somebody had to."

He bit his tongue.

Literally.

He needed to taste the blood to keep from speaking his mind.

Romeo needed that bit of pain to bring clarity.

"Tell me," he asked her, "how did she react to that? Being told to... shut the fuck up."

"Oh, that's when she came around."

387

"How so?"

"She gave us until tonight to fix things."

Romeo wasn't sure he wanted to hear any more, but knew he had to. "How, exactly?"

"Her scalpel."

"Her scalpel?"

"Yep."

"I don't follow."

Juliet looked over her shoulder at the IV bag hanging from the ceiling. "Are you still a bit cloudy, sugarplum? I can dial back the pain meds."

Romeo jerked at the zip ties again. "Just explain it."

"She said, those two trust her scalpel."

"They trust her…" Romeo didn't realize he was thinking aloud until the words hovered over him like a thinly veiled cloud. "Did she say who that person was? Her scalpel?"

"Nope, and I pressed her on it. Don't doubt that for a second. I told her if we were going to see this thing through, we'd need to know, but she insisted it wasn't important, not to us. That's when she told me what we needed to do."

"…to fix things?"

Juliet nodded. "To fix things. Tonight."

If tonight was the *tonight* Romeo thought it was—and his days and nights were both a bit hazy—there was only one thing happening tonight that he knew about that could possibly play into all this. "She's leading them to the Fall Ball, isn't she? Drawing them."

Juliet didn't answer that, but she didn't have to. It made sense. If they were stupid enough to venture into the center of the viper's nest, they'd be completely isolated, surrounded by players. Not just any players, but top-level players who wouldn't think twice about ending them to add a few more points to the leaderboard. Manipulating the press to hide all the rest was easy. She'd clean up the story, get it to play out in some way that made sense. For her.

"She told you how to find the Fall Ball?"

Juliet nodded. "Yep."

"But why would they go? They gotta know that's a death sentence. Walking in there. Why not just take what they've got to the feds?"

"Dunno," Juliet replied. "She said I go to the ball, I make them disappear, I get our points back. How the rest plays out don't much matter to me."

Romeo let those last few sentences sink in. "Juliet, baby, I heard a lot of *I*'s and *me*'s in that last statement, not no mention of *we* or *us*."

The ambulance was racing, probably pushing a hundred miles per hour, but Juliet gave it more gas anyway. The engine screamed and jerked forward. He barely heard her over the roar, and part of him wished he couldn't.

"The thing is, her scalpel can fix a lot of this stuff, can shut those two down for sure, but you made a lot of noise over the last few days, and there's no way to blame it all on them. When people start to string things together, they'll realize the Hollanders couldn't possibly have been in all the places they needed to be to account for everything that's happened, only some of those places. For it all to work, to tie things up nice and neat, they'd have to have been working with someone. Someone who wasn't afraid to get loud. Someone akin to a sledgehammer."

Romeo jerked at the zip ties again. "Juliet, baby, that ain't the way."

"You always said you wanted what's best for me, sugarplum. You said you'd do anything for me. How many times you tell me you'd die for me?"

Again, Romeo yanked on the zip ties. He put his entire body

into it, but the belts around his waist held him firm to the gurney. "Juliet, this ain't—"

Reaching back, Juliet twisted one of the valves on Romeo's IV. He felt a warmth enter his veins.

"I'd hate to see you hurt yourself, sugarplum. Maybe it's best you sleep for a bit while I drive. This'll all be over soon enough."

77

Driving through the night and the better part of the day, Brendan and Abby finally exited the highway at a little after six in the evening and wound through back roads before reaching their destination.

Roland Ludlow's house sat atop a hill at the end of a cul-de-sac in an affluent suburb of Chicago known as Oak Brook. A stone Tudor more akin to the English countryside, it would have appeared out of place if it weren't for the ancient live oaks peppering the yard and partially concealing the home from the street. With the setting sun, the streetlights had begun to tick on, same with decorative lighting around the property, bathing the home in subtle pools of light.

A man was in the driveway, loading bags into a matte black Range Rover.

Brendan and Abby parked on the street and walked up the driveway, making no attempt to hide their approach. When he saw them, he didn't seem surprised. He picked up another bag and shoved it into the vehicle. "She knows you're coming. Probably has eyes on you right now." He gestured at two security cameras pointing at the driveway. "Doesn't matter who owns them. She's got her fingers in everything."

"You know who we are?" Abby said, slightly surprised.

"Of course I do. I'm frankly surprised it took you this long to get here. Another ten minutes and I'd be gone." He eyed the .380 tucked in the waistband of Brendan's jeans, but didn't seem phased by it. "For the life of me, I don't understand why you'd come here, but she said you would and here you are." He loaded the last bag in the back and closed the door. "Crazy bitch doesn't seem to know how to get things wrong."

Abby stepped closer. "You said *she*. Not them. Not the players. You said *she*. Do you know who's behind all this?"

When Ludlow didn't reply, Brendan pushed harder. "It's Robin Church, isn't it? That's her name?"

At the sound of a triple chime, Brendan's heart thudded.

It came from Ludlow's phone.

Leaning against the back of the Range Rover, Roland Ludlow read the message and shook his head. "I didn't sign up for any of this."

"What does it say?"

"Well, it's a *Spice*. Nothing mysterious about it. Like I said, she knows you're here. She wants me to walk you back to your car and shoot you both. Make it look like a murder-suicide. Apparently you've outlived your usefulness." He shrugged. "Not like you're the first. Ain't that how it goes."

Already knowing the answer, Abby asked, "Are you going to do it?"

"I'm done being her dancing monkey. I earned enough; I'm getting out." Ludlow rounded the vehicle to the open driver-side door, reached in, and tugged the hood release. Back in front, he raised the hood, took a moment to study what he found, then ripped a small black box from the engine compartment and tossed it to the lawn where it landed next to the Range Rover's stereo and several other electronic components Brendan didn't recognize. Ludlow took one last look around the engine, appeared satisfied, and closed the hood. He glanced at his watch, a wind-up Timex that might have belonged to his grandfather it looked so old. "You clearly have questions. I'll give you ten minutes, then I'm gone." He nodded at the cameras. "Inside, not out here."

Ludlow didn't wait for them to answer. He went up the path to the front of the house, leaving the door open behind him.

The interior of the house was open-concept, warm and inviting yet something was missing. Brendan didn't realize what that was until Ludlow led them to the kitchen and motioned for them to sit at the table. There was a hutch against the wall filled with family photographs. Roland Ludlow had an attractive wife and a daughter of around eight. She had her mother's long dark hair and chestnut eyes. A beautiful smile missing two of her front teeth.

Ludlow lowered himself into a chair. "I got them out four days ago." He nodded at Brendan. "About the same time you and your friends were going through our offices downtown. That's when most everyone split."

To Brendan, that felt like a lifetime ago. He couldn't imagine it had only been four days.

Abby let out a soft gasp. "Brendan..."

He turned to find her pointing at a body on the floor near the back corner of the living room. A dead man of maybe thirty-five. There was a butcher knife sticking out of his chest.

"That's the second one she's sent for me in as many days. I put the other one out in the toolshed."

He said this matter-of-factly. He might have been rattling off a recipe for pumpkin pie.

An old video camera was mounted to a tripod a few feet from the dead man, pointed at a well-worn recliner. Cables snaked back across the room to a 65" flatscreen hanging on the wall.

Ludlow snapped his fingers and drew their attention back to the kitchen table. "Sit."

They did.

On the corner of the hutch sat a pile of electronics amid a tangled mess of cords—two phones, two tablets, laptops, smart watches, three smart speakers, a Wi-Fi router—all of it powered off.

Studying them both, Ludlow drummed his fingers on the tabletop. He'd chewed the nails to the quick. He looked at his ratty index finger like he was considering going back at it, then leaned back instead. "You know she's stealing from players, right? Do you know where she's hiding the money?"

"She's paying it back out to the higher levels—bronze, silver, gold, and platinum," Abby replied. "Someone else called it wealth redistribution."

Ludlow waved a dismissive hand. "She's paid some of it back out, but that's pennies compared to what she hauled in. I'm asking if you know where she stashed the rest."

Brendan's heart thumped. A deep rattle as if to punctuate what Ludlow had just said, because when the man put it in those simple terms, something clicked in the back of Brendan's mind, something he should have caught much earlier. "She's funding the loans…" he said in a voice that was almost dreamlike. His mind was racing now, putting pieces together.

"What loans?" Abby asked.

"We found a bunch of defaulted loans on INTENT's books. The borrowers on those loans were all bogus. Isaac Alford and Joel Hayden were behind them. Shell companies, mostly. They emptied those accounts and hid the money at the bank in Laos. From there it was meant to be laundered, then paid back out to them somehow."

Ludlow nodded. "So you found the bank in Laos?"

"Notakopi," Brendan told him. "Hundreds of millions of dollars. The part I couldn't figure out is why nobody complained about the missing money. We assumed it was because the lenders on those defaulted loans only contributed small amounts, but that wasn't it at all, was it? *She* funded those loans. Robin Church. That's why nobody was looking for it. All that money came from the app." Brendan's eyes grew wide. "She planned to store the money at INTENT, in their peer-to-peer lending system. It wasn't supposed to leave…Isaac Alford stole it from her."

Ludlow was smiling now. "He yanked all that money right out from under her. Put it in the one place she couldn't reach."

"…that's why she killed him," Abby said. "All of them."

Ludlow sat back in his chair. "She's generous until you steal from her. Then she can become a righteous bitch."

Brendan blew out a breath, considered all of this, then looked back up at him. "Yeah, you never know who you can trust."

The shot was loud.

Ludlow slammed back into his chair, then slumped forward. Dead.

When Brendan's hand came up with the .380, smoke was still coming from the barrel.

78

Abby screamed.

It was short.

Cut off.

Like it tried to get out along with a gasp, and both got caught.

Brendan dropped the gun on the tabletop and grabbed her wrist. "Abs, that wasn't Ludlow. *It wasn't Ludlow.*" She was still breathing heavily when he nodded toward the framed photographs on the hutch. "Look—the small picture in the back."

She didn't see it at first, then she did. Most of the photos were of Ludlow's daughter; a few included his wife. Only one had all three, and it was buried deep behind the others. Abby stared at it for maybe ten seconds before turning toward the dead man on the floor in the living room. "That's Ludlow..." she whispered.

"I think this guy was like Romeo and Juliet. Some player sent to kill him. We must have surprised him before he had a chance to leave or clean up or whatever he was supposed to do."

Brendan rose and rounded the table. He didn't see the stun gun in the man's hand until he was next to him. Abby saw it too. "Check his phone."

He'd placed his phone facedown on the table.

Brendan retrieved it. When the lock screen appeared, he held the phone in front of the man's face until it vanished. The *Spice* was still there. It simply said—

I want proof Ludlow is dead.

Brendan set the phone back down on the table. He didn't want to touch it. He didn't want to be in this house, but he knew they couldn't leave, not yet. He didn't will himself to look back at the dead man on the floor in the living room, at Ludlow; his subconscious did that all on its own just as it made him cross the room until he reached the body with Abby trailing hesitantly behind him.

Ludlow's blank gaze stared up at them both, and before Brendan realized what he was doing, he knelt and closed the man's eyes. When he stood, he found Abby studying the video camera.

"I haven't seen one of these in maybe ten years," she said. "It uses VHS tapes."

"It's not connected to the Internet. There's no way to access or erase it remotely."

Brendan studied the buttons, then rewound the tape and clicked PLAY.

There was a flicker of static, and Roland Ludlow appeared on the large television.

"If you're watching this, I'm dead." He paused and smiled slightly. "That is not something I ever expected I'd be saying. I've had a lot of *unexpecteds* over the past few months, but here we are. If you're with law enforcement, maybe this will be useful; if you're working for her at least do me the courtesy of watching through to the end

397

before you destroy the tape. Maybe you'll change your mind." He stared at the camera a moment, then continued. "I'm not going to say her name for obvious reasons." He held up a smart speaker for a second, then tossed it off to the side. "She's listening. What I'm about to tell you might slip past her as long as I don't say her name—she's got bots listening for that, it would draw her right in. You best keep that in mind, too. She's listening to *everything*."

Brendan glanced at the pile of hardware on the hutch near the kitchen and thought about all the devices in their own home before Ludlow's voice drew him back.

"We didn't start out expecting to hurt anyone. Well, at least I didn't. Writing peer-to-peer lending software is boring. When I suggested we code what would become the app you know as Sugar & Spice, I was just looking for a way to keep my team engaged. The app was something to keep us busy between the mundane stuff. Truth or dare for adults. What harm could come from that, right? There were six programmers on my staff, and five didn't give a shit. Wanted no part of it. She was interested, though, and that was enough to keep me on the idea. She was by far my best programmer, and I was curious where she'd take it." He rubbed his chin. "Before I go into the app, you need to understand something—she might have been the most skilled coder I'd ever encountered. Barely an adult, but she improved INTENT's software a hundred times over. Could do it in her sleep. I'd put these complex problems in front of her, and not only would she find a solution, she'd eliminate a thousand lines of code and streamline the entire process. Watching her work was like watching Mozart compose. It was inspiring. That may be the real reason none of the others wanted to participate in the app—they were intimidated and didn't want to get shown up.

"It was easy enough to write the code—just a bunch of text prompts stored in a database doled out as users played along. A kid could write that, I guess that was our real problem—me *and* her—we wrote that initial code in twenty minutes and needed to take it further. *It wasn't hard enough.* So we began to challenge each other—our own version of truth or dare. I dare you to incorporate GPS. I dare you to read in data from the user's other apps, use that to shape what S&S gives them. I dare you to read their e-mails, their texts, whatever personal thoughts they put in writing—use that. Okay, well, I dare you to *listen*—find some way for the app to listen to the user's conversations in real time, get their innermost thoughts, use that. Done. How about we listen when they fuck their partners—use that. Hell, we've got a camera, we can watch, right? I want to watch. We can use what we see, too. We have their health data. Their financial data. We know what they buy. We know what they eat. We know their friends. We know…everything. With each revelation, came enhancements. At some point *we know* became *we can. We can* make them do this. *We can* make them do that. *Do you have any idea what that's like?* Having the power to tell someone what to do and watching them do it? In real time from their own phone? That…that made us feel like gods. That was like a drug. She got off on it as much as I did, don't ever let her tell you otherwise. She was the one who came up with the whole payment system. I remember her saying, 'you need only sex, drive, and money to rule the world and we've got the first two, how do we get the third? How do we use *that?* Well, at this point, I imagine you're intimately familiar with *how* so, I don't need to go into all the details." He paused for a moment and gathered his thoughts. "Initially, we only rolled the app out to INTENT employees. We kept it in-house. It was only meant to be a game, right? And that's all it was until the day it wasn't. The day she posted it to the various app stores. I told her to take it down, but I won't lie—it was a half-assed request. I knew she wouldn't, and I didn't push. I was as hooked as she was. I wanted to see what would happen. Neither of us expected it to take off as fast as it did. People will do *anything* for money. A woman in San Francisco stood naked on the Golden Gate Bridge. We had some guy jerk off in front of the fountain from *Friends*, the one in Central Park. We told people to fuck on buses, trains, and planes…like any drug, you build up a tolerance, you need more to get high. Each *Spice* became more daring than the last until we ran out of places to go with it." He fell silent, looked down at the floor, then back at the camera a moment later. "I was the one who asked if she thought we could get someone to kill another person. I'm not proud of that. The thought came into my head and popped out my mouth before I could stop it, and she was nodding right along before I finished my sentence. I won't go into the details, but the short answer is yes. Like I said, people will do anything for money, for sex, for power. When you've got access to everything on someone's phone, it's like being in their head. It wasn't hard finding the right person to ask any more than it was hard to find their victim. Someone who deserved to die. I think that's when her and I started to see things a little differently. I was okay with doing it once. She wanted more. That was about the same time Isaac Alford found our money. We'd hid it good. Trust me, when you've got access to the code for an online financial company, hiding some money isn't hard. The problem was, we didn't have *some money*, we had a *lot* of money. If he'd come to us and just wanted in, I think we could have worked something out, but instead, he stole, and man, you don't fuck with her like that. I knew better. Isaac should have known better, but he did it anyway."

The video flickered and Brendan thought that was the end of it, but Ludlow reappeared. He must have stopped the recording to piece together what he wanted to say next because when he returned, he leaned into the camera, his face awash with sincerity.

"I never agreed to kill Isaac. Cindy either. That was all her. I'm no saint, I did some bad shit, but they were friends and that was crossing a line. I began wondering when she'd paint a target on my back, and if you're watching this I had a right to be paranoid. If you're watching this, it means she wasn't willing to stop when I asked her to stop. *When I told her she had to stop.* It means she's taking it all to another level. Part of me is glad I won't be around to watch that play out because I know where her head's at, I know how she thinks, and that's scary as fuck." He licked his lips and slumped back in the chair, tried to force a smile. "Whoever you are, whether you destroy this tape or not, please tell my wife and daughter I love them both more than anything. I'm sorry I brought all this down on us. I'm sorry I brought it down on anyone."

Brendan was so caught up in the video he didn't realize Abby had knelt next to Ludlow's body.

On a chain around Ludlow's neck were four metal trinkets—bronze, silver, gold, and platinum—each containing a number.

Sugar & Spice™

Sugar
When was the last time you lied?

79

Romeo woke to the sounds of laughter.

Complete darkness.

He was still tied to the gurney, he was sure of at least that, but where the gurney was in the world, he had no idea.

The air was thick.

Still.

Slightly medicinal, but tinged with an underpinning of copper.

Hot and stuffy, like being trapped in a barrel or a box, only that wasn't it at all. This was something else entirely.

"Juliet?" he muttered from cracked lips. "You there, sugarplum?"

She didn't answer, and when he held his breath to complete the silence, he heard nothing to indicate she was with him in that dark place. There was only the laughter.

Muffled.

Distant.

Only…that wasn't laughter, was it?

No.

Now that he gave it a better listen, it wasn't laughter. It wasn't even coming from a person. It was something metallic—scraping. Measured. Careful.

Romeo's brain was sluggish, flushing out whatever cocktail Juliet had put in his IV, and that was probably why two plus two didn't quite equal four, but instead felt like it could be some other number entirely. That was why the idea that he could still be in the ambulance hadn't occurred to him in those early moments after waking. Probably because the ambulance had been a cacophony of noise when they'd been driving, nothing like all this quiet.

Nothing like the stillness.

When the back door opened and Romeo caught a glimpse of some Black man standing there in the instant before the Black man pointed a high-powered flashlight at him, Romeo realized the laughter he'd heard, the scraping, had been that man picking the lock. He knew that because he also caught a glimpse of the man stowing his lock picks in the pocket of his coat and retrieving a .9mm from the ambulance's bumper before he extended his arms, crossed the gun under the hand holding the flashlight, and pointed both directly in Romeo's eyes.

"I'm Agent Curtis Brown with the FBI. Let me be the first to welcome you to Chicago."

Romeo squinted at him. "How 'bout you get the light out of my eyes?"

The man did no such thing. Instead, he tilted his head slightly and spoke into some sort of radio, maybe an earbud like they used in the movies. "I've got him. Bringing him in now." He stared at Romeo for a long time, then finally said, "Someone doesn't like you very much. A call came in on my personal cell; I've got no idea where she got my number. Told me you were Hollander's accomplice. Told me exactly where to find you."

Although Romeo's brain wasn't quite running up to snuff, the pieces of what was happening started to click. The bitch who had been on the other end of his phone calls, the one who took away all the points and money he'd earned the hard way and then dangled said funds in front of Juliet, had demanded a sacrifice.

You made a lot of noise over the last few days, and there's no way to blame it all on them. When people start to string things together, they'll realize the Hollanders couldn't possibly have been in all the places they needed to be to account for everything that's happened, only some of those places. For it all to work, to tie things up nice and neat, they'd have to have been working with someone. Someone who wasn't afraid to get loud. Someone akin to a sledgehammer.

Yeah, all that came back to him, too.

"Let me guess," Romeo managed. "Robotic voice? No caller ID?"

Brown didn't respond to that, didn't have to. The answer was all over his face.

"Lovely lady," Romeo muttered. "Fucking cunt of a lady."

The FBI agent climbed up into the ambulance and ran the light around the interior. When the beam reached the gurney, he studied the zip ties and belts holding Romeo in place. He then shined the light back in his face. "You want to tell me your name?"

Romeo squinted. "No, sir. I do not think I do."

"If I cut you loose, you going to give me trouble?"

That might have been the stupidest question the man could have asked.

Nope. I won't give you no trouble at all. Don't mind me if I smash your nose with my elbow as soon as you free my arm. Pardon my reach when I relieve you of that gun. So sorry about the bullet in the skull.

Romeo didn't answer him because he simply couldn't while keeping a straight face. Instead, he turned his head, away from the light.

"Because here's the thing," Brown said. "I don't need you alive.

All of this is far easier to explain if you're not rotting away in some cell thinking of ways to distort the narrative. Especially with lawyers and the like trying to paint you as some sort of victim to get their faces on TV and line their pockets. You struggle. I kill you. My report is typed and submitted by this time tomorrow. Quick review board decides the shooting was just, and I'm back to status quo. From my end, that's way easier than you spinning lies for the next twenty to thirty in hopes of seeing daylight."

As he said all this, Brown got himself a good look at the taped-up wound in Romeo's belly, the mess of filthy bandages littering the floor, the empty vials of painkillers, antibiotics, and whatever else Juliet had pumped in through Romeo's IV. This man might have been talking game, but by the end of his little speech, he had a good handle on the score.

Romeo took the opportunity to use the light spilling across the inside of the ambulance to study the place he'd last seen Juliet. He pictured her sitting in the driver's seat, leaning forward to get a good look at the road over the steering wheel. He pictured his burner phone in her hand. The phone she had not left behind.

"You cut me loose," Romeo told him. "I won't give you any trouble. I own what's mine, what I did. But here's the thing, I'm small potatoes. You can bring me in, lock me up, hell, I might even tell you a little bit about what I know, but what do you think will happen when you walk out of that interview room after our little talk and have a sit-down with your boss? He's going to ask you one simple question; one you will not be able to answer. He's going to say, 'Okay, but who was pulling this guy's strings? Who was really running this shit show?'" Romeo paused for a second. He needed to get his words right, and his brain was still a little mushy from the meds. He glanced out the open ambulance door, at what looked like a very empty parking lot. "You here alone, Agent?"

There was a flutter behind Brown's eyes. It was brief, but it was there.

Romeo said, "Let's assume you got backup incoming, but they ain't here yet. That gives us a window. An opportunity. You and I, we work out a deal. I tell you exactly where you can find the lovely lady behind all of this, hell, I take you to her, then maybe you agree to let me go. You don't have to break no laws or nothing, just turn your back for a second, give me an out. You can even come after me, all fair-and-square like. I'm just asking for a chance, here. I've been used, Agent." He jerked at one of the zip ties. "Why you think they served me up like this? I'm a patsy. You bring me in by my lonesome, and that will all come out soon enough. You'll have to explain how you wasted time with me while your real perp skipped off. *But you work with me*, I help you get *her*, and you've got yourself a solid collar. You got the kind of arrest that puts your ass in a corner office."

Brown leaned back slightly on his heels and wiped his chin with the back of the hand holding the flashlight. At least a minute of quiet dropped between them, weighing as heavily as the smell of Romeo's spilled blood drying around the inside of the ambulance. Finally, he tapped the barrel of his .9mm on the metal frame of the gurney, three quick taps. "I'm listening."

80

Abby's fingers trembled as she tugged the chain from where it was partially obscured under Ludlow's shirt and spread the four metal squares out so they could read them clearly:

Bronze 73
Silver 9
Gold 149
Platinum 180

Brendan retrieved the dead man's phone from the kitchen table, opened a browser, and keyed in the numbers as an IP address:

73.9.149.180

The browser hung for a second, then the screen flashed black and was replaced by an animation of the Sugar & Spice logo, which morphed into the outlines of a man and woman dressed in formal wear holding each other in an intimate embrace. Below that appeared:

The party's started, but it's far from over.
Dress to impress and come on over.
There are no limits, there are no rules,
There are no boundaries and there are no fools.
You've earned the right.
You are the elite of elite.
The Fall Ball awaits you,
A night of decadent heat.

Brendan and Abby were still reading when the camera's flash went off on the back of the phone, turning the palm of his hand bright red. He didn't realize the camera had taken a picture until an image of Abby and him looking down at the screen replaced the text. That was quickly followed by their names appearing superimposed over the image.

When the phone rang, he nearly dropped it. The harsh ring was like the bite of a snake striking with hostile malice, the blade of a razor opening his flesh. The caller ID listed no name, didn't even say UNKNOWN CALLER, and the number made no sense, as if it originated in some far-off place.

Brendan didn't click *Answer*, he knew he didn't, but the call connected anyway.

A female voice on speaker, electronic, disguised—*"Is Ludlow dead? I want to see. Show me."*

Brendan twisted the phone toward the body on the floor.

"And the other one?"

He showed her the dead man at the kitchen table, held it there for a moment, then twisted the phone back, brought it close to his lips. "What the fuck do you want from us?"

"You don't get to ask questions. You're only breathing right now because I've let you."

The phone screen flashed again. The image of Brendan and Abby vanished, replaced with a new one.

Abby let out a soft gasp.

Hannah and Stuckey both stared at the camera, their eyes wild with fright. Both were gagged, sitting on a concrete floor with their backs against an old stone wall. The kind you'd find in the basement of a house built long before the use of concrete or cinder blocks for foundations. Their hands and feet were bound with thick rope, and dried blood speckled their clothes and faces. There were bruises too. The entire left side of Stuckey's face was purple and swollen.

When Hannah moved, when her head twitched with a short-lived spasm, both Abby and Brendan realized this wasn't a photograph at all, but a live image.

The screen went dark for a moment, not because the camera failed but because someone stepped in front of the lens as they crossed the room. It wasn't until the person drew near Hannah and crouched that they realized it was the girl they'd come to know as Juliet. She'd pulled her hair back in a greasy ponytail, she was still wearing the same clothing she'd had on when they left her in the freight car. Brendan had no idea how she escaped the police, and it didn't really matter because she was there now, hovering over their friends, and she was holding a very large knife. She made a show of it, pointing the tip of the blade at the camera and slowly twisting the handle between her fingers with this deliberate impatience. Like she wanted to get on with things, but someone else was holding her leash. She brought the knife to Hannah's cheek, pressed it against her trembling skin. Hannah pinched her eyes shut and held back cries that desperately wanted to escape.

With a quick flick of her wrist, Juliet drew the knife down, opening a cut about an inch long. With that, Hannah did cry, she fucking screamed.

The image vanished.

The screen went blank.

The female voice returned—*"I'm sending a car for you. One hour. If you're not in it, they're dead. Bring Ludlow's video tape."*

She disconnected.

The phone slipped from Brendan's fingers and clattered when it struck the ground.

His heart was racing.

When Abby spoke, her voice was low, distant, yet her words surrounded him from all sides. "Brendan, we go, and she'll kill us. All of us."

"We could leave right now." He nodded at the video camera. "We take that tape, this guy's phone, whatever else we find in this house, and put it in a locker at the bus station, call the news networks and the police—tell them what we have, where to find it—then we vanish. Make it look like we got on one of the buses, but maybe steal another car, head to Mexico or Canada, or Europe, or—"

Abby squeezed his hand. "We don't have our passports, and even if we did we couldn't use them. She'd know. Running is expensive, and we have no money. How long do you think we would last?"

Brendan wasn't listening, he just kept going. "Maybe we walk it into the FBI office where that agent, Bellows, works. Or go to another FBI office—maybe New York, or Indianapolis, someplace they wouldn't suspect we'd go."

"We barely made it here," she told him. "We're exhausted. We're not thinking straight, and if we run, that's only going to get worse. We run, and she kills Hannah and Stuckey, we see their bodies on the news later tonight or tomorrow... I don't know about you, but I

411

couldn't live with that. We can't spend the rest of our lives looking over our shoulders. We have to…see this through."

The woman standing before him wasn't the woman he'd married. She wasn't the woman he'd spent the last thirteen years of his life with. This was someone different, someone stronger, someone *complete*. He could think of no other way to describe her. It was like the woman he thought he knew was only an illustration and this Abby was rendered from stone, every inch intricately revealed in perfect detail. There were no secrets between them, not anymore. She was an extension of his body, he an extension of hers.

Brendan stroked her cheek. "Abs, I can't lose you. I feel like I finally found you."

Abby's eyes locked with his, and he knew she felt it too.

There was so much there. So much happening behind them. He saw his life with her, every second they'd been together. Every laugh. Every fight. Every tear. Every heartbreak. With all his being he wanted to see into the future, their future. Whether that was only a few more hours or five decades, but there was no hint of what was to come, there was only what they had been. While that terrified him, it also brought solace, because he couldn't imagine what his life would have been without her.

"Whatever happens, I love you," Brendan told her. "I always have, and I always will. Everything else…whatever problems we might have had, whatever stumbles, they're meaningless. They've done nothing but make us stronger. The silliness with—"

Abby placed her finger over his lips, silencing him. "You're right. It doesn't matter. I love you too. My judgement may have gotten clouded over the past few months, but I've never lost sight of that. I've always loved you."

She took him by the hand and led them through this stranger's house, through the master bedroom and into the spacious bath, to the large walk-in shower dominating the far corner. She reached in and turned on the water.

When she kissed him, he hadn't expected it. It was tentative at first. She leaned in and gently brushed his lips. When he returned the kiss, when he wrapped his arms around her, and returned the kiss, there was a heat neither of them had felt in a decade. Part of Brendan's brain told him it was because it was their last kiss, but he pushed that thought away because that wasn't right at all.

It was their first kiss.

They shed their clothing and stepped under the water where they made love. After, they held each other until the hot water was gone. Even then, they didn't want to let go.

81

Exactly one hour later, a black town car appeared in Ludlow's driveway, and it wasn't alone.

Dozens of people stood silently outside. They were on Ludlow's lawn, in his driveway, along the quiet residential road. At least three had guns and made no attempt to conceal them. All were holding their phones. Some seemed lost in the displays. Others were watching Brendan and Abby. Others still were filming, holding their phones out and recording as they stepped from the house and started for the town car idling at the curb.

The air filled with the sound of the triple chime, playing out in some unholy chorus.

"Just keep walking," Brendan whispered in Abby's ear. "Try not to look at them."

They reached the car without incident and climbed in the back; several boxes were on the floor.

The driver eyed them in the mirror. "She's provided clothing for you. You're expected to change. We're fifteen minutes from our destination, so please be quick about it."

Before either of them could respond, a black privacy screen rose between them. The doors locked and the car rolled forward.

The crowd didn't attempt to stop them, but instead parted as they drove down the road, and closed again behind them.

Brendan couldn't shake the feeling they were being swallowed.

The boxes were from Bergdorf Goodman and held a Brioni Tuxedo for Brendan and a stunning black velvet and lace Giorgio Armani dress for Abby. Other boxes contained shoes and accessories, including an Omega watch that probably cost a year's worth of Brendan's salary and a Van Cleef & Arpels diamond necklace valued at twice that.

They redressed in silence, discarding the clothing they'd scavenged from Ludlow's closets after their shower at their feet. Abby looked amazing, and he told her so.

They encountered very little traffic. Even the lights seemed to be on their side—green the entire way. Brendan couldn't help but wonder how much of that fell to chance and how much was *her*. His mind had conjured some godlike image of this woman waving a magic wand over all things electronic. Although he knew it wasn't true, he couldn't shake it. He tried to memorize the streets, but his brain was buzzing with so much chaos he quickly lost track. It was clear they'd left the better parts of Chicago behind them, though. Wherever they were, only a handful of the streetlights were working. The asphalt was cracked and riddled with unpatched potholes. Many of the buildings were boarded, and those that weren't had bars over the lower windows. All looked abandoned. There was graffiti everywhere, from random phrases and images to gang tags. The roads and sidewalks were deserted, yet Brendan knew they were being watched. Shadows seemed to scurry away moments before the headlights found them. Eyes looked down at them from the dark windows above.

If they were at war (and Brendan was under no illusion they were not), they'd traveled deep behind enemy lines, their presence far from stealth.

Another right.

Two lefts.

The burned-out carcass of a pickup truck on blocks at the corner.

They drove halfway down the block and came to a stop.

Brendan expected to hear the triple chime, to hear a GPS say, *You have arrived at your destination*, but there were neither of those things.

Brendan and Abby peered out the window, at the sign marking the tall, stone structure beside them, the only building lit up on the street:

Robert Inverness Church
All are welcome!

"Robin Church," Brendan muttered, taking in the words. "I'll be damned. It's not a person, it's a place."

The church was old, far older than the surrounding buildings, certainly older than the overgrown abandoned park to its left or the square structure to its right with the collapsed roof and gaping holes where the windows once were. At least a hundred years older than the brick tenements on the opposite side of the street, the ones with crumbling concrete steps leading to heavy doors chained and padlocked. Unlike those surrounding buildings and places, the church was alive. Lights flickered from behind stained glass, and a trickle of smoke curled toward the sky from one of the many chimneys. Brendan got the impression the church had been built long before all else and would still be standing long after the rest was gone.

"Do you hear that?"

Brendan nodded. "I can feel it."

And he could.

Loud thumping bass, rattling his chest.

Music.

The knock on Brendan's window caused him and Abby to jump. A Black kid of maybe thirteen was staring at him through the glass. He tried the door handle, and when he found Brendan's door locked, he motioned for him to roll down the glass.

Brendan still had the .380, it was tucked in his tuxedo pants at the small of his back. He felt its presence, close, yet out of reach, as he lowered the window.

The kid held up his phone, snapped a picture, and studied the screen. When the triple chime played, his eyes lit up and he whistled. "We've got ourselves some VIP platinum players, here! Welcome to Robin Church, Mr. and Mrs. Hollander. Head on inside. All food and beverages are complimentary." He either knew their car or the driver, because he knocked twice on the roof and waved toward the front.

Another car pulled up behind them. Brendan realized it was a Rolls-Royce, the gray paint polished to a mirror-like finish. After a few seconds, the driver tapped their horn.

"Come on, now. We don't want to keep anyone waiting."

There was another knock, this one on Abby's side of the car.

Another kid.

He looked younger than the first.

Brendan thumbed the door locks, and the two of them got out, the video tape looking like a clutch purse in Abby's hand.

The older boy pointed at the front of the church. "Straight up them steps. Just follow the music. Enjoy."

The moment Brendan and Abby started in that direction, the older boy's phone let out the triple chime again. He showed the screen to the younger one. There were smiles, and a fist bump. The town car drove off, vanishing around a corner two blocks down.

Crossing the street, Brendan and Abby climbed the stone stairs to the massive wood door of the church, the music growing louder with each step. At least nine feet tall and held together with intricate black ironwork, it easily could have been the door to a fortress or some medieval castle.

"Do we knock?" Abby asked, studying the alcove. "Or should we just go in?"

Before Brendan could answer, the door swung open and a woman wearing a black lacy evening gown bolted out laughing wildly, her high heels dangled from the fingers of her left hand. She took quick stock of her surroundings, and padded down the steps, waving at one of the boys dealing with the cars. A moment later, a man in a vintage tuxedo appeared. When he spotted the woman on the sidewalk, he stumbled over to her and pressed his lips to hers in a drunken kiss.

Music blared from inside.

Some nonsensical techno beat.

The door started to swing shut. Brendan grabbed it by the edge. He held it for Abby, then followed after her. Together, they disappeared inside.

82

"You coulda cuffed me in front, that woulda been the neighborly thing to do."

Romeo was in the back seat of the FBI agent's car, half sitting on his hands because when they were behind his back, his knuckles lined up perfectly with the exit wound in his flank, jabbing with every bump and bounce like a hot poker. Not that sitting on his hands was much better. That put pressure on his wrists and caused the way-too-tight cuffs to bite into his skin.

The fact that he was feeling all that told him whatever painkillers Juliet had given him were making their way to the exit, and the worst was yet to come.

"Who shot you?"

Romeo almost replied, *Oh, that was Skinny Bitch*, then he realized that might not mean much to this guy. Super Federal Tommy-On-The-Spot Special Agent... Brown? Is that what he said his name was? Romeo was having trouble holding on to the man's name, and that had him bothered because it meant his recent memory problems weren't because of the waning painkillers but more likely from the infection, and if the painkillers were wearing off, that meant the antibiotics probably were too and any clarity he might have now could be fading with them. Just putting that thought together made his head hurt. "It was the wife. She shot me."

"Abby Hollander?"

Romeo nodded. "She's a tough nut. Tougher than her old man."

Whoever had Brown's ear must have said something, because Brown straightened up in the driver's seat, went quiet for a second, then said, "Copy."

He made a left turn followed by a right a few blocks later. Romeo tried to get a look at the street signs, but most were either missing or painted over. "You still tracking my phone?"

Brown shot him a glance in the mirror, one that said, *no, we're out trolling for Girl Scout cookies, you dumb fuck*, then went back to the road without answering.

Romeo knew he was tracking the phone, and it was leading them right to Juliet; that wasn't the point of the question. The point of the question was to engage this man. Get him talking. Get his guard down. Brown seemed to be having none of that, and Romeo was sure they were getting close to their destination, which meant he didn't have much time to turn things around. "I like that you're doing this without backup, going in all Dirty Harry like. That takes some balls. I've never been much of a team player, either. Not till I met my Juliet, anyway. She changed that in me. Filled a hole I didn't know I had."

Brown stared straight ahead.

Said nothing.

Romeo eased his bad thumb under his thigh, counted silently to three, and rolled his weight on it in one measured movement. He felt the knuckle go for the second time in a day and bit back the pain. Then he said, "Going into a potential firefight alone, though? Hell. They must pay you good over there at the FBI. Or is it the other way around? They don't pay you enough, so you gotta do something like this to right the scales?"

With his thumb out of place, he pulled his left hand from the metal cuff, then he made a fist, rolled it, and forced it back in. That one hurt a bit more, but it was all good.

Brown made another right, and when he did, Romeo caught the sweep of a second pair of headlights making the turn behind them. Careful to keep his hands down, he twisted around in the seat to get a better look out the rear. He couldn't make out the car, they were hanging too far back. Some kind of sedan. Romeo turned back around and leaned forward. "You got a tail? Or are you traveling with company after all?"

Brown gave him a quick look in the mirror again but kept his mouth shut.

Romeo wanted this guy to be a lone cowboy. Killing him would be hard enough, but if there were more behind them, that changed things. Made his work exponentially harder. "FBI usually works in pairs, right? So how many you got in the car behind us? Two or three?" When Brown didn't answer, Romeo added, "I'd guess three. Your partner and another pair."

They made another left.

So did the car behind them.

Under his thigh, Romeo massaged the feeling back into his hand.

The neighborhood had gone decidedly sketchy. All run-down and forgotten. Like everyone packed up what little shit they owned and went on to someplace greener, leaving an empty husk behind. Although, they weren't quite alone—Romeo caught a curtain in a second-story window of what looked like a shitty apartment build-ing ruffle and drop back in place. Someone else was watching them from behind an abandoned gas station.

Whoever was tracking Romeo's phone was feeding directions to Brown through an earbud. That had to be what was going on, because Brown was doing nothing but driving and listening to some voice in his head. He hadn't looked at his own phone since they got in the car, and best Romeo could see, he had no other electronics up front with him.

"When we get there, you gotta promise me you won't hurt Juliet. She's gone a little astray, but that's only 'cause of her current circum-stance. Once we get in there, she'll have my back. And when she sees I'm with you, that means she'll have your back too. You'll see. You'll want someone on the inside. If you're planning on bringing in the cavalry and storming the place all Normandy-like, that ain't gonna work. You'll have to go surgical. Strike from inside."

When they turned right again, Romeo waited for the sweep of headlights from behind. When it didn't come, he twisted in the seat again. Whoever had been behind them was gone. Either they didn't take the turn or had dropped off earlier and Romeo missed it. No way to know for sure. "I got you. You're going Dirty Harry style. Making a solo run at the castle," he said at a whisper, although he knew Brown heard him.

They drove a few more blocks before Brown slowed and stopped the car in the middle of the street. He shifted into park, and while it was clear he was assessing the surroundings, it was also clear he was listening intently to whoever had his ear.

Romeo had never been to Robin Church, but he knew of it.

They all knew of it.

Like Oz's mythical castle.

Juliet was in there; he was sure of that. So was the woman who robbed him. Skinny Bitch and Abercrombie, too. They were all in there.

Romeo licked his lips, tasting a sweetness that hadn't been in the air for days. He leaned forward again. "Let me ask you a question, Super Special Agent Brown, do you think of yourself as a sledge-hammer or a scalpel?"

"Sit. Back," Brown instructed.

Romeo did no such thing.

He brought his arm up and around Brown's neck so fast, the loose handcuff smacked the man in the side of the head. Romeo jerked his arm back, squeezed. When Brown tried to pry him off, Romeo pressed his knee into the back of Brown's seat, got more leverage, and pulled harder. Brown gagged. Spit. His legs cracked against the bottom of the steering wheel, flapped, and finally went still. It was over in under a minute, but it was a hard minute and Romeo had to catch his breath when it was done.

He found the handcuff keys in Brown's pocket and rid himself of those. He was about to climb out of the car when he had another thought.

Digging in Brown's ear, he fished out the earbud, wiped it on his shirt, and placed it in his own ear. Then he said, "It's you, isn't it? You ungrateful bitch. I just took out your scalpel. Now I'm coming to play with you."

83

Inside, the music was deafening. This relentlessly pounding dance beat marred by synths and loose guitar riffs. There were vocals, but they were short and clipped, samples thrown across the bed by the DJ whom they didn't spot until they reached the end of a short hallway and found themselves at a wall of people.

The DJ was suspended from the church's soaring ceiling on a large platform, surrounded by turntables, equipment, and amps. He wore a black cape with red lining, an oversized Red Sox jersey, and black tuxedo pants like some hip-hop vampire. His heavily made-up face was alabaster white behind wraparound shades. As he worked the turntable, he pointed at nobody in particular in the crowd below him, his body jerking and thrashing with the music. Through a haze created by smoke machines, lasers and flashing lights cracked the darkness with illuminations timed with the thumping bass. Strobes created a random lightning effect that came and went.

The crowd of at least a thousand writhed in a twisted, drunken dance. The air stunk of alcohol, sex, and sweat. There were banners and signs everywhere announcing *Sugar & Spice Version 2.0 out tonight!* Below that was a list of feature updates:

- *Automatic currency conversions!*
- *The ability to write and direct Sugars AND Spices to other users!*
- *Sugar & Spice user proximity alerts! If there are other S&S users in the room, you'll know! Hit them up with a private Spice!*
- *Increased referral credits for every new member you recruit!*
- *Automatic push of the Sugar & Spice app to all your contacts - It's anonymous, they won't know it came from you, but you'll still get the referral credit!*

We have over 1 billion users - who's ready for 2 billion?

"Brendan!" Abby shouted over the music. She was pointing at a wall of television monitors on their left. They started at the floor and filled every inch to the ceiling at least thirty feet above. There were videos of people having sex. Others simply displayed empty rooms. Others still showed photos of people with their Sugar & Spice level and total points and stats—how many *Sugars* they'd completed, how many *Spices*, overall ranking in the app versus other players—like baseball cards. As these images shifted and morphed from one person to another, there were occasional shouts from the crowd, pointing, as people spotted themselves or those they knew. In the center of all the smaller monitors was one large screen, at least ten feet across. A photograph of Brendan and Abby dressed to the nines was at the top. He realized the picture had been taken the night he and Abby had gone to Menton's. Some clandestine shot either taken by an employee or one of the nearby tables. That seemed like a lifetime ago. Directly below the photo were five words, flashing with the beat—

1,000,000 Points! Dead or Alive!

Beneath that line was a long list of players. Following each of their names, it simply said *0.0 Miles.*

Brendan immediately understood he was looking at a leaderboard listing the players closest to his and Abby's current location. All of them, right there in this room.

As that realization struck him, all the smaller monitors went blank and came back with the same video—Abby undressing in her agent's bathroom on a hundred screens.

As Abby gripped Brendan's arm, the crowd on the dance floor cheered. Some held up their drinks toward the monitors in a mock solute, others just kept on dancing as if all of this was perfectly normal.

In Brendan's hand, Ludlow's phone vibrated—

Unknown Caller:
If you stand there until someone recognizes you, you're dead.
Back left corner. Now.

Every inch of Brendan's body screamed for them to run. Head back the way they'd come, push through those doors, and just run. But he also knew they'd never make it. They'd only survived this far because the woman he thought of as Robin Church had let them survive. The moment they ventured off script, she'd alert one or more of these people to their exact location. Hell, she'd probably throw an actual spotlight on them and have the DJ point them out. They wouldn't reach the door. They'd die right there on the dance floor, and most of this crowd wouldn't miss a step.

Brendan showed the message to Abby, pointed toward the far corner, and after a moment's hesitation, they worked their way through the crowd. The mattresses started about midway back. Plush, king-size mattresses up against the outer walls littered with bodies in various stages of dress or undress, some entwined in the throes of sex, others were tied up, bound with straps of leather or metal restraints, many were blindfolded as hands groped every inch of their flesh. There were smaller freestanding monitors scattered about displaying random *Spices*—

Have intercourse with a stranger.
Submit.
Kiss whoever is to your left.
Perform oral on the first person to tap your shoulder.
Dominate.

As the messages changed, this hedonistic orgy eagerly changed with them. Brendan realized there were leaderboards here too, and all these people were earning points with each debaucherous act, hungry for more. Deeper into the room there were racks, swings suspended from metal works, and even machines designed to perform various sex acts. Crowds swarmed, either watching or waiting their turn to participate. Cameras were everywhere, the images projecting on the walls, ceiling, and floor.

They were near the back corner when Brendan felt the barrel of a gun push into his side below his ribs. That was followed by warm breath and a familiar voice nestled against his ear, "Hey, Brendan."

Kim Whitlock.

84

"Straight ahead!" Kim shouted over the music. "Through that door on the far left!" As if to emphasize her point, she needled the gun deeper into his side, and with a hand on the small of his back, shoved him in that direction. Abby had no real choice but to follow.

The door had a security card reader on it, identical to the ones at the INTENT offices. When Brendan stopped in front of it, Kim gave him another nudge. "It's busted, just go through."

Above the door was a camera. The lens twisted in their direction, constricted.

Someone was getting a better look.

The metal fire door wasn't locked.

Brendan stepped through with Kim at his back, Abby behind them. When the heavy door swung shut, the loud music became nothing but a muffled rhythmic thump. They were in a narrow hallway, lit by bare bulbs above, spaced every seven or eight feet.

Kim turned and took a few steps back, until she was facing Brendan and Abby with an arm-length between them. She looked

Abby up and down. "Pleasure to finally meet you. I'm Kim Whitlock. I imagine your husband has mentioned me?"

Brendan's face was bright red. "Kim, what the fuck?"

She turned back to him and held out her palm. "I was told you have a gun."

When he didn't hand it to her, Kim let out a long sigh and snapped her fingers. "Geez, you two with the long pauses. She said I'd have to shoot one of you, and I told her, 'no way, Brendan's smarter than that, he gets when he's lost. He'll be compliant.' But no…"

Making a show of it, she thumbed the hammer down on the revolver and started to squeeze the trigger.

Brendan held up his palms. "Okay! Okay." Reaching around to his back, he pinched the .380 between two fingers, slowly brought it around, and dropped it in her hand.

Kim looked at the gun for a second, then slipped it in her pocket. "Any other weapons? Smartwatches, earbuds, electronics of any kind?"

They both shook their heads.

"Okay." She gestured to her left. "Head down that hall, I'm right behind you."

Someone had fastened a bolt lock to the top corner of the fire door, but when Kim tried to throw the bolt, it was misaligned with the eye and wouldn't lock. She tried a couple of times, then finally gave up and came after them.

The hallway ended at stone steps descending into gloom, polished smooth from years of use.

"Down."

Holding the walls, Brendan and Abby did as they were told. With each step, the air grew colder, slightly moist, and when they reached the basement level, a dehumidifier was chugging away in the far corner.

"Keep going," Kim instructed. "Straight ahead."

White holiday lights hung from the ceiling, strung between various pipes for HVAC and plumbing.

They passed an open door. Brendan only got a quick look, but it was enough—some kind of living space. He spotted a couch and tables, a small kitchen against one wall, and a queen size bed against another, neatly made, complete with throw pillows. There were even a few artsy prints on the walls.

"You've been living here?"

Kim didn't answer him, but he could tell by her expression she had. She twisted the lock on the door and pulled it closed. "Keep walking."

"You owe us some answers," Abby told her.

"Keep walking."

"You framed my husband for your disappearance, made it look like he killed you, and you've been hiding here the whole time?"

Kim raised the gun as if ready to strike Abby with it, then managed to get her temper in check. "You'll have answers soon enough. Hurry up."

At the end of the hall was another door. Metal, like the previous fire door, with another camera mounted above and a card reader to the right of the knob. Set in a steel frame mounted in a cinderblock wall like some underground bunker. Someone was watching here, too. The door unlocked with a loud *click* as they approached.

"Inside," Kim instructed.

The knob was cold, and when Brendan gave it a twist and opened the door a rush of chilly air poured out, at least fifteen degrees colder than the hall. There was a buzz, too. The underlying sound of hardware, fans, and motors. As they stepped into the large room they were surrounded by racks of computer servers from floor to ceiling with thick network cables bundled together and snaked tight against the rafters. Fluorescent bulbs hummed between it all, bathing the entire space in harsh white light.

Kim pointed at a metal plate on the wall. "Touch that, both of you."

Abby frowned. "What is it?"

Kim blew out a frustrated breath and tapped her finger against the metal. There was a quick spark with a barely audible pop. "It will rid your body of static electricity. Can't be too careful in here. Touch it."

Abby did, followed by Brendan, both creating soft sparks of their own.

"Kim!" a woman shouted from the far end of the room. "Get them over here."

85

As the seconds ticked by, Romeo waited for *her* to respond in the earbud. His puppet master. The woman who giveth and the woman who taketh away. The woman who had his Juliet somewhere inside that church. Because that would make sense. She owned an insane number of law-enforcement officers, why not an FBI agent? Why not Super Federal Tommy-On-The-Spot Special Agent Brown? He'd come along for this ride easy enough. That meant he was at least willing to dip his toe in the dark half of the pool. The voice that finally replied wasn't *her*, though, it wasn't even a woman.

"Brown? Report."

Brown no longer had use for his Glock, so Romeo relieved him of it, then he plucked Brown's phone from the center console and studied the main screen. It was secured with a six-digit code, but Romeo didn't need to open it to check for the Sugar & Spice app, he found the man's score to the right of the time, under the battery indicator. Brown was still a newbie, less than a thousand points. He wasn't a player; he wasn't much of anything. Romeo gave the score three fast taps, then two slow ones, then another two fast. That bypassed the phone's lock screen and took him right to Sugar & Spice. Clicking through the various menus, he brought up the support tab, clicked on *Create Ticket*, and thumbed in the following:

This here is Romeo. You've got more than one something that belongs to me. If you don't give it all back to me, I'm going to huff and I'm going to puff and I'm going to burn your whole fucking church down around you. XOXO

He backspaced over that last bit, deleted it, then keyed it back in only because he knew Juliet would like it, then he clicked SEND and climbed out of Brown's car. He'd forgotten about the earbud when the other voice came back.

"Brown? I'm ten minutes out. What the hell is going on?"

Romeo started in the direction of the church and raised his index finger to his ear, touched the small device. He was pretty sure he didn't need to do that to talk, but he'd seen it in enough movies to know it couldn't hurt. The movement tugged at his gut wound, but it didn't hurt anywhere near as bad as before. Juliet had done a bang-up job. He cleared his throat, "This here is Romeo, who do I have the pleasure of speaking with?"

There was a momentary silence, then: *"This is Agent Marcus Bellows with the FBI. What have you done with Agent Brown?"*

"Agent Brown and me had ourselves a slight disagreement as to how to proceed. He decided to sit this one out. What's your 10-20?"

"My…"

"Your location, shithead. Where the fuck are you? Do you have eyes on me?"

"I'm not telling you—"

"If you weren't in the car right behind us, I strongly suggest you get your ass down here with about a hundred of your closest friends. I think I'm gonna have to do something very bad."

Agent Marcus Bellows didn't like that very much and began to voice his concerns, but Romeo heard none of it. He took out the earbud, tossed it to the ground, and crushed it under his boot without missing a step.

Two Black kids who looked no older than the stain on the pocket of Romeo's favorite jeans appeared to be running double-duty as some type of security on the church and a valet service. Romeo slowed his approach enough to catch their procedure with some facial recognition. Boy One did the scanning. He signaled Boy Two to take the cars away. When the passengers of said car went up the church steps, Boy One flashed a hand signal to Boy Three up top, who opened the door. None of them appeared to be packing, which meant they probably were and just knew how to hide it.

If Boy One was bothered by the fact that Romeo walked up to him without a car, he didn't say nothing. Instead, he held up his phone and took a pic of Romeo's battered face. While it was processing, his gaze landed on Romeo's wrists. The handcuffs were gone, but the red marks left behind were not, and anybody with a shred of street smarts recognized those lines. To his credit, he didn't say nothing about that, either, didn't even linger on it, but Romeo knew he'd made a mental note and would share his newfound intel the second he got the chance, just like he'd tell whoever that the crazy large man's tee shirt was all bloody and his face was banged up pretty good.

Boy One lowered his phone. "Says here you're not eligible to enter. You need to be a platinum member. According to this, you don't even have…" His voice trailed off for a second. "I'm not sure what this means. I've never seen it before."

Romeo smiled, knowing full well his smile didn't do much in the way of easing someone's anxieties. His smile had a habit of doing just the opposite of that, which was all right by him. "I hate to be a Karen, but I need you to go ahead and make a call to your supervisor, son. I ain't here for the party. I'm here to work some shit out with *her*. I'm not the patient sort, so be quick about it."

Another car pulled up and stopped about ten feet from the two of them. With the headlight glare, the occupants were shadows.

Romeo couldn't help but wonder if Agent Marcus Bellows was in that car.

Brown's phone vibrated with an incoming message—

Hello, Romeo. Would you like to try a Sugar or a Spice?

"Oh, I don't think we have time for petting above the sweater." Romeo mashed down *Spice*.

The phone went quiet, then there was the triple chime and—

You step inside this church, you'll be dead in ten steps. Then I'll make your Juliet suffer. She might live longer than you, but she'll spend that time begging for death.

Or

You can put a bullet in your own head. I'll kill Juliet fast. I can't let her go. None of the loose ends are leaving tonight.

Romeo let out a loose sigh and told Boy One, "You're gonna want to run, son. Take your friends with you. You don't want a part of what comes next." The boy's phone rang. Romeo snatched it from his hand, held it close to his face, and said, "I think I'd rather dance."

The door of the church opened less than an inch, and the barrel of an AR eased out and pointed at him. Romeo side-stepped, grabbed the barrel, and yanked. He felt the gunman thump against the opposite side, then he hauled his leg back and kicked the center of the door, sending it crashing back against the man a second time. Romeo was still holding the AR when the door swung open, and the man slammed against the opposite wall. Romeo gripped the weapon with his other hand near the center for leverage and brought the stock up in a wide arch, catching the man under his chin. There was a satisfying crunch, then the man dropped in a heap at Romeo's feet.

86

Brendan didn't realize they were standing in a giant Faraday cage until after Kim had ushered them deeper into the space. When he looked back at the room's only exit, he spotted the metal framework lining the walls and ceiling. Thick bundles of network cables snaked through and vanished behind another rack of computer CPUs and hard drives, this one secured behind a secondary cage. At the center of the room was a single workstation surrounded by computer monitors. Behind the desk, pecking away at an ergonomic keyboard with lightning speed, was a beautiful woman with long brown hair and deep, dark eyes.

Kim brushed the hair from the back of the woman's neck and gave her a kiss. "This is my girlfriend, Ana Morales."

Brendan recognized the woman from the photograph Kim had shown him at dinner.

Abby recognized her for other reasons. "You're the woman Roland Ludlow talked about."

Without looking up from the center screen of her immense workspace, Ana held up a finger, then went back to typing.

While her screen was filled with code that might as well have been gibberish to Brendan, the others all had video feeds. There were shots of every conceivable angle of the church above, interior and exterior, the crowds, every intimate act caught on camera. But it didn't end there. Some of the monitors were divided up into dozens of small squares, each with another feed, and as Brendan got a closer look, he realized those were coming from the app itself. Cell phone cameras. Computers. Home security cameras. Nanny cams. Robot vacuums. Hacked feeds from all around the world. Tiny text over each image displayed the player's name, location, level, and points.

Ana finished typing whatever she was working on, gave the block of text a secondary look, then clicked ENTER. Lines of code began flying across the screen at the center of her desk.

Satisfied with whatever that was, Ana settled back in her chair and scanned the feeds on her wall of monitors. "Ah, Roland, even in death the bastard can't keep his mouth shut. She held the palm of her hand out. "Tape, please."

Abby stared her down. "Where are Hannah and Stuckey?"

"Tough till the end, huh? You weren't so tough when I put you in that hotel room. When I had some guy fuck you. I'm curious, are you Abby right now or Emily?" She reached into a camouflage bag near her feet and pulled out a stack of printed pages. "I've gotta admit, it's pretty good. Kept me guessing, and that's not easy to do."

Abby's notebooks and Mac were in there too.

"How did you get my book?"

"That sniveling little tool took it before she torched your house. She figured it might be worth something after you're dead. I guess we'll see." She dropped the pages back into the bag and held her hand out again. "Tape."

Abby gave it to her.

From a shelf under her workstation, Ana took out a bulky square device, pressed it against the VHS tape, and pulled the trigger. A red light came on, there was a soft hum, then quiet again. "Magnetic eraser," she told them before shoving everything back on the shelf. "Bye, bye, Roland." She let out a soft sigh. "Now, where did I leave his family…" Her finger froze in the air, made a fist, twisted. One of the video feeds slipped across the various monitors, centered on her main screen, and expanded. Brendan realized she was wearing a haptic controller glove.

Roland Ludlow's wife and daughter were standing on a subway platform, nervously looking up at a clock on the wall.

"I heard what he told you," Ana said. "Funny how everyone has their own version of the truth. Shit hits the fan, and he decides to play the innocent. He got off on pulling the puppet strings way more than I did. Then he lost his balls when Isaac Alford stole all our money and things went sideways. It's a little tricky to pay players when you don't have access to your funds. Instead of working the problem, he panicked. That's why he's dead on his living room floor and I'm right here in the captain's chair—*I don't panic.* I solve the problem. I solve every problem."

Ana looked back at the video feed of Ludlow's wife and daughter on the subway platform and asked Kim, "Do you want to clean up this loose end, or should I?"

"I'll do it."

Kim leaned down, clicked a button marked *Spice*, and typed—

Push them on the tracks. 10,000 points.

Ana read the message. Backspaced over the points and changed it to 20,000. "Why not?"

"You can't do that," Brendan said.

"Of course I can." Ana's finger hovered over the ENTER key. "I can do whatever the hell I want."

Before Brendan or Abby could stop her, Ana clicked the key. On the screen, at least half the people standing around the platform looked down at their phones. Although the video was silent, Brendan knew the triple chime also played, because Ludlow's wife's face shot up in alarm in the half second it took for multiple hands to reach out and shove her forward. She and her daughter vanished over the edge. Those around her didn't bother to look to see if either survived; instead, they all buried their faces back in their phones. Brendan realized they were trying to figure out who collected the winnings.

Ana quickly typed another message. "I'm giving all those people points. A happy player is a returning player."

"You're fucking crazy," Abby spat out.

"I'm a risk management savant. The wife knew too much, she had to go. The daughter is all cute and cuddly now, but I let her live, and in ten years she's hunting me down like some deranged Lara Croft. Fuck that noise. Better to plug the hole now. Besides, a kid growing up without parents is doomed from the start. I did her a favor. If I'd taken care of Isaac when he first tingled my radar, you wouldn't be standing here, and I wouldn't be in this mess."

"I don't understand," Brendan said.

"Of course you don't. Because you're a simpleton. Let me explain it to you in terms you'll understand. Isaac stole all my fucking money."

"The defaulted accounts at INTENT."

"When Isaac realized Ludlow and I were parking the funds we confiscated from Sugar & Spice players in lender accounts at INTENT, he set up bogus borrowers, took the money, and defaulted on the loans so he could pocket the cash. He knew I couldn't tell anyone, and the bastard was quick about it. Spread it out over hundreds of accounts he knew I couldn't touch." She gestured around the room at all the equipment. "Even with all this. He picked that bank in Laos because they use hexi-encryption. That's more robust than AES 512. That's not next level. That's next next next level. Uncrackable. I couldn't steal it back. I needed you to do it for me."

87

Brendan felt the blood leave his face.

"Oh," Kim said. "He put that together quick. I thought you'd have to explain it to him."

Brendan found himself looking at Kim as things clicked into place. "You highlighted the fraud at INTENT. You put the spotlight on Alford and Joel Hayden. You got us to the bank in Laos. You purposely steered Stuckey and me."

"We needed you to seize the funds," Kim said flatly. "Identify the accounts and lock all that money up nice and tight behind a good ol' U.S. of A. FCID wrapper."

"What's an FCID wrapper?" Abby asked.

"It's like an electronic bag or box. Once assets are placed inside, they can only be accessed by the authorized party at FCID."

"And that's you?"

"Him and Stuckey," Kim told her. "It takes both of them."

With one eye on her monitors, Ana said, "I'm going to make this simple for you. You give me my money back, and I'll let you walk out of here. Like I said, I'm a problem solver. You need to decide if you're part of the problem or part of the solution."

"I'm all over the news," Brendan told her. "I'm sure my access has been revoked."

Kim smiled. "If poor Mary hadn't died, maybe she would have done exactly that. Unfortunately, she never had the chance. Not before you and Abby killed her."

Ana's fingers flew over the keyboard. Her screen filled with headlines about the explosion in Brookline. The deaths of Assistant Director Mary Dubin and her husband. Nearly every story pinned responsibility on Abby and him. "I can even make all this go away."

"How?"

"Oh, I've got a guy." She waved an arm in front of the monitors filled with Sugar & Spice players around the world. "There's very little I can't do. If you want to live another hour, you know what *you* need to do."

Ana's phone rang.

She pressed it to her ear, listened, then muttered, "He's where? Okay, put it where he'll see it—make a statement—then end him. I want that to be the last thing that good-for-nothing piece of shit sees." She hung up. "Fucking Neanderthal."

Three of Ana's monitors blinked and switched to the timer announcing Sugar & Spice v2. There was less than ten seconds left. "Got a lot of balls in the air tonight. Who's ready to take this one to the next level?"

Kim stroked her hair and hovered over her. "Do it."

Ana waved her controller glove through the air, then quickly typed some commands into her keyboard. "We're live in three, two, one...done." She leaned back in her chair.

All the phones in the room lit up. On the one nearest him, Brendan saw a progress bar slowly cross the screen, then there was the triple chime. That was followed by another sound, five notes. A new chime. As it played, Ana waved her finger through the air like a conductor. "It grows on you, doesn't it?"

She returned to her keyboard, fingers flying. One of her monitors went blank, flashed, and returned with a graphic of the world with the title *Sugar & Spice v2 Rollout/Central Hubs* across the top. White dots littered the continents, thick in the populated areas, less so in the more remote corners. Brendan understood enough about the Internet to know these hubs were servers owned by the Internet service providers across the globe. The dots around Chicago and the central United States had gone green, slowly spreading.

Ana studied the image for a moment, then tapped the edge of her desk impatiently. "Timetable, people. Let's keep things moving." She clicked a button on her desk and spoke into a microphone. "Bring them in here."

88

Romeo was still standing at the church entrance when the phone in his back pocket got hot. He shifted the AR to his other hand, took out the phone, and checked the screen, half-expecting to see a new message from her. Instead, there was a progress bar. When it finished, the Sugar & Spice logo appeared with some new chime and a graphic informing him he'd been updated to version two.

"Well, lottie-fucking-da," Romeo muttered, shoving the phone back in his pocket. He barely heard himself over the thumping base and electronic squeals someone considered music.

There was a shout from outside. Romeo was pretty sure it was the kid with the scanner, but he slammed the door before he got a good look. He caught a glimpse of a car sliding to a stop outside too. It had one of those floodlights mounted on the driver-side near the mirror, and that screamed law enforcement.

Romeo had spent his entire life under the impression churches never locked their doors—sanctuary for the needy and all that—but this door had two dead bolts and a heavy slide lock up at the top.

He twisted both dead bolts, slammed the slide home, then beat the hell out of all three with the AR until there was no way they were coming undone. It'd be easier to take the hinges out.

Satisfied no new players would be walking on the game board, Romeo turned and got a better look at what was going on inside.

He was either standing at the mouth of heaven or hell, depending on where someone's idea of a good time might land. Every inch of the church's interior was packed with people. Drunk. Sweaty. Some dressed in tuxedos and formalwear, others in tee shirts and jeans, others still wearing nothing at all or some combination of all the above. The floor was sticky with spilled booze. A DJ presided on a platform high above the crowd, wearing some ridiculous get-up. There were screens everywhere filled with porn, player stats, or crap about the app. Half of them were touting *Sugar & Spice v2!* flashing and pulsing. Romeo was taking that in when they all switched to, *Coming, in three, two, one*—then came loud pops with strobes flashing in time, colored lights, all simulating indoor fireworks. The crowd screamed, and nearly everyone raised their phones as the progress bar he'd seen moments ago on his own ran across all the others. When version two completed its installation, the screams and shouts only grew louder as everyone cheered the coming of their personal hedonism and no doubt insane wealth—Romeo remembered the kid outside telling him only platinum members were permitted access to the party. One point, one ounce of platinum, was worth around a thousand bucks. These people didn't look like the kind who rolled with only one point.

His wound had opened again. He felt the blood running down the side of his leg. When he lifted his shirt and checked the bandage, it was growing dark with blood. He didn't dare peel it off to see the wound itself, there was no point in that. What will bleed will bleed. No point in crying over spilled blood. A stuck pig was right twice... that one wasn't right, but it still made him smile.

Someone kicked him. A hard shot, right in his left kidney.

Romeo managed to keep his balance and turned just in time to see his assailant steadying himself for another blow. Romeo side-stepped, the man went wide, and Romeo grabbed his forearm as he stumbled. He pulled the man closer as he brought up his right knee, caught him in the gut. The air left him with a choked gasp. Romeo gripped the sides of the guy's head, twisted, and snapped his neck. He'd barely had time to straighten up when a message vibrated on his phone—

You were warned.

"Yeah, well fuck you too." He brought the AR around, aimed, and shot the DJ in the center of his frilly white shirt. To his credit, the DJ got his hand off the turntable without skipping or scratch-ing the record, then his head lulled forward and seemed to study the growing red stain in his chest before he toppled back, flipped over the railing, and landed somewhere in the middle of the dance floor. The music never stopped, and if there were screams, Romeo couldn't hear them over the racket. That would change soon enough as he raised the AR, set it to single shot, and started for the crowd, shouting Juliet's name.

89

A door opened at the far end of the room. Two large men appeared with Hannah and Stuckey in tow. They forced Hannah and Stuckey inside, half-dragged them toward the group, and shoved them to the floor a few feet short of Ana's workstation. Their wrists were secured with zip ties. Both were badly bruised. The blood around the cut on Hannah's face had dried a crusty black.

"Oh my God!" Abby tried to go to them, but Kim leveled the gun.

"Don't."

Brendan's eyes met Stuckey's single good eye; his other was swollen shut. "Hey, buddy," Stuckey managed before coughing and pressing a hand against his ribs.

Brendan turned on Kim with complete disgust. "Jesus, Kim. He was never anything but good to you."

"That's true, right up until the part when he figured out who my girlfriend was and asked for a shit-ton of money in exchange for not indicting me along with her. For me, that's when he crossed the line. It was that last night in Chicago. I knew it was time for me to pull the pin. I made myself disappear and came here. I figured the cops would blame one of you." She raised an eyebrow. "I guess you won that particular coin toss."

Brendan tried to process that. It meant the guilt trip Stuckey had poured on him, making him think he was responsible for whatever happened to Kim had been a ruse. Not only did he lie to him, but Dubin, the police. Not once did Stuckey raise his hand and point out she'd committed a crime and he'd confronted her, instead, he led them all to believe Brendan had done something to her.

Stuckey's gaze remained locked with Brendan's for another second, then dropped away and Brendan knew it was true.

Ana produced a USB fingerprint reader, plugged it into her CPU, then brought up the FCID secure website before turning to them. "Stuckey, you're up first." She nodded at Kim. "He does anything stupid, shoot Hannah."

Hannah had taken a beating too. There were bruises on her face, her neck, and what was visible of her shoulder under the torn corner of her shirt collar. She trembled at the mention of her name, her head twisted first to Ana, then to the screens in fast jerks, like some wild animal boxed in looking for a way out. It was only when she looked at Abby that the trembling stopped. Like she found comfort there.

When Stuckey rose and went to Ana's workstation, Brendan said, "It's over two hundred million dollars, Stuckey."

"I'm not dying for it."

"She'll kill us anyway."

Stuckey ignored that and typed his username and password. When prompted, he pressed his thumb to the reader. The monitor flashed, and his photograph appeared followed by his home screen. Logged in, he went back to Hannah.

Ana brought up a secondary login window.

Kim waved the gun. "Your turn, Brendan."

Abby squeezed his hand. "Stuckey's right, it's insured. Just do it."

Brendan's legs felt like rubber as he stepped to the workstation, keyed in his data, and pressed his finger to the reader. A moment later, he was logged in too. He returned to Abby and wrapped his arm around her.

Ana pulled the keyboard close and went back to it. She expanded multiple windows, read carefully, then smiled. "We're in." With several keystrokes, a series of numbered accounts appeared, the balances containing more zeros than Brendan could count. They expanded, minimized, moved. Ana was moving like a machine. Transfer windows appeared. She keyed in account and routing numbers. Repeated with the next account, the next. Kept going. Nearly five minutes passed before she clapped her hands together and grinned wildly at Kim. "We are *so* back in business, baby!"

"You have what you want," Brendan said. "You need to let us go."

Kim kissed the top of Ana's head, squeezed her shoulder, then pointed the gun at Abby. "Not until that bitch admits it."

Abby's eyes filled with confusion. "Admits what?"

Kim's gaze burned into Abby. "Stow the theatrics, and tell your husband what you did."

Abby was clearly confused. "I don't understand…"

Ana shook her head in slow frustration, like she was getting tired of having to explain everything to everyone and just wanted to get back to whatever she'd been doing before. She keyed something in on the main terminal and waved her controller glove through the air. Her central monitor began to fill with all the naked photographs of Kim. "Are you seriously going to pretend you're not responsible for these?"

If Kim was embarrassed by the display of nudity, she gave no indication. She wasn't even looking at the pictures, her hateful gaze was fixed on Abby. Her grip on the revolver tightened enough to turn her fingers red. *"You made those,"* she finally hissed out, her voice filled with venom.

"I don't…"

Ana grabbed both sides of her keyboard, lifted it up, and slammed it down on the desk with enough force to make them all jump. "They're fakes. When you thought there was something going on between my girlfriend and your husband, you found her social media accounts, downloaded every image you could find, then frankensteined them back together with a bunch of nudes you got from God-knows-where. Then you plastered them all over the web to try and ruin her. Don't you fucking deny that! Don't you dare! Own it, you stuck-up pretentious bitch!" She grabbed one of Abby's notebooks from the bag and held it up. "You even had the balls to write about it in your new fucking book!"

Abby's mouth fell open, but no words came out.

"Did you seriously think there wouldn't be repercussions for that?" Ana fumed. She slapped her keyboard again, and the video of Abby undressing flashed across the screen. That was followed by a quick montage of the news—the press conference when Kim was first reported missing, others where it was implied she was believed dead. Brendan's photograph. Abby's. Wanted.

Ana shook her head, disgusted. "Shoot her. Just fucking shoot her."

Kim's leveled the revolver.

Abby managed to get out, "I wrote about it—one of the characters in my book did that to another one—but I didn't do it. I would never…"

Kim thumbed back the hammer.

Beneath the naked images, video flashed at lightning speed—police surrounding the abandoned Tesla on the highway. Total chaos at the train yard. Firefighters in the street, the burned-out husk of her home smoldering behind them. The ruin of Hannah and Stuckey's house across the street. Brendan and Abby's photographs again. All the carnage pinned on them. All because of—

"Oh my God," Abby breathed, the realization striking like a sack of bricks. She twisted toward Hannah. "Tell me you didn't... I let you read that part of the book, but I didn't think you'd do it. *I thought those pictures were real!*"

Hannah's mouth fell open. Her eyes glistened with tears at the sudden betrayal. "Abs, how could you?"

They all stared at her.

"Hannah read that part of my book. She must have gone home and done it." Abby's face bounced from Kim to Ana and back again. "She didn't tell me. She wouldn't. She knows I would have stopped her. It was her. I wouldn't even know how to do that!"

Brendan eyed the gun. He wanted to make a play for it while Kim was distracted, but she was too far away. She'd get at least one shot off before he was able to reach her, and the gun was still pointed at Abby.

Gun or not, Hannah looked like she was about to attack Abby. "That's bullshit! You *showed* me that section of your book, let me read it, then you showed me the pictures, all proud of yourself after figuring out how to stitch them together. When you said you planned to put them online, I told you it was a bad idea, you'd regret it. Find some other way to get even—I tried to talk you out of it!"

"You made those!" Abby insisted.

"You're just trying to save your own skin."

"I wouldn't even know where to start."

Ana blew out a frustrated breath. "Enough." She reached into the bag and retrieved Abby's MacBook. Clearing a space on her desk, she plugged in a thick USB cable and attached the other end to her CPU before powering on the Mac. "I'm going to keep this really simple," she said as the screens filled with boot-up data. "I'll run a search for the files. If they're on here, Abby gets the first bullet."

"What if she deleted them?" Kim asked.

"Won't matter. I wrote this code. When you delete a file, it doesn't go anywhere, the pieces just get scrambled on the drive. This software searches at the bit level. Unless you destroy the drive, there's always trace left behind. If Abby created them, we'll find them."

A moment later, Abby's Mac lit up, not with her home screen, but with the same message that had been there for days over an image of a skull and crossbones:

The contents of your computer's hard drive have been encrypted within a locked file. This file will be deleted if you do not pay $10,000 in bitcoins to us, the new owners of your data. Should you notify authorities, your data will be deleted immediately. We are not located within your country. You have no recourse. Failure to comply will result in the deletion of your data. Do not turn off your computer or reboot. Doing so will result in the deletion of your data. Do not attempt to back up. Your backup will be infected as well, and all data will be deleted. We will provide payment instructions shortly. Say hello to your friends for us – you just infected them too.

"What the hell is this?" Ana said, scanning the text. The meaning of what she'd just read registered a moment later—her face went white as she yanked the cords out of her CPU with enough force to snap away one of the ends. "No! No! *NO!*" but it was too late—the ransomware message appeared on her center monitor, then the others. She frantically clicked at the keyboard, but it did nothing. The only monitor that didn't change was the one detailing the transmission of the new Sugar & Spice app around the world. She was still trying to understand the significance of that when they all heard what sounded like gunshots from somewhere else in the church.

90

Humans were animals.

Romeo came upon that decision when he rounded the corner into the main room of the church and the first person to spot the AR in his hand was a sixty-something fat man against the wall fucking some woman half his age who wore nothing but a cut-off tee shirt that said, *Real Men Love Tater Tots* across her small breasts. He was taking her from behind, caught sight of the assault rifle, and kept fucking even as Romeo pointed the gun at him. If he wasn't pressed for time, he might have let the man finish, but instead, he shot him in his creased forehead. The woman had her eyes shut through all this and didn't realize anything was wrong until said fucking ceased. Romeo shot her as the look on her face began a transition from puzzlement to fear, one it would never complete.

Gunshots in a crowded space brought on all kinds of odd reactions, particularly when everyone was drunk, there was loud music playing, and simulated fireworks had just rocked the room. For the most part, there was no reaction at all. Music kept playing. People kept dancing. Of the three or four people who saw what happened, only two had the sense to run and vanish deeper into the crowd, the others just stood there. One woman was still swaying with the music, albeit off the beat, her eyes growing large as her alcohol-saturated brain slowly pieced together what happened. Romeo didn't shoot her. Instead, he shot two people to her left. When they dropped, she finally screamed.

Others turned then, saw her, saw Romeo holding the gun, and he finally got the reaction he was hoping for—panic.

Romeo shot three more people at random, and the panic began to spread through the crowd like dominos toppling across a table-top. Switching the AR to a three-shot burst, he raised the barrel, sighted on the rack of equipment on the DJ platform above, and pulled the trigger. The equipment erupted in a burst of sparks, and the music abruptly stopped. There was a blissful silence for half a beat, then the screaming really kicked in as the crowd rushed the locked doors at the same time.

"Party's over, people! You don't have to go home, but you can't stay here!" Romeo shouted before mowing down four others. "Juliet! Where the hell are you, baby? Talk to me!"

On his far right, some guy in a tux shattered a stained-glass window with the heel of his highly polished loafer, only to find bars on the other side. Romeo didn't shoot him, either. Instead, he shot the woman standing to the man's left holding his tuxedo jacket.

All the movement opened up Romeo's gut wound further, and when he looked down, his pant leg glistened and there was a trail of blood on the alcohol-sodden floor. He wasn't light-headed yet, but he knew that was probably coming sooner rather than later, so he pressed forward, toward the center of the makeshift dance floor. Some woman made a play for the AR—she grabbed the barrel only to find rifle barrels got damn hot when recently fired. When she peeled her hand away (leaving bits of skin behind), Romeo shot her in the throat, then shot two other people at random to clear a path toward what looked like a large ice sculpture in the middle of the room. Partially melted, it had once been the Sugar & Spice logo but now looked more like two number fives with the tops half-missing.

He didn't see Juliet.

Not at first.

And when he did see her, it took a moment for his mind to register what he was looking at. He briefly wondered if that was from the blood loss or flat-out denial, decided it didn't matter, and stumbled over to her on legs that didn't want to work anymore. To his credit, Romeo managed to keep hold of the rifle as he dropped down next to Juliet's motionless body.

She had been tied to the base of the ice sculpture. Propped up against it like she was sitting on the floor, her legs splayed out in a wide *V*. Her face was frozen in stunned silence, and if not for the small bullet hole in the center of her forehead, Romeo might have convinced himself she was perfectly fine. Just resting. She wasn't resting, though—he knew before his finger stroked her cold cheek she was gone. Her unblinking eyes held no light.

A sign had been taped to her chest, her fingers wrapped loosely around the edges to give the impression she was holding it. It contained three words—

I failed her

While that stoked an anger within Romeo greater than any he'd ever felt, it was matched by the thought of all these people—people who had danced around her dead body, *his Juliet's dead body*, like she was nothing more than some party prop.

With a shaking, bloody finger, Romeo reached out and closed her eyes.

Had he been thinking clearly—*had he been thinking*—he might have realized this was some sort of trap. It wasn't until he heard a shot and the bullet tore through his left shoulder he realized he might be in trouble. He blindly pulled the trigger on the AR, the triple-burst struck the ice sculpture from below and shattered it in an explosion of white icy shards, then Romeo rolled, ignored the pain, sighted, and ended the man who had shot him.

Romeo stumbled to his feet, managed to cross the room, and braced himself against the wall.

She was here.

That fucking bitch.

That cunt.

The woman who strung him and Juliet along, played them, and decided she could just throw them away like yesterday's garbage.

His eyes fell on Juliet.

The lifeless husk that was once his Juliet.

His heart twisted with an ache so deep he wanted to tear his chest open and rip it out to make it stop. Breathing without her felt wrong.

"I'm right behind you, baby doll," Romeo said softly. "Wait for me."

This church would be their shrine, their temple, their monument.

Candles burned on tall wrought iron stands to his left, the surrounding floor was covered in drips of red wax. Romeo gripped two of the candle stands and toppled them to the floor. He watched as the flames fought to live, then found the wax, all the alcohol spilled throughout the night, and set the floor aflame. The quickly spreading fire brought on new screams, new panic, and that gave Romeo new life. "I've got one bit of business to finish, baby doll, then I'm right behind you."

With that came one simple realization. As clear as if Juliet had whispered it to him.

Only one door looked like it went deeper into the church.

91

At the sound of gunfire, Kim's head jerked up. The shots had come from upstairs. She listened intently for a few seconds, then turned to the two men who had brought in Hannah and Stuckey. "Go see what that was. Don't let anybody get down here."

With a nod, they were gone.

If Ana heard the shots, she gave no indication. She was frantically typing. Her face moved from the keyboard to the locked screens, to the map displaying the version 2.0 rollout, and back again in quick, spastic movements. She was breathing so hard it sounded like she'd just run a marathon.

"What's it doing?" Kim asked Ana. "Can you stop it?"

"It's infected," she muttered back. "It's all infected..."

"Why don't you unplug everything?"

Ana rolled her eyes like that was the stupidest idea she'd ever heard. "That wouldn't stop it. It's not just here anymore. It hit the distribution server and went out with the app update. Fucking thing is everywhere." She keyed in something else, and the map updated.

The dots nearest their current location switched to red and were spreading across the map as quickly as the others. She didn't say it, but it was clear that was the virus, chasing the app, spreading.

On the desk, Ana's phone dinged. When she picked it up, Brendan caught a glimpse of the ransomware message on the screen before she threw the phone against the wall. "It's getting in every-thing! Every fucking device with the app!"

Kim's voice fell low. "What about the money?"

"Who gives a shit about the money?"

"We need that money," Kim insisted.

Ana had stopped typing. She was gripping the edge of her desk like a vice. "I don't think you fully understand what's happening. This is going to hit every single user of the app—millions of people. It will brick their phones, their computers, all the servers feeding them. Forget about the money—the ransomware riding the back of my software update could take down the Internet!"

She drew in another breath, then grabbed the gun from Kim and stomped over to Abby. She jammed the gun against Abby's temple. "You fucking bitch! You did this! You knew your Mac was infected!"

Abby tried to twist away from her, but Ana only pressed the gun harder.

"You're hurting her!" Brendan shouted. "Stop!"

"Oh, I haven't started to hurt her."

Ana snatched the gun away, pointed it at Brendan, and pulled the trigger.

The bullet ripped through Brendan's thigh. His leg came out from under him, and he dropped to the floor. The pain came like a hot spear. His hand went to the wound before he realized he'd moved, and blood seeped out between his fingers.

Upstairs, a fire alarm sounded.

Stuckey lunged.

He tucked his restrained hands to his side and shot up from the floor, leading with his shoulder and the momentum of his considerable bulk. With three steps, he was on her. He caught Ana in the gut and sent the much smaller girl crashing back against her desk, but not before she managed to pull the trigger again.

92

Loud alarm.

No sprinklers.

Not in this old building, Romeo thought. *It's a fucking tinderbox. A place like this wants to burn.*

The fire spread quickly. It lapped at the alcohol on the floor—turning stains into puddles of hot flames. Thin tendrils reached out, explored, found wood, of which the old church had plenty—saturated with a hundred years of oil and polish. Then there were the people—many had spilled drinks on themselves and others as the panic spread and the fire sought the alcohol out like some hungry beast that hadn't eaten in months. The air had become a haze of gray smoke, thickening with each second.

In a half-daze, Romeo marveled at it all. The efficiency of those flames. He listened to the screams and wails as some burned and others were trampled trying to get out, only to find the main entrance blocked and the windows barred. Those screams were music. They were a symphony. They were a song for his Juliet.

All the television screens had switched to a skull and crossbones image with some long block of text. He didn't bother to read it, whatever it said didn't much matter. The picture was good, though. The picture felt *right*.

When two men with automatics came through the door in back as Romeo approached, Romeo knew she'd sent them. He just knew. Just like he knew when he raised the AR and pulled the trigger without taking the time to aim the bullets would find them. And they did. Both men dropped. It was divine intervention. It was his Juliet guiding his hand.

Romeo shot two more people at random and when he pulled the trigger again, there was only a click. He discarded the assault rifle, picked up an empty champagne bottle, and cracked it against a tabletop. He rotated the makeshift weapon in his palm and knelt next to one of the men who'd come out that door. Blood bubbled from the man's lips and down his chin, but he was still alive. He was alert enough to recognize the bottle for what it was when Romeo showed it to him, then pressed it against the side of his neck.

"How many more of you does she have back there?"

The man stared up at him, wide-eyed. "Help...me..."

"How many?"

When he opened his mouth to speak again, no words came out. There was only his final breath.

Romeo considered taking the man's gun, hell, both guns, then he heard Juliet's voice, clear as rain.

You don't need no gun, baby. Keep the bottle. You'll want to cut her. Nice and slow. Go through that door down into the belly of the beast, that's where the rot lives.

He stood and went through the door, oblivious to the screams behind him. The crackle of the fire in the rafters. The chokes and gasps as even the oxygen fled the church, leaving all else to die.

He'd gut her and dance on her corpse.
For his Juliet.

93

Stuckey slammed into Ana, Ana crashed into her desk, the desk rolled beneath them both and they ended in a heap on the floor amid the shattered monitors and a twisted mess of cords and computers.

The revolver tumbled from Ana's grip and skittered across the floor.

Abby went for the gun.

So did Hannah—although her hands were zip-tied, she lunged for the weapon.

The two women reached it at the same time, grappled, and Abby came away with it.

"Shoot that fucking bitch!" Hannah shouted at her.

Stuckey rolled off Ana and gave her a clear shot. "Now, Abby!"

Abby didn't fire, though. Although she trained the revolver on Ana, her eyes were on Kim.

She realized Kim was clutching her chest. Her face was stark white, filled with confusion. She never looked down at the place she'd been shot, instead, her eyes locked with Ana's, the woman who shot her. Even as she collapsed, she kept looking at her. It wasn't until her last breath left and her head lulled to the side, she finally looked away.

Ana scrambled off the fallen desk and crawled across the floor to her, oblivious to the shards of glass embedding in her palms and knees. "No, Kim. No!" She managed to get Kim's head in her lap and began to sob in her hair.

Abby raised the revolver and fired.

First, she shot the CPU that had been under the desk, then she turned to the racks of servers and unloaded the remaining shots into the hardware, unleashing a shower of sparks. When the gun was empty, she tossed it aside and went to Brendan. She managed to get his arm over her shoulder before she realized Stuckey was on Brendan's other side. "Lift on three?" he told her.

Together, they got Brendan to his feet.

He tried to tell them he couldn't stand, much less walk, but the words didn't come out. The world swooned, tilted, and went white.

Stuckey slapped him. "Stay with us, buddy."

When the room righted itself, he spotted Hannah at the door. She'd figured out the electronic lock and yanked it open.

She nearly ran into Romeo.

He was standing in the hallway, covered in blood holding half a bottle, a maniacal expression chiseled into his face, his eyes gleaming with hate.

94

Skinny Bitch holding up Abercrombie with some big Black guy who'd been beat to hell. Some blonde woman he didn't know.

Romeo glared at them all.

He stood in the center of the hallway, his wide shoulders and large frame nearly reaching wall-to-wall. His chest heaved as he sucked in air, not quite able to get enough.

That's just the smoke, baby. Seems it followed you downstairs. Fire's coming too, but you're okay. You're just fine. You're a goddamn machine.

"Yeah, baby doll."

His throat was filled with gravel, soot, and snot, and with those two words, a cough tried to climb out. He swallowed; it tasted both bitter and sour.

Someone had put a hole in Abercrombie's leg. He was dripping all over the floor. If a vampire sucked him dry, he might have had more color than he did now. When he turned his head, his eyes followed on a delay. The bullet probably nicked an artery. He wasn't long for this world.

As those thoughts rambled around Romeo's head, he thought about the hole in his own shoulder, his ruined gut, and realized he couldn't feel either of those anymore. He'd be willing to bet that was Juliet's doing.

The blonde woman went to the floor and came back up holding a revolver. She pointed it at his face. "Get the hell out of our way!"

The thing about revolvers is the barrel was visible, and even through the thickening smoke, Romeo saw the gun wasn't loaded. He twisted the bottle between his fingers and nodded toward the room behind Blondie. "Is she in there? The one behind all this?"

"Yes."

That came from Skinny Bitch.

No hesitation.

No fear.

She might have been the smallest runt in their litter but one look in her eyes told Romeo she was running the show.

Respect.

"I'm not here for you," Romeo told her. "Our business is settled. I only want her."

"Tell us how to get out, and she's all yours," Blondie demanded, waving the empty pistol.

Even as she asked the question, there was a loud bang as something collapsed upstairs and the first flames appeared behind him at the far end of the hallway, near the steps. They chewed through the plaster ceiling and started down the walls. Romeo figured the partiers were still trying to get out upstairs, but he couldn't hear them screaming no more. The fire burned as loud as a locomotive up there.

"There ain't no way out, not no more. Best you find a quiet spot and make peace with that."

When it was clear they weren't going to get out of his way, Romeo raised the bottle and pushed through them.

That's when he saw her, huddled on the floor.

She saw him, too.

95

Brendan's vision swooned, and when he tried to breathe he sucked in nothing but smoke. He coughed and heard Abby shout, "In there! Hurry!"

Although she shouted and was inches from him, still holding him up, she sounded like she was a million miles away.

Brendan caught a glimpse of the stairs at the end of the hallway in the moment before they shoved him through a doorway. The stairs were completely blocked, part of the ceiling collapsed, and every inch was on fire. It might have been the entrance to hell, and maybe it was.

They were in Kim's small apartment. The one he and Abby had found when they first came downstairs.

Abby and Stuckey carried him over to the bed and set him down as Hannah closed the door and frantically looked around until she spotted a small bathroom off to the side. "I'll get some towels and try and seal the door."

"Wet them, if the water is still running," Stuckey instructed.

He crossed the room and went to a narrow window high up on the wall.

As Brendan slumped back on the bed, he found himself looking up at the ceiling. Portions had already gone black, and dark smoke was drifting from between the rafters.

It's like an animal, he thought. *Feeling things out before going in for the kill.*

"I can see people out there!" Stuckey shouted back. "Firetrucks. Police." Brendan twisted and saw him fumbling with the window's twist-locks.

"Don't!" Abby quickly told him. "If you open that, you'll let air into the room, that will bring the fire right to us."

"We don't have a choice," Hannah said. She was back at the door, stuffing towels around the bottom.

"There are bars on the window," Abby said. "Even if we get them off, I don't think you'll fit."

Brendan knew she was talking about Stuckey, and when Stuckey didn't reply, it was clear she was right.

"We need to do something. The door is getting hot," said Hannah.

Brendan managed to point at the ceiling, at the smoke.

They all followed his finger.

"There's no other way out of here," Stuckey finally said. "We've got to open the window and call for help—hope they've got some way to get the bars off and get the three of you out."

"I'm not leaving you here!" Hannah cried.

"Abby's right. I won't fit." He turned to Abby. "We close the window as soon as we get their attention. If we do that, we can minimize the fuel for the fire and buy some time."

Brendan tried to sit up, couldn't.

"You three get out," Stuckey said. "It's either that or we all burn to death. We need to move."

When Abby nodded and went to the window, Hannah buried her face in Stuckey's shoulder.

She was still holding him when Abby said in a defeated voice, "The window is nailed shut."

96

Romeo closed the door behind him.

He knew the fire was coming, and while it would eventually come through that door, it would come from above first. The smell of it was everywhere, and portions of the ceiling had already gone black.

A quick scan of the room told him there was no other way out.

Ruined computer hardware was everywhere, punched through with bullet holes, trashed on the floor, an overturned desk and all that was on it. Shit had gone down in this room. That became abundantly clear when Romeo got a better look at the woman on the floor and the lifeless body of the other woman she held in her arms; she'd taken a slug in the chest.

"What's your name?" he asked her, his voice gravelly, sandpaper dry and layered in soot.

"Ana."

She was stroking the dead woman's hair, her face streaked with tears.

Romeo waved the broken bottle around the smokey air. "You did all this, or her?"

She replied in a meek voice. "If I say it was me, will you kill me?"

"Was it you?" he asked again, his voice forceful.

"Yes." She nodded at the broken bottle in his hand. "I'm also the one who killed your girlfriend. You have every right to kill me, and I want you to." She looked down at the dead woman. "I've got no reason to go on. I don't want to be alive without her. I want this pain to be over. Please, kill me."

Romeo started toward her, ready to do just that, when he spotted his burner phone on the floor, the one Juliet had taken before leaving him in that ambulance. He bent down and picked it up. It still had power, the battery indicator said it was at 13 percent. Unlike every other phone in the building, it didn't have the Sugar & Spice app installed, that meant it hadn't gotten bricked like all the others.

When he thumbed the screen a picture of Juliet came up. Then he realized it wasn't a picture, it was the frozen frame of a video. She'd recorded something on his phone. Romeo swallowed and keyed PLAY.

Juliet smiled, steadied the camera against something, then leaned back. She was in the driver's seat of the ambulance. "Hey, baby. You're in rough shape. Do you know what septic is? I think that bullet put a hole in your gut. Not a big one, but a hole, and that's where the infection is coming from. That's why every time I clean things up and patch you, things come back worse. I can't fix it. I ain't got the know-how or the supplies even if I did. You need a doctor. Without a doctor, you're gonna die. It won't be quick, neither, this could go on for days. I can't live in a world without you, which means I had to make a decision. I called that woman and talked things out. She told me if I leave you in the ambulance, she'll get help to you. They'll get you to a doctor. They'll fix you. I know that means the police. I know they'll lock you up after. But I also know you'll be alive and that's what matters. This Juliet needs her Romeo." She smiled weakly. "She also wants me to come to her, told me where. She said if I do, she'll make good on the money she owes us. I'm gonna use that to set us up, just like we said, then I'll use more of it to get you out of wherever they plan to try and cage you. I'll get you to me. There ain't no other way. If I take you to the hospital, they'll lock us both up. We won't get out. We won't get what's owed to us. We'll die in there. This is the only way. I gotta trust she ain't lying 'cause I got nothing else to bank on. If you're watching this video instead of holding my hand, *instead of sitting on our beach with me*, that means it all went bad. I want you to know I love you more than anything, more than peanut butter, like you told me once. If I'm dead, you were the last thought on my mind, and I clung to that as long as I could. I love you, baby."

Juliet reached for the phone and the video ended, her frozen image on the screen.

Romeo was crying, he didn't much care who saw. He didn't give two shits if the woman responsible for all this saw. He knelt in front of her and held the broken bottle up to her face.

"I'm gonna ask you a question, and you're gonna answer it truthfully, understand?"

She nodded.

"This here's a *Sugar*, just like one of them questions from your app." He placed his other hand on the head of the dead woman. "If you could, would you trade your life for hers?"

Without hesitation, the woman who called herself Ana nodded. "I don't want to live another second without her."

Romeo let that sink in. "It's hell, right? Being here knowing they're gone?"

She nodded. "It's worse than dying."

"Let me see her." Romeo reached for the dead woman, got his hands under her shoulders, and pulled her from Ana's grasp. She resisted at first, but he was far stronger, even in his current state. Her hands dropped away, and she fought back the sobs. Romeo leaned her body against a broken computer rack across from them. If not for her bloody mess of a chest and the glazed-over look in her dead eyes, she might have been just sitting there, just like Juliet upstairs. He sat back on his heels and got a better look at her. "She was a beautiful woman."

Ana nodded. "Yeah, she—"

Romeo reversed the broken bottle in his hand and jammed it into the dead woman's face. It sunk into her cheek and the soft flesh around her eye with very little effort. When it was good and in there, he gave the bottle a rough twist, pulled it out, and mashed it into her again.

Ana screamed.

She lunged forward, but he was ready for that. Romeo punched her hard in the chest. "Stay the fuck back!"

He stabbed the dead woman again.

Again.

He kept stabbing her in the face until there was no face.

He kept stabbing her until he was out of breath and could barely raise his arm, then he threw the bottle across the room and watched it smash against the far wall. Ignoring the pain in his ruined gut, the pain in his shoulder, he twisted around and sat next to Ana, directly across from the dead body. When Ana tried to hit him, he grabbed both her hands and held them still in one of his much larger, meaty fists. With his free hand, he grabbed Ana's chin and twisted her head forward. "Look at her! That's you! That's all on you!"

She said something, but he couldn't make it out. He didn't much care what she had to say.

Holding the woman still with one hand, Romeo fumbled around on the ground, found his phone, and held it inches from her face with Juliet's frozen image looking back at them.

He said, "You want to die? I'm not gonna let you. We're going to sit here until the fire takes us. I'm going to keep you alive as long as I damn well can. I want you to spend what time you have left thinking about what you done."

Romeo thumbed PLAY on the video, and it started over.

Juliet's beautiful face.

Her beautiful voice.

As she spoke on the small screen, he heard her in his head too, as sweet as an angel, *More than peanut butter, baby. That's how much I love you.*

Above them, the ceiling was hidden behind a blanket of torrid smoke. Flames tentatively found their way into the room and began to feast.

97

With Hannah in his arms, Stuckey coughed and looked back over to the window. "Who the hell nails a church window shut?"

"What would Emily do?" Brendan managed in a voice so weak he was surprised Abby heard him.

She did, though. Her gaze fixed on him before she frantically looked around, grabbed a small lamp from the table beside the bed, and yanked the cord out of the wall. Then she scooped up one of the pillows and shoved it toward Stuckey. "When I break the window, we all need to start yelling, as loud as we can. The second we get someone's attention, and they know we're down here, you need to cover the opening with the pillow. Understand?"

Stuckey nodded, kissed Hannah on the forehead, and got back next to the window.

"Shield your eyes!" Abby reversed the lamp in her hands and swung the base toward the glass, turning away as she did. It struck with a hard thud.

The glass shattered, but didn't break away.

"Fucking safety glass!" she swung again, then a third time. With the next, the glass dropped out in a single piece and smashed on the floor. A rush of air roared into the building, and Brendan had this insane image in his head of the fire sucking through a straw.

The three of them were at the window then, shouting.

As he yelled, Stuckey grabbed the metal bars on the opposite side and tried to break them free, but they didn't budge.

Hannah spotted the flames first and pointed at the ceiling above the door. "It's coming in!"

"They can't hear us!" Abby shouted back.

"Hey!" Stuckey screamed, his face right up against the bars. "We're in here!"

All three shouting again.

Screaming.

Brendan tried to make sense of it all, but the words blended and seemed to drift away. He didn't realize he'd passed out until he twisted his head back toward the window and saw a fireman on the other side attaching a cable to the bars.

He blacked out again.

This time when he woke, Stuckey, Abby, and Hannah were holding him up, passing him headfirst through the window. Other hands had him from the outside.

His feet and legs were hot.

My God, I'm on fire! I'm—

He passed out again.

Missing time.

Bright lights.

Many voices.

Ambulance.

When his eyes fluttered open, he was in the back of an ambulance. The door was open, and Abby was crouched next to him with a blanket over her shoulders, holding an oxygen mask to her face.

"He's awake!" she called out behind the mask, then began coughing.

Brendan's head felt like it weighed a thousand pounds. He managed to twist enough to get a look out the open doors. Hannah was standing there draped in a blanket with her back to him. It looked like she was holding a mask too. Beyond her was the church, burning so hot and bright it hurt Brendan's eyes to look at it. Flames leaped to the sky from where the roof had been. The rafters were nothing more than blackened twigs. Fire crawled up what remained of the walls. There were people everywhere—cops, firefighters, Sugar & Spice partygoers who managed to get out. Water sprayed from at least half a dozen hoses, but it was a lost cause, Brendan could tell that much from the firefighters' slow, defeated movement. They were still going through the motions, but the church could not be saved, it was clear any attempt at rescue was over. A moment later, the church imploded. What remained of the walls collapsed inward, sending a large black cloud into the air with a thud that shook the earth.

"Stuckey..." Brendan managed in a faint breath.

Nobody heard him.

All went dark again.

Sugar & Spice™

Sugar
ERROR 572 [APPLICATION FAILED TO LOAD]

98

Labored breathing.

Beeps and bings.

When Brendan woke, it was with heavy eyes to a wall of white. It seemed every light in the room was on and beating down on him, dialed up to eleven, the bulbs unable to burn the power fast enough and about to burst with an irate hum. He might have stared into those bulbs for ten seconds or ten minutes. In those first moments, he had no grasp of time any more than he knew where he was or how he'd gotten there. When focus came, it was the warmth of someone's hand in his he found first, and when he managed to twist his head to the side, he found Abby. His glorious, beautiful, loving Abby. She was asleep, her face resting on his chest, numerous sheets and blankets between them. Something covered his mouth, and to say getting his hand there to move it was a challenge would be an understatement. His brain sent the command to his limb several times before anyone answered the door and decided to follow orders. When his fingers found the mask, they fumbled over the plastic, finally gripped the corner, and managed to tug it away from his face.

"Abs…"

His mouth was so dry his tongue felt like it had swollen to twice its normal size, this foreign thing taking up residence in his face. Swallowing brought no relief, there was no moisture to speak of, only what might have been shards of glass, and his brain flashed briefly to that church window when it finally broke away.

"Abby," he managed on a thin breath, "where…" Then his voice was gone again, not quite ready to wake up.

Abby stirred, smacked her lips, and her eyes fluttered open. First only thin slits, then wide as she realized Brendan was awake. "Oh my God…" She fumbled around the side of the bed, found the nurse's call button, and jabbed it down a few times before tossing it aside, dropping on top of Brendan, and squeezing him in an immense hug. "I thought you'd never wake up! You lost so much blood, you—"

"…how long?"

She brushed the hair from his face. "Three days. The bullet nicked your femoral artery, and you lost a lot of blood, too much. When we got to the hospital, they immediately took you to surgery." She started shaking her head, her eyes filled with tears. "I didn't do a tourniquet, I don't know why I didn't do a tourniquet. I just wasn't thinking, I—"

"Shhhh," he told her. "I'm okay. I'll be okay. Is there water?"

Abby nodded, grabbed a plastic cup with a straw from the bedside table and placed it in his mouth. "Not too much, take it easy at first."

Brendan drank about half before twisting his head to side when he couldn't stomach more.

Abby set the cup back on the table and hugged him again.

A nurse came in, picked up a clipboard attached to the foot

of the bed, and studied the displays of the machines surrounding Brendan's bed. "Welcome back to the land of the living, Mr. Hollander. I've notified your doctor, he'll be in here shortly." She took a penlight from her breast pocket and brought it to his eyes, asked him to follow it as she waved it around. "Looks good."

As she was leaving, Abby asked her, "Our friend Hannah is in room 213. Can you let her know he's awake?"

The woman nodded and was gone.

Brendan turned back to Abby. "Stuckey? Is he..."

Again, Abby's eyes filled with tears. Words at first fought her. When she finally did manage, what she said wasn't what Brendan expected. "Stuckey's alive." Her voice tried to break up again, but she pushed through it. "The firefighters used this hydraulic thing on the window and managed to open it up enough to get him out. He inhaled a lot of smoke and got some second-degree burns, but he'll recover. There was a moment there where we didn't think they'd get him out. I had to hold Hannah back, she was hysterical, it was terrible. The fire was everywhere. All around him." She wiped the tears away with the back of her hand.

"Jaws of life."

"Yeah, that's what they called it." She sniffled. "None of us would have gotten out without him. The building started to come apart around us. Pieces were dropping right outside the window. Nobody heard us yelling—the fire was burning too loud. Stuckey found a box of Borax laundry detergent and threw it on a chunk of roof that was burning in the grass. It lit up bright green. That's what got their attention. Five more minutes and...well, he saved all our lives."

There was a knock on the door.

When it opened, Agent Bellows tentatively stuck his head inside, caught a glimpse of Brendan, then asked Abby. "Is he okay to talk?"

Abby's face clearly said, *No*, but Brendan nodded. "It's all right."

When Bellows slipped in and closed the door behind him, Abby's eyes narrowed. "He's medicated and just woke up. Anything he tells you is off the record, you understand? If you want to do some official interview, it needs to wait."

Bellows's right forearm was wrapped in a thick, gauzy bandage. Some of the hair on the left side of his head had been shaved away. The skin was puckered with angry red burn marks. "He's not in trouble, Abby. Not anymore. We'll get an official statement in the coming days to close things out, but he's no longer a suspect." Bellows gestured toward the empty chair on the opposite side of Brendan's bed. "May I?"

The fact that Bellows called Abby *Abby* rather than Mrs. Hollander told Brendan the two of them had not only spoken before but had gotten to know each other, at least a little bit, in the three days Brendan had been unconscious.

Bellows settled into the chair and rubbed his bandaged arm before speaking again. "Itches," he told them.

"You were there?" Brendan managed.

"My office got an anonymous call that night. We were told your partner had been left in an ambulance outside the city. They told us where to find him. I sent an agent to follow up—Curtis Brown— good man. He found Romeo tied up in back. When Romeo offered to flip on Ana Morales, I told Brown to follow through." Bellows's eyes welled up with guilt. He rubbed both his temples. "Romeo somehow got the better of him… Brown got us to the church, though. If he hadn't, a lot more people would have died. He was a hero."

Brendan swallowed. "How…many?"

"Forty-seven dead. A third of those shot, the rest from the fire. Hundreds injured. Many treated on scene, others right here at Memorial. Brown wasn't the only hero here. The two of you brought this whole thing down. Sent Dr. Bixby with those files. The recording from Mr. Morland…Stuckey… You should know, he told me you were innocent every chance he got. He's a true friend." He looked at Abby for a moment, then back to Brendan. "A lot of people had that app installed. An *insane* number of people were blindly following orders in exchange for payment."

"Like Romeo and Juliet…" Brendan said softly.

Abby and Bellows traded a knowing glance, then Bellows said, "Their real names were Earl and Monica Portwitz. Earl did some time at Clinton Correctional in upstate New York for a few home invasions. Monica was a high school dropout who worked at a diner not far from the prison. Best we can tell, they met in 2018 when he got out, and they've been on the road ever since. Dropped off the radar. Earl's had a bench warrant out for years, since he first failed to report to his parole officer. I've got a feeling when VICAP is back up, we'll be able to piece together what they've been doing over the years. Not much we can do until then. And like I said, they weren't alone. Ana Morales amassed quite an army worldwide. Foot soldiers, just like them. We're hoping to reconstruct her app's database and piece together everyone who was on that woman's payroll. It may take some time, but we'll get them all."

"Follow the money," Brendan said softly.

"Follow the money," Bellows repeated. "That's the plan but it's slow going with power out in most of the world."

Brendan must have appeared puzzled, because Bellows gave Abby an odd look. "Oh, he doesn't know, does he?"

She shook her head.

Bellows leaned in closer. "When the Sugar & Spice update went out attached to that ransomware virus, nearly half the phones in the country went dark. Other devices followed—computers, servers, thermostats, cameras, toasters—the virus spread like a wildfire through anything connected to the Internet." He gestured around the room, at the lights and the machinery beeping behind Brendan. "Most hospitals are running on generators. To say we have an infrastructure problem right now would be a severe understatement. Damn near everything is down. The folks at DARPA managed to put together a patch in record time, but rollout has been slow going." He settled back in his seat for a moment, a content expression on his face. "I'm not gonna lie, three days without a phone constantly buzzing in my hand has been like a vacation. My wife and son broke out the board games last night. We've been forced to talk instead of text. Part of me hopes this outage goes on for a bit. I think we all need a break." He smiled at Abby. "Your wife told me how she tricked Ana Morales into installing the ransomware virus on the Sugar & Spice servers. You're married to a very clever woman."

"Are we in trouble for—"

Bellows broke in. "Knocking the world back to the Dark Ages?" He shook his head. "Outside this room, nobody knows it was you. There's no point in putting that spotlight on you. Best to let blame die with the app. I think the two of you have been through enough."

Brendan didn't hear the door open, nor did he know how long Hannah had been standing there. The cut on her cheek had been properly bandaged, and she had another on her arm. She slipped into the room and closed the door. She looked horribly tired. "Your doctor is coming."

Abby got up and hugged her. "Have I told you I'm sorry today?"

"For lying and nearly getting my face shot off? No, you have not."

"I'm sorry," Abby said, squeezing her tight.

"Next time you find the need to tell some psycho I doctored pictures of her girlfriend and plastered them on the web, I'd appreciate a head's up."

"I'm sorry," Abby said again.

"So it was you?" Brendan asked her.

"WWED," Abby replied.

"Emily is one hardcore bitch."

"You have no idea."

When the doctor came in, he took one look around the room and said, "Everybody out."

Bellows rose and patted the corner of Brendan's bed. "I'm in town for two more days to wrap things up here, then I'm back to Chicago to help unravel that mess. I'll stop back by before I head out."

The doctor took in Bellows's injuries and frowned. "You should be resting, too. Not working."

"Story of my life." Bellows waved him off as he stepped through the door.

Hannah followed him, pausing at the door. "I'm thinking all this might be some kind of sign."

"Of what?" Abby asked.

"We might be getting too old for Game Night."

"Out," the doctor insisted, practically shoving her through the door.

Brendan gripped Abby's hand tighter. "Can my wife stay?"

"I've given up trying to run her off. She hasn't left your side in three days. She's been here so much I think she's eligible to collect benefits if they ever get the computers running again."

For the first time, Brendan noticed the pillow and blankets piled in the chair near the window. The notepad and pen on the table beside it. Writing. Always writing.

Abby nuzzled her face against Brendan's ear. "I'm not going anywhere."

"Then I know everything else will be okay," he told her. "What would Abby do. That's all that really matters to me."

TWO MONTHS LATER

99

"When was the last time you had sex?"

Sitting on the couch in what they still considered Donetti's office, Brendan and Abby shifted a little closer together, both their faces flushed. Brendan wasn't about to mention the elevator on their way up. Nor would he mention last night in the back seat of their car any more than he would bring up the swimming pool at the hotel they'd been staying at while their house was being rebuilt.

Dr. Bixby frowned from his leather chair opposite them. "She really opened with that?"

Abby shrugged. "It seemed like a valid question at the time."

"Well, sex doesn't define a relationship, but it is a good indicator of a relationship's health. I take it things have improved on that front?"

"Wait a minute," Brendan interrupted before Abby could answer. "I thought we all agreed we wouldn't let this devolve into a therapy session."

Bixby raised both palms defensively. "Sorry, hazard of the trade. Let's start over. How have the two of you been?"

"We have been splendidly wonderful." Abby beamed.

"Well, that's good to hear. You're back to writing, I take it?"

"I finished the new book two days ago. All longhand. Six notebooks. I have no idea what that means as a printed book, and things are still up in the air with my publisher, but I'm sure we'll get it out eventually. I honestly think writing it helped me get through all this."

"Writing can be very therapeutic. As beneficial as talking to your partner or someone like me. It's a release. Some of our worst issues stem from holding in emotion and thoughts, not allowing them to escape. That can be no different than a powder keg or a tea kettle. You've got to let the pressure out."

Okay, Brendan thought. *This is all sounding very much like a therapy session.* He cleared his throat. "How have *you* been?"

Bixby let out a soft laugh. "You would think a significant event like the Big Blackout would trigger all types of anxieties and send half the population in for therapy, but apparently it had the opposite effect. Since things have come back online, many people have decided they don't need to be as *connected* as they were before. That seems to have reduced anxieties rather than escalated them." He waved that off. "I'm not complaining. I bought an old flip phone with exactly zero Internet access, and I haven't been happier. I can place a call when I need to, people can reach me, but I'm not buried in a screen anymore." He glanced at the table and at Brendan and Abby's hands looking for phones they no longer carried. "I see you've joined the ranks of the unplugged, too?"

"When Brendan quit FCID, we realized we didn't need any of that stuff anymore. We still have laptops, but that's about the extent of it."

"I check e-mail maybe once a day," Brendan told him. "It's fantastic. No more jumping whenever some box in my pocket vibrates."

"You quit FCID?"

Brendan nodded. "Me and Stuckey both quit. We started a private consulting firm. We've got a handful of clients, all local. No more travel. No more nights or weekends. We rented a small space not far from here and put a sign on the inside of the door that says ALL WORK STAYS HERE. We don't take anything home with us anymore." He smiled at Abby. "Home is for *us* time."

"Well, that's wonderful. Good for you."

Abby said, "We never had a chance to properly thank you. If you hadn't picked us up and agreed to drive us to Chicago…"

He waved her off. "It was the right thing to do, and I was happy to help. If you have anyone to thank, it's my patient, the girl you met at the diner."

"Elsa," Abby said. "How is she?"

"Are either of you familiar with Miss Hall's School in Pittsfield?" Brendan shook his head. Abby said nothing.

"It's a boarding school near the Berkshires. One of the best in the country." Bixby drew a little closer. "While Elsa was staying at Hampton House, she wrote an essay about surviving an abusive household. It was extremely emotional. Moving. Insightful. She was kind enough…strong enough…to allow me to have it published in a peer journal. A week after the essay released, I received a phone call. Apparently, someone read it and offered Elsa a full scholarship to Miss Hall's. The folks at the school couldn't tell us who her benefactor was, only that her room and board were fully covered through graduation."

Abby squeezed Brendan's hand. "That's wonderful."

"It certainly is," Bixby agreed. "Our sessions are online these days, but we still speak twice each week. She asks about you a lot. Told me to say hello. Speaking of the past, that reminds me—" He twisted around to the desk, found a notepad, and turned back to them. "That FBI agent came by a few days ago. Bellows."

"Bellows?" Brendan hadn't spoken to him in weeks. "What for?"

"Asking about the two of you, actually. Well, Donetti's interactions with you."

Brendan shifted slightly.

"He was curious if Donetti took any notes, maybe left something behind."

"Did she?"

Bixby's expression shifted, grew colder. It was as if all the warmth he felt at discussing Elsa drained away, leaving behind a different man. His gaze settled on Abby. "He seemed particularly interested in your time at Northeastern. Your degree."

Abby stiffened.

Bixby tapped his pen against the corner of the notepad in much the same way Donetti had during their first session. "You told her before becoming an author, you were an event coordinator. That's what you told Bellows, too."

"Because it's true."

"But your degree from Northeastern is in computer sciences. It seems odd to get a programming degree and then work in hospitality."

"Not really," Abby told him. "Harland Hotel hired me because of my programming degree. They needed someone to rewrite their scheduling software. It was supposed to be a one-off project, just a contracting job, but when I finished, they asked if I'd be interested in the event coordinator position, and I accepted. I was good at programming, but I didn't enjoy it. I wanted to be around people. It seemed like a better fit."

Bixby nodded. "Yeah, Bellows told me that too. But he seemed fixated on the programming thing. I pressed him and he slipped. He told me the scheduling software you rewrote, your programming experience, was with a computer language called Python. He said that's the same language the ransomware virus was written in."

Before Abby could say anything else, Brendan placed his hand on her arm. "That's a complete coincidence. We never discussed Abby's major with Donetti. Aside from telling her we met at Northeastern, we didn't bring it up at all. Bellows couldn't possibly believe Abby was involved."

Bixby's gaze remained on Abby; he tilted his head like an inquisitive dog. "The money still hasn't been found…"

"The two hundred million."

"Much more than that, according to him. The two hundred million only covers what that guy Isaac Alford tried to steal. It doesn't begin to touch all the money that woman siphoned out of Sugar & Spice users' bank accounts and credit cards. It doesn't come close. Bellows said there are billions missing."

"And he thinks Abby took it? That's ridiculous. She was one of the first to get infected. She got that virus from her agent."

"The agent she visited two days earlier."

Brendan opened his mouth to argue, but Abby silenced him with a touch. "None of what you just said came from Bellows, did it? An FBI agent wouldn't share that kind of detail with a civilian. Not on an open investigation."

It was Bixby's turn to go quiet.

"It came from Elsa. Your patient," Abby pushed. "This is her theory?"

A flicker passed behind Bixby's eyes. "Elsa is a very impressive girl on her way to becoming an impressive woman. Not unlike you."

"So it wasn't Bellows?" Brendan pressed.

"Bellows was here. He may have asked some questions, but it's Elsa speculating," Abby answered before Bixby could. "The real question is, how much of Elsa's theory did you share with Bellows?"

"My God, that mind of yours…" The sparkle returned to Bixby's eyes. "Elsa is curious about who covered her scholarship, understandably so," Bixby said. "I explained to her some questions are best left unanswered. I told Bellows Donetti left nothing behind, and I knew very little about you. He hasn't been back."

"I don't have the money," Abby stated flatly.

Bixby said nothing. Not at first, then he leaned back in his chair. "I like to think whoever does is doing something good with it. Putting it toward world hunger, the climate. Education. That's what someone like Elsa would do."

"Well, let's hope someone like Elsa has it, then."

"We can only hope," Bixby echoed.

The three of them rose and went to the door. Embraced. "We should stay in touch," Abby said.

"I'd like that."

Brendan and Abby were back in the elevator, the doors closed, before either spoke again.

"You…didn't take it, right?"

Abby only smiled.

She kissed Brendan's cheek and pressed a folded sheet of paper into Brendan's hand. In Abby's neat script it simply read:

Spice

In four hours you will be boarding a plane to a private island in the Caribbean, where you will spend the next two weeks alone. Get to know your wife. Allow her to know you. There is much to be discovered. It's only when you stop searching, stop exploring each other in both mind and body, that the adventure comes to an end.

* * *

Author's Note

It's been a minute since my last book, I'm sorry about that. A few years ago I got a call from a guy named James Patterson, he's this former ad exec who occasionally dabbles in fiction. You may have heard of him? He'd read The Fourth Monkey and enjoyed it enough to ask if I'd like to write something with him. That resulted in a book called The Coast to Coast Murders, an insanely twisty psychological thriller that debuted at number two on the *New York Times* bestseller list and is currently working its way up the ranks with the folks in Hollywood as a series. I think we both expected that title to be a one-off, a distraction, but we had so much fun crafting it we decided to do another, and another, and another... by the time I looked up, Jim and I had written five books together, and nearly two years had passed since I turned something over to my editor.

Oops.

Ask anyone in this business, and they'll tell you how important it is to stay in front of your audience. During those two years, my wife pointed that out a few times, so did my various agents. I told myself next week, next month, next... Oh shit, two years. There's really no excuse for that. I mucked up.

Here's the thing, though. During those two years, I *was* writing. Not just with Jim, but on my own. I'd crank out a book with Patterson, then write one for myself, then another with him, then another for me... I wrote and wrote and wrote, I just never hit Send. Four titles in total. Books I haven't shared with anyone.

As a reader, I imagine that sounds counterproductive. As a business person, it sounds downright stupid. But as a writer...well,

497

honestly it was refreshing. It brought me back to when I wrote my first book. A time without deadlines or expectations. In those early years, I wrote simply for the enjoyment. You made the words, Dada, my five-year-old would say, and in her mind, that's all it was about. Making the words. That's the part she understands, because she enjoys making the words too. I regularly find her sitting on the floor in my wife's office stapling the pages of her latest title together, complete with illustrations. At five, she's figured out how to tell stories with a beginning, middle, and end—a concept I didn't grasp until my twenties. When she finishes with one of those books, she shows it to her mama and me, then puts it up on a shelf in our library, content with knowing she wrote it and it's there. On some level, I think I took inspiration from that. She was writing for herself and somewhere along the line, I'd forgotten how to write for me.

An odd thing happens when you start getting published. A lot of people raise their hands and tell you what you're doing wrong, what they'd do differently. Those voices grow louder with sales. It's easy enough to ignore some of that, not so easy when those people are making a movie of your book. Or when a publishing house reminds you of what they're spending on marketing and, "Hey, with that in mind, think you can cut this scene? Or maybe have the character do this instead?"

Ultimately, I understand I'm creating a product, and the people involved in the sale of that product deserve a say. I understand it, that doesn't mean I have to like it. So when I wrote the book you just read, I first decided not to share it with anyone. I tucked it away in a quiet spot, took a special comfort in the fact that I made the words, the words I wanted to make, and went on to another project. And another, and…yeah, we've covered that.

That brings us to today.

At some point, I hit Send.

I'm not sure what changed. I don't think it was anything in particular. I just woke up one morning, and it felt like the right time. Maybe it's because the night before I had downloaded some app and read the Terms of Service. Okay, I read the first few lines, then moved on because who has time for all that? I read the start of the Terms of Service, and that reminded me of the last time I'd done that—right after the incident that sparked the idea behind this book.

My wife and I were having dinner discussing her latest acquisition—a large house on a mountaintop in Georgia she hoped to renovate and turn into a short-term rental. The house had seven bathrooms, all in need of work, so I suggested a company called BathFitters. I imagine you've seen their commercials. They basically install a shell over outdated baths and showers. A quick cosmetic fix when there are no plumbing concerns to address. That night, both of us noticed something strange—ads for BathFitters started popping up on our phones, our computers. Keep in mind, neither of us actually typed the word BathFitters into a device, I only said the word verbally. That sent me down a rabbit hole— were our devices listening and targeting advertising? I quickly learned the answer to that was YES, and I allowed them to do it by blindly agreeing to various Terms of Service. Our phones, our apps, all listening and sharing information. I don't have anything against BathFitters. Who can fault them for taking advantage of the latest tech? I'm not sure I can even point a finger at our various devices—after all, they asked me if they could do it, and I said yes. That put the blame squarely on me. I felt like I let a stranger into our lives. While this stranger was arguably helpful (showing us ads for things we need rather than random ads), it was still an intrusion. And it got me thinking...what if? The two biggest words in any author's toolbox.

For the record, my wife and I have a fantastic marriage. We're partners in every sense. We've never downloaded an app as a marital aid, but what if? Yeah, that's how this process works. I quickly met Abby and Brendan and learned about their problems, wrote them all down. Turns out they didn't read the Terms of Service either, and things went sideways.

I suppose *Behind A Closed Door* can be seen as a cautionary tale. We live in an age of tech, and sometimes it's not so easy to determine who's in charge. If there's a moral there, it wasn't intentional. For me, this book was just more literary popcorn. Dada made the words. First they were mine, now they're yours.

I promise I won't disappear again.

Not for long, anyway.

Until next time,
jd

New Castle, NH
July 21, 2023

Bookclub Questions & Discussion Topics

Created by author, Christine Daigle (*christinedaiglebooks.com*)

SUGAR

1. Have you ever skimmed or not read the terms and conditions of apps or technology that you use frequently? (Let's be honest. No one reads these). How does *Behind a Closed Door* exploit our fear of not reading the fine print? Were there moments in the novel that made you reflect on your own digital habits and the permissions you grant to applications?

2. Could you survive your daily life without your technology? In what ways does the novel comment on the power and influence of technology in our daily lives? Did the portrayal of the dangers of blindly trusting technology resonate with your own experiences or views? Do you think your technology is listening to you right now?

3. Paying the consequences for agreeing to something we haven't read or haven't understood is something that could happen in the real world. Has anything ever happened to you because you didn't know what you were signing? Or maybe to someone you know? If so, how did you or the person you know deal with this experience in terms of explanation, rationalization, and closure?

4. How do Abby and Brendan rationalize their decisions to comply with the app's requests? What would you have done in their position?

5. How did your feelings towards the app change as the narrative progressed? Were there moments where you empathized with Abby and Brendan's decisions?

6. Hannah says, "You're letting an app run your life." Abby becomes dependent on the app to help her with her writing. What do you think are the costs and benefits of using technology to assist with creative work? What about dependence on technology in other aspects of our lives?

7. Dr. Bixby says, "If you free up some thought real estate with modern technology, the brain will utilize that space for something else. Instead of thinking about a map, I might be composing a sonata…" Do you agree with this statement? Why or why not?

8. Which task assigned by the app surprised you the most? Why?

9. Were there moments in the story where you felt Abby or Brendan should have stopped participating in the app's tasks? Which moments stood out?

10. There's a saying among writers that goes, "Write what you know." What do you think drew from the author's real-life experience that made it into Abby's experience? Was there anything you learned about being an author that was interesting or surprising?

11. What do you think about the idea of a peer-to-peer lending company? Would you lend out your money to a vetted stranger, cutting out a traditional financial institution? Why or why not?

12. "Brendan got the impression the church had been built long before all else and would still be standing long after the rest was gone." How did the setting of Robert Inverness Church contribute to the atmosphere and tension of the events that take place there? Discuss the juxtaposition of a century old building built for the pious in a pre-technology age with the modern high-tech debauchery going on inside. What do you think humanity and technology will look like a century from now? Two centuries?

13. Dr. Bixby says, "sex doesn't define a relationship, but it is a good indicator of a relationship's health." Abby and Brendan start off the novel in couples' therapy, partly because of a lack of physical intimacy. How did Abby and Brendan's relationship grow or change throughout their experiences with the Sugar & Spice app? Do you think they benefitted from using the app? Do you think they would have ended up in the same place relationship-wise without using the app?

14. The Sugar & Spice app Abby and Brandon use is comparable to the type of apps we use at the present time. How might spicing up their relationship have played out differently ten years earlier? Ten years later?

15. The screens at the Fall Ball showed "photos of people with their Sugar & Spice level and total points and stats". The gamification system of the Sugar & Spice app, using points to keep score, upped the competitiveness between Abby and Brandon, and between other players. How and where has gamification creeped into our lives? Does it push us to do things we wouldn't typically want or need to do?

16. The novel addresses the concept of personal boundaries and the influence of external forces (like technology and other people) on challenging and redefining them. How did peer pressure and societal expectations influence the characters' actions throughout the book? In particular, how did Hannah and Stuckey affect Abby and Brendan's relationship?

17. What do you think is the backstory on Romeo and Juliet? What were they doing in the years between when Romeo got out of prison, and they met at the diner where Juliet worked? How did they get to where they were at the beginning of the novel?

18. Were there any characters outside of Abby and Brendan that you felt had a significant impact on the story or its themes? What would this story look like if these characters were the main characters with the narrative lens focused on them? How do you think the novel might give us a different perspective on the events if they were told by Stuckey and Hannah? Kim? Ana?

19. Abby and Brendan both imagine their futures together at different points in the novel. How do you imagine the future for Abby and Brendan? Will their relationship continue to strengthen or fall apart?

SPICE

20. The novel has been compared to "50 Shades of Grey" and David Fincher's "The Game". How do these comparisons manifest in the storyline and character dynamics?

21. How does the novel comment on the idea of seduction and the lines between consensual engagement and coercion?

22. How does the novel tackle themes of morality and the lengths one would go for a thrill or pleasure? Have you or someone you know done something for a thrill that didn't turn out the way you expected?

23. How is the theme of "desire vs. consequence" explored throughout the narrative?

24. How did the author mix elements of eroticism with psychological thriller? Did it feel balanced?

25. Abby says that in her romance novels, "The sex is implied, but it happens behind closed doors. Off camera...Sometimes it's better to let the reader's imagination fill in the blanks." Discuss the title "Behind a Closed Door." How does it tie into the overall themes of the novel?

26. Which scene or moment in the book left the deepest impression on you, and why?

27. Dr. Donetti says, "Now, we need to talk about the sex thing." Abby and Hannah are very different in their sexuality. Hannah is experimental and up for anything, whereas Abby is more traditional and shy. At least at first. How does Hannah push Abby to be more adventurous? Do you think Hannah is trying to be a good friend, or is she purely driven by ulterior motives? How does Abby's attitude toward sex change?

28. Thriller novels tend to treat romance and sexuality according to certain tropes. Do you think that's the case in "Behind a Closed Door"? What do you think about the balance between violence and sexuality compared to other thriller novels you read? How do you think "Behind a Closed Door" is the same or different?

29. Sugar or Spice? Go back and pick one or more of the Sugar & Spice prompts to answer as a group. Ready? Ok.

For more on J.D. Barker, visit:
www.MasterOfSuspense.com